REPEAT THE INSTRUCTIONS

Books by R. Vernon Beste

Repeat the Instructions

The Moonbeams

R. VERNON BESTE

:

Repeat
the
Instructions

HARPER & ROW, PUBLISHERS

NEW YORK AND EVANSTON

FIRST EDITION

LIBRARY OF CONGRESS CATALOG CARD NUMBER: 67-25255

H-R

LADY MACDUFF'S SON: What is a traitor?

LADY MACDUFF: Why, one that swears and lies.

SON: And be all traitors that do so?

LADY MACDUFF: Everyone that does so is a traitor, and must be hanged.

SON: And must they all be hanged that swear and lie?

LADY MACDUFF: Every one.

SON: Who must hang them?

LADY MACDUFF: Why, the honest men.

SON: Then the liars and swearers are fools; for there are liars and swearers enow to beat the honest men, and hang up them.

LADY MACDUFF: Now, God help thee, poor monkey!

—*Macbeth*, Act IV, sc. II

REPEAT THE INSTRUCTIONS

1

"Who?"

"Dr. Sherngold. He says he knew you in Berlin."

To Huskion, his mind still half engaged with the figures in front of him, the name meant nothing. It was ten years since he had been in Berlin.

"I suppose you had better put him on."

Reluctantly he pushed the file aside and sat back. The hairs on the back of his neck told him plainly the Umgee boys were up to some villainy in these estimates and he was impatient to tease it out.

"Mr. Huskion? Helmut Sherngold. We met at Mr. Lampson's in Berlin. I was with the Swiss delegation, you remember?"

The accented voice struck no chord in his memory. He must have been to at least fifty of "Knocker" Lampson's parties and met innumerable Swiss at them, not to mention Kurds, Uzbeks and Laotians.

"Can't say I—"

"I'm sure you would if you saw me," Sherngold cut in quickly, ingratiatingly. "We had such very interesting conversation. Such good talk."

"It's a long time ago."

"Indeed, yes. But I remember. And in Berlin you are remembered also."

"I doubt it," Huskion said, smiling derisively to himself.

"But yes. I have today come from there. People speak of you. You know Herr Roesinck? And Herr Mullbricht . . . and his so beautiful wife, Gerda?"

"Good grief, are they still around? I should have thought they would have been liquidated years ago! Especially Ferdie Roesinck."

"No, no, far from it. They ask to be remembered to you when they know I come to London."

"Remember me to them when you see them next."

"I will. And, Mr. Huskion, will you have dinner with me tonight? And your wife, of course. You are married now, yes?"

"Yes, but I'm afraid we are booked for tonight."

"What a pity. I looked forward so much for some talk with you. Perhaps we could have a drink together before you go home? Unfortunately, I am only here a little while."

When Huskion evaded this, the Swiss pressed, not offensively but with a soft persistence. Anxious to be rid of him and lacking the courage to be downright rude, Huskion reluctantly suggested they meet at his club. As soon as he hung up he regretted the impulse. Berlin and the people he had once known there meant nothing to him now.

"I'm meeting Dr. Sherngold at six-fifteen at the Progressive, Gilly," he said into his intercom. "Don't forget to remind me before I go."

"As if I would."

"You would. Ring my wife and tell her I'll be half an hour or so late."

2

"Shall I make an index card for Dr. Sherngold?"

"God forbid! Now let me have some peace. No calls and head off any nuts trying to see me."

"I'm sure that means me."

"Especially you, Geoffrey."

The short plump man in shabby tweeds and wrinkled gray pullover, who had entered from the outer office as Huskion was speaking, looked down at him across the Ministry of Works desk. Thick lenses magnified his dark eyes, in which a habitual glint of malice warred with the benignity of his round, pink baby-smooth face and grizzled hair. Both men held the same rank, Assistant Secretary, but Geoffrey Wigstall was twenty years the senior and would be retired in another eighteen months.

"Tridon bumf returned."

Wigstall dropped a large manila envelope on the desk. Procedure with Top Secret files was that they had to be sealed into an envelope and this enclosed in another before being delivered personally. "Tridon" was Top Secret.

"Any devastating comments?" Huskion asked, slitting the envelopes and removing the file.

"You're joking, of course. Now it's in the technical phase, you're the only one who understands those ghastly polysyllables and ridiculous signs. Farce for the rest of us to look at 'em."

Huskion unlocked the khaki-colored fireproof cabinet that stood behind his chair and put the folder away.

"Your pal Dillon got his, didn't he?"

"Is the verdict out? I didn't see the midday paper."

"Thirty years."

Huskion, relocking the cabinet, let out a long low whistle without turning round.

"That *is* steep!"

"Too steep?"

3

Huskion dropped back into his chair.

"Hard to say. With three-quarters of the case held in camera, we don't really know what he did."

"The judge let fly rather. It seems Dillon gave away all our agents in the satellite countries. Fellow ought to be hanged for that. I bet the blokes he ditched would have been damned glad to get away with thirty years."

"I don't think I could take thirty years of prison stench. Ever smelled it, Geoffrey?"

"I haven't had your advantages." Wigstall smiled thinly. "What were you in for?"

"After I came back from Cyprus I got roped in to do some lecturing at Wandsworth and Lewes. I nearly packed it in after the first one because of that stink. It hits you the moment you step inside the walls, a stale corruption that even the disinfectant that's swilled everywhere can't kill."

"Just you remember it, my boy, the next time you're tempted to flog your safe keys to the Russkies. I gather Dillon was paid handsomely for his traitoring and has salted it away very neatly. Altogether a real cunning skiver. How did you rate him?"

Huskion frowned. He had hardly known Dillon, just one official contact and half a dozen social ones, when both were in Berlin. The coincidence of their tours of duty in Cyprus hardly counted, for then he had been engrossed with Penny.

"He was a bloody bore. Always ramming his ideas down your throat."

Behind their thick lenses, Wigstall's eyes stilled in astonishment.

"About communism?"

"Nothing so interesting. Food reform. He's a compost fanatic. Says we're all being poisoned by artificial fertilizers."

"The Dartmoor diet should give him a new slant on that!" Wigstall chuckled. "Queer, isn't it, the way there's always

4

something cranky about unreliables?"

"About all of us."

"No, seriously, Roy. That's the kind of way-outness that should have made Security suspicious."

Huskion smiled.

"Come off it. What about Havelock's spiritualism or His Nibs' paper folding? People would start remembering odd things about us, too, if we landed up in the dock at the Old Bailey. Dillon wasn't just a nut, he was damn good at his job, you know."

"Oh, I didn't know you'd worked with him."

Huskion had not meant to imply this. A tug of caution pushed him to the edge of denying that he had but he was suddenly revolted that he should disclaim a totally innocent association because of the absurd atmosphere of suspicion that blew up whenever a traitor was caught.

"Only once," he said reluctantly. "In Berlin one of my chores was to keep tabs on prohibited materials being slipped under the Iron Curtain. Dillon got the dope on a shipment of titanium that had been bothering us and we were able to cut it off rather neatly. I remember, when I first met him, wondering what such a drip was doing in Intelligence." Huskion grinned. "I didn't know much about Intelligence freaks in those days, you see. Dillon stayed with it until we had our birds safely caged. And damned useful he was, too."

"Why should he do that? The Russians were paying him to help them."

"So were we. He had to be able to deliver in both directions, I suppose, or he would have been no use to either side."

"Filthy times we live in, don't we? I wonder if we caught him or the Reds shopped him?"

"I think our policemen are wonderful."

5

"Just as well, as we'll probably be seeing a lot of them."

"Oh, God, not Spinwell?"

Wigstall nodded.

"Stands to reason. Master Dillon has shaken Security from end to end. Now there'll be questions in the House, demands for an inquiry, every kind of jazz. I'll bet our gallant Captain RN, retired, is even now preparing to sluice the scuppers for what he calls unreliable elements. You can't really blame him, this coming so soon after that fool Philipson's defection."

"But Philipson was never within shooting distance of anything secret. He hopped it because he was crazy about that girl."

"As you say. But he was in the department and now he's in Hungary and being made a prize exhibit by the Hungarians."

"Hogwash!"

"True, but it must be like having a piece of sandpaper sewn in his underpants, to Spinwell. I've a hunch he'll be busier than a blue-arsed fly and twice as silly."

"So what do you advise? We pay off our mistresses and only go to opium dens when there is an R in the month?"

"Wouldn't that be rather excessive?" Wigstall smiled. "But I've definitely decided to have milk instead of lemon with my tea. See you in Pentonville."

He went out, using the door that led directly into the corridor, instead of the one through the outer office. Huskion's brows contracted in annoyance, for he liked to keep that door for his private use. The door was to him what carpets were to some of the other men, a status symbol. It would not have been there if the Ministry of Works had their way but Fairmile House had been taken over during the war and continuing doubts about its future had kept it out of their drab hands ever since.

Not that the room looked like anything but a government

office with its regulation desk, two chairs, gray-green linoleum, coat stand and filing cabinet. But where the walls met
the ceiling there was some fine plaster embellishment, which
even a thick coating of sooty dust could not obscure.

Absorbed in taking apart the handsomely dressed-up estimates put in by the Universal Magnetics Group, Huskion
lost all sense of time. He delighted in these battles of wits
with contractors, especially on new projects when there was
no past experience to act as a guide and he had to rely
solely on his skill and prescience. With figures he had a rare
gift, not unlike the art expert's whose suspicions of a picture's genuineness are alerted on sight by some incongruity
in the composition.

This was a neat piece of poodle faking, he found, labor
costs being inflated subtly throughout, which was normal,
and the cost of the electronic timing and recording gear
included twice, once as a whole and once broken down into
its elements, which was anything but. Together these
sleights of hand added £430,000 to the bill and took the
contract over £2,000,000. Huskion knew that Universal
Magnetics were not being exactly dishonest. Their part of
Tridon's electronic "hardware" was full of problems and
with so much that could go wrong they were simply ensuring
against ending up in the red. That was fair enough, but
they were not going to be allowed to con him with a phony
estimate because they knew Tridon's security rating meant
no other firm was tendering.

He was reaching out for the phone to ring Gellatly at
U.M.G. when he saw to his surprise that it was five past six.
Gilly had been so conscientious about not disturbing him
she had not even brought him his tea. She had also gone
without saying good night. Instead she had slipped a note
under the door between their offices.

7

5:30 (well, nearly!)

Got to dash. Meeting Simmy. If there's anything that wants doing, leave it in the usual place. Will be in early in the morning to do it. Don't forget you have Dr. Sherngold at the Progressive at 6:15.

'Bye.

He had forgotten Sherngold.

2

What was called the waiting room at the Progressive was a corner with two battered armchairs and a magazine-littered table opposite the porter's desk. From one of these chairs the man who greeted him ejected himself as Huskion stepped through the door.

Because of his own height, the man seemed small to Huskion, but in fact he was taller than average, with very wide muscular shoulders and a thickset wrestler's body. The instant recognition was flattering.

"I'm surprised you know me after all this time," he said as they shook hands.

"But you look exactly the same. You do not know me? In Berlin I do not wear spectacles. And my hair is flat. Like this."

He whipped off his heavy horn-rimmed glasses with their faintly blue-tinted lenses and pressed down his blond wiry crew-cut hair with his other hand.

"There."

9

The eager questioning in Sherngold's gray eyes, like a puppy asking for a caress, was disarming. Out of politeness Huskion pretended a memory. In fact, he could not place him at all.

Huskion took the Swiss upstairs to one of the windowed alcoves that fringed the gallery bar.

Sherngold was easy to entertain. His English was fluent, though inaccurate, and he liked using it. What his job was, Huskion was not quite sure, but it seemed to have something to do with electronics and to take him everywhere.

He was also remarkably well informed. Mixed up with gossip about mutual acquaintances from his Berlin days was much shrewd comment. He spoke familiarly of giant firms like I.R.M., Philips, Siemans and Mitsubishi, of the direction their research was taking and its chances of success.

Except in one particular, it was common knowledge to Huskion. He knew the picture from the outside but Sherngold spoke about it in terms of the men involved, of the pressures that decided the direction of their work, of their struggles for power and who was winning or losing. Even if it was only gossip it gave flesh and blood to the faceless facts he already knew. Sherngold told his anecdotes well, mostly in a tone of aloof cynicism but punctuating those he found amusing with quick explosive laughter.

"Where did you pick up all this dirt?" Huskion asked curiously.

"I travel a lot and I listen. In my job it is necessary that I know which of the beans are making five."

He did not actually say what he did but Huskion gathered he was some sort of purchasing agent, specializing in primary products but interested in anything that was temporarily in short supply.

The doctor did not look as high-powered as he sounded. In fact, as he rocked gently backward and forward on the bench seat, the jacket of his silk suit rucked up round his ears, one stubby leg drawn up over his thigh, the ankle clasped between his powerful, hairy, sunburned fists, he did not look like a businessman at all.

"Good God!" Huskion said, glancing at his watch and seeing it was already twenty past seven. "I have to go."

"So soon?"

"I've already stayed much later than I intended."

"But we haven't arranged how I can give you the presents."

"Presents?"

"From your friends in Berlin."

Huskion, who had stood up, looked at the Swiss curiously.

"I have no friends in Berlin who would be likely to send me presents," he said quietly.

"But I told you. We were talking of you, of what a jolly chap you are, yes. We are laughing at the things Herr Roesinck tells us you and he have been doing when you are in Berlin. And when I say I will call you when I am coming to London, yes, Ferdie jumps up and says I must take little gifts from them, 'to show the old buzzard we remember him,' he say." Sherngold frowned. "I'm sure he say buzzard but it is not right, is it? Maybe he meant bastard but pronounce it badly."

Huskion smiled. That was exactly like Ferdie Roesinck. Particularly the "buzzard." His English was a quaint mixture of formal officialese and Edwardian public school slang. "Buzzard" was his favorite endearment.

"I shall have to return the compliment."

"Yes, but when I give you them? Would you and your wife come to dinner with me tomorrow? It will have to be my hotel or a restaurant, I'm afraid. The worst part of my work, Mr. Huskion, is that it makes a gypsy of me, yes. Home is the place to meet one's friends but for me it happens only two-three times in a year."

11

He had taken off his tinted spectacles and set them carefully on the table, pressing the earpieces about the stem of his sherry glass.

"Why not come and eat with us? A spot of English home cooking will give you back your zest for a five-star hotel existence quicker than anything."

On his way to the tube Huskion wondered with a certain sardonic amusement whether Sherngold thought he had cleverly wangled the invitation. He was not sure why he had fallen for it. For one thing, having someone in the house he could enjoy talking to would be a relief from Lambert. Also, he was feeling guilty because he was now so late. Penny was certain to be furious and his only counter to that was to make her even more annoyed by telling her he had invited a complete stranger to dinner. She wouldn't like it but it was part of her job as his wife to entertain business friends he brought home. One of the signs their marriage was falling apart was that they hardly entertained at all, hardly did anything together, in fact, except live in the same house.

And then there was bloody Lambert Henderson. For months he'd been screwing himself up for a showdown with Penny about him. He'd promised himself he'd get it over tonight before Lambert came in; now, once again, it would have to be put off. Maybe his real reason for inviting Sherngold for a drink had been to give himself yet another excuse for not facing it.

When he got home, Lambert was there, of course, elegantly posed in front of the fireplace, his arm resting on the mantelshelf, showing off his wrist watch with its heavy gold bracelet.

Lambert always looked as if he were posing. Even in motion he seemed to be passing through a series of poses, seeking one that pleased him before coming to rest.

And Penny, instead of being annoyed, treated his lateness facetiously.

12

"You've reached the age, darling, when men get kept late at the office," she said. "I only hope she's more attractive than that dumpy Gilly thing."

Penny never laughed and rarely smiled. When she was amused, as now, a glow came into her large brown eyes and spread down over her placid features. If her beaky imperious nose had been a little smaller, she would have been extremely beautiful in a high-cheekboned, *Vogue*ish way.

"Lambert says as an Assistant Secretary you ought to be able to manage a beautiful spy, Class 11, at least."

Knowing that they had been talking about him made Huskion scowl as he poured himself a sherry. He could not delay much longer letting Penny know that he objected to having Lambert under their feet all the time. It irritated him even to look at them together. They were a real pair. Penny as usual draped out prettily on the sofa and him behind her in his well-pressed suiting and Dior tie. They looked as phony as an advertisement for the joys of home ownership. He knew that for Penny to arrange herself gracefully was quite natural—if they had not married she would have been a model—and for all he knew Lambert's stances were, too. Neither had troubled him until he began to see them as complements of each other.

"Really?" he said. "Perhaps you could get the Russians to lay one on for me, Lambert, through your contacts."

The barb caught, for Lambert's weak face went pink. He earned an apparently comfortable living as an adviser on antiques and interior decoration, a business which depended on having the right "contacts."

"She might have sent you home in a better mood," Penny said, when Lambert did not answer. "Come on, let's feed the brute."

His crack at Lambert had caused no rancor in her and she spoke quite gaily, getting up and slipping her arm through his to draw him to the table where the meal was already set out. Looking down at her, a picture floated up in his memory of the night in Cyprus when he had been struggling to find the courage to propose to her and she had known it and her eyes had shone with the same private unmalicious mockery as now. The gaiety that had attracted him then had in recent years been so submerged by her complaining self-centeredness that its reappearance caught him by surprise. But her next words drained the warmth from his response.

"Fix the salad, Lambert."

It was a measure of the foothold Lambert had achieved in their home that he had taken over some jobs entirely.

"The judge really clobbered Dillon, didn't he?" Lambert said, as he deftly tossed the salad in the wooden mixing bowl he had insisted they buy. "I suppose he deserved anything he got but wouldn't it be more civilized to shoot him than shut him up for thirty years?"

His voice was deep and well produced, like an actor's, its resonance offsetting his general air of effeminacy.

"Would you rather be shot?"

"I'm a fearful coward, you know," Lambert said hesitantly, "so I suppose I wouldn't have the guts to actually *choose* to be shot. But I'm sure I'd rather be killed painlessly than spend the rest of my life in prison."

"Suggest it to the Home Secretary. Dillon won't serve more than twenty years anyway if he earns his full remission."

Lambert laughed shortly.

"From where he's sitting I doubt if he can see the difference."

"What about his wife?" Penny asked.

"What about her? She hasn't been charged with anything."

"Have you noticed, though, how sentences are getting heavier?" Lambert queried. "Is it just another kind of inflation? Or are we getting nastier?"

"The judge apparently believes in the deterrent effect of

14

punishment. He was thinking of blokes like me who haven't dirtied their hands yet."

"How will she live, now?" Penny cut in, not having been listening to them but pursuing her own thoughts.

"Lord knows."

"There's all that money Dillon has stashed away. That should keep her going for quite a while."

"I don't think she'll be able to touch that. The police will be watching to see if she does."

"But how will she be able to manage?" Penny persisted. "There's the children, too."

"She'll manage. People do, you know."

"The Russkies will look after her," Lambert said with cheerful disinterest. "Or her family. Or someone. She can get a job. Or go on National Assistance—and that will cost us more money!"

"Your guess is as good as mine. You were with me the only time we met."

"You say so but I can't remember it at all."

She could never remember people, their names or their faces, until she had met them several times and this exasperated him unreasonably. His own memory of people he had met even fleetingly was exceptional. That was why his inability to place Sherngold had so puzzled him.

"It was at some godawful function, the Queen's Birthday or something. She drank lemonade, had two arms, two legs and only one head."

So far as he could remember she'd had a rather intent, studious face, too, and wore her hair in a bun.

"Even I could remember her from that." Lambert grinned.

"But don't you see that this thing could have dropped on her from nowhere? She couldn't have known what he was doing unless he told her. How could she? I don't know what Roy does. I don't know where he's been this evening. If he

15

told her he was out with the Foreign Secretary when he was doing his nasty little spying, she would have believed him. Or even if she knew he was lying, she would think he was being secretive because of his job. And it would be just like a man to carry on without a thought of what would happen to his wife if he were caught. That's what's so unfair."

Lambert leaned over and patted her arm.

"We are being feminist tonight, dear, aren't we? But don't worry, in a few weeks we shall hear that Mrs. Dillon and the kids have been whisked away to spend a life of ease sunbathing on the Black Sea, won't we, Roy?"

"I'm not bothered one way or the other. I've my own worries. All this hoo-ha over Dillon means there'll be a Security blitz in the department. And that's always tiresome when it's not downright dotty."

"But you said yourself that the Security was comic when . . . what's his name . . . your little clerk . . ."

"He wasn't my clerk."

". . . ran off to Germany."

"Hungary!"

Another maddening thing about Penny was the way she never quite got her facts right.

"You know perfectly well what I meant!"

Lambert walked round the table, collecting their plates and shuffling them together ready for washing up, while Penny served the sweet. Looking at him, Huskion thought: He's missed his vocation, he ought to have been a blasted butler.

"But surely Security is the key," Lambert said. "Plugging the hole before the leak occurs. Lashing out heavy sentences after it's happened isn't much help. Fellows like Fuchs or Dillon or anyone like Roy, in touch with really important secrets, aren't going to be worried whether they're likely to get five or fifty years if they're caught, because they don't think they will be."

"Roy would be scared stiff if he thought he might get five months, wouldn't you, darling?"

"How well you know me!"

"If I had your job I should go mad worrying in case I'd left out the plans of some dreadful bomb for the charwoman to pick up." Lambert shook his head. "I just couldn't stand it."

"Well, I couldn't stand yours," Huskion said rudely. "So that makes us quits."

Penny had settled herself back on the sofa.

"You two can wash up now," she told them.

When Penny's woman was coming the following morning, they left the dishes in the sink, but three days a week she came in the afternoons and then they put away all the crockery before they went to bed. If Lambert was there, he wiped while Huskion, in rubber gloves, scrubbed away in the sink. It gave Huskion a sense of satisfaction, of superiority even, that Lambert should dry the dishes after he had washed them, as though wiping was somehow inferior to washing.

"How was your wife this weekend?" he asked.

Lambert's wife was in a mental home, incurably insane. Though she often did not recognize him, he went to visit her every Sunday. When she knew him it was worse, for she either sobbed uncontrollably at the sight of him or abused him in the foulest language for shutting her away. But he would not give up going to see her. Huskion thought this masochistic.

"Quite well. And very quiet. They told me she'd had a cold during the week. But she was quite better."

This seemed so wildly irrelevant he nearly burst out laughing. For anyone else in the same plight he would have been brimful of sympathy but he could not feel that way about Lambert.

Lambert had left and they were preparing for bed when he told her about Sherngold. Penny was sitting at her dressing table, beginning the nightly lustration of her face and neck with a succession of creams from jars laid out in higgledy-piggledy confusion in front of her. This was the only time he ever knew her to look mucky and unappetizing. Even when she blinked awake in the morning, she looked cool and fresh. She had that kind of skin.

"Not tomorrow, darling," she said mildly. "I'm going down to Godalming with Lambert to see a house he's titivating up so I won't have time to prepare anything."

"Then you can't go," he said firmly. "I've invited him for tomorrow and tomorrow it is."

She did not reply until she had wiped the grease from her eyelids with a tissue.

"All right," she said, to his surprise. "What shall we give him?"

They discussed the meal, Huskion making a list for her of things she would need to buy and would probably forget. He thought Sherngold would like a traditional English meal of roast beef, Yorkshire pudding and horseradish sauce and, Swiss appetites being what they were, the quantity of everything was important. Probably the doctor would prefer to drink beer but even if he did, there was no reason why they should not have something more civilized and so a couple of bottles of Margaux had to be ordered as well.

"For hors d'oeuvres Lambert can bring some of that terrine he gets in Old Compton Street. Grapefruit is rather dull."

"Lambert's not coming."

Penny turned away from her mirror to face him.

"Why not?"

Huskion had a picture of Sherngold watching Lambert with amused cynical eyes, as he fussed about the temperature of the wine and the way the cutlery was set out, wondering exactly how they managed their *ménage à trois*.

18

"Because I don't want him."

She nodded and turned back to the dressing table.

"Then it'll have to be grapefruit," she said, dipping her fingers into a jar and scooping out a yellowish grease which she spread on her cheeks. "You are a devil, though, Roy. Why didn't you tell the poor man when he was here? Now he's got to find someone else to have dinner with. You know how he hates eating alone."

They were in bed and Huskion, who always read for a few minutes before going to sleep, had just opened his book, when she said:

"It'll be rather fun. Why don't you bring people home more often, Roy? We don't meet nearly enough new people."

Huskion thought he could not have been more wrong about her reactions.

3

"That was most excellent," Sherngold said, as he folded his napkin, firmly pressing the creases down with his muscular fingers. "For someone like me—a stone that rolls, yes?—it is most nice to be in your charming home."

He smiled and bobbed his head awkwardly toward Penny. All the evening he had been slightly tense and ill at ease, as though conquering shyness. This Huskion found puzzling, for there had been nothing maladroit about the doctor at their first meeting. But tonight he had noticed it as soon as he had met him at St. James's Park station, a rendezvous chosen by Sherngold. On the platform and in the train his attention had kept wandering, his eye never still but constantly examining the other people traveling with them.

"I'm glad you liked it," Penny said, "now you two can talk while I make the coffee."

The two men stood up as she rose and Sherngold moved quickly to open the door for her. For such a thickset man he was very light on his feet.

As she went out, she shot a quick look at Huskion. She was genuinely pleased with the evening. During the day he had wondered several times if her easy acquiescence to his bringing Sherngold home had not been from guilt, an act of contrition because she and Lambert had become lovers. Her look reassured him.

When she had greeted Sherngold in the hall, Penny's eyebrows had lifted slightly. The house was an estate agent's ten minutes from the station and Huskion as usual did it in nine, in a long-legged lope the Swiss had found hard to match. He had arrived flushed, his forehead shining damply, the badly tied brown paper parcels he clutched in his arms making him look like an overheated Father Christmas. Gerda Mullbricht had sent them a large doll, handsomely decked in gaudy peasant costume. She could hardly have chosen anything more inappropriate. Under the influence of Lambert, Penny had been gradually changing their furniture for well-matched period pieces, and among this "finicky good taste," as Huskion called it, the doll stood out as harshly as a boiler suit in a Balmain collection.

From Ferdie there was a bottle of vodka and an ill-made ugly cigarette box in polished wood that played the chorus of a sentimental drinking song when the lid was lifted. Instantly it brought into Huskion's mind a picture of Ferdie's lean, cynical, almost demonic face, as he bawled out an obscene parody of the words. The tune had been a great favorite of his and he delighted in composing these parodies in several languages. It was remarkable he should have remembered something so trivial after all these years.

"Brandy now . . . or will you wait and have it with your coffee?"

Huskion went over to the serpentine-fronted sideboard and fished out three goblets, remembering that he must be careful not to stand them on the polished top.

21

"We will wait for your most charming wife, yes?" Sherngold said, eying the three glasses. "You have a most beautiful room, so many beautiful pieces."

He had taken off his tinted spectacles and laid them on the table in front of him. Without them, his eyes had none of the misty, unfocused distress usual to weak sight but were alert and bright.

"My wife's doing," Huskion said carelessly. "She's become quite a collector."

"An expensive hobby, yes?"

"It can be. Especially if you haven't the flair. Penny's quite good at it."

In fact, he did not know whether she bought her pieces cheaply or not. She had some money of her own and earned a little buying and selling oddments with Lambert. "Lambert's little fiddles," Huskion called these transactions but he had no idea how much they amounted to.

"You have good fortune, a clever wife, a beautiful house—"

Huskion laughed.

"That's hers, too. She inherited it from an aunt. It would be worth quite a bit if it had a garage. Even as it is, we could never have afforded it if we had had to buy it."

"You joke."

"I wish I did. Not that we would have bought it from choice."

"But money is no trouble to you, yes?"

Huskion blinked. The Swiss seemed to have grown larger. He was leaning forward, elbows on the table, holding his glasses and gently tapping the heavy sidepieces together beneath his chin. He had lost his uncomfortable tenseness and was relaxed and assured.

"I know about these things, you see," Sherngold added.

"About money? I thought you were an electronics man."

"Electronics, too. But not all I would like to know. Particularly about Tridon."

Huskion's stomach contracted sharply in shock. So far as he knew, nothing had been published about Tridon. The project's very name was Top Secret. But since they had now reached the estimating stage the code name had been bandied about pretty extensively. There were half a dozen places where he might have picked it up. Sherngold had probably dropped it to impress him, in the same way as he had reeled off his other inside information at the Progressive.

"Really?" Huskion said cautiously. "And what's Tridon?"

Sherngold laughed, put his glasses on the table and sat back in his chair.

"So you do not know? Ferdie said you were one who held your lips tight. You know he used to try to squeeze—no, pump, yes?—you?"

"We tried to pump each other. You know what Berlin was like then. But I don't think either of us was very serious about it. There were so many pleasanter things to do."

"I'm sure so. And profitable, yes?"

Sherngold was still smiling but there was menace behind the upward curving of his lips. Suddenly Huskion felt, here in his quiet Wimbledon house, the chill suspicion-laden atmosphere of Berlin. Had the Swiss sought him out in the hope of learning something that would put the mockers on Ferdie? And if so, why? To serve his own ends? Or were Roesinck's East German masters gunning for him?

"We had a lot of fun, if that's what you mean," Huskion said quietly. "But I don't think you do."

Sherngold laughed pleasantly.

"It's all so long ago. What does it matter now what went into your account at the Helmstedt all—"

"What's the Helmstedt?"

"You banked with Helmstedt, yes?"

Huskion nodded.

"I am puzzled, Mr. Huskion, wondering why you choose

23

it, yes? It is a good bank, of course, of good reputation certainly, but small."

"It was convenient. We all used it."

"All? Dillon and the others as well?"

At the mention of Dillon's name, Huskion felt his sweat glands overflow. Yet there had been nothing loaded in Sherngold's tone. To cover up, he picked up the ashtray from the table and walked across the room to empty it in the little bin that stood beside the small writing bureau.

"I don't know about Dillon," he said levelly—though he did because he had seen him in the bank many times—"but all of us in Commercial used it because it was just across from the office. Not that they had the use of our money for long. We were all regularly broke by the middle of the month."

"They don't use it now. Only one Englishman banks with them now."

Huskion took a piece of scrap paper from the bureau and carefully wiped the ashtray clean. He did not look at Sherngold but could feel his eyes on his back.

"Well, they wouldn't, would they? The office in Grubenstrasse was closed down years ago."

"So, of course."

"How did you know I banked there?"

He was looking at him now as he came back to the table with the ashtray. The doctor did not drop his gaze, following him across the room, not staring him out exactly but giving nothing away.

"We all knew. We make jokes of how you bank at the Helmstedt. We laugh much about it, you remember, yes?"

"No, I don't remember," Huskion said lightly. He put the ashtray down on the table in front of the Swiss and carefully straightened it. "I don't remember, because there were no jokes. And if there had been, you wouldn't have heard them, because we never met in Berlin. Did we?"

Sherngold was not in the least disconcerted.

"You are right, Mr. Huskion. I make the pretense. You forgive me, yes?"

Huskion was on the point of saying that if he was after information about Mullbricht and Roesinck he was unlucky, because he had none. But he changed his mind and kept silent. From the kitchen came the chink of china, as Penny set cups and saucers on the trolley.

Sherngold picked up his glasses and settled them on his nose.

"You have a big balance in your account at the Helmstedt," he said crisply, "fourteen thousand and nine marks."

Huskion laughed.

"You've got the wrong man. I haven't got even fourteen thousand marks in any bank, let alone the Helmstedt."

Sherngold took out a small memo book and rapidly leafed through the pages until he came to the one he wanted.

"Fourteen thousand and nine marks and forty-eight pfennigs. In your account as of the seventeenth of this month." He closed the notebook and returned it to his breast pocket. "It could be more, Mr. Huskion, much more, very much more."

Huskion felt neither angry nor fearful. Curiosity, incredulity, flat disbelief at the crudity of the approach were the thoughts uppermost in his mind. So this was the way it was done, directly, without finesse, the bait laid out raw and naked, without the least attempt to tart it up.

"The nine marks forty-eight pfennigs might be right," he said.

"My friends are interested in Tridon," the Swiss continued as though Huskion had not spoken. "For that they will pay much, yes?"

He spoke casually but watched Huskion closely. And

Huskion knew it, knew that the eyes behind the blue-tinted lenses were wide and strained. He wondered whether the man thought he was going to slug him or, at least, start blustering. He tried to still the nerve twitching at the corner of his mouth.

"You would not be involved, you understand." Sherngold's voice was urgently persuasive now. "Nothing to do at all. Nothing to make copies of. Nothing to steal. Nobody to meet. All you have to do is this, yes?" Clasping his hands together, lacing the fingers tightly, he emphasized each point he made by pressing his fists against the table's edge. "You sometimes take your car to work, yes? And you bring home papers to work on, sometimes, yes? One day when you have taken your car, yes?, you will bring home with you a file. It is one my friends are interested in, yes? About Tridon, yes? So, it is important, yes? So, you put it in the boot and lock it most carefully, yes? But when you come home, you feel tired, yes?, too tired to work. So you leave the file locked in the boot and put the car in the garage. Right? In the morning it is still there, just as you left it. And that is all."

There were questions Huskion wanted to ask. Like how the trick could be worked as he garaged his Morris at a big open filling station, where there was a constant coming and going. And how much was the "very much" Sherngold's friends had in mind? Especially that. But that kind of curiosity a civil servant with top secrets in his care was not permitted to satisfy.

"Get out!"

The Swiss or whatever he was spread his hands in a gesture of acceptance and stood up. On his feet he spoke tranquilly, obviously neither surprised nor put out.

"So. The routine is understood, yes?"

Kicking his chair back from under him, Huskion stood up, fists clenched. With a graceful, weaving motion, Sherngold slid away from the table toward the door, his arms slightly bowed hanging loose at his sides, the palms of his hands facing forward, fingers crooked.

"No, no, please, Mr. Huskion," he said gently. "You will hurt yourself. And perhaps your so beautiful furniture breaks, too, yes?"

There was neither threat nor mockery in his tone, just plain statement, the pleading of common sense. It made Huskion feel his clenched fists were utterly ludicrous, not only because he sensed that Sherngold could snap him in two like a stick of macaroni but because in Sherngold's world of ruthless murder, sabotage and betrayal, indignant Boy Scout postures were immediately exposed for the shams they were. That this indeed was Sherngold's world, the reality behind Spinwell's idiotic suspicions, questionnaires and screenings, hit him suddenly. His flesh crept.

"Your hat's in the hall."

He said it quietly but his voice sounded dry and cracked. It was the only thing he could think of to say but at least it did not make him feel a fool. Sherngold simply nodded and went out.

Huskion followed him to the door of the living room and waited there. To have crossed the hall and opened the front door would have seemed melodramatic and he wanted, now he knew the score, to play it as coolly as Sherngold. Or at any rate as coolly as he was able.

With his hand on the latch of the front door and still with his hat in his hand, Sherngold turned and faced him.

"I am going," he said, smiling, "but there are still fourteen thousand marks in your account at the Helmstedt. That's nice, yes?"

He went out, shutting the door behind him, miscalculating the distance slightly, so that it went home with a slight bang. The noise it made hung congealed in the empty hall.

Huskion did not move. When Penny wheeled in the trolley with the coffee, he was still standing near the living-room door.

"Where's Rumpelstiltskin? In the loo?" she whispered and then, as he turned toward her, "Roy, what's the matter?"

The shock had gone right home now. He was white and trembling. To cover his disturbance, he grinned and told her what Sherngold had said, trying to make it sound rather a joke. It helped him to get a hold on himself but did nothing to cure the ache in his guts.

"Well, of all the nerve!" Coming to her at second hand and in the way he had told it, she was more amused than shocked. "And I suppose he wasn't a Swiss at all but a Russian."

"I suppose so," he said. Hearing her glibly put into words what he had not got round to thinking, sharpened the gnawing in his stomach.

"Poor dear. It has shaken you, hasn't it? Here."

He was fumbling with his address book. Penny was beside him, holding out a goblet, into which she had poured three fingers of brandy. He took it from her and swallowed it like a medicine. A moment of nausea followed before the warming spirit found its way into his bloodstream.

Going over to the telephone, he started to dial a number.

"Who are you phoning?"

"Spinwell. I seem to have lost his home number—a Freudian lapse if ever there was one, that. I've got to get it from the office."

Like a nervous tic his facetiousness covered his anger with himself. He should have had all the numbers where Spinwell could be reached.

"Are you going to tell him about tonight?"

"Of course."

"Is that being clever?"

28

With the soft burr-burr of the ringing tone in his ear, he was wondering that himself. When the night operator answered, instead of asking for Spinwell's number, he dropped the receiver back on its cradle.

He had to think. If this story wasn't pat when he spoke to Spinwell, he'd be in for any amount of tiresome questioning.

"What do you mean?" he asked.

But he knew what she meant. Her father being a career diplomat, she had sucked in the Civil Service code of "keeping your nose clean" with her mother's milk. Get into a mess and, innocent or guilty, the dirt stayed with you for life.

"You don't have to say anything."

That had been in his mind, too, when he'd put the telephone down. He'd gladly duck it if he could.

"I can't just sit on it."

"Why not? You remember Pops saying—"

"Oh, for God's sake! What does your father know about this sort of thing? It's not some piddling divorce case!"

She shrugged her shoulders and began to pour the coffee. She could bitch but her nature was too languid, too little concerned with all that lay beyond her touch, to argue.

"Well, I think you're being silly . . . starting a flap in the middle of all this Dillon brouhaha."

Unconsciously she underlined what she said by taking up the evening paper from where he had thrown it and spreading it over the arm of the couch before stretching herself out comfortably. The large headline across the front page read, CABINET MEETS ON SECURITY. There would be a flap all right.

"But they ought to be warned," he said uncertainly. "He may try it on someone else."

"They'll only chuck him out the same as you did."

Slowly he stirred his coffee trying to see how it would look to Spinwell.

He couldn't tell him anything about Sherngold, where he

29

was staying in London or his telephone number, whether he was in fact Russian, not even the organization he purported to be working for, let alone the one he was. He could see how skeptically Spinwell might take this.

It was all so thin, fishy almost. Inviting a man home to dinner at their first meeting and then agreeing to pick him up at a tube station he never used. Spinwell would be curious about that. It made him look a proper Charlie, the complete naïve idiot. As they did so little entertaining, explaining why he had brought Sherngold home at all would be even more difficult. He couldn't think why he had. Then he realized he knew perfectly well. And let them find that out and he would be marked not only as a clot but as having a mucky marital background as well!

The more he thought of it the more sticky it looked. He had not been very bright to kick Sherngold out so briskly. It had seemed the discreet, the proper thing to do, but Spinwell might think it would have been more on the ball to keep the doctor around somehow while he got through to Security and asked for instructions. Or, if that had not been feasible, at least strung him along until he'd wrinkled something concrete out of him.

That was the trouble. There was nothing concrete. If only there were, the rest could be ridden out, probably unnoticed, if Spinwell and his mates had something good and hard to concentrate on. As it was, they were liable to pan any old bit of dirt in the hope of washing out a grain or two of gold.

"There's the money," he said suddenly. "The money in Berlin."

That at least was tangible.

"But you didn't believe him?"

It had not occurred to him that Sherngold could have been bluffing.

"Really, Roy! They'd hardly give away all that money—

30

how much is fourteen thousand marks?"

"Nearly thirteen hundred pounds."

"Give away thirteen hundred pounds for nothing."

That was reasonable, what anyone would think.

"Besides, you should have known it wasn't true," Penny said, "because you haven't got a bank account in Berlin."

That was the rub. She was wrong. He had an account at the Helmstedt, though he'd forgotten it long ago. Presumably the statements were still being sent to Nicosia, for he had not notified the bank when he left Cyprus. And now accounting for its existence could be tricky, very tricky. He could hear Spinwell's toneless voice saying, "But, Mr. Huskion, you always closed your bank accounts when you moved. What made you keep this one in Berlin?" Well, he could say there had only been about twenty marks in it anyway and he had left it because he expected to be posted back to Berlin. No, he'd better not try that, for Spinwell would know there was as much chance of being reposted to an old station as winning the pools. And the other bit about not bothering because there was so little in the account squeaked like a wooden leg, it was so false to his character.

The truth, that he'd kept the account alive for the black market deals he'd planned with Spiller Martin, didn't bear thinking of. That the deals—which were no more than off-white anyway—had not come off and the account never used after he left Berlin would only be a small mitigation of the sentence Spinwell would pass in his mind.

Spinwell would never understand what it had been like to be in Berlin in those days, with every second man a spiv, with ten times your salary in his pocket. Martin, a second-rater with a shrewd cold eye for the main chance, had slung in his government job within three months of arriving in the divided city to go in for what he euphemistically called "the import-export business" and, in no time at all, had been

31

swanning about in a Cadillac. Knowing he had an uncle who was a Mincing Lane broker, Martin had sought him out. Martin had a market for coffee on the other side of the Brandenburg Gate. Over a lot of varnish-colored German brandy in the brash neon-lit club in the Ku-damm Martin claimed he owned, they had fixed up the details. All he had to do was to get the coffee shipped to Amsterdam; Martin would take over from there. The profits he promised were immense.

Then instead of back to London he had been posted to Cyprus. In Nicosia and upgraded, it had all looked rather different and he had written to Spiller bowing out.

"You've decided not to say anything, then?" Penny asked when instead of going back to the telephone he sat down and began to crack his knuckles.

"I haven't made up my mind yet."

"Don't do that, darling."

"Sorry."

He pulled his hands apart and let them drop to his sides.

"I thought I'd cured you of it." She smiled.

"Nerves."

"I think you're right to sleep on it. You won't feel so shot up in the morning."

He nodded.

"Whether I go to Spinwell or not, this is Top Secret, you know," he said after a while. "We won't talk about it any more. Especially not to anyone else." She cocked an eyebrow and he added, "That means Lambert."

"Poor dear. He would have found it so exciting. He leads such a humdrum life."

He looked at her lying on the couch, gracefully languid and relaxed, mockery, amused, tolerant and remote glowing beneath the smooth planes of her face. She doesn't give a damn for him, he thought, or for me, for what we feel or suffer. It is not cruelty or hate or any emotion. We just have no existence. Except as possessions with special functions, no different in fact from the manicure set on her dressing table. She was as self-contained, as unattached, as a cat.

For the rest of the evening he was very quiet. When Penny switched on the television, he could not give his attention to the play and went into his room and attempted to read. But he couldn't focus his mind on a book either.

"I wonder why they picked on you," Penny said, as they were going to bed. "I mean, I wouldn't have thought you were the bribable sort."

He grunted and went into the bathroom to clean his teeth. When he came back she was in his bed. The abnormal evening had excited her, whereas it had deadened him, so that their sex gave him no pleasure.

Afterwards, when Penny was patting the last layer of cream on to her face, he got out of bed and took two Seconal capsules, something he had not needed to do for a very long time. Usually he was asleep within ten minutes of putting his head on the pillow.

4

In the morning he had a slight headache but it disappeared as soon as he gulped down his first cup of coffee.

Though what had happened the previous night was there in his mind, there was no time to think of it as he went through the routine scramble of shaving, dressing and getting his breakfast of toast and coffee. From the water he boiled for his coffee, there always had to be enough for him to make Penny a single cup of tea.

"What's the weather like?" she asked sleepily, when he took it up to her.

"Not too bright. But it's not raining." He was at the door by the time he had finished speaking.

It was all they ever said before he left for the office in the morning.

He was biting into his second piece of toast and marmalade when it came to him that sleeping on his problem had settled it irrevocably. He could not go waltzing into the office and announce a spy had tried to buy him as something they might like to know, as he had when I.C.I. offered him £6,000 a year to join them. Last night had been the time for action. Now there was nothing for it but to clam up.

He was angry with himself for not having seen something so obvious. But also, now the decision had been made for him, as it were, he was relieved. His career was going well but it was still green. To have it known Sherngold had approached him would mark it, however innocently and correctly he had acted. All the same, the deceit had an unpleasant taste.

At the office he found Gilly with a long face, listlessly sorting out his correspondence. She had round, prettyish features that advertised her feelings as brightly as an electric sign.

"What's the matter with you?"

"Just the miseries. Simmy's got the job. He goes to Durrington in a fortnight."

"I thought that was what you wanted, so you could get married next summer?"

The file she was looking for was in the top drawer of the cabinet and being so short she had to strain up to it, her shoulders dragging her cardigan high above her thick rump. She always wore a cardigan; in the summer over cotton dresses, in winter as the top half of dun-colored twin sets.

"But I shall hardly see him at all until we do."

"Nonsense, it'll give you a lovely excuse for hopping down there and spending weekends together. And very nice, too. There is a certain piquancy in being immoral in Worthing."

"Horror!" She was smiling now. "You're being nasty because you thought I was miserable at leaving you."

"Oh, God, so you will. You'll have to find me someone nice to take your place."

"Well, it won't be for a year at least." She fitted the last letter into its file and stacked the folders on his blotter.

"There's a meeting at three. Top priority, to take precedence over all other business. You're all right for it. You have no appointments for this afternoon."

"Hell, what's it about?"

"No idea. I was just to warn you. Official summons will be along later, for Eyes Only, I expect. It's in Number Five."

That meant it was a big meeting, for Number Five was the largest room in the building and used only for large-scale conferences.

"You're clear today except for Mr. Gellatly at eleven-thirty," Gilly said as she went out.

He was soon absorbed in routine work, so that he did not think of Sherngold until he pushed aside the folders on his desk when Gilly brought in his coffee. He was thinking idly how odd it was the man should have come to him, when it hit him with the sharpness of a blow there was one pitfall to keeping quiet he had overlooked, the 14,000 marks in the Helmstedt Bank.

He sat back in his chair. Steady, he told himself, think it right through, don't panic.

If they were there, he could not keep quiet, it would be too dangerous. But how could he know whether they were or not? Only by asking the bank. But it would take at least a week before he could expect to hear from them. And in a week it would be more disastrous to speak out if the money were to be there than to do it now if it weren't.

He could not check his Helmstedt account. To do so, he would have to tell them his present address and thus admit that he knew the account was still alive. Which would be fatal if it turned out the money was there and it became known. An Assistant Secretary without private means engaged on Top Security projects who had over a thousand pounds in a bank within spitting distance of the German Democratic Republic which he could not explain would be in for a lightning transfer to unclassified work, if nothing worse. And his chances of ever being anything but an Assistant Secretary would be nil.

But there was no way it could be discovered. Unless he were to be investigated in depth as a security risk. And there was no possibility of that. There had never been a whiff of a leak about any of his jobs.

And all of this presupposed that the money existed. Common sense shrieked that it didn't. Fantastic sums were splashed around to try to lift the lid off secrets but, even so, 14,000 marks was surely too much to chuck away as ground bait before finding out if there was a fish in the stream. It just could not be there. It would be nice to know for certain but since that was impossible he had to trust his reason.

All he had to do was to keep his sense of proportion and not let so simple a thing as deciding to forget an extraordinary experience get on his nerves.

Nevertheless, the notice for the afternoon's meeting, which was handed to him by Gilly when she came in to collect his coffee cup, jolted him.

He had supposed without really thinking about it that so large a conference would be about some administrative perennial, like a new method of calculating officers' expenses. But it was on Security and everyone down to Assistant Secretary was commanded to be present. Substitutes would not be allowed.

Huskion initialed the notice and sealed it in a fresh envelope. He did not put it in his "OUT" basket but gave it to Gilly to deliver personally when she showed in Gellatly at eleven-thirty.

The Universal Magnetics Group had no patience with soft diplomacy in their negotiations, preferring to take them the tough way, head on. It was typical that Gellatly should come to see him in his office when any other firm who had had an estimate rejected would have laid on a lush lunch to soften him before they broached their business. Gellatly, a wiry middle-aged Yorkshireman, was one of the shrewdest of the Umgee men, his slow deliberate speech camouflaging a brain that worked with computerlike speed.

For an hour they batted figures back and forth and shuffled drawings across the desk. Gellatly stone-walled stolidly but gradually the areas of disagreement were narrowed to three. All were problems to which the eggheads had evolved a number of solutions. Huskion wanted the contract based on the simplest and cheapest. Gellatly said flatly this was unacceptable. In practice, it might be found that none of the theoretical solutions would work, owing to snags that only became apparent when the hardware was assembled.

"It might just as easily go the other way. You might find a means of doing it for half the cost. Anything new is a bit of a gamble."

"A bloody bad gamble you're offering, a thick ear to nothing," Gellatly said. "You'd be after us to hand back the extra profit before we knew we'd made it. Remember Ferranti?"

Huskion grinned. He liked Gellatly. They continued to wrangle until Huskion was convinced that Universal Magnetics would rather not have the contract than take it on his terms. Slowly they maneuvered toward the inevitable compromise. Gellatly was not satisfied until they had drafted exactly what the escape clauses should cover.

By then it was nearly two o'clock and they went to a pub and ate a couple of sausage rolls each with their beer, which Gellatly paid for. But he let Huskion buy their second drinks.

They did not talk shop but about music. Gellatly was a hi-fi enthusiast but unlike most was interested in what he heard, not simply the quality of the reproduction. Penny had said several times recently that they ought to get rid of their old radiogram and buy a decent hi-fi and he asked

Gellatly his advice about the minimum apparatus necessary. He would have been chary of doing this with any other supplier with whom he had just settled a million-pound deal, in case they offered to supply him with it at cost or even to give it to him. But Gellatly, as he expected, offered nothing more than to send a diagram of his own apparatus.

He got back to the office five minutes before the meeting was due to start. As he strode along the corridor to Number Five he whistled, feeling rather pleased with himself, his spirit light with the loose confidence of having done a job well.

The conference room was already full with far more people than could be seated at the long shiny table. All but two were men. Those who had not found a place at the table sat on a second row of chairs ranged round the walls. Huskion took one of these in a corner near the door.

How his colleagues had disposed themselves, he thought, was an indication of their characters. At the table, apart from section heads whose rank demanded they should be there, were the chronically insecure like Havelock who needed the reassurance of every scrap of authoritarian trapping to get through the day, the livelier of the newer men whose clamor to be noticed had not been heard, and those who had not yet admitted to themselves they would never reach the peak and from habit still went through the motions of climbing. Behind them were the sure-footed, confident men, who knew that this meeting could give them nothing and to take a back seat when it lost them nothing was also a means of acquiring merit, and men like Wigstall who, though the same age as Havelock, had cynically settled for playing out their time as effortlessly as possible as well as the genuinely diffident who had not yet plucked up the courage to push themselves forward or, perhaps, had not yet had their eyes opened to the need to. This division ran true with the

39

women, too, for the brusque and mannish Miss Hornchurch of Statistics sprawled across the upper end of the table while the plump Miss Poole, her yellowish badly tinted hair slightly awry, sat next to Wigstall, beaming happily at his bitchy chaffing.

Spinwell was seated on the right of the chairman's empty high-backed armchair, books and papers arranged with ambitious neatness before him. There was no place for a secretary and no tape recorder on the table, indicating that no official note was to be taken.

At three minutes past three the Undersecretary came quietly into the room and took his place beside the Security man. The murmur of talk stilled.

"I think we'll have the windows open," he said, looking round with distaste. Most of the men were smoking, the majority pipes. "The risk of your succumbing to exposure to fresh air is doubtless great but less, I think, than that I shall be suffocated by this cozy fug you have created. At any rate, I am willing to take the risk."

There was a slight titter, followed by much scraping of chairs, as those nearest to the windows hauled up the heavy sashes. With the fresh air came a tracery of noise, the distant hum of traffic, birds singing and sudden bursts of high-pitched voices faintly heard.

Smiling benevolently, His Nibs waited for them to settle again. Sir Nigel Inigo Bertrand's parents had quite inadvertently chosen his nickname at his baptism and some of the variants with which he had been saddled during his schooldays had made him curse them heartily for their thoughtlessness. But in its present form it was admirably suited to an Undersecretary. At fifty-nine, within nine months of retirement, his skin was still very smooth and pink. His eyes were pale blue and babyish but his long thin nose was very shrewd. He brushed his fine-textured snow-white hair upward in two wings about the bald center of his head. His

40

manner was slightly fey, even eccentric, which went oddly with the fearsome tales that were told of his ruthlessness when he had been a young man carving out his career. Huskion, who respected him greatly, thought he had not changed, not mellowed but grown more subtle, affecting eccentricity as something that was expected of undersecretaries.

"Since we all know why we are here," he said, letting his gaze range round the table, "I think we should plunge straight in, yes, straight in. Lay on, Spinwell, lay on."

Spinwell had a strong, resonant but quite colorless voice and a delivery, unvaried in pitch or pace, that made concentration on what he was saying a burden. In minutes his audience was betraying signs of inattention, doodling, examining their fingernails or letting their gaze rove over the ceiling, tracing out the intricate repetitive pattern of the plaster. For three-quarters of his speech, they remained like this but then the pencils ceased to scratch, the fidgeting gave way to a frozen stillness and their eyes focused on him. Even the flat fence of his utterance could not obstruct their interest in something so close to them.

"Thank you for setting out the position so succinctly," Sir Nigel said smoothly, when Spinwell sat down. "What is now before us seems to fall into two parts or, like Gaul, into three if we include the details for tightening up existing procedures. About those I'm sure we all agree and the necessary changes will be embodied in new instructions. That brings us to the proposal to put all files in the Central Registry, not only those of limited availability but even Top Security. Well, gentlemen? . . . And ladies?" he added with a faunlike leer toward Miss Hornchurch.

There was complete silence for about a minute while everyone either assumed an ostentatiously blank expression or shot covert glances around them to see if anyone was going to speak. It was Hornsby of Contracts who did. After paying the minimum of courtesies to Spinwell he criticized the scheme as impractical. He did not question that central control might not be securer but the procedure suggested for withdrawing files, especially those with top classification, was so complicated—and indeed had to be if it were to be foolproof—that it would add greatly to the work of those who had to use them, who were already overloaded. Inevitably this slowing up would work right down through all grades and reduce the tempo of the whole department.

When he had finished, Spinwell started to answer but His Nibs stopped him with a wave of his hand and looked round the table for the next speaker, nodding to Philipson, one of Administration's assistant secretaries, who had raised his finger.

Philipson questioned the soundness from the standpoint of Security of expanding their present Registry to cover all classified material with no more protection than a formula on its withdrawal. At present the Registry was in the charge of an E.O. (Executive Officer). He knew that Civil Service rank and Security rating were not synonymous but they would be deluding themselves if they were to think there was no connection at all. The responsibility for the ordinary files of the department was one thing, the responsibility for its top secrets something infinitely more important. If, however, it was intended to put an officer of a rank equal to this greater responsibility in the Registry, it had not been mentioned by Captain Spinwell. If that was the intention, it raised a number of issues that ought to be considered. If it wasn't, then he did not see that Security would be effectively increased despite the extra work the proposed scheme would involve—about which he agreed with Mr. Hornsby.

This time the silence was immediately broken by chairs being shunted, throats being cleared and other signs of people who had opinions they would like to air. Sir Nigel affected not to hear them.

"Yes, yes," he said quickly, "most cogent what you've said. Both of you. Something that needs thinking about. In depth. For that we ought to have a piece of paper—don't you think? —so that we all know what we're talking about. Captain Spinwell, will you be good enough to give us a piece of paper on your proposal?"

Spinwell nodded. The only indication that he had been taken completely by surprise by the suggestion, and would have rejected it if His Nibs had given him the opportunity, was his stony face becoming a shade stonier.

He had been neatly outmaneuvered. Huskion had been puzzled why Hornsby and Philipson should have been so eager to knock Spinwell's reorganization plan. Now he saw they had been selected, primed and planted by His Nibs for this demolition job precisely because they were not involved, to ensure that the clash left no work-clogging feud behind. He wondered if Spinwell knew, even now the trap had closed, how it had been done. Probably not, for if he had that kind of gumption he would not have tried to bullock the thing through. He would have known he had to gain His Nibs' support first, that the old man would never allow the filing system, the department's highly sensitive nerve center, to be tampered with on a snap decision.

Most of the people in the room, as onlookers, recognized that Spinwell had been adroitly defeated but were unconcerned because the issue only touched them lightly. Their interest lay in what was coming.

If they expected Sir Nigel to complete Spinwell's destruction in the same deft way he had begun it, they were to be disappointed. He had no intention of presiding over the meeting while they baited the Security man like terriers with a crippled bull. In the interest of the department he could slip the fury of their injured dignity as easily as Spinwell's thoughtless rushes.

Before speaking, he played several arpeggios with his fingers on the edge of the table and cleared his throat.

"What we have discussed so far has concerned the department. Our third part concerns us as individuals." His eyes ranged over those sitting opposite him at the table and then dropped fleetingly to the papers in front of him before he continued in a voice that had less than its normal urbanity. "Captain Spinwell quite properly gave his outline in general terms but I see no reason why we should not say bluntly what is in all our minds. Loyalty is taken as an attribute of all who accept government service. In the past this was unquestioned and the trust it implies rarely betrayed. Recent events, of which the Dillon affair happens to be the latest, have shown that this assumption is no longer valid, that where the safety of the state is at stake such naïveté is plain folly. I hope none of you is thinking that the number of us who have or indeed would betray the trust we hold is infinitesimal compared to those whose loyalty is steadfast. True though that is, it is not an argument of any cogency here. It is the damage alone that counts. If our security is endangered, our strength weakened, through the pillage of our secrets, where else can the fault lie but in the inadequacy of the protection we give them? I am not saying we are all tarred with Dillon's brush. But there is one brush that marks us all here to a greater or lesser extent: opportunity, the right of access to the department's secrets. I suppose none of us believes there is anyone in this room who would abuse that right, who is either actually or potentially a traitor. But can we say we are more certain of it than the men who sat in similar secret conferences with Dillon or Blake or Fuchs and were convinced of their loyalty? We cannot. And we cannot leave it there. We have to move closer to that certainty or we ignore our plain duty."

Sir Nigel's pointed tongue slid over his lips, then he pursed them with a quick convulsion of the muscles. The stillness

44

and silence in the room was extraordinary and, although the day was warm, it suddenly seemed chilly. Cigarettes smoldered unregarded in the saucer ashtrays and most of the pipes being sucked were dead—to attempt to relight them was unthinkable in that frozen atmosphere. It penetrated even Miss Poole's homely placidity so that she dragged her cardigan tighter round her meaty shoulders.

"What we need is a better measure of the loyalty of each and all of us. That is what Captain Spinwell has been telling us. That is what the phrase in the jargon of his trade, the necessity to deepen our screening technique, means." His Nibs laid his hands on the table with the fingers spread wide and pushed them away from him, before going on speaking slowly and flatly. "As civil servants we accept in return for certain benefits—though these become fewer year by year —certain limitations to our personal freedom such as preclusion from political activity. These prohibitions are well defined, we are aware of them and if we do not wish to accept them we do not enter the Service. What you are being asked to acquiesce to now is a new condition, not a lengthening of the normal prohibitions, for what is required of us cannot be codified as 'dos' and 'don'ts.'"

Having draped his meaning in officialese to ease the shock, he now proceeded to strip it bare. None of them should in future consider anything private in his life or outside the proper interest of Security. This meant Security needed to know all about their and their wives' families, their friends, their leisure pursuits, the places they frequented, their household budgets, their bank accounts, every brick and stone, in fact, out of which they built their lives and what was more, should this information be given, not to resent its being checked. He outlined the demand that was being made on them grimly without attempting to add gloss, almost as though he was attacking the proposal. But he wasn't.

"There are some countries, as you well know, where this

45

probing of the private life is a commonplace. Inevitably it produces much injustice for it seeks the unprovable, a negative. Sometimes it is done in secret." He placed the palms of his hands together in an attitude of prayer and tapped his chin with his fingertips once or twice. "This I would not have here, though not because it adds to the possibility of injustice, for I doubt if it does." He smiled, a double-beamed smile that went inward as well as out. "A more practical objection is that such comprehensive prying cannot be concealed from its target for very long and is therefore not secret. For any of us to find ourselves, without forewarning, under surveillance would be disastrously demoralizing. It is a paradox of this age that freedom frequently needs to be defended by the same detestable weapons as threaten it. When this has to be, it is best that the weapons should be in the hands of free men who hold them to be destestable and voluntarily acquiesce in their use only because they are convinced they are necessary. Therefore, now that you know the scope and purpose of the positive screening we have in mind, I hope you will cooperate freely with Captain Spinwell. It is hardly necessary for me to add that the personal data you furnish will be treated with the strictest confidence and will be seen by no one except those officers directly concerned with assessing the department's Security ratings." He carefully spread his fingertips along the table's edge, as he had when he began to speak, but this time he did no piano-playing mime but let them rest.

"Not all of you may feel you can do this. That is understandable. I am not sure whether I could have myself, even a few years ago. Certainly the young man I was when I entered the Service would not have accepted such a condition. But the world is very different now from what it was then and we can only trust our secrets to men who can live by its onerous terms. You'll need to be tough and dedicated and have a strong character to see you through. There'll be no rewards. You will only be winning the right to continue with the job you are doing already. And, of course, you all have a choice. Not all the mansions in the government's house are secret. You must search your hearts and your consciences and then decide for yourselves. You have to make up your own minds but if any of you have a difficulty that you feel a talk with me might help to solve, my door is open to you. That is all, I think."

Sir Nigel patted his papers together. Clearly there was going to be no discussion, the meeting was over. Except of course for the idiot question.

"If we opt out of d-d-deep screening will it affect our future, with the S-s-selection C-committee, I mean?" asked Offington of Administration, an untidy, long-jawed, horse-toothed man whom large meetings affected oddly, causing him to stammer nervously over the simplest sentence while compelling him to speak whether he had anything to say or not.

Sir Nigel was already on his feet.

"Your crystal ball works as well as mine," he said, smiling pleasantly. "Unfortunately mine doesn't tell me what Appointments Boards will base their selections on in the future. If it had in the past I might have been able to head off some of their choices I see before me now."

The tension dissolved in the titter that followed. Sir Nigel nodded and went out quickly. Immediately everyone got up and began to move toward the door.

Huskion, not wishing to be caught up in talk with any of the others, was one of the first out of the room. He went back to his office, taking the stairs up to his floor two at a time.

"Mrs. Huskion phoned," Gilly told him. "Shall I get her for you?"

"Not just now."

47

"Mr. Frobisher and Mr. Lyons both want to see you. Mr. Haley brought up the Meridian contract. They'd like you to let them have it back as soon as you've been through it, as they want to get it off tonight. It's on your desk with the file."

"Right."

"Nice meeting?"

"Hilarious."

Going through to his room, he sat down at his desk, pushing aside the Meridian folder.

After a few minutes he decided the meeting had altered nothing. The only unexpected thing that had come out of it was the extent of the activity Security had been driven into.

For the first time he was genuinely thankful he'd kept his mouth shut about last night. Spinwell's pack would have made a real meal of Sherngold's bribery attempt, pretending it was the first fruits of their new vigilance. And the greater the furor the blacker the mark he would have been left with when it all fizzled out.

The screening in depth he shrugged off. It would be unpleasant but it was better to look over your shoulder knowing the watcher was there than to wonder if he was or not. There was the Helmstedt account, of course. But if everything else was all right, he doubted whether the screening would go that deep. Ten years was a long time. And in any case, it didn't matter because the money couldn't be there.

His life was tidy, nothing in it anyone might think odd or undesirable. He was neither a homo nor a womanizer, he drank very little, and as for gambling, he did not even do the pools, just had a small bet on the Derby and Grand National. He went out little, to the theatre half a dozen times a year and the cinema, mostly locally, about as often. Every fine Sunday morning he played tennis on the courts at the bottom of his garden and, on alternative Saturday evenings in winter, bridge at parties organized by the tennis club. Ana-

48

lyzing it in this way, he was mildly surprised his life should seem so terribly dull and ordinary. The only ways he seemed not to be average were that he and Penny had no children and took winter skiing holidays in Austria.

And a man had come to his house last night intending to make him a spy.

There was a halfhearted tap on the door that led out into the corridor and Huskion, looking up, was surprised to see Spinwell come sidling round it. The Security man always carried himself so stiffly that it was difficult to believe he had spent most of his Navy days at a desk in Bath and not on ceremonial duties with the Guards. Huskion had often wondered if the rigid back was the result of an accident and the expressionless face the work of a brilliant plastic surgeon, for neither seemed quite natural.

"Mind if I come in?"

"You are in."

Spinwell came over to the desk, pulled out a chair and sat down.

"Smoke?"

He watched Huskion take the cigarette, then closed the packet and put it back in his pocket. If he had not forgotten that Spinwell didn't smoke Huskion would not have taken the cigarette. How was smoking interpreted for Security rating? Implying a nervous and unstable temperament? Extravagance? A tendency to drug addiction? Reckless regard for health?

"Enjoy your party?" he asked.

"Came to see you about that," Spinwell said in his toneless voice. "His Nibs laid it on too thick. Altogether too thick. Enough to scare everyone stiff."

"Has it?"

Spinwell squirmed a little in his chair. Because of his posture the movement seemed old-maidish.

49

"Don't know. Haven't seen anyone else yet. But it's not the idea at all, you know."

"You mean you don't want us to allow you to spy on us?"

"Well, not in those terms. That's what I meant—"

"Aren't you going to tap our phones?"

"Possibly but—"

"Open our letters?"

"Perhaps but—"

"Vet our friends?"

"Look here, Huskion, if you keep on asking questions to which you want yes and no answers when I haven't yes and no answers to give you, we are going to waste a lot of each other's time," Spinwell said, with quiet dignity. "All I want is to be able to do these things *if necessary*. It does not mean that you will be watched every minute of the day. Or that you will never have a letter I have not read or make a phone call that is not listened to. What it means mainly is filling in a much fuller questionnaire about yourself, something that will give us a rounder picture of you."

Although his tone had not changed, he was pleading. To him the meeting had obviously been a complete debacle.

"So for a start there'll only be the questionnaire, no narking into our private lives, is that it?"

"No, it isn't," Spinwell said curtly. "Some or all of the other means may be needed to fill in the picture, give us a feel of the texture and . . . and complete the pattern."

"You make it sound quite cozy. What does the Association say about it?"

"They'll beef, of course, they always do."

"That's their job, to protect us."

"Protection is my job . . . and yours . . . protecting the whole bloody country. Making trouble every time it lands us in some personal inconvenience doesn't help. I shouldn't

50

have thought you were the sort of chap, Huskion, to go squealing to the Association."

"I'm not."

"Good. The Association'll be dealt with. I seem to spend most of my time fighting them anyway."

"I'd lend you my shoulder to weep on but work presses. What is it you want with me?"

"Your cooperation. We can't lay these deep screenings on throughout the department all at once because we just haven't the resources. They will have to be phased. I want to begin with you."

Huskion let the stab of shock dissolve before replying.

"Why pick on me?" he said.

Spinwell apparently didn't notice the fright in his voice for his lips tweaked as though he were attempting to smile.

"Don't be so damned modest. Tridon being our Top Secret you picked yourself."

Of course. It would have been where he would have chosen to start if he had been in Spinwell's shoes.

"I'll shoot the questionnaire along to you tomorrow. We'll take it you're the subject for screening in depth as of now."

Huskion had not bargained for this but he could think of no reason for trying to put it off. Or any point in stalling. Two or three days or even weeks would not make him a better or worse slide in the microscope.

Spinwell wanted to run through the current Security routine and availability of Tridon and the other classified files Huskion kept. While they were doing this Penny phoned.

Lambert had managed to get hold of two tickets for the first night of a play because they were redoing a room in the house of one of the backers. It was very important as this man could be a very useful contact with the theatrical crowd.

"It means you'll have to eat on your own. But everything

51

will be ready for you. You can either have the chicken cold or put it in the oven for half an hour on 350 to warm. Unless you'd rather eat at the club."

"I'll come home."

"I'm sorry to spring this on you, darling, but it couldn't be helped."

"That's all right. Enjoy the play."

He hung up. Lambert was one thing he could not put off dealing with. Not any longer.

"Who puts these figures in in ink?"

Spinwell was holding one of the Tridon files, flipping over the pages of technical specifications.

"I do."

"Why don't you have them typed?"

"For one thing because some of the mathematical signs we use aren't on the typewriter. For another, figures give my girl the vapors although she claims she has always known twice two made three and a half and didn't learn it here."

Spinwell looked suspiciously at him and then at the page as though seeking reassurance before accepting this as a joke. With a flash of insight Huskion saw the cross Spinwell bore. His lack of technical knowledge frightened him and he dreaded making a fool of himself with those who stepped light-footedly through incomprehensible calculations.

"Without the figures all this would be meaningless, wouldn't it? And she never sees them, is that right?"

"Usually. If I am dictating to her I tell her the space to leave. But sometimes she copies something I have written. Then she would. Why?"

"Just trying to cut down the number who have access to the data."

"You could do better than just her. There's Wigstall and Baldwin, they're really passengers now."

"That would only leave you and His Nibs."

"And the eggheads and such."

"They're not my worry. I meant in the department. The fewer the better there. I'll see if His Nibs will agree to drop them off the list."

They checked over his other files. Huskion pointed out three projects that were only nominally secret and ought to be downgraded and Spinwell noted them down. Clot though he was, he was efficient in his limited way. It was his ramrod back and quarter-deck manner that were so off-putting. The suggestions he made for simplifying some of the procedures and to keep a stricter grip on material graded "Secret" and "Confidential" which was apt to get passed about rather too freely were good. And now that he was confident of Huskion's cooperation, he was able to make them without seeming to hector.

"How are spies recruited?" Huskion asked suddenly.

"With money."

"Always?"

"Yes, though sometimes politics and blackmail come into it, too."

"But a Red wouldn't want money to work for Russia?"

"Might not. But they'd make him take it all the same. So as to have a hold over him. They don't like idealists and want no favors from them. Then if the chap becomes a liability or makes too many demands and they shop him, he can't show up as a hero even to himself."

"Does that happen often?"

"It happens."

"I can see the blackmail. That's how they got Vassal, wasn't it?"

"And with Harrison at Portland it was simply money. He was a drunk and so it was easy. It's a neat system of carrots and squeezes."

"But how do they pick on these chaps?"

"Usually they don't. Except when they spot a likely candidate for blackmail. It's the spy who comes to them with secrets to sell or give away."

Huskion frowned.

"Surely that's very haphazard? That way they only get the secrets they are offered, which may not be ones they want very much. I mean, how do they go after something they want?"

"That's the sixty-four-thousand-dollar question we're all trying to answer," Spinwell said, looking at him hard. "Are you interested in spies?"

"Not until today. You've shown the relevance of Reds, drunks and homos but if it's all hit and miss as you say, I can't see where your knowing if I have one lump or two in my tea helps you to assess my loyalty."

This time the corners of Spinwell's mouth definitely twitched.

"That would be really telling." He stood up. "Let me have the questionnaire back as soon as you can."

After Spinwell had left he locked away the files. It was easy now for him to throw himself into clearing the routine stuff on his desk, for being so close to the Security man had made him feel better. Obviously the positive screening in depth would be considerably less awesome in practice than in theory, about 90 percent flannel. Unless there was some definite suspicion, the surveillance would be no more than token.

On his way home he kept his eyes open for followers. It surprised him to see how different people's faces were. Every day he must pass hundreds, perhaps thousands, without noticing their infinite variety, just registering them as so many blobs in space. He supposed that, for spies, this seeking an enemy among those who shared their waiting at the bus stop or sat beside them in the train became a part of their lives.

He saw the man first as he was leaving the station though he hadn't thought he looked like a policeman then. He had just noticed how very few men were wearing hats. He was wearing a hat; otherwise it was unlikely he would have remarked him. A narrow-brimmed trilby hat set straight on his head and low down, almost resting on his ears.

At this time in the evening there were never many people in Bridle Walk and such as there were were mostly the same type, residents like Huskion on their way home from the offices, their friends or their children. Therefore, the man in the hat was conspicuous, for he was square and thick and his feet made no sound on the pavement. Opening his gate, Huskion turned and looked back down the Walk. It was then he noticed that he looked like a policeman. The man did not check his pace but altered his course, going diagonally across the road to the other side.

Huskion went quickly up to his front door and let himself in. Without even stopping to drop his umbrella he raced up the stairs to the front bedroom.

With his pulse thumping not entirely from the speed with which he had taken the stairs he cautiously sidled round the wall until he was able to see out the bow window from behind the triple mirror on the dressing table.

The man was still on the other side of the road. He had stopped two houses farther along in the shadow beneath one of the plane trees that lined Bridle Walk and was unfolding a newspaper. Propping one of his solid shoulders against the trunk of the tree, he began to read, apparently resigned to a long stay.

Spinwell had got the first of his token ploys smartly off the mark.

5

He was putting away the cutlery after rinsing it through when the phone rang.

A couple of times he had got up from his solitary dinner and gone to the window to see if the man was still there. He was but it no longer disturbed his pulse.

He could see him now through the angular branches of the monkey puzzle tree next door as he went to the phone table in the window. A tedious and uncomfortable life he must lead, having to hang about in all weathers. Curious that a Security job should be thought glamorous.

He picked up the receiver.

"Mr. Huskion?"

The question came before he had time to say hello. The voice was light but very clear and a little breathless.

"Yes."

"I'm Mrs. Dillon, Kay Dillon."

"Who?"

"Pat Dillon's wife. We met, oh, a long time ago, in Nicosia."

His brain split open in a white sheet of flame, stunning him. He stood stock-still, gripping the receiver, gawping at nothing.

"Are you still there?" she asked when he did not speak. "I must see you. Now."

"You can't!"

His voice was thick with panic.

"But I must! Really I must!"

"Why do you want to see me?"

"I can't tell you over the phone."

Blast her! Suddenly anger cleared his brain. Saying a thing like that! If the line was tapped— He had to get shot of her.

"Look, come and see me at the office. Phone my secretary tomorrow and she'll give you an appointment."

That at least would make it obvious to any listener that they had no secret association and he wanted no part of one. And if she did come to the office Spinwell could listen in on what they said to prove he was in the clear.

But she would not play.

"No," she said firmly. "I must see you tonight. Please, I've come a long way."

He remembered the papers had said she had gone to stay with friends in a secret hideaway after the trial.

"I'm sorry about that but you should have got in touch with me first," he told her coldly. "I'm going out now."

"Then I'll come to the house and wait until you come back."

His panic returned.

"No! You mustn't do that!"

"But I must! I must see you tonight. I don't care what I have to do but I must see you!"

She was not hysterical but spoke with desperate determination.

Ever since his first panic he had kept his eyes on the immobile watcher beneath the plane tree on the other side of the road, had even spoken softly, his lips close to the mouthpiece, as though fearful of being overheard by him. She had to be stopped from coming to the house.

"Where are you?" he said.

"At the station."

"Wait there. I'll meet you."

Without waiting for her to reply he crashed the receiver down onto its cradle and almost ran into the hall. He was back in a moment, clamping his bowler on his head as he strode across to the kitchen. He let himself out the back door, closing it behind him but leaving it unlocked. There he waited for half a minute listening and looking.

The air was full of evening sounds. In one of the neighboring gardens a lawn mower chattered. The clunk of tennis balls meeting catgut and voices intoning the score came from the tennis courts.

He made his way across the browning lawn and through the gap in the laurel hedge that screened the patch of kitchen garden. At the door in the fence beyond, he paused with his thumb on the latch.

If a real watch were being kept on him, there would be a man covering the narrow alley between the gardens and the tennis courts. The chances were, though, that with the operation being so hurriedly laid on Spinwell did not even know of this second exit.

He pulled open the door and looked quickly up and down the alley. Being little used, it was much overgrown but as far as he could see was completely deserted.

Walking rapidly he moved as quietly as he could, bending his back to keep his head low. He did not want to be seen by any of his neighbors pottering with their compost heaps and caught up in polite natter.

The alley did not continue through to the main road but

ran up between the last two houses into Bridle Walk. At this point he would be in view of the square man in the trilby if he happened to be looking toward the end of the road and not at the house.

To make it more difficult for the man to recognize him at that distance, he took off his bowler before going out into Bridle Walk, holding it close to his chest and away from the watcher.

He made his way past the last house to the main road, keeping close to the wall and restraining an impulse to look back. Turning the corner he stepped into the first shop doorway and pretended to be absorbed in the window display.

He gave the square man about twice the time he needed to cover the distance to the corner before deciding he had given him the slip.

There were few people around the station, for the homeward rush was well over. Even the newspaper seller had gone to the pub or to his supper, leaving late travelers to serve themselves from his remaining stock.

Kay Dillon was waiting in the shadows of the cavernous entrance just behind the news vendor's stall. She came forward to meet him.

"I'd have known you anywhere," she said. "You haven't changed a bit."

"You haven't either."

But he didn't mean it, for she was not a bit like his memory of her. The rather peaky girl had coarsened and thickened into a bossy Woman's Institute matron.

"Come on," he said, "let's go somewhere where we can talk."

He lurched off, leaving her to trot beside him.

"How's your wife? Penny, isn't it?"

"All right."

He spoke shortly, glowering. The bloody cow wasn't going to trap him in polite social small talk.

59

He did not take her to the pub near the station which he sometimes used but to one in the street by his garage where he was not known. On a Wednesday night there were few people using it. In the private bar there were three men talking to the barmaid, who looked round incuriously when they came in. He sat her down at one of the tables along the wall under the window as far from the men as possible.

"What can I get you?"

"Oh, nothing alcoholic. A fruit juice, please."

"Lemon, orange, pineapple, what?"

"Orange, please."

He ordered a beer for himself. While he waited for the drinks a young man with a tousled mop of fair hair came in and climbed on the stool beside him.

"Evening," the young man said cheerfully and when Huskion nodded, "Weather keeps up anyway. Smoke?"

He flipped open a packet of Players and, when Huskion refused, drew one of the tipped cigarettes out of the packet with his teeth and lit it with a massive petrol lighter embossed with an RAF badge in enamel.

"Quiet in here tonight, isn't it?" he said, still playing with the lighter. He was one of those wiry youngsters who seem incapable of keeping either their hands or their tongues still.

"Yes," Huskion said, picking up the drinks and taking them over to the table. He could feel the young man's eyes on his back as though he were hoping for an invitation to join them.

"I can't drink it, you know," Kay said, looking at the orange juice. "It's synthetic. I ought not to have let you buy it. But I suppose you had to get me something as we're here. I'm very sorry, really I am."

She had a handkerchief in her hands which she was twisting and plucking at the border. The waste of the drink or her social gaucherie was distressing her painfully. It was completely idiotic but also pathetic and touching.

"You've been through it, haven't you?" he said with involuntary sympathy.

"It's been dreadful."

It was a plain statement. Her rather shiny, reddish face did not change, nor did her fleshy shoulders droop in self-pity. It was as though what she had suffered had taken her beyond the range of sympathy and become part of her, like the color of her eyes.

"What did you want to see me about?"

"It's about Pat. I want your help."

He looked at her coldly.

"What makes you think I'd give it even if I could?"

"But you knew him. You can't want him to stay in prison for the rest of his life."

"He knew the risk he was taking. And the damage he was doing to the country. Now he has to sweat it out."

She didn't flinch or begin to snivel. He guessed there had been tears in plenty but their comfort had gone along with the need for sympathy.

"I know how it looks to you. But Pat must have believed what he was doing was right and good or he couldn't have done it. He may have been mistaken. But so have other people without being sent to prison for thirty years."

Her sincerity was pathetic.

"There's nothing can be done about that now."

"Oh, but there is!" she said, eagerly. "That's why I had to see you. The Russians are willing to make an exchange for Pat."

"I don't believe it," he said incredulously. "And what the hell has that to do with me?"

It took him some time to drag the story out of her.

"So this is it," he said at last. "Your solicitor came to you today and—"

61

"No, not our solicitor. That's Mr. Filby. But he couldn't come. I told you," she explained painstakingly. "So he sent Mr. Broughton."

"Well, it doesn't matter," Huskion exclaimed irritably. "Your solicitors tell you that the Russians would be willing to exchange several British and American agents they hold for your husband. That's right, isn't it?"

"Yes."

"There's a meeting at the F.O. tomorrow morning at which it could be discussed. Right? And you want me to do what I can to see that this exchange is considered then, favorably if possible?"

"Please do it. If only—"

"Wait! I still don't understand why you should ask me to do it."

"Well, Mr. Broughton said—"

"Oh, so it was his idea?"

"No, not exactly. He made me go over the men whom Pat had worked with or known or been friendly with who . . . who . . ." she hesitated, "who had become influential. Then we went through the list to see who was best. Mr. Broughton is very clever, he'd been on Pat's case since the beginning though I hadn't seen him before. He agreed you were the one who could do it. You have got on so well, you know."

"But damn it all, I'm not in the Foreign Office, have absolutely nothing to do with it."

"But you'd know who to go to, how to make the right approach." She gave him a queer little smile that was both superior and pleading. "You're not like Pat, you're part of the inside network, know all the right people."

For the first time he heard Dillon in her, chip-on-the-shoulder, sneering. He felt a quiver of anger but even as it shook him the pathos of her arrogance in believing that anyone would be willing to help her treacherous husband for the asking, touched him.

"You'd better get yourself some other solicitors, if yours have been feeding you this kind of bull," he told her brutally. "There's no chance of Dillon's being exchanged. Even for the Kremlin."

"Why do you say that? There are such exchanges. Look at Lonsdale and Wynne. And then there was Powers and some man the Americans had."

"Those were different. Lonsdale was a Russian. Your husband is British. The government would never hand over a British subject to the Russians. He'll not be able to get out of serving his sentence that way."

This went home, breaking through her composure. The set line of her lips suddenly slackened like a violin string that had lost its purchase. Her eyes filled.

To avoid looking at her, Huskion turned his head away. He saw the young man with the cigarette lighter who had joined the other men at the bar, looking at him. They were laughing and he hoped that Kay was not going to break down completely and make a scene. He turned his eyes to the window. Outside the silver dusk of the evening sky was melting into a grapelike purple.

"God, I must go!" he said, jerking to his feet. "Look, I'm sorry about you." He was leaning across the table, speaking quickly, quietly, close to her ear. "But I wouldn't have helped you even if I could. You ought to have known that. So please don't try to see me again."

He went out in a rush, turning away almost before the last words were out of his mouth. He sped down the street in a jog trot and even when he reached the main road and had to slow down to avoid being conspicuous, it could hardly be said he was walking, he was moving so fast.

Gritting his teeth, he cursed himself for a fool for not

63

having thought of its getting dark. It would have been simple to have put on a reading lamp before he went out. If the house remained in darkness much longer, Spinwell's man would become suspicious.

When he reached the alley, he broke into a run, crashing his way through the brambly weeds. A surprised courting couple jumping apart as he floundered past so startled him he nearly fell. He dropped his pace a little then.

But when he reached the house he darted headlong across the garden to the back door without pausing to fasten the gate into the alley.

He switched on the neon light in the kitchen and flopped across the table, gripping its sides and gasping for breath.

The light from the kitchen spilled through the door into the living room and would be seen by the man under the plane tree. He hoped the watcher would think he had been pottering in the garden until now.

When he got his breath back he went into the living room but was careful to leave his bowler behind in the kitchen in case Spinwell's man had taken advantage of the dusk to come closer and was now in the front garden with a full view of the room. After switching on the light in there he went upstairs and looked out the window.

He could not see anything very distinctly because it was now almost dark. The man under the plane tree was easy to see, however, for he had taken off his jacket and his shirt gleamed whitely in the gloom.

As he watched, the Danish *au pair* girl from Claremount, the house immediately opposite, came tripping out and ran up to the man and flung her arms round his neck. They went off down Bridle Walk clinched tightly together.

It seemed hardly likely that the man in the white shirt could be Spinwell's myrmidon. Either the token surveillance only operated during daylight and he had gone home or he was, indeed, lurking in the front garden shrubbery.

He went down into the kitchen again, took a carrier bag from the pantry and put his bowler hat in it, carried it through into the hall, hung the hat in its place on the stand and slipped the carrier into the cupboard under the stairs. Penny would have thought he had come home drunk if she had found his hat in the kitchen. He was too tidy a man to leave his things about the place.

Back in the living room again he poured himself a stiffish whiskey and soda.

The thought that there might be somebody beyond the black walls of the windows watching him was less disturbing than he would have imagined. If there was anyone there he had no sense of eyes following him. He did not draw the curtains because the idea of someone trying to peer through a chink was somehow far more nerve-racking.

All the same it made it difficult to enjoy lingering over his drink and he finished it quickly.

His thigh muscles were throbbing from his unaccustomed running and he had a sharp intermittent needling pain in his left calf which made him wonder if he had strained a tendon. He decided to have a hot bath and go to bed with a book without waiting for Penny to come home from the theatre.

He had, after all, had quite a day.

6

No more weird events came along to plague Huskion during the rest of the week. Or the next. Or in the one after that.

He saw no more of the square man in the trilby. After about ten days had gone by and he was sure he was not being followed, his interest flagged and he began to spend more time reading his paper than memorizing the faces of his traveling companions. He had hinted jokingly to Spinwell about the size of the square man's feet but the Security man had only looked at him blankly.

And as Spinwell didn't mention it, he presumed Kay Dillon's phone call had not been tapped.

Spinwell's questionnaire was a formidable affair with which he wrestled to give conscientious answers to queries like: "List the friends with whom you are on visiting terms, setting out the frequency of your contact. If known, give their occupations and political affiliations (if any)."

Most of the questions were similarly tiresome, worrying only in that they could not be answered accurately because the data asked for changed from day to day. But in one he felt the point of the probe.

"Give the names and addresses of any bank(s) where you have, or at any time have had, an account."

He punctiliously omitted none but juggled the order slightly so that the Helmstedt appeared inconspicuously about the middle of the list.

His recent experience had robbed him of the lighthearted contempt with which he usually approached this kind of form filling. To the question: "To your knowledge or have you any reason to suspect that any of your acquaintances have contacts or links with residents in Iron Curtain countries?" he had put down a simple "No." Before he had entertained Sherngold at dinner he would have been tempted to name all the Cabinet Ministers with whom he dealt.

He used the screening in depth as the reason for asking Penny to see less of Lambert or, at any rate, stop him from using the house as though it were his home. His first attempt was comically abortive.

"That's nastily mean of you, grudging him eating with us," she snapped, though he hadn't mentioned food. "And anyway he always brings something. I expect because he senses how your mind is working."

When he had protested that was hardly the point, she paid no attention. She defended Lambert as though Huskion were attacking his character, instancing numerous generous acts and contrasting them with what she called his "meanness."

The wrangle went on for several days. Each exchange took them closer to inflicting irrevocable wounds on each other and ended with them slumping into bed raw with anger. He had asked her as reasonably as he could, couldn't she see that a *ménage à trois* background was impossible for a civil servant in his position?

"Don't be ridiculous," she had said, looking down her nose, and then walked out of the room.

This moving away, refusing to do battle, whenever he tried to uncover the causes of the tensions between them was a defense she had developed. Anticipation of this slipping away beyond his reach increasingly inhibited his capacity to say plainly what was in his mind.

The quarrel went far beyond the tidying up of his home life for the benefit of Spinwell or the "having it out and dealing with it" he had had in mind before that arose.

"You're just making all this up about the screening," she had said. "The truth is you're jealous, jealous of me, because I'm working with Lambert."

"If you mean, I don't like your being lovers or having tried to be," he had retorted, "you're right."

The "having tried to be" clearly touched her. Huskion, too, was hurt. It was one thing to have surmised it, quite another, a shock, to learn it was the truth.

In the end, without anything being settled or agreed, an uncomfortable and insecure truce came into being. Lambert came to the house only once or twice a week, at any rate when Huskion was there. And Penny announced that she would be going out more often in the evenings on business. And of their marriage there was nothing left but the sex rather perfunctorily performed.

At the office he was covering for two men who were on holiday and since he was always fully loaded this meant he did not get away until after six on most nights. If he had been less busy he might have noticed that there had been a subtle change since the Security meeting. There was noticeably less gossip between executives, less inclination to chat about the affairs of the office and to make ribald comments about each other. And there was a notable falling off of social contact; even men who had regularly lunched together found excuses for not doing so.

After two or three days he hardly thought of Sherngold or Kay Dillon. He did not actually forget them but the menacing shadow their appearance had momentarily cast melted.

Then one afternoon he was dictating to Gilly, ignoring her pouting glances toward the clock as it was after five, when the phone rang. Gilly reached over and answered it.

"It's Goodhews," she said.

He made a note on his pad and took the receiver from her. "Hullo, Smithson," he said.

But it wasn't Smithson on the line. Or anyone else at Goodhews.

"You haven't checked your bank account, Mr. Huskion." The words were spoken softly, chidingly, the Middle European accent unmistakable. "And our deal is waiting to proceed, yes?"

He banged the receiver back on its cradle as though it was burning his fingers.

"What's the matter?"

Gilly was staring at him.

"Eh?"

"Are you all right? You look very groggy."

"No . . . no, it's nothing."

He scrabbled among the papers in front of him trying to restart his numbed mind. But all he could do was stare at his fingers twitching at the papers.

"We'll finish this in the morning," he blurted out at last.

Gilly immediately forgot her concern for him and beamed happily. "That's a mercy," she said cheerfully, as she gathered up her things. "I'll get these done tonight. I thought you were going to be grim and want them all."

After she had gone he sat still, staring in front of him, his hands on the desk clasped so tightly his muscles were taut right through to his shoulder blades. Except for the faint tap-tap of Gilly's typewriter there was a graveyard hush in the room.

He had not moved when five minutes later the telephone jangled again. Automatically he started and stretched out his hand toward the receiver. Then he froze. Slowly his head came up, fear dragging at his features.

Again the bell jangled. If he didn't answer, Gilly would be in to find out why.

Very gingerly, as though he were handling something wild and dangerous, he picked up the receiver and waited.

It was only Gilly, unsure of an outline. She had to repeat the sentence twice before he was able to answer sensibly.

He hung up and leaned back in his chair. The ringing of the bell had cleared his head. He knew what he was in for now.

Taking out a handkerchief he wiped the dampness from his palms and forehead. Whenever his phone rang in future he would never know whether it was Sherngold's voice he was going to hear.

And there was nothing he could do about it.

When Gilly came in with his letters, he was still reeling. He signed them without reading them through.

"I'm off now," she told him as she went out. "I'll switch the phone through to you before I go."

He was on the point of calling after her that he didn't want the phone. Then he was hit by the futility of trying to escape that way. There was his phone at home, a much greater hazard if Spinwell had got around to tapping it.

And at that moment he recognized what the phone call meant to him, how it had changed everything. Spinwell had to be told.

But not now, not at this minute. He did not feel capable of even telling the Security man the facts coherently, let alone arranging them so they would not be too damaging.

The one thing against waiting till the morning was that he did not know whether Sherngold would.

It could be that he would find the doctor standing next to him on his way home. Or waiting for him on his doorstep. He would know what to do then. Being able to imagine either happening told him. It also told him, because he could imagine it, that that was not the way Sherngold was going to act.

If he only knew Spinwell had not tapped his phone, he could face an evening waiting for it to ring, expecting what he would hear when it did. But if Spinwell heard the tape of that call before he told him about the doctor, then he was deeper in the mire than ever. It would look as though he had opened up only because he suspected that another ear had been on the line.

He phoned Penny and told her he was working late and would be dining at the Progressive.

"Are you going out?" he asked.

"I don't know. I might go to the pictures with Lambert. If there's anything worth seeing, that is. Why?"

"Oh, nothing. It's just that I expect to be pretty late."

It was all very cool in tone, for that was how they had become.

After he had hung up he collected the papers he had been working on and put them away. All the routine of clearing up he went through meticulously in order to steady himself.

As he bought a paper, he looked carefully round. There were several doorways and buttresses in Fairmile Place that could have given cover but so far as he could see neither Sherngold nor any other watcher was concealed in them.

Casually swinging his umbrella he walked toward White-hall, crossed it and continued on to the Horseguards. Keeping in the very center of the arch he walked out on to the parade ground and directly across to the Guards Memorial. All this time he was careful not to look behind him. When he reached the memorial he turned sharp right toward the Mall. Now, without turning his head, he could see spread out across the parade ground the people who were taking the same course as he had. As most of those coming through the arch struck out diagonally to the left or right toward the Mall or Birdcage Walk, there were not many of these. Just seven, five men and a woman with a child. He slowed his pace a little so that he could examine the men and be sure of recognizing each of them again. None of them was Sherngold.

In the Mall he waited for a break in the traffic but made no effort to identify any of his possible followers among the others waiting to cross. As soon as he was on the other side he went rapidly toward the Palace until he reached the steps leading up to Carlton Terrace Gardens. He stood still for a moment looking out at the traffic, his umbrella resting across his shoulder. Then he bounded up the steps two at a time.

From the top it was possible to see the whole expanse of the steps and be unobserved behind a clump of bushes. In five minutes only two people came up and three went down. The two who came up were a cloth-capped overalled workman carrying a bag of tools and a dapper, potbellied man in a sporty curly-brimmed bowler with a monocle bouncing against his midriff, who was puffing badly by the time he reached the top.

Neither of them had been among the five who followed him across the Horseguards.

He had promised himself a stiff whiskey as a bracer when he got to the Progressive but instead he ordered a sherry, which he took along to the same alcove where he had talked to Sherngold, and sipped it slowly. These maneuvers had whetted his mind and the knowledge that he had not been followed was satisfying, like a victory.

After a stodgy meal during which he hardly noticed what he was putting into his mouth, he took his coffee into the library where he could be sure of not being disturbed.

Very deliberately he reviewed his problem dispassionately as though it did not involve him personally. He began with the facts, from Sherngold's first phone call, trying to recall not only what he had said then and later but the actual words he himself had used and what he had had in his mind. He also visualized the doctor as clearly as he could, noting down and memorizing a precise description of him.

But setting out the problem did not solve it. His situation was the same as it had been three weeks ago, except that the extra time lag could only be explained by the plain truth. He cursed himself for a fool for hanging up in a panic instead of arranging a meeting with the Swiss. Then he could have gone to Spinwell and left the Security man to take it from there. It all looked so easy when it was too late.

He no longer doubted the money was at the Helmstedt. The date of its deposit would corroborate his story, anyway. That he hadn't checked whether the money was there or not because he hadn't wanted to know sounded terribly weak but it couldn't be helped.

However it sounded, he had to tell the truth now, without trying to rearrange the facts or omitting anything. He had no other choice. It was a fire trench he would not be able to cross undamaged. Even so, his feeling was of relief rather than dismay.

It was half past ten when he left the club and joined the homeward-bound theatregoers trooping into Piccadilly Underground. He did not follow his usual route but got out at Putney Bridge and took a bus, leaving it a stop before Wimbledon Station. Then by a detour he entered Bridle Walk from the opposite end from the main road.

He approached the house cautiously. The road appeared very empty, its quietness emphasized rather than broken by the soughing leaves of the plane trees and the distant pounding of a pop record from an upper window. The only light in the house was in the hall. Dark shadows from it were thrown among the shrubbery making it difficult to see if there was anyone lurking there. Looking from right to left with narrowed eyes, he hurried up the path and turned round. There was no one there.

He let himself in and stood still for a moment before hanging up his hat, listening. He was surprised to hear himself breathing hard as though he had been running.

"Roy?" Penny called sleepily from the bedroom as he reached the landing.

"Yes."

He went into the bedroom and switched on the light. She looked up from her pillow, blinking.

"You're late."

"Yes. Did anyone phone?"

"No."

"No one at all?"

"No."

"It didn't ring once all evening?"

"Not once. Who were you expecting?" Her eyes were wide open now, staring at him warily. "Lambert's in Bath," she added, betraying her train of thought.

Curiously, it troubled him to know Sherngold had not rung. He had been so sure the doctor would not leave him alone, now he'd started to apply the pressure. To have miscalculated again filled him with unease.

As he brushed his teeth he racked his brains for an explanation. It could be that his dodging about during the evening had upset the doctor's plans; but he didn't think so. That meant Sherngold had something in mind he had not thought of. Which was anything but a pleasant conclusion to go to bed on.

To quiet his nerves he took a couple of sleeping tablets.

In the morning he was coming downstairs from giving Penny her cup of tea when the postman delivered the morning mail. What with the furry tongue the sleeping tablets had left and the unpleasant day he had to face, he was not feeling too good. He took the letters from the wire basket behind the door and sorted them. It was his practice to take his to read on the way to the office, leaving Penny's and any advertisements on the hall stand.

There were five letters, one from his father that he put into his pocket, one from Penny's sister in Edinburgh which he immediately tossed aside with two that were obviously circulars or bills. The fifth was quite a large envelope with a strawboard back which he was about to throw down with the others thinking it was an advertisement, when he saw it was sealed and, out of curiosity, slit it open with his thumb.

In it was a photograph, a half-plate enlargement, not a good photograph, for it had been taken in poor light and was very thin and gray. But the people in it were perfectly recognizable.

It was of him and Kay Dillon in the pub at the moment he was handing her her orange juice. He was smiling. It could have been a polite smile. Or one of friendly intimacy. Which way it was taken would depend on what the viewer was looking for.

For a second he stood gaping at it in a mindless vacuum. Then the hall seemed to spin round him and he blacked out in blind panic.

What he did in the next few seconds he never knew. He certainly did not remember tearing up the photograph. His first conscious memory was of being in the kitchen stuffing the torn pieces into the sink disposal unit and ramming the envelope down after it.

Then he collected his hat and umbrella and hurried out of the house.

In the street he walked rapidly, his long legs swinging, head thrust forward. However bad the day had seemed before, he had never imagined it could be as terrible as it was going to be.

He had not even thought of mentioning Kay Dillon's dunning him with her idiotic request. Their pathetic meeting had been quite meaningless, of no relevance to him at all. But the photograph had. Whatever chance he may have had would go when he showed up as a target for blackmail as well as bribery.

But who could it be? And how had it been taken? No one had known he was going to the pub that night so a camera could not have been hidden beforehand. But he would swear none of the people there had a camera. And in any case they were all strangers. Then why? The envelope had not contained a note demanding money, only the photograph. Presumably that would come later. The thought sickened him.

Unable to contain himself while waiting for the train he walked up and down the platform, ignoring the smiles of acquaintances. Twice he had to take off his hat to wipe the sweat from his forehead.

He was sitting in the train, his paper still folded on his lap, too shaken even to make a pretense of reading, when the truth burst upon him.

It was so obvious he could not understand why he had not seen it at once.

There was no blackmailer. Or rather no unknown one. The photograph had been sent by Sherngold.

That explained why he had not tried to contact him again yesterday. There had to be a further softening up. The carrot had been refused, so now the squeeze had to be applied.

Immediately he felt better, less frightened now that what was happening to him had lost some of its Kafkalike quality.

Kay Dillon's appearance had not been an irrelevance but a piece of the whole.

Once again he cursed himself for being such a panicky fool. Destroying the photograph would make him as popular as a bedbug with Security.

But he need not have worried.

At the office, on top of his correspondence, was another strawboard-backed envelope. It was prominently marked "Personal," so Gilly had left it unopened.

It was a different photograph, though it had the same thin gray underexposed texture as the first. It had been taken just before he had left the pub. He was leaning across the table, his head close to Kay's, looking very earnest, conspiratorial even.

The picture gave him a queasy sensation. It made him see what a hell of a chance he was taking. It wasn't just a matter of telling the truth and taking the consequences. He had to convince Spinwell it was the truth.

7

Sir Nigel Bertrand's room was the largest and pleasantest office in the building in summer. In winter it was drafty and the elegant fireplace visitors always admired smoked whenever the wind was in the east or northern quarters.

On its broad mantelshelf His Nibs arranged the produce of his paper-folding exercise. Today Huskion saw it was elephants he was making. A procession of buff, pink, green and white ones marched trunk to tail along the length of the mantelpiece. While waiting for Huskion to be shown in, he had taken another piece of paper from the stock he kept in his top right-hand drawer and was deftly folding yet another between his long aristocratic fingers.

He nodded Huskion to a chair. His baby-blue eyes examined Huskion shrewdly while his fingers moved with the assurance of a craftsman certain of his mastery.

"What are your hobbies?" he asked disconcertingly.

Huskion blew out his cheeks. He had come to His Nibs because when it came to it he had found he could not face

Spinwell cold, on his own. There was a better chance of Sir Nigel's understanding, as a civil servant, why he had acted so crazily than Spinwell, a sailor turned policeman.

"None really. I play tennis at the weekends. I suppose work's what I enjoy most."

"Damn fool. Like all you young chaps. Live on your nerves. Think you don't need to relax 'em. You're looking damned peaky. You should try origame."

"What?"

"Origame. This." He held up the paper. "Paper folding. It's a Jap word. They've made a science of it. Damn clever, the Japs. Ever tried it?"

"When I was at school we had a craze for tearing paper into patterns."

"Never tear in origame. Just fold."

He put the figure he had folded on the desk in front of him. It stood there on its own, the trunk raised, large ears drooping.

"Very neat," Huskion said.

"Yes. Invented by some American feller. I think I've got hold of it now. You ought to have a go. I'll send you a book on it." He reached over and took another sheet of paper from his drawer. "Something to do with all these damn forms we don't use anyway. Now what d'you want to see me about? This screening lark of Spinwell's?"

"In a way, yes."

As succinctly as he could he told his story. He had it all so clearly in his mind that he was able to do it without stumbling and strictly in sequence. When he reached the point where Sherngold had suddenly asked him about the money in his Helmstedt account, His Nibs's fingers had stilled and he set the crumpled paper on his blotter. Huskion ended by handing him the photograph.

Sir Nigel studied it thoughtfully.

79

"Very pretty," he said. "How did they get it?"

"I haven't an idea," Huskion answered hopelessly.

"Security'll work it out. You don't need me to tell you you haven't been very clever?"

"No."

Sir Nigel played several arpeggios on the edge of his desk.

"I think I'll lunch on this," he said crisply. "Yes, I'll lunch on it."

He let Huskion go without throwing him a comforting phrase or even a smile, committing himself to nothing.

Worrying about it over his lunch, Huskion saw he had little reason to expect sympathy or help from His Nibs. If he allowed himself to be involved, it would only be out of a certain *esprit de corps,* and there was precious little of that left where secrets were concerned. If he hadn't been within touching distance of retirement and so fireproof, he would almost certainly have bundled him off to Spinwell right away. That he hadn't was the one bit of cheer. After all, it wasn't much he wanted. Just to be steered through his first interview with Security.

He had to sweat on it for more than an hour after he came back from lunch.

A little after three o'clock His Nibs came into his room from the door into the corridor. He was at his feyest, white wings of hair flying, and moving with dapper jauntiness on the balls of his feet. His icy caution had evaporated over lunch and he smiled and waved Huskion back to his seat.

"Sit down, sit down."

Having settled himself in the chair opposite him, Sir Nigel planted his elbows on the desk and rested his chin on his hands gnomishly.

"You've broken so many of the damn rules, what d'you say to breaking a few more?"

80

Huskion blinked but said nothing.

"I mean this thing is bigger than a department matter." He beamed apparently guilelessly but Huskion saw that all the ice had not melted from the baby-blue eyes. There was a hard appraising calculation in them. "We might be a little naughty and by-pass the excellent Spinwell. Go to a specialist."

Huskion's stomach griped.

"Scotland Yard?"

Sir Nigel patted the tips of his fingers together.

"No," he said slowly. "They'd only come back to Spinwell. The people I have in mind are experts in this kind of skullduggery. They'll work on their own."

Huskion nodded.

"Now, I'm going to leave this note on your desk." He fumbled in his waistcoat pocket and drew out a slip of paper and laid it down in front of him. "It is a name and telephone number. When you have memorized them you will destroy it at once." He smiled. "They're all quite ridiculously melodramatic, these Security wallahs. Oh, yes, and when you ring the number you mustn't do it from the office. You must use a public call box."

Again Huskion nodded.

"When do I phone this man?"

"This afternoon, of course, my dear chap, this afternoon."

His Nibs stood up. And now when he spoke from well above Huskion's head he was not smiling and his voice was brusque with authority.

"If you would rather go to Spinwell, that is up to you. But you must do it today. Otherwise I shall forget that you have spoken to me. And if you don't, but use that number, I shall also forget it. What is more, you must not mention it to me again. Or tell anyone else that I knew anything about it. If you do I shall deny it." Suddenly he smiled. "Not that I think you'd feel the need to as you'll be in most competent hands."

The operating theatre jargon seemed to amuse him, for he chuckled as he went toward the door. Huskion stopped him before he reached it.

"What about Personnel, sir?"

"You're remarkably obtuse," Sir Nigel said, a shade irascibly, turning back to face him. "If you should adopt a certain course"—he seemed pleased with the phrase, for he repeated it, rolling it round his tongue—"yes, a certain course, the management of the affair will be outside the walls of this building and thus it seems improbable that Personnel will be involved. Ultimately, of course, there will be a report for Security but, unless your nose isn't as clean as you say it is and I'm being a damn fool, it probably won't be available to grades below Undersecretary. Does that dot the i's and cross the t's for you?"

"Yes, sir. And thank you."

Sir Nigel had the door open.

"I'll send my girl along with that book on origame on Monday," he called over his shoulder for anyone in the corridor to hear. He obviously thought this rather clever, for he winked at Huskion before closing the door softly after him.

Huskion sat at his desk staring in front of him. What His Nibs had offered him was a chance to wipe out his idiotic mistakes, a chance he had not expected or even imagined existed.

He took up the note Sir Nigel had left. On it was written a Notting Hill number and the instruction "Ask for Mr. King."

After memorizing the number he took out his cigarette lighter and burned the note, being careful to pound the embers into dust as he had seen it done in TV thrillers.

On his way to the call box at the end of Fairmile Place, he passed Spinwell in the entrance hall coming in. They did no more than nod to each other but seeing the Security man took some of the edge from his exaltation. It reminded him that he was still outside the pale though now it was with His Nibs' connivance.

Before the bell had trilled twice the receiver was lifted and a voice, accentless but authoritative, gave the number.

"Mr. King, please."

"Huskion?"

"Yes, sir—"

"No names!" the voice snapped. "And no explanation is necessary." Though it had not been raised nor loaded with a threat it was extraordinary how decisive the voice was, cutting like a whip, making argument unthinkable. "Tomorrow at eleven you will come to 37c Finlay Street. That is off the Portobello Road. From Notting Hill Gate end you'll have no difficulty in finding it. Understood?"

"Yes."

"Then repeat."

What the hell, thought Huskion. He felt the blood ride up his throat and the muscles of his jaw tighten in anger.

"Repeat the directions, please," the voice said when he didn't answer at once, not softening or encouraging but in exactly the same tone as before. "It's immaterial how big a fool you think me."

Huskion did as he asked.

"Right. One other thing. Use your car."

There was a click and the line went dead.

He left the box and walked slowly back along Fairmile Place. A week ago he would have considered this finger-on-the-lip cloak-and-daggery comic but there had not been anything funny about that cool impersonal voice.

The following morning being Saturday he put on a sports

83

jacket and slacks, his usual dress for weekends. He had debated whether to wear a business suit but had decided against it. It would have been bad for his morale to have got himself up specially, for the cool Mr. King made him feel inferior.

Without explanation he told Penny he would not be in for lunch. She looked at him out of the corner of her eye but said nothing. Usually on Saturday mornings they went round the shops together and had coffee at Grunler's, a Swiss patisserie, popular with the locals. She obviously took his brusque, unexplained breaking of their routine as all of a piece with his recent behavior.

He was approaching Putney Bridge when he became aware of the scooter. All up the Fulham Road it followed him and into Shepherd's Bush where he circled the green.

There had been a number of other vehicles he had noted in his mirror as possible shadowers but they had either peeled off into side turnings or passed him. He was dawdling, for the traffic was much lighter than he had anticipated. Yet the gray scooter did not overtake him. Judging by the getup of its wiry begoggled rider, it was not from lack of power, for he wore the leather jacket and round skid lid more usual to ton-up tearaways than sedate scooterists.

To find out if the scooter would follow, he made a second round of the Bush. As he approached Wood Lane for the second time and the lights halted the traffic, he was able to turn his head and look back. The scooter was no longer behind him.

But halfway up Holland Park he had a shock. The scooter was tailing him again.

He decided that if it continued to follow him right to Portobello Road, he would not go to Finlay Street but phone King and ask for instructions.

The scooter remained behind him all the way up Holland

Park, keeping quite close now, as though unconcerned whether he was seen. As Huskion turned off at Notting Hill Gate, the rider suddenly opened his throttle and the scooter surged past and wove its way through the traffic in front of him. In thirty seconds it was out of sight.

Because of the Saturday morning market, parking was tricky. After about five minutes, though, he found a spot in a side street, just pipping a fat woman with a dog and two glum children in a Mini for the place and earning himself a heavy scowl for jumping her.

He located Finlay Street but did not go up it immediately as he still had some time to kill before eleven o'clock. Instead he drifted among the market stalls while he looked around for anyone resembling the scooter rider. Assured that he was nowhere about, he turned into Finlay Street just as his watch showed the hour.

Number 37c turned out to be a shop, one of three that had been built in what had once been the large front garden of a hideously ugly Victorian house. Huskion looked at the three shops with misgiving.

Number 37a was a secondhand dealer's with an assortment of fishing rods, toys, watches, football boots and electrical components all thick with dust in the window. Next to it was the Bestyet Fish Saloon all brash pink marble and bronze displaying a notice "Frying Today, 12 o'clock." Number 37c had a large temporary fascia board on which was written in phosphorescent paint, "Amusements Unlimited." It was apparently an old-established concern, for peeling gold leaf on the window offered repairs to steam organs. Inside could be seen a higgledy-piggledy collection of pin tables and fruit machines.

It did not seem credible that this could be the place. He saw now why King had made him repeat the address.

He pushed open the door and went inside.

85

A round bald-headed bookie type in a ginger suit was talking in a loud voice to a tall cadaverous jacketless man who was listening to him with his thumbs in the pockets of his shabby unbuttoned waistcoat. While he talked the bald-headed man was banging balls round a pin table and shaking it vigorously.

"And you know what?" he was saying, "yer won't credit this, yer won't. After the fifth he was skint and he come up to me, straight up, he come up to me and said—"

But Huskion missed what he said because a young man in his early twenties who had been leaning against the wall just inside the door swung himself round and asked him:

"And what can we do you for, guvnor?"

The young man had sideburns that ran halfway down his cheeks, long hair that had been curled at the ends and flowed over the collar of his corduroy zip jacket. He was also none too clean. But his eyes were sharp, very sharp.

"I've an appointment to see Mr. King."

"Check." The young man nodded. "You're the bloke that rang about the Conservative fete, ain't you? Come with me."

"How'd you be able to earn a crust with crap like this," the bald-headed man was saying indignantly as they went out through a door at the back of the shop. "The bloody tilt's fixed." He gave the machine a vicious kick and all the bells on it began to ring.

At the end of a long passageway the young man opened a door and stood aside for him to enter.

"Mr. Huskion," he announced, adding explosively, "sir!"

"Thank you, Perkins."

Huskion recognized the cool voice he had heard on the telephone.

"Sir!"

The young man went out smartly, closing the door behind him. The military heel clicking went oddly with his barrow-boy appearance.

Huskion hardly noticed his withdrawal for he was taking in the room. It was about fifteen feet square and very scruffy. It was uncarpeted and, though the floor had once been covered with a greenish linoleum, this had been worn away in many places, exposing scored, dirt-gray boards. In two of its corners leaned several cupped pegs, painted with red and white rings, for holding coconuts in fairground shies. The poles and string netting that went with them lay along one wall while the container for the shies' ammunition, also brightly painted in red and white, stood in another corner. Above a fireplace choked with rubbish was a mold-pocked lithograph of what appeared to be a solar-topeed soldier of the Boer War standing on a sand dune valiantly waving his rifle aloft in defiance of the shells bursting in the sky around him. On another wall was a highly colored souvenir of the Jubilee, portraits of Their Majesties King George V and Queen Mary, leaning slightly askew as though endeavoring to avoid contact with each other, with the legend "1910-1935."

For furniture there were two chairs, a filing cabinet and a solid writing table, all Ministry of Works issue and scrupulously clean. King sat at the table beneath the solitary window, the lower half of which had at one time been whitewashed, seemingly needlessly for the accumulated grime on the upper half made it equally as opaque.

"Sit down, Mr. Huskion," he said. "You were four minutes late."

"I was making sure I hadn't been—"

"You weren't. It was one of my chaps on the scooter, checking you weren't tailed. It was keen of you to spot him. Very keen." King's tone was detached, objective not commanding. Nor was there any blame coloring what he said next. "But going back on your tracks as you did at Shepherd's Bush was very stupid. Never do that again if you suspect you are being followed. Gives the game away, that does, shows you know you're being tailed. Best thing is to stop and buy something, and then go home. But a packet of cigarettes or a pound of tea is no good. It depends on how far you've come, of course, but it has to be something that would justify you coming that distance, something you could not buy every day, a hacksaw, say, or a pair of budgerigars."

Huskion looked at him. He wasn't being funny.

His eyes were getting used to the murky light and despite the shadows he could see King plainly now. He judged him to be in his middle forties, short and spare. He had the tanned yellow-gray skin of a man who has spent many years in the tropics. His eyes were shiny-black, set close to his long thin nose; his mouth above a pointed chin was thin, too. A sharp ferrety face, a mask for thought. His clothes, an ill-made blue serge suit beginning to shine, a rounded buttoned-down collar and cheap red tie, and the way his crisp, pepper and salt hair was dressed, brushed forward and then turned back in a quiff, only needed topping off with a greasy cap to complete him for running the coconut shy on Hampstead Heath. But his authority definitely belonged to the Ministry of Works furnishings.

"Now, Mr. Huskion, I propose to put you in a room with a pencil and paper so you can jot down in note form the chronology of everything that has happened since this man Sherngold contacted you. It should not take you more than ten minutes and it will save time in the end."

"That won't be necessary," Huskion told him sourly. "I may not be very bright in dealing with spies but I've had some training in making reports. I'm ready now."

"That remains to be seen. Well, get on with it."

Huskion had been over the ground often enough to be sure of himself. As soon as he began to speak, King picked up a ball-point pen and pulled a scratch pad on the blotter in front of him. Every now and then he made a note, writing very small and putting a number, which he carefully ringed, by the side of each note. Huskion found it disconcerting that he rarely looked at him, it was almost as though he were talking to himself. Adding to the general bizarreness, a heavy odor of batter frying in slightly rancid oil began to seep into the room.

He ended, as he had with His Nibs, by putting the photograph of himself and Kay Dillon on the table. King glanced at it and then without a word got up and got a folder from the filing cabinet.

"Tell me if you recognize any of these."

He dropped a photograph in front of Huskion and when he shook his head covered it with another, and then another. Most of them had obviously been taken in a hurry, usually in the street, though one seemed to show the corner of a cinema foyer and one had a background of cages that might have been the Zoo. All were of men and none seemed to be aware of the photographer. The seventh picture caused Huskion to lean forward in his chair.

"That's him!"

"Who?"

"Sherngold."

There was no mistaking the thick wrestler's figure. The picture showed him about to enter a waiting car, the door of which was being held open for him. The photographer had not had much time, for Sherngold was moving fast, but he had caught him whole with one leg raised and his face toward the camera.

King did not query the identification but, without a word, put the photographs back in the folder and returned it to the cabinet.

"Who is he?" Huskion asked.

"He has dozens of names. The best we have is Lieutenant

89

Colonel Pavel Semenov but I wouldn't like to say it was his real name. Mostly he operates in Europe but he's turned up once or twice in the States. He's a thumping good spy and must be pretty high in Soviet Intelligence by now."

While he was saying this he had gone over to the red and white crate containing the balls for the coconut shy. He took hold of each side of it and lifted. It came apart. The rails of the crate were the sides of a tray on which the balls were piled. Underneath was a tape recorder.

King ran the tape back, then went over to his chair dragging the remote control lead behind him. He sat down and flicked the switch. Huskion heard King saying "Well, get on with it" and then his own voice telling how Sherngold had rung him on that August afternoon, three weeks before. After a few moments King clicked the switch and the recorder cut off abruptly.

"Tell me about Roesinck and Mullbricht."

"What do you want to know about them?"

King looked at him. Huskion knew he would not ask that kind of question again.

"Everything," King said evenly. "What they looked like, what they did, what they said, what you did together, where you met, where you went together, who were your mutual acquaintances, what their backgrounds were, how they dressed, what their incomes were, and anything else of importance."

"But I don't know all that," Huskion said, aghast. "Even if I ever did I'd have forgotten it by now."

"Then just tell me what you remember."

The curious thing was how much he did remember, things even he didn't know he had noticed at the time. King had a way of asking a question just as his mind was going blank that turned up the corner of the skin time had grown between him and his years in Berlin. In ten minutes he was seeing it

90

all so clearly it might have happened yesterday.

When he thought he had squeezed him dry, King started the tape running again. When it reached his next note he again switched it off and started more questioning. Each time, before he set the tape going again, he carefully scratched through the note he had just dealt with.

They had got about halfway through the list when Perkins came in with a tray of slablike ham sandwiches and a jug of coffee. The coffee had been made from essence and tasted filthy. King paused just long enough to pour the coffee into a couple of cracked cups and wolf a sandwich, masticating the meat rapidly between strong, very white teeth. If he had any small talk he was clearly not wasting it on Huskion, for he immediately set the reels turning again. He did not smoke either and there being no ashtray on the desk Huskion had not lit up. But after he had choked down the sandwich he decided he was not going to be intimidated in that way any longer and lit a cigarette.

Not all the exchanges between them were pleasant. Huskion was exasperated by the apparent pointlessness of some of the questions. And some were definitely insulting.

"Don't you believe what I say?" Huskion burst out angrily at one point.

"When you convince me you're telling the truth."

"I'm not in the habit of lying," Huskion said, and immediately wished he hadn't for it sounded weak and pompous.

"We all lie," King commented coolly. "Sometimes unknowingly but mostly with intent."

Nothing ruffled him. Provocation did not disturb his patience nor resentment his determination to lay bare the facts. Huskion hated him. He had shrunk from Spinwell because he had thought him incapable of understanding. King was ten times worse because he understood too well, picking out actions, motives, baldly for what they were, stripping away every extenuating gloss. This ripping away of the small shreds of self-justification that had solaced him made him feel naked, diminished.

"I'm not interested in the truth," King told him when he protested. "It's made up of more things than I've time to guess at. But I can use facts."

Of course, he spotted the significance of Huskion's Helmstedt account still being alive and dragged out of him the reason. He asked a lot of questions about Spiller Martin and his import-export activities. To Huskion they seemed to have no relevance, except to make his ever thinking of joining in these shady deals look totally despicable.

Even when the last note on King's list had been crossed off and he laid aside the remote-control switch of the tape recorder, he was still not finished. There followed questions on his background. Not just a general outline but questions designed to expand the facts tabulated in his dossier which King had evidently studied. Huskion presumed His Nibs had given it to him.

"Well, that's that," King said at last. "You've a good clear mind, Mr. Huskion. That always helps."

Huskion said nothing, being too wrung out either to be rude or to say thank you.

"There are a couple of things you might like to know. The photographs in the pub were taken by the young man who followed you in there. The lighter he was flashing about was also a miniature camera. I'll get some pictures for you to look at to see if you can identify the feller among them. It's not important but it's nice to know the other team. The chap watching your house was one of theirs too, not Spinwell's. Probably there to get the pictures if Mrs. Dillon went to your house."

"Was she in it?"

92

"I doubt it. If she was, she would have had to be acting when she came to see you. Do you think she could?"

"No."

"Nor do I. Any more than I think the man who conned her about Dillon being exchanged came from her solicitors."

"Christ, what a filthy thing to use her like that."

King, looking at his fingernails, which in contrast to the seediness of the rest of his appearance had a manicurist's polish—Huskion noticed that the backs of both his small hands were much scarred as though from burning—made no comment.

"Anything else?" he asked.

He was cool, detached and impersonal as ever and Huskion knew he would never like him but now that the questioning was over he was at least treating him as an equal.

"Why did Sherngold leave me alone for three weeks after seeing me?"

"For several reasons. First, to see if you went to Security about him—"

"How would he have known if I had?"

King looked at him for a moment before replying.

"It's only possible to guess, of course," he said, "but they probably thought it out like this: Semenov knew that we knew he was here. I'm pretty sure now he deliberately let us spot him. Any sudden activity by us would have warned him the game was up. As an added spur, he even let us think we had a chance of getting him, for the Embassy has not covered him with diplomatic immunity. He's supposed to be here as a private citizen. Of course, he was running no risk in trailing his coat like that because he couldn't be nailed for anything on the evidence of your word alone."

"I see."

"Then you had to be given a chance to get at the money. If you had drawn some of it, they had you hooked."

"But why the hell should they think I'd be such a damn fool?"

If King had any ideas about that he kept them to himself. "Another reason for their keeping out of the way was to soften you up by letting you think you had seen them off. Then, when Sherngold popped up again suddenly and they threw the photographs at you, they hoped you'd crack."

Huskion nodded.

"Mind you, that's pure assumption, what it looks like. They may have had quite a different idea."

"Such as?"

"There's the rub. I don't know. In this game there's always the one that hasn't been tried before."

"Well, whatever they expected is up the spout now you're on to them."

King grunted noncommittally.

"Do you ever go to the office on a Sunday?"

"Very rarely. Only in an emergency."

"Then we'll have an emergency for tomorrow. I'll see you in your office in the morning. Eleven o'clock suit you? Right. That's it then."

He didn't smile. But then he hadn't smiled before, not even once. His was not a face for smiling. But his control of his features was quite unlike Spinwell's blankness of expression, for he could convey nuances of feeling subtly, without changing the tone of his voice or altering the keen, shrewd line of his lips. For all its abruptness, the dismissal was not hostile but held a certain moonlight friendliness.

"Why do you want to see me tomorrow?" Huskion turned at the door to ask.

"I want some time to think about what you've told me."

Huskion nodded and went out.

Perkins was in the corridor waiting for him. Without a word he led him through into the shop. Apparently, business

94

was not brisk on Saturday afternoons, for there was no one in it except the cadaverous man leaning on a pin table studying an early edition of the *Evening Standard* and drinking steaming tea from a thick earthenware mug. He did not look up as they went through. Perkins did not open the shop door for Huskion and only acknowledged his "Good afternoon" with a barely audible "Hi!"

It was half past four when he arrived back at Bridle Walk. If the clock had shown five hours later he would not have been surprised.

Propped up against the telephone was a note from Penny telling him she had gone out with Lambert. He crumpled it up and dropped it in the wastepaper basket. He knew she had deliberately not said where she was going because he had not told her where he was off to when he went out in the morning.

He wandered round the house feeling aimless and rudderless. He thought of going to the club to play tennis but when he looked out he saw that was impossible because the clouds that had been building up all the afternoon had begun to weep a fine drizzle that would at any moment turn to steady rain.

The dampness had an autumnal tang of death darkening the dried-up foliage of the garden as though in mourning for the summer. He stood in the window looking out at it, no longer tired but drained and lonely.

He wished he was the sort of man who could go out and get thoroughly drunk, a spurious idea for he had not been drunk more than half a dozen times in his life and then only at parties. And never once enjoyed it, for the extra glass that made other people forget their misery only made him vomit.

Instead of risking anything like that he went into the kitchen, cut a plateful of thickly sliced bread and cheese heavily larded with mustard pickle and swallowed it with a pint of beer.

Afterwards he took his briefcase into his room and began to work. For those who have the stomach for it, work is also an escape—without a hangover.

8

Fairmile Place, naked of cars on Sunday, had the eerie hush of an evacuated city awaiting bombardment. Huskion parked in the place reserved for His Nibs' official limousine and got out.

He had not been followed either by one of King's outriders or by anyone else. One of the reasons why King had chosen the department for their meeting, he guessed, was because it did not matter who knew he was there.

"I'm expecting a Mr. King," he told the messenger on duty in the hall. It was ten minutes to eleven by the clock on the wall behind the desk. "Send him up to my room, will you?"

The instruction was unnecessary. King was already in his office, sitting in his chair with a pile of Top Secret files in front of him. The safe gaped open beside him.

"Hullo," he said, "you're early."

"I suppose if I hadn't been all those would have been back in the safe."

"No, but if you're to work with me, you'll have to be more precise in your timing."

He was not in the least flustered. Nor was Huskion after the first shock of surprise at seeing him there. He knew how he had got in. His Nibs must have given him the key to his private entrance through Fairmile Mews. And also the key to his safe in which were kept the duplicates for Huskion's.

Thinking that King was expecting him to ask how he had got in, he deliberately said nothing in the hope that he would explain and give him the satisfaction of telling him not to bother. But he didn't.

"Any number of people handle some of these files while others have very few names on them. What decides this?" he asked.

Huskion explained the system they used with Top Secret documents, the personnel who theoretically had access to them and those who did in practice. King crossed off a numbered list of questions on a scratch pad in the same way as he had the day before. But if he had a tape recorder with him, Huskion could not see where he had hidden it. He was becoming bored with the questioning routine.

Suddenly there was a slight noise in the outer office, a footstep or a chair being moved. Huskion was not conscious of it until King held up his hand for silence and at the same time whipped the files across the desk so that they were in front of him, as though it was he, and not King, who was looking at them.

Huskion started to get up to see who it was but King signaled to him to stay where he was.

"But the production rate you're asking for isn't feasible," he said evenly, as though he were continuing a discussion. "Not with all these changes your people have made. It's not a question of the availability of the materials, they're something we can fix. It's the wiring. That's all skilled handwork.

Of course, if the total run was long enough it could be automated. But even then—"

The door opened and Spinwell was there taking in the scene. Especially the yawning safe and the pile of folders on the desk.

His face was as wooden as ever but his eyes flickered uncertainly.

"I didn't know you were coming in today, Huskion."

"I didn't know myself."

"We're on the phone, you know."

"I'm sorry but it never occurred to me to let you know."

"You're damn lucky I came in. Hearing voices I might have decided it was someone who had broken in and called the cops."

"That would have been quite a party. Oh, this is Mr. King. Captain Spinwell, our Security chief."

"How d'you do," King said casually without getting up. Spinwell nodded.

"What are you doing here on a Sunday, Spinwell? No home to go to?"

"Standing in for my duty chap. His wife's having a baby."

"Good God, do Security men have children? You'll be claiming to be human next."

"Are you staying long?"

"About half an hour or so. That should about do us, Mr. King?"

"If that's all it'll take to convince you I'm right," King said and, to Huskion's surprise, his teeth gleamed whitely against his yellowish skin in the broad grin of a salesman gently joshing a customer.

"O.K. I'll leave you to get on with it."

Spinwell went out and they heard the door of the outer office close.

"I'm sorry about that," Huskion said. "I'd quite forgotten

about reporting I'd be in today. It wasn't necessary when I'd been in on Sundays before."

King grunted and went over to the door into the outer office and looked inside. Then he went across to the one that opened into the corridor.

"Where's the lavatory?" he asked.

Huskion told him and he went out.

"He's gone," he said when he came back.

"You were damn lucky it was I and not Spinwell who came in and found you sitting at that desk with the safe open," Huskion told him nastily. "He'd have clobbered the life out of you before you had time to reach for your warrant card."

"It's nice to know there's a modicum of security here. I should have thought it would have been simpler to break in and take what they wanted instead of offering to buy it from you. However, let's put this stuff back in its hutch and talk about that."

It did not take King longer than three minutes to tell him what he wanted. Only it wasn't what Huskion wanted. He had thought that once he had told all he knew about Sherngold, that would be the end of it for him. But, instead, he was to be more deeply involved.

"What you mean is, I'm to be one of your bomb throwers," he said slowly, "temporary, acting, unpaid, of course."

"Of course. Only you won't be given any bombs to throw. As you only made your school second eleven as a wicket keeper, you wouldn't be accurate enough."

King was prepared to be funny, too, if that was the way Huskion liked it.

"I'm just to sit tight until Sherngold contacts me again?"

"No. I think we'll prod him a bit. I want you to go to Berlin and pick up that money. Have you any leave due to you?"

Huskion hadn't but King told him it didn't matter. In his

rummaging through the files he had learned that a Dutch firm had tendered for a large quantity of condensers the G.P.O. needed. Huskion could go out to Eindhoven to look over the factory. When Huskion pointed out that there was no chance of the firm's getting the contract, King told him that didn't matter either.

"It's not the easiest place to get to Berlin from but it's the best we have."

"Why do I have to go to Berlin at all?" Huskion objected. "Wouldn't it be simpler if I just drew a check transferring the money to my bank here?"

King drew a slim, silver cigarette case from his inside breast pocket, offered it to Huskion and took one himself.

"Much simpler. But is it what you'd do if you were about to sell top secrets?"

"I don't know," Huskion said hesitantly.

"Of course you wouldn't. It would be much too dangerous for you to have all that money suddenly appearing in your account. Sherngold would immediately suspect you."

What they would expect him to do as soon as he had assured himself the money was in the Helmstedt, King told him, would be either to leave it where it was or remove it to a safer place. Which he chose to do didn't matter but drawing it out and stashing it away somewhere, say in a numbered account with a Swiss bank, would be slightly the better.

"What makes you so sure it's there?"

"Semenov . . . we may as well continue calling him Sherngold. Better to do that so you won't think of him as anyone else. If he's in it, they're treating this seriously and wouldn't be so silly as to bluff about the money."

"When do you want me to go?"

"Tomorrow."

This Huskion said was impossible but King overruled him. It was best for him to be out of the way for a day or two so that Sherngold could not make another approach until they were ready.

King mapped out a timetable that would take him until Friday. It was necessary, he said, for Huskion to spend at least one day at the factory and also to keep his hotel room for the whole week so that he could attach the bill to his expense chit. This meant that he could not fly home from Zurich but must return to Eindhoven to settle up. Even using airplanes—King was more familiar with the Continental airways than Huskion was with London Transport—this roundabout route meant much tedious traveling.

"Who pays for all this hopping about? I can't put it on my expenses, can I?" Huskion asked. "Should I take it out of the money in the Helmstedt?"

"That's a good idea, a very good idea." He didn't actually smile but it was obvious he was pleased. "Of course, if you run yourself into any expense over this we'll take care of it."

They went upstairs to His Nibs' room on the next floor. While King returned the duplicate set of keys to the safe, Huskion kept watch. It gave him a slight thrill to be acting stealthily, creeping on tiptoe like a genuine cloak-and-dagger man. That his secrecy would be official and he would be working in an aura of danger that held no meance promised a certain compensation for his disappointment at not being rid of Sherngold.

King left by the front door. After being seen by Spinwell, to have sneaked out through Fairmile Mews would have been idiotic. His presence could be accounted for by his having slipped past the doorman unseen, but if he were not seen to leave either, it would be a coincidence Spinwell would not like.

As he was now going to be out of the office for the next week, Huskion went back to his room to see what he could clear up before leaving. But first of all he called Spinwell to tell him that, although his visitor had gone, he would be staying on. Later he rang him again to let him know he was off to Holland.

"Just to put you in the picture," Huskion told him cheerfully. "Wanted to make sure that any of your bloodhounds trailing me would have the fare. Be embarrassing if he had to borrow it from me."

Now that he had the protection of a genuine mauler he felt safe taking on a paper tiger like Spinwell.

"That fellow come from Holland?"

"Good God, no. Mings and Wyatt of Sheffield."

"Not very clever, strewing all those Top Secret files under his nose even if he's British," Spinwell said nastily, and went into a homily on the need to work to strict rules when handling the files even inside his office. Huskion reckoned he deserved it for being so cocky.

It was six o'clock before he left Fairmile Place and he was none too pleased when he reached home to find there was only the usual cold snack they had on Sunday evenings waiting for him. As he had had only a couple of sausage rolls and a lager for lunch he was ravenously hungry.

"If you'd told me you weren't coming home, we could have eaten this evening," Penny said coolly, not looking at him, her attention engaged with checking her hairset in the mirror above the sideboard.

"Why don't we do something different tonight, have a celebration?" Lambert suggested. "What about eating Chinese at Lin Tong's. We haven't done that for ages."

Sunday was one of the days when Lambert came. Despite their row, it was accepted that he dropped in on them after visiting his wife.

"What should we celebrate?" Huskion asked icily. "Your being here? Or my being at the office all day?"

Penny turned her head toward Lambert warning him not

103

to answer. There was a martyred resignation about the look that made Huskion clench his teeth.

His nerves were on edge and the blackness of his mood deepened as they ate. Penny and Lambert pretending there was no "atmosphere" only increased the awkwardness between them.

To get away from them, he went off to his room as soon as they had eaten on the pretext that he had work to do.

As soon as he heard the front door close behind Lambert he went into the living room and told Penny he was going to Holland. She was patting the cushions straight and tidying up before going to bed.

"You'll not have enough clean shirts," she said without looking up. "Unless you'd like to run a couple through yourself tonight."

"I don't want Lambert living here while I'm away."

"Is that what's eating you?"

She emptied an ashtray onto a piece of newspaper. He could not be sure she was not smiling to herself behind the placid composure of her face.

"I don't give a damn what you do, with whom or how!"

It was his stomach speaking. But it was true, though he had not put it into words even to himself. He didn't care.

"But not here, d'you understand? Not in my house."

She was looking at him now and she was not smiling. When she spoke her voice had the cutting edge of an ice dagger.

"It happens to be my house. If you don't like what I do in it, you can leave it."

She went out of the room and upstairs, as always moving unhurriedly away from unpleasantness. Only this time she had had the last word.

He knew she understood his saying "living here" had been exaggeration for effect, his bad temper speaking. Her retort had not been in kind, but had a ring of unsuspected truth.

He didn't attempt to placate her but, glowering, packed his suitcase ready for the morning as she prepared for bed. Normally Penny saw to his things when he was going away.

They didn't exchange another word, not then nor in the morning. When he took up her tea, she opened an eye and watched him put it down on the bedside table. Instead of asking her usual question about the weather, she deliberately turned on her side with her back toward him.

9

In Berlin, as Sherngold would be footing the bill, Huskion booked himself in at the Tusculum on the Kurfürstendamm.

The drive from Tempelhof had stirred him nostalgically. The new buildings were in keeping with West Berlin's special flavor, a little too bright, too thrusting, uncertain, like a small boy putting his tongue out at a giant but not quite sure whether he's far enough away to be safe.

Detained by the eager hospitality of his Dutch hosts, it was now Wednesday afternoon and too late to go to the bank. Not that it mattered, for he had made up his mind to stay the night in Berlin and to hell with King's schedule.

At Thomas Cook's he booked a plane for Zurich. Then he strolled slowly down the Kurfürstendamm looking for Spiller Martin's bar. He didn't know whether he still owned it and he had only the haziest idea where it was located in the interminable boulevard.

He had walked almost half a mile before he came on it. It was called the Tender Trap. He couldn't remember if that was new but a lot of the neon was. It was like that inside, too. And larger. A floor of the next building had been taken in to make room for dancing. It was very dimly lit.

A white-coated barman was leaning over the bar reading a paper. He looked up at Huskion, evidently not expecting customers so early.

Huskion asked him if Martin was there. His German was so rusty that even this simple request came out haltingly. Not that it mattered, for the barman was English.

"No," he said, "Mr. Martin don't never come here as early as this."

"What time d'you expect him?"

"I don't expect him. But he looks in most nights. Mostly after midnight to pick up the divi—"

"I'm an old friend of his. I need to see him before that. Do you know where I might find him?"

The man shrugged.

Huskion fumbled in his wallet and laid a ten-mark note and his card on the bar. He had once seen Spiller Martin do this. He did it awkwardly, feeling a fool to be acting like a character in a second-rate TV crime series.

"Haven't you a number where you can reach him in an emergency?"

"Oh, if it's an emergency—"

He stretched out his hand and picked up the note, folding it carefully before putting it in his pocket. For some reason the way his bait had been taken made Huskion feel ashamed.

He was able to see the first two numbers dialed but then the man turned the phone away from him: 91 was the local exchange, so Spiller could not be far away, probably somewhere on the Kurfürstendamm.

"You're in luck, he'll talk to you," the man said, passing him the handset after two or three minutes' explanation to someone at the other end.

A secretary kept him hanging for a few moments but when Spiller came on he shouted his pleasure at hearing from him again. When he learned that Huskion was leaving the next day he cursed that he was tied up for the evening. If he could come back to the Tender Trap about one o'clock, though, they could make a night of it. Huskion was non-committal about this, pleading that he had to be up early.

"Have you any idea where I could get hold of Ferdie Roesinck?" Huskion asked.

"Who?"

Before the question there had been a slight pause and the tone was cautious.

"Ferdie Roesinck."

"Haven't a clue, old boy. We don't see many of these East Berlin bods now. What did you want him for?"

"Just a beer. We went around quite a bit when I was here."

"It's different now, with the Wall."

They chatted for a few more minutes, mostly about how Berlin had changed, where he ought to go that night, and the places where he would be assured of the best by mentioning Spiller's name. Spiller, at least, hadn't changed.

He went down into the Kurfürstendamm and hailed a cab, telling the driver to take him to a beer hall off the Hardenbergstrasse, one of four or five where Ferdie was often to be found. It was a long shot, ten years was a long time.

The beer hall had been rebuilt as a luxury restaurant, and there was not a soul there he knew. But in the third place he tried there was a face he recognized, an old thin face, much lined, with a pendulous nose above thick lips, which had already been so worn when he had known it that the last ten years seemed not to have touched it at all. He remembered Huskion; or said he did.

"Herr Roesinck? No, he doesn't come now because he's an East Berliner, you understand. But he's well. At Easter I was over there to see my brother—though I don't know why

I should trouble myself to queue all day for a permit to go to him, the fool likes the Communists. He told me Herr Roesinck often goes to the Spartacus where he works."

Huskion asked him for the address and his brother's name.

"Many of our old customers go to the Spartacus now. You remember Herr Grosse, who always laughed so much he got hiccoughs? And Herr Stillemann? And Herr Mullbricht? Oh, yes, and many others, too. My brother thinks the Wall is good because it prevents them coming here to be poisoned by American dollars," he said bitterly.

"If I should see your brother, is there any message you would like me to give him?"

"What is there to say to a fool like that?"

He added two marks to his tip when he paid for his beer but the old waiter refused them.

"The service does not justify it," he said with dignity.

At the hotel they told him there was no difficulty for foreigners to go into the Eastern Sector but it wasn't advised. But at Uhlandstrasse station he found this no difficulty to be relative. All the subway stations in the Eastern Zone were closed and he would have to get out before the train reached the Wall and go through the checkpoint on the corner of Friedrichstrasse and Zimmerstrasse.

In fact the crossing was easy enough. On the surface it was just like any other frontier, though the formalities were rather more punctiliously observed.

But as he walked across no man's land toward the East German barrier he felt uneasy. The brooding hostility at either end was unhealthy and the air had an unnatural chill as though the strip were haunted by the spirits of all those who had tried to come this way and never made it.

He knew King would break a blood vessel if he knew where he was going. But it was King's own fault. He wanted him to behave naturally. And Sherngold would see it as only natural

109

he should want to see Ferdie Roesinck.

The People's policeman who examined his passport was young and courteous and returned his papers with a smile. All the same, he could feel his heart jumping as he slipped them away in his breast pocket.

Going up Friedrichstrasse he turned into Leipsiger Strasse and then across the Platz der Akademie. These streets were broad and open but in contrast to the thrusting hysteria of the Western Sector had a drab defensiveness. Though the night was warm with a glitter of stars in the sky, there seemed to be no strollers, only people hurrying, shoulders hunched, looking neither right nor left. He wondered whether any one of them would have stopped long enough to direct him, if he hadn't looked up the way to the Spartacus on his street map.

The Spartacus was a traditional beer cellar that had probably been there in the Kaiser's time and didn't seem to have been changed much since. It was spacious, paneled in dark oak, and was reached from street level by a handsome staircase also of oak. Despite its being full, it had an air of seediness, of having come down in the world, the dim lighting suggesting a saving on electricity rather than an aid to intimacy.

As he walked slowly down the stairs he saw several men eying him narrowly and it increased his queasiness. He began to hope Ferdie wouldn't be there and he could go back to the Tusculum. King could not think him a bigger fool for coming here than he felt.

One of the men he had seen watching him detached himself from the bar and came toward him. He seemed to be the manager and, without a word, waved him toward a table on the far side of the room when he asked for Roesinck.

Ferdie was sitting with two men, looking boredly round the room while one of them talked and the other vigorously

110

nodded agreement. When he saw Huskion crossing the cellar, after a moment's incredulity, his face lit up, and he was out of his chair and coming round the table to greet him.

"Roy!" he yelled and slapped him hard on the back, adding in English, "What are you doing here?"

There was no doubt about his surprise or the genuineness of his pleasure. His boisterousness caused heads to turn at nearby tables.

He introduced Huskion to his companions as an old English friend. They stood up and smilingly shook hands, shuffled a little uneasily, looked at each other, bowed politely, and taking up their beer steins, moved away. The implication of the glance was obvious. They didn't want to be seen hobnobbing with a foreigner.

Ferdie cocked an eyebrow at Huskion and watched them go with amused contempt.

Ferdie had not worn well. He had the elegant good looks to which age usually adds distinction but it had made of him a ruined boy with heavily pouched eyes and veined cheeks. On the surface his manner was as gay as ever but, in repose, a dispirited tiredness settled on his face.

"I see you're thriving."

"Surviving, anyway," Ferdie said cheerfully. "What brings you to the Spartacus?"

They sat down and Ferdie ordered drinks.

Huskion told him he was on a sentimental journey, seeing Berlin again and looking up old friends.

"Nothing official?"

"No."

"Then your friend is wasting his time."

"My what?"

"Don't look round. He's sitting three tables to your left. He followed you in."

Huskion laughed.

"You're getting paranoic, Ferdie, seeing secret policemen under the bed."

"How else d'you think I've survived?" He said it as though it was a great joke. "You're probably right. He's probably only keeping an eye on you because you're foreign."

While pretending to be absorbed in their reminiscent chatter, Huskion, as unobtrusively as he could, shifted his position so he could bring the tables on his left into view. When he called the waiter over to order more beer he was able to get a good look at the man.

He was sitting with his stein of beer in front of him, smoking a long thin German cigar, the kind that is made by wrapping the tobacco leaf round a straw, and looking idly round the smoke-laden cellar.

Ferdie was right. The man had been on the platform at Uhlandstrasse. Huskion had not consciously noticed him but since the days when he was on the watch for Spinwell's bloodhounds his mind had taken to registering faces. He was sure of this one, even though the man had then been wearing a narrow-brimmed greenish felt hat, with a small feather in its band. The hat was now on the chair by his side.

Huskion wiped his clammy hands on his handkerchief. It was hot in the cellar. But it wasn't that that was making him sweat.

He kept the conversation going with Ferdie while he tried to sort out who could have had him followed. And why? Spinwell, King, Sherngold—the number of people interested in him was getting uncomfortably long. He eliminated Spinwell. He didn't know he was coming to Berlin. Even if he had known, he hadn't the forces to lay on a shadowing operation.

But King knew. Could the blond man be there for his protection like the scooterist? Or because King didn't trust him?

There was still Sherngold. But how the hell could Sherngold know he was in Berlin before he had been to the bank?

One thing only was certain. The man wasn't German.
Checkpoint Charlie, the crossing at Friedrichstrasse, was
barred to Germans.

He did not work all this out coherently or very quickly. By
the time he had got this far he was calmer. There was nothing
he could do about it, anyway, now the man was there.

They were on their third beer when Huskion began softly
to whistle the tune on the cigarette box. Pretending to be
absorbed in flipping the lid on his stein to the rhythm, he
watched Ferdie covertly. He was almost through the chorus
before Roesinck's face came alive and he joined in the last
line.

"You remember that old thing!" He laughed and punched
Huskion in the chest. "So many years ago, and you remember
it! It's so long, I can't remember the words."

"Which version? You wrote a lot."

"Oh, yes, very dirty, weren't they? I can't remember the
German at all. The English was 'A little girl went to the pond
for a duck'—no, it wasn't pond, was it? What was it? Lake?
I forget."

"Be sensible for once and tell me where I can get one of
those wooden cigarette boxes that play a tune when you open
it. Know what I mean?"

"Anywhere on the other side of the Wall. All the souvenir
shops have them," Ferdie shrugged.

"No, I wanted something better than junk. A man I know
brought a beauty back from Dresden a couple of months
ago."

"In Dresden, perhaps. Here we don't have things for
tourists."

"No? But you still have a lot of people coming through the
Wall. Why only the other day I had a chap in my office called

113

Sherngold, a Swiss, who said he'd met you when he was here."

Ferdie could not remember the doctor and when Huskion described him he shook his head.

"There are many who look like that around here," he said, "but they are Russians not Swiss. And none of them is called Sherngold."

He wasn't acting. If he had been innocently trapped into sending the cigarette box, there would have been no reason why he shouldn't have admitted it, unnatural if he hadn't asked whether Huskion liked it. And if he had been privy to the plot he would hardly have been so unfeignedly pleased to see him.

At about half past ten the fair-haired man got up from his table and Huskion thought they'd boobed about his being a policeman. But he only went over to the telephone kiosk in the corner of the room, coming back immediately afterwards and settling himself down again.

Now that he'd learned what he'd come for, Huskion wanted to get away. It wasn't that he didn't like Ferdie but there was such a gulf of time between them. He was as bored by Ferdie's scurrilous stories, about West German politicians he had never heard of, as he had been by his filthy songs. And Huskion's detachment from the Berliner's political urgency about every upheaval in the world irritated Ferdie.

When Huskion stood up to go, his attempt to make him stay was loud but halfhearted. But they went through the motions, exchanging addresses and promising to write.

At the top of the stairs Huskion turned round and waved to him across the smoky cellar. The fair-haired man had got up from his table and was putting on his hat.

Huskion's head was aching slightly from the beer and the stuffy noisy atmosphere and the night air had a pleasantly cool freshness. He felt like walking, so, instead of making

114

directly for Checkpoint Charlie, he turned up across Platz der Akademie into Unter den Linden before going back down Friedrichstrasse.

He was no longer worried about being in the Eastern Sector. He didn't even bother to look round to see if the KGB man was following him. He knew it was a KGB man because he had made the phone call. That clinched it. With calls from the Eastern Sector to the Western having to be routed right round the Russian Zone via Dresden, it wasn't feasible that one of King's men would risk using the phone. And any man of Sherngold's would only want to ensure that he had no trouble. So he walked past Volkspolizei, who eyed him suspiciously, with a carefree, almost provocative, unconcern.

The phone call itself gave him a slight twinge, for he guessed it meant a car and some quiet men would be waiting for Ferdie when he left the cellar. But Ferdie would survive the grilling. He had, after all, chosen to live where such things were part of the way of life.

Back in the Western Sector, he threaded his way through the fringe of loiterers gazing at the Wall beyond the checkpoint. He understood the curiosity of tourists doing the sights but what brought the Berliners there? There was something ghoulish about their patient staring, as though they were waiting for the moment of drama that would set the world alight, waiting and hoping.

He took a taxi to his hotel. The Kurfürstendamm, bright with color and activity, deepened his melancholy. It was as unreal, as false, as the gloom in the other half of the city, an expression of subservience to America as the other was of Russian dominance. That was the trouble with the damn city; it wasn't divided at all. Each half was a mirror of the other, grotesquely distorted.

He decided to give the Tender Trap and Spiller Martin a miss. Spiller stank too strongly of Berlin.

The next morning as he approached the bank in Gruben-strasse, he suddenly lost his nerve and began to tremble as he had when Kay Dillon had phoned him. If it had not been for the KGB man trailing him, he would have walked past it.

Not wanting to look a fool, he took a grip on himself and pushed open the door and walked slowly across the black-and-white tiles to the nearest grille.

It was still early and there were only a few people in the bank. A man turned away from the counter and strode toward the door stuffing a wad of notes into his wallet. The cashier looked after him and then shifted his gaze to Huskion. Huskion had the sensation that all the clerks were looking at him, that even the clock on the black wall was a gigantic eye.

Everyone behind the counter seemed youthful and not one had a face he recognized. The teller took his request to see his statement noncommittally and then disappeared round a partition. He was gone several minutes. While he was away Huskion leaned on the counter and looked the other customers over. The KGB man hadn't followed him inside the bank.

When the teller came back his manner was brisker, more deferential.

"Would you be good enough to give us a specimen of your signature on this piece of paper, Mr. Huskion?" As Huskion signed, he added, "I'm sorry to give you this trouble but it is a long time since you have been here, sir."

The clerk's smooth tones told him what he'd come to Berlin to learn. That kind of soft soap wasn't wasted on twenty-mark accounts.

The money had been paid in—or so the statement showed —in the most damaging way, in three unequal installments over eighteen months. The first was the smallest, DM.3,680, and the last, deposited on the day he'd taken Sherngold home to dinner, for DM.6,165, the largest. Fourteen thousand marks in all, just as Sherngold had said.

The spacing of the payments was nicely calculated. They neatly covered the time he'd had Tridon.

"There's nothing wrong, is there, sir?" the teller inquired anxiously. He realized Huskion was staring at the statement.

"No, not as far as I can see," he said, pushing it back under the grille. "Will you let me have a checkbook?"

He separated out fifteen hundred marks, reckoning that that should cover his expenses. If it was a bit over he wasn't worried. The rest he stuffed away in his inner pocket.

Back on the pavement he paused for a moment while he sorted the notes into his wallet. Sherngold would know about his withdrawal soon enough from his source in the bank but he wanted the KGB man to have something to report. Now came the difficult part. He had thought it out over his breakfast and it had seemed easy enough then. But now he had to do it.

Seeing Grubenstrasse that morning, though, had been a shock, it was so changed. Half the rickety old houses, including the one where he had worked, had disappeared under huge concrete office blocks. But the Konditorei where they used to have their elevenses was still there. And that was what mattered.

Casually he crossed over to it. Hatless, with a copy of yesterday's *Times* under his arm, he hoped the picture he presented to his tracker was of a man with time on his hands who had just completed a piece of business he needed to think about over a coffee.

Like everything else in Berlin the coffeehouse had been given a facelift with bright new tablecloths and neon-lit showcases but was substantially as he remembered it. The same dumpy frau, the proprietor's wife, sat at the cash desk, only slightly altered by a couple of extra chins. She gave him

117

a faint puzzled smile, evidently recognizing but unable to place him, and he smiled back.

Probably because of the new office blocks, the café was fuller than he'd expected at this time in the morning. He managed to find an unoccupied table at the back of the shop and ordered a coffee and a slice of Black Forest gâteau, a specialty of the house, and a favorite of his when he used to go there regularly.

These had been brought to him when, to Huskion's relief, the KGB man came in and sat down with his back to him at a table in the middle of the room. There had always been the possibility he would wait outside. His guess that, despite the risk, he could not afford to do that in case his quarry was meeting someone in the café had been right.

It was the same man who had been at the Spartacus, though he had changed his green hat for a black felt and put on a dark belted raincoat with a fur collar. He didn't look toward Huskion. Knowing he was there and alone was enough.

Huskion found the rich cream and kirsch-soaked strawberries of his cake too sickly sweet for his stomach. Even if he hadn't grown unaccustomed to such goo, his midriff was fluttering too violently to welcome meeting anything, even the coffee.

No matter how he felt, he told himself, he'd got to sweat it out. The timing he had worked out was all-important. So he sipped his coffee and pretended to read his paper. Cautiously he worked a five-mark note onto the table beneath the paper, calculating that would cover the bill.

Precisely at 10:30 he called the waitress over, ordered another coffee and asked where the lavatory was, speaking loud enough for the blond man to hear. Leaving the folded copy of the *Times* beside his half-eaten cake he strolled to the door she had pointed to.

118

Beyond it a flight of wooden stairs led down to a stone-flagged passageway. On the wall was a notice, TOILETTEN, and a finger pointing to the left.

Huskion turned right. That way led out into an area and up to a side alley by way of a short flight of steps, the delivery entrance for the café. He and his friends had often used it instead of going back through the shop.

A worry that gnawed at him was that the entrance might have been blocked up. But the door at the end of the passage opened easily and he was in the area. A moment later he was darting up the steps.

And there was the snag.

The area was separated from the alley by a row of spiked iron palings with a gate let into them at the top of the steps. As Huskion remembered, this gate had always been open. Now it was secured by a chain and a heavy padlock.

He looked at it stupidly for a moment. But only for a moment. Using the padlock as a foothold he hauled himself on top of the railings and jumped.

His leg seemed to twist and he landed awkwardly, going down on one knee. His trousers had caught in a spike and made a great gash in the cloth.

A plump, jolly-faced man walking down the alley apparently found his mishap amusing, for he was grinning broadly when Huskion looked up from dusting his knees. He didn't seem to think it strange that a lanky man in a city suit should be clambering over spiked railings, only funny that he should fall down. Huskion grinned back sheepishly and stood examining the tear in his trousers until the man was well past him. He must not look as though he was running away.

As soon as he felt the man was far enough off he went out into Grubenstrasse and took a taxi to Tempelhof. His trousers bothered him but he'd no time to do anything about them.

He didn't know how long it would be before the KGB man found out he'd ducked him but he doubted if it would be more than ten minutes. So long as he drew the wrong conclusion from his having no luggage and went back to the Tusculum in search of him, it would be too late for him to catch him at the airport. If the plane left on time.

All the same as soon as he'd collected his bag, which the hotel had deposited for him with Pan American, he made himself as inconspicuous as he could for the few minutes he had to wait before the Zurich flight was called.

The plane was on time. Sherngold's man had not shown by the time he passed the barrier. He hoped he had enjoyed his coffee.

Several passengers stared at his torn trousers as they walked out over the tarmac though he probably imagined more eyes were on them than actually were. He certainly hadn't imagined the air hostess who hovered over him obviously would think she should be able to help him.

"An accident," he mumbled, feeling his cheeks redden, "just an accident."

"You're not hurt?" she asked, her eyes lighting up hopefully. Clearly she would know what to do if he were.

"No, no."

But now that she mentioned it, he realized that the slight stiffness of the skin that he felt on his knee and his right shin must be dried blood. Just grazes, they couldn't be anything more than that.

He was caught completely unprepared when he had to change planes at Frankfurt, having assumed he was on a direct flight. For an hour he squirmed in anxiety in case there was a later flight out of Tempelhof that connected with the Lufthansa for Zurich. But if there was, the blond man didn't make it.

At Zurich, instead of taking the airport bus from Kloten, he escaped into the privacy of a taxi, telling the driver to take him to an outfitter's. He bought and changed into a pair of dark-gray Daks. If they didn't go with his jacket they didn't make him look as peculiar as the high-breasted Continental suit they tried to sell him.

There was no point in his rushing to find a bank, for he could not leave until the morning as both the evening planes for Amsterdam were full. It had also started to rain hard.

He booked in at a hotel on the Ute Quai overlooking the lake. Nervous to be carrying so much currency on him, he sealed the wad of hundred-mark notes into an envelope and gave it to the hotel manager to put in his safe.

And then he had nothing to do.

To ease the bruising on his leg he had a long soak in a hot bath. When he went downstairs again his odd trousers made him feel conspicuous among the sleek transient businessmen in the public rooms. That he should be so conventional annoyed him without easing his embarrassment.

To escape he put on his raincoat intending to look at the town. But he got no farther than the Platz on the other side of the bridge at the end of the lake. In that downpour he would be soaked through in an hour and he didn't want to look like something that had been fished out of the water when he went to the bank in the morning.

Retracing his steps he found a restaurant on the corner of Bellevue Platz. Even with a good dinner inside him he felt no more cheerful. When he came out from the restaurant he decided Zurich, with its double trams, almost empty at that midevening hour, grating between the puddles pitting the Bellevue Platz, was a dreary provincial place, somewhere to get away from.

In the morning the rain had given way to blue skies and the lake and quais had a clean, invigorating sparkle. With the change in the weather, his gloom dribbled away to a specter at the back of his mind.

The bank he'd selected from King's list was in the Bahnhofstrasse. Its façade of marble, stainless steel and copper was of such daunting opulence that he hesitated before entering. He felt out of his element and guilty, too, to be pretending the money was his.

Making the arrangements to open a numbered account, however, was astonishingly easy. The depositing of the thick bundle of notes was treated briskly as though such transactions were everyday affairs. Which, he thought in surprise, they probably were.

As he walked back along Bahnhofstrasse toward the lake, the luxury shops and splendid façades on either side of the wide boulevard no longer seemed oppressive but to express a sensibly ordered security. He would have liked to spend the bright autumn day exploring Zurich. But he had no time. As it was he would have to stay the night at Eindhoven.

It was not quite dusk but dark enough for lights to be on in upper windows when he arrived home on Saturday to an empty house.

There was no reason why Penny should have waited in for him, no way she could have known what time he would be back. He had looked forward to dropping into her lap the little hexagonal watch he had bought for her—and paid duty and purchase tax on. It wasn't meant as a peace offering. Just something he knew she'd like.

As she wasn't there, he felt cheated, as well as tired and hungry.

He went upstairs and bathed, after which he felt better.

It was not until he went into the bedroom to get some clean clothes that he discovered Penny had moved all his things into the spare room.

10

"Hullo! Who're you?"

From a teapot with a chipped spout she was watering three exotic-looking plants he didn't remember seeing on the window sill behind Gilly's desk. The eyes she turned toward him were large and brown, several tones lighter than her hair, which was brushed back with unfashionable severity from her forehead. The style suited her deep high-cheek-boned face.

"Calshott, Deirdre Calshott. Miss Langham's been transferred and I've taken over from her. You're my boss?"

"One of them."

"Oh, I've already met Mr. Wigstall and Mr. Havelock."

"It's a damn nuisance having her whipped away without warning but I suppose we'll survive," Huskion said, unconscious of the rudeness. "Where's she gone, anyway?"

"Durrington."

She followed him into his office. There was a row of flower pots on the window sill there, too.

123

"Miss Langham showed me how you liked your correspondence arranged. I think you'll find it's all right. She left you this note."

He glanced at the piles of folders on his desk and nodded. "There's just one thing, Miss . . . Miss . . ."

"Calshott."

"Calshott, I don't like my office looking like a greenhouse. I get nervous in case one of those bits of ivy gets loose and strangles me."

"I rather wondered whether you would like them. I'll take them home. I wouldn't like to give you nightmares."

This time she smiled.

She was a damn sight more decorative than Gilly. The yellow-gold blouse with a floppy bow at the throat that she wore under a tan jersey suit was a long way from Gilly's inevitable dun-colored cardigans.

Still he wished Gilly had been there. Her note burbled about a vacancy having come up that would let her be with her Simmy and added, characteristically, as an obvious afterthought, she was sorry to be dashing off without being able to say good-by. Her defection was one more jar to the familiar pattern of his life.

He had already gone to bed when Penny came home on Saturday and all through Sunday they had been politely cool to each other. She said nothing about turning him out of the bedroom and, as so often recently with anything important, his will was paralyzed and he could find no words in which to speak of it. Lambert's coming in as usual in the evening and pretending that it was no different from any other Sunday seemed to stamp the new situation as permanent, making it still more difficult to mention.

The odd thing was that it was losing the trivia of marriage, the ordinary mundane things they did for each other every day without thinking, that hurt most. Over his breakfast

124

he had debated whether he should take her up a cup of tea as usual, not knowing whether she expected it. As Penny had slung him out of the bedroom, he didn't feel inclined to go barging in holding the cup of tea as though it were an olive branch. And he was damned if he was going to knock on the door like a footman. Deciding in cold blood not to do this small thing had weighed like a stone on his insides, for it seemed to make their estrangement complete, more irrevocable than their sleeping apart.

After a week away there was enough work on his desk to take his mind off his depression. His Nibs had been fairly blitzing the categories. Huskion found that three of his projects had lost their Top Secret ratings and about ten others had been downgraded. Not, he thought, before time.

The Calshott girl turned out to be quite efficient and apart from putting *z* for the *s* in the suffix -ise—something he detested—her spelling had none of Gilly's unforeseeable vagaries. But neither did she have Gilly's happy acceptance that she was less than perfect.

"The dictionary says that either *s* or *z* may be used," she told him bluntly. "It's a matter of preference."

"I prefer *s*."

"Oh, that's all right. I thought you were telling me I was wrong."

"Don't worry, young woman, I expect I shall. Often."

"But spelling is my job," she said, going a faint pink. "I don't want you to think I'm inefficient. I'll always use an *s* in future."

He supposed he'd get used to her in time.

As he was going out to lunch, Wigstall caught up with him and they went down the stairs together.

"I trust you painted the Netherlands red at the Treasury's expense?"

"Vermilion."

"You're young enough to take it. Dutch debauchery is something stodgy to my jaded palate. What d'you make of Deirdre of the Sorrows?"

"She's hardly the right coloring for an Irish tragedy queen, is she?"

"But sad, don't you think, to be so earnest? An improvement, though, on that other big-bummed hoyden, a definite improvement. In your absence Havelock and I borrowed her to do some small chores."

Strange, Huskion thought, how things came to be established. Wigstall and Havelock had given up using Gilly because her anarchic attitude infuriated them. Now they took for granted that her replacement was his secretary and they could only borrow her at his convenience.

The phone box in Fairmile Place and all the booths at Charing Cross Post Office were in use so he walked on to a pub in St. Martin's Lane where he had a snack before calling King at Notting Hill. He had rung the number twice on Sunday and been disconcerted when there was no reply. It had affronted him and sapped his confidence to know that a Security department he depended on could go off on a Sunday leaving its exchange unmanned.

Huskion reported what he'd done in Berlin and Zurich, holding nothing back. He had expected to be bawled out about going into the Eastern Sector but King let this pass, though frost settled on the silence as he waited for the comment that never came.

"You'll need a new suit" was all he said. "Send me the bill."

"I was going to. What happens now?"

"That's up to the other side. They have to make the next move. When they do, let me know at once."

"Can I have another number? One where I'll be certain of reaching you."

"This one will do that."

"No, it won't. I tried it twice yesterday."

"Yesterday it wasn't necessary for you to reach me."

Before he could argue further King hung up.

He walked back to Fairmile Place nursing annoyance and a feeling he'd been let down. All things considered, he'd done damn well by King. He didn't expect to be given a medal but the bloody man could treat him with common decency. Damn it all, did he think he liked waiting to hear that soft voice on the phone, not knowing what was going to appear in his mail, wondering what trick Sherngold would play next?

Huskion had hardly sat down at his desk before Spinwell came in to see him.

"Thought I'd have a word with you before you got your head down," he said.

Which meant that he'd had the messenger in the lobby warn him when Huskion came back from lunch.

"Everything go all right in Eindhoven?"

"Yes."

Spinwell obviously wasn't interested in his trip but was congenitally incapable of making a direct approach. Huskion let him blather for a couple of minutes and then asked him tersely what he wanted.

"About your girl," he said, lowering his voice.

"What about her?"

"How well do you know her?"

Huskion leaned back in his chair.

"Intimately. We've been engaged in a passionate liaison ever since we met at nine-six this morning—give or take a minute."

"I rather thought you must have asked for her specially," Spinwell said, adding bleakly, "you see, I was against her appointment."

"Well, well! What's wrong with her? Or is a certain kinkiness in spelling now evidence of a Security risk? Tell me all about her."

Spinwell did just that, as flatly as a policeman giving evidence.

Deirdre Ann Calshott was now twenty-seven. She had been educated at St. Philippa's, an unremarkable choice of her parents, for Major Calshott was a professional soldier and St. Philippa's specialized in giving the daughters of parsons and soldiers a sound grounding. She had done well there, getting a good "A" level pass in English and just scraping others in French and history, and "0" levels in maths, chemistry, biology and needlework. Shortly after she left school, Major and Mrs. Calshott had been killed in an accident in the South of France. She inherited a small house at Harley Wintney but very little else as the Major's pension died with him and the Calshotts had invested their cash in a joint annuity. In eight years with the government, she had been variously employed in the Board of Trade and Supply. Her salary scale was loaded with a bonus for French and all her superiors had given her exceptionally good reports.

"I seem to be lucky to get her," Huskion said. "What's your beef? Do you think, like Lady Bracknell, losing both parents smacks of carelessness?"

Spinwell eyed him stolidly, evidently trying to place Lady Bracknell. He had probably only heard of Oscar Wilde as a homosexual.

"She's not English," he said woodenly.

"Don't tell me she really is Irish?"

Spinwell didn't exactly show surprise but his neck stretched upward another half-inch out of his collar.

"Did she say she was Irish?"

"She didn't say she was anything. Skip it. What is she?"

"That's it, I don't know. She's not the Calshotts' child. He found her in a DP camp when he was serving in Germany and adopted her. She could be Russian, German, Bulgarian, anything."

"Doesn't she know?"

"Apparently not. She was only a baby when Calshott found her in a camp he liberated. It was thought she was six or seven then but it wasn't known when she became separated from her parents, nor even what her name was. In the last six months of the war, with all Germany collapsing, these camps became a shambles. By the time we reached them what records there were had either disappeared or been destroyed. According to Calshott—he sent a letter to the Appointments Board at the time she applied to enter the Service—she was ill when he found her and so shocked it was six months before she uttered a word. And then it was English, not surprisingly, for it was the only language the Calshotts used to her."

It was difficult for Huskion to relate the rather stiff English manner of the brown-eyed girl sitting in the outer office to such a bizarre infancy.

"Quite a story."

"Yes. So you see why I thought there must be some special reason for her being appointed, after I'd given her the thumbs down?"

Huskion laughed.

"I suppose it didn't occur to you that your objection might be thought daft?"

"A line has to be drawn somewhere."

"Which at once produces borderline cases."

"You know the form now, anyway."

"Don't worry." Huskion grinned. "If I see her trying any Mata Hari tricks on His Nibs I'll let you know at once."

It was quite a gift, the way Spinwell let any ribbing run over him as though it didn't exist.

"A good idea would be," he said, "for you to continue

writing in the formulae and calculations on Top Secret stuff, even though a 2 in "O" level maths shows Miss Calshott can add two and two."

Spinwell stood up.

"Enjoying my questionnaire, Spinwell?"

"It's being worked on."

"Good. I wouldn't like it to have been shoved away in a pigeonhole after all the hours I spent on it. In my own time, too."

Spinwell at the door looked back at him, his lips cracking open a fraction in what he may have meant to be a smile.

"We never like to disappoint our customers. And we get there in the end."

When Miss Calshott brought him his tea, he asked her to get her book. The memos he dictated to her were not important and could very well have waited but what Spinwell had told him had intrigued him enough to want a closer look at her.

It was still hard for him to believe, though he did not know how he expected her tragic infancy to show. It had certainly not broken her spirit. She was wary of him as was only natural but not at all intimidated. Deliberately testing her out he dictated at a pace that would have had Gilly squealing at the second sentence but she took it quite coolly. And it was not because she was too frightened to protest, for she was quick enough to tell him when he mumbled.

"Settling in all right?"

"Oh, yes. But all the names are new to me. I mean, I don't know who's important and who isn't."

"Start with me," Huskion grinned. "Oh, and by the way, if either Mr. Wigstall or Mr. Havelock wants you to do things for them, you'll be too busy."

She looked at him, her large brown eyes rounded.

"But I work for them, too."

"Technically, but I don't think they'll press it unless you let them. So be diplomatically busy. I want to keep you for myself."

She turned away from him without answering. Suddenly he wished he hadn't said it. It sounded so ridiculously petty.

"Of course, you'll help them all you can in an emergency," he added weakly. "I only meant they'll snow you under if you let them."

"I see."

He looked at the door closing behind her, still feeling uncomfortable. Her priggish efficiency was going to take some effort to live with. One thing was certain, it would never be possible to think of her like Gilly, as a piece of the office furniture, cozy and familiar. But, as Wigstall said, she was attractive, much more attractive than he'd thought at first sight.

"What did you make of our Voosborg friends?"

His Nibs had come into his room by the door into the corridor. Under his arm he carried a large manila envelope.

Huskion assumed that His Nibs must know that his trip to Eindhoven had been a blind but the inquiry seemed quite genuine. Taking his cue, Huskion also played it dead-pan, explaining the setup of the factory in detail.

"It was quite an eye opener," he ended. "We have nothing here in electrical assembly to touch their highly automated production line. I got the impression they were having trouble finding orders large enough to keep it fed. That's why their prices are so low!"

His Nibs nodded, his dolly-eyes sparkling with amused malice.

"How sad it won't do them any good. There's no justice, there really isn't. Our masters at the Treasury have spoken. The G.P.O. must shop at home for their bits and pieces. Still, your journey's not been entirely sleeveless. What these

Dutchmen are doing will make a nice stick to beat our fellows with. Nothing like a good scare that they may lose a contract or two to foreigners to make them pull their socks up."

"Right. But I doubt if I'll be able to get any of them to within five percent of Voosborg's price."

"Do your best, my boy, do your best." He dropped the manila envelope on the desk. "Number three of the Tridon files. Only you and I will have access to them now. There really is no point in Wigstall and the others checking them any more."

"I see you've regraded some of the other files, too."

"Been in need of a shake-up." He gave a sudden smile. "Spinwell has his uses, you know."

Alone again, Huskion felt a new respect for His Nibs. Not by a single sidelong glance or gesture or tone in his voice had he betrayed that there was secret knowledge between them. It was a great piece of dissimulation. Huskion found it too good, for it seemed to deny completely they had ever shared this knowledge. He was too conscious of his loneliness to want to lose anyone who had once been friendly.

He did not take the Tridon folder from its double-envelope Top Security covering until he was clearing his desk before going home. Before locking it away he glanced at the minute sheet.

As he read his brow corrugated in a puzzled frown. Dropping the folder back on his desk, he sat down and read it carefully. When he had finished he looked through the rest of the file, his fingers riffling through the pages in nervous panic, his face white and drawn.

After he'd been right through it, he flopped back in his chair, staring straight in front of him for some minutes before getting up and walking round the room. He was breathing in short gasps that ended in a wheezing sound. But he hardly noticed this or even that he was on his feet, his movements involuntary, disoriented, his eyes blank with stunned bewilderment.

It was not a Tridon file!

Every formula, every calculation, every assessment, everything about it had been changed. Except the cover.

11

It had been done extraordinarily well.

He had to admit that, after he'd gone through all the Tridon files a second time the next morning. For they had not been made into gibberish by the alterations. The figures made sense.

Only they didn't add up to Tridon. The picture they gave was no more like Tridon than Stephenson's Rocket was like a modern diesel.

Very cleverly the files began at the point where they had been just over a year ago. Then the project had been on the verge of being abandoned. It wasn't that it wouldn't work— expert opinion was emphatic that it would—but it was too clumsy and too expensive. An electronic pile driver, His Nibs had called it, for delicately cracking nuts. Then had come the breakthrough converting the pile driver into a tiny, exquisitely poised instrument with a weight of pounds instead of hundredweights.

That was Tridon.

134

But now all mention of the breakthrough had been deleted from the files. They were a wholly fictional record of the development of His Nibs' pile driver. And they were so minutely detailed that he would have accepted them as genuine if he hadn't known the true ones. Even his and Wigstall's and Havelock's and His Nibs' handwriting had been beautifully forged on the minute sheets, the notes they had written in the real files being rephrased just sufficiently to make them fit.

It was very impressive. And bewildering. For these phony files were not dummies prepared for a purpose he didn't understand.

The faking was still going on.

On his desk that morning had been letters from two of the firms who were employed on Tridon. They had apparently come in with the rest of the mail, as they had the department's date stamp on them. And each letter was arrant nonsense, totally unrelated to the ones he'd sent them over a week ago, which they purported to answer. But they fitted the forged files.

Last night he'd no more than flicked through the other files on the project in the safe to confirm they had all been altered. He'd been too shaken then to go through them properly, had, in fact, been gripped by an urge to run from them, to be on his own.

On his way out he'd been startled to find the Calshott girl still sitting at her desk in the outer office, waiting for him to leave. Brusquely he had shooed her off home. It was when she had looked at him oddly that he became aware of his bronchitic breathing and made a mental note to go along to Boots in Piccadilly to get something for it. If he didn't deal with it soon, it would probably develop into a bad chest cold, for he'd had it hanging about for some time. He'd first noticed this tightness in his chest when he was standing at the top of the stairs as he was going into the Spartacus.

Instead of going home, he spent the evening at the Progressive. Over his dinner he tried not to think of the spurious files and concentrate on his paper but his mind kept wandering back to them. Afterwards he sank into an armchair in the almost deserted library and tried to fathom it out.

It wasn't the monkeying with the files that bothered him—though he couldn't say he liked it—but that he hadn't been warned that was worrying. It could be, of course, the plan had only been worked out while he was away. But he saw at once that that wouldn't wash, for King had said nothing about it when he called him. Nor had His Nibs.

There was nothing he could do but carry on as though the files were genuine. The whole damn business had started because he'd thought it would be clever to keep his mouth shut and now he was stuck with it. There wasn't anyone he could talk to now. Barring King, who wouldn't be interested in his feelings.

By the morning the shock had worn off and he thought he was getting far too jumpy. It was plain silly to panic because he hadn't been told the files had been altered and didn't understand why they should have been. After all, all he was being asked to do was to act quite naturally as though nothing had happened.

That should be easy enough. And would be if he could shake off his queasy feeling that he'd lost his roots and was treading on air.

As he put the Tridon files back in the safe, he still puzzled over them. Why on earth had they been made? Such elaborate deviousness had to have a purpose. Somebody was intended to see them. The Russians? But how? Was a courier going to "lose" the phony files where an interested party would find them?

The idea amused him. He saw, too, that it had its uses.

If the Russians could be conned into believing the British were capable of getting all that hardware into orbit they might take it they had lost their lead in rocketry.

"I'm afraid I jumped on you rather last night," he said to Deirdre Calshott when she came in with her book in answer to his buzz. "I'm sorry. Seeing you still there threw me."

"That's all right." She had a way of looking down and straightening the hem of her skirt over her knees when she was nervous. "You hadn't said you wouldn't want me any more."

"You hadn't asked, Calshott, you hadn't asked."

"I didn't mind staying."

"I minded. I'll keep you late when there's a need. But your time is half past five. Just shove your head in the door to say when you're pushing off, that's all."

"But you may want some calls . . . "

"I'm not so damned helpless I can't twiddle a dial. Now let's get down to work, Calshott."

She didn't exactly pout but her jaw set tight. He wasn't at all displeased he'd needled her.

He saved the two Tridon letters until he had dealt with the rest of his correspondence. Then he replied to them in the terms of the phony files. Making them as apparently genuine as the rest of the inventions gave him a certain satisfaction. Taking a hand in the game was better than being the ball that was batted about.

"I don't like being called Calshott." She had closed her book and stood up and was looking toward him. "If it's to be a single name, I prefer Deirdre."

It was not so much a protest as a quiet assertion, spoken softly, her expression neither mutinous nor defensive.

"I bet they called you Calshott when you were a prefect."

"I'm not a prefect now."

"That's a relief. You had me worried once or twice yesterday." He was diverted to see her cheeks pinkening and grinned. "All right, Deirdre it shall be."

"I suppose I'll get used to you in time," she said as she went out.

It amused him to hear her echoing his thoughts about her.

When she brought him his letters for signature, he kept back the Tridon ones, slipping them together with the carbons into their files. Before he left he took the files along to His Nibs. Usually only exceptionally important letters would be shown to him before they were dispatched. All that was important about these was that they should not be posted or Universal Magnetics and General Metals would think he was off his rocker. Presumably some scheme had been evolved for seeing they didn't leave the premises but Huskion didn't see how he could lose by making it easy.

He left punctually and arrived home earlier than he'd been for months. If Penny interpreted this as a gesture asking for forgiveness for skipping dinner the previous day without letting her know, she made no sign.

He didn't know what he'd expected or hoped or wanted or how he would have reacted if she had been more forthcoming. Mainly, he'd wanted to share with her the lightening of his spirits that had come during the day as he got a grip on the Tridon nonsense.

Nor was the rest of the evening any less disastrous. They talked brightly while they ate, impersonally about the day's news and a murder trial that was claiming much space in the papers. Huskion tried to bring a more intimate note into these exchanges by telling her about Deirdre Calshott but Penny ignored this and immediately began to talk about the play that had opened the night before. Such talk was more depressing than silence.

Afterwards they sat on either side of the television set watching a play he found excessively boring.

138

The sensible thing would have been to go to his room. But this he obstinately refused to do. It would be playing Penny's game, to leave her alone and shut himself up with a book, as though he were a lodger.

When she finally unwound herself languidly from the couch and went over to switch the television off, he said:

"Don't you think we should talk?"

"Isn't it rather late, Roy?" she yawned.

"That damned box has been on all the evening."

"I didn't know you wanted to natter. You should have turned it off."

"You seemed to be enjoying it."

"Yes, it was rather good, wasn't it? I think the plays have been improving lately." She was at the door. "I shan't be long in the bathroom, if you're planning an early night."

It would have been useless for him to try to stop her. And what the hell did he want to say to her anyway? Reconciliations were born of compulsive need bursting out in a shared emotional explosion. Even if it hadn't been laughable to imagine Penny responding to that kind of drama, it wasn't what he wanted either. But, equally, he didn't see what words he could use to ask for what he did want, which was, he suddenly saw, some solidity, a sure base he could retreat to and feel secure, himself, recognizable and known. Or, even if he could make her understand this, whether she would be willing or capable of giving him anything like that.

The next day was Wednesday, the day of the week Sherngold seemed to favor. Since his last call, Huskion's fear of hearing his voice whenever he lifted the receiver had slowly melted away. Now it returned sharply as ever, his heart giving a little leap every time the phone bell whirred.

He, of course, didn't know that Sherngold would contact him at the office. He had, in fact, carefully noted everyone who came near him on his way to Fairmile Place, in case

139

someone attempted to slip him a note. No one had. And, so far as he could judge, no one had followed him.

This furtiveness had its effect on him and his nerves were on edge by the time he reached the office. To add to his jumpiness his telephone was particularly busy. He vented some of his irritation on Deirdre, snapping at her and making her retype two unimportant interdepartmental memos, because he detected where she had rubbed out mistakes.

The fright he felt each time he reached for the phone was followed by something very like disappointment when the voice in his ear was neither foreign nor whispering. He wanted an end to the suspense. As the day wore on though, he realized the suspense was his own creation. He expected the call because by now Sherngold must know he'd withdrawn the money. But, as usual, Sherngold was unpredictable.

Neither on Wednesday nor during the rest of the week did the Russian try to contact him.

Each day there was something on his desk to be added to the phony Tridon files, letters, memos, reports from non-existent committees. All these meant work but none so much as a minute from His Nibs asking for an appraisal for the Minister. After abstracting the facts for this, which meant going through all the files, he put aside writing it up until the weekend. Then it would at least provide an escape from Penny and Lambert.

All this faking was giving someone else a lot of work. He guessed that the missives he was receiving mirrored the papers going out on the genuine project.

By the end of the week, any comfort he had gained from helping with the fraud had oozed away, partly because what he was doing he did blindly and partly because the way the thing grew was menacing. Outwardly it was so completely genuine it corroded his confidence in what was real so thoroughly that he checked his other projects to see if they were phony, too.

He toyed with the idea of going away for the weekend to see if a change of scene would restore his balance. But going off alone to skulk in a seaside hotel or country inn seemed pointless. And, in any case, cut across his instructions to behave naturally. What he needed was something to take him right out of himself. But making the diagnosis was simpler than finding the cure. He didn't fish or shoot or like motoring for its own sake. He made a tentative approach to a beefy Assistant Secretary in his middle forties named Potter, who spent the summer weekends getting excessively damp sailing a Flying Fifteen and who had several times suggested he join him on the Hamble. But Potter wasn't going down to his cottage at Bosham that weekend because gales all along the south were predicted for both days.

So he stayed at home. To his surprise, it turned out to be less depressing than he'd feared. The daylight hours he spent at the tennis club, exhausting himself playing half a dozen sets each day, seeing little of Penny except at meals. Even Lambert's normal defeated Sunday expression after seeing his wife and prissying with the cutlery failed to irritate him as much as usual. Huskion wondered whether it was all the exercise that had made him so tolerant, whether his sense of being pushed further and further into limbo was not partly due to a sluggish liver.

Certainly, as he worked in his room that night on His Nibs' appraisal, the shenanigans over Tridon seemed less sinister. If he hung onto himself, they would work themselves out, fall into perspective, in time. His was not to reason why, but obediently to fake and lie. It would all be over soon.

All the same the ringing of his phone still made him start sometimes. Though, characteristically, not when the expected happened.

141

He was in the middle of dictating to Deirdre and he held the receiver suspended while he completed a sentence.

"Huskion."

"You found the account correct, yes, Mr. Huskion?"

At the sound of the silky, purring voice, Huskion felt the nerves tighten down his body. He gripped the receiver so hard his knuckles were as white as maggots.

"Yes!"

"So now we can deal, yes?"

"I don't know."

"Oh, yes, Mr. Huskion, I'm sure you do." The voice was still soft but it no longer purred silkily.

"No."

"The telephone is not the way to discuss private things, Mr. Huskion. And like me you are a busy man, yes? But it is good to have a break in the air sometimes in the middle of the day. And there are such beautiful parks in London. Especially St. James's Park. You walk in St. James's Park sometimes?"

"Sometimes."

"Tomorrow lunchtime would be good for us to meet, yes? You enter from Birdcage Walk, by Buckingham Palace, you know, and go along the south side of the lake. Just before you reach the bridge are two large trees with a seat under them. It is a very nice spot. Tomorrow at one." Then after a pause, "At one, Mr. Huskion."

"I'll think about it."

"Oh, yes, Mr. Huskion, you must think about it. I shall think about it, too. So, tomorrow, Mr. Huskion. I am sorry I could not ring you before but I have been very busy. At one, Mr. Huskion."

The line clicked and the dialing tone whirred in his ear. Slowly he dropped the receiver back on its cradle and stared in front of him, his face stiff and set.

142

"Our concern is not with the completion date, which is satisfactory, but when deliveries will start and their flow thereafter," Deirdre read from her book. "That's as far as you'd got."

Her voice gave him a sharp shock, as though he'd been roughly shaken from a deep sleep. He looked down at the letter on the top of the file in front of him and collected his thoughts. He wanted to talk to King at once but it would seem odd to Deirdre if he sent her away with only half his letters done. He had to act naturally.

He began to dictate. His voice sounded very queer, dry and reedy. To hide his shock, he lounged back in his chair, trying to look easy.

But halfway through the next letter he had to sit up straight because his chest was playing up again. By the time they had finished the constriction was so bad he was gripping the desk as he gulped in air in short wheezing gasps.

"Go out and get me"—he was finding speaking an effort—"or send a . . . messenger . . . Get me some ephedrine."

She was standing with her notebook and pencils held in front of her regarding him speculatively, as though trying to make up her mind about something. He fumbled in his pocket for some money.

"Breathe out," she said.

"What?"

"Breathe out. Empty your lungs."

"Damn it all," he gasped, "I'm trying to . . . fill 'em!" He dropped a pound note on the desk. "Here's the money."

"Do as I say. Breathe out. As hard as you can."

She had put down her book and pencils and was leaning over the desk toward him. He made a face at her and blew out his cheeks.

"No, harder. You must do it till it hurts."

He tried again, feeling the blood bound up into his head

143

with the strain. When he let his diaphragm go, air rushed into his lungs.

"Again. But you must do it harder. Really empty your lungs."

After half a dozen exhalations the constriction had eased a little. He was still gulping in air but not in such short painful gasps.

"It seems to be going away," he mumbled.

She nodded.

"Would it make you more comfortable if I massaged your back?" she asked diffidently.

"I haven't a clue."

"Shall we see if it does?"

"All right," he said ungraciously. "It'll be exercise for you anyway."

He took off his jacket and straddled a chair, facing the back, as she directed. Deirdre ran her fingers lightly over his shoulders and the base of his neck and then began to knead the muscles.

"Ouch! That hurts!"

"Yes, I'm sure it does. You're all knotted up," she said, continuing to press her fingers hard and rhythmically over his shoulders.

In a couple of minutes the acute pain that had stabbed him when she first touched him had given way to an all-pervading ache across his neck. It stayed there after she stopped massaging him and began to run her hand down his spine, examining each vertebra with the tips of her fingers.

"You've made me ache like hell," he grumbled.

"It'll wear off. Now relax, let yourself go quite limp."

Her hands left him and he heard the rustle of materials being rubbed together behind him. The next second she had gripped his shoulders and planted her knee on his backbone. Getting as much purchase on his shoulders as she could, she jerked him back sharply, pressing her knee forward at the same time.

"Hoy!"

"Sorry. Just one more. Let yourself go."

"D'you know what you're doing?"

"Not really, that's why I'm going to try only once more."

"You nasty little sadist!"

But he let himself relax. This time when she hauled on him he felt his bones crack. Immediately she released him and again he heard the rustle of material.

Swiveling his head round to see what she was doing was painful, for his neck muscles were tender from their pummeling. She was smoothing down her skirt. He grinned, realizing that to ram her knee into his back she would have had to pull it up round her waist.

"I ought to have looked round before."

"Your life must be full of regrets."

She was flushed and a little shiny from her efforts. Two or three hairs had come away and lay on her brow like cracks in porcelain and a light frill of perspiration hung on her upper lip. Instead of the questioning doubt which he had come to believe was their only expression, her large eyes were bright and pleased.

"Shouldn't I have some of the pleasure as well as the pain?"

This time she really did smile, a small tucking of the corners of her mouth.

"I think it worked that time."

"Where did you learn this devilish karate or whatever it is?" he asked as he slipped on his jacket.

"My mother had asthma. Her osteopath showed me ways of giving her relief when she couldn't go to him," she said. "She was chronic, though. Hasn't anyone told you how an attack of functional asthma can be stopped by getting control

145

of your breathing as soon as it starts?"

"Asthma?" he queried, frowning. "I haven't got asthma, haven't had it since I was a kid. This is just a chest cold I've had hanging about for . . . oh, a couple of weeks or more."

She looked at him as though she didn't believe him.

"Well, it seems to be easing, whatever it is. Your breathing's better."

That was true. He'd gone back behind his desk but had not sat down. Resting his hands on the back of his chair, he was concentrating on emptying his lungs after every intake of air. The rhythm of his breathing was definitely slower and less urgent.

"And now you'll know what to do if it happens again," she said.

"Let you kick me in the back."

"I wasn't thinking of that." She didn't smile this time, but picked up her book and pencils before adding with a slight edge, "If I don't get on with these, I'll have you complaining about my staying late."

As she went out he remembered he had to speak to King.

"But, damn it all, what the hell d'you want me there for? All you have to do is to pick him up," Huskion said angrily.

He was in the call box in Fairmile Place.

"He won't be there to be picked up," King told him.

"But I told you he's arranged—"

"Somebody will be there. But it won't be our friend. He's too spry to take that kind or risk. That's why you must go."

"Why can't it be one of your men?"

"Because whoever is going to meet you in the park will know how to recognize you."

"Yes, but look here—"

"Not now, Huskion. There's no one else who can do this but you, so you will have to do it. Afterwards I'll listen. Right?"

Huskion didn't answer at once but King said nothing else.

"All right," he said at last. "What d'you want me to do?"

"Nothing," King said, and then went minutely into what the nothing was.

"Will you be there, too?"

"We'll be keeping an eye on you," King promised, though this didn't fully answer the question. "Afterwards I'll see you."

"At Notting Hill?"

"No. Come out of Fairmile House at five past three. Someone you know will be getting out of an official car. Cadge a lift in it to Custom House."

"But that's right down in the City."

King ignored this irrelevance.

"It would be useful if you could dream up a reason for seeing someone in Customs," he added, and rang off.

Frowning unhappily, Huskion hung up. On the steps of Fairmile House he stopped for a couple of minutes, carefully exhaling. Though he hadn't hurried, the twenty yards he'd walked from the call box had made him puff. He found that by this conscious effort his breathing returned to normal almost at once as Deirdre had said it would.

It was nearly six before Deirdre brought him his letters. By then he was feeling much better, the leaden pressure on his lungs had disappeared. And, instead of being nonplused and worried by having to meet one of Sherngold's men tomorrow, he was beginning to feel some anticipatory titillation at seeing some action.

"Your tenses were a bit wild, so I altered them," she said.

"Showing off your education again, Calshott? It would have been more tactful if you'd let me think your impeccable grammar was my own. Bolstering my ego is part of your job."

"Doormats come from the M.O.W., requisitioned on the

appropriate form," she told him tartly, for the first time answering his chaff in kind.

She stood at his shoulder pointing out the alterations in the letters as he read them. The hand she rested on the desk was very feminine, with long fingers ending in well-cared-for oval-shaped nails, hardly seeming to have the strength he had felt in it when she had massaged his neck. He liked having her close to him.

"I haven't said thank you for pounding me so effectively, have I?" he said, signing the last of the letters and dropping back on his chair.

"You looked awful. I was scared I was doing it all wrong. You can never tell with asthma anyway. It can go as suddenly as it comes."

"How about a drink to celebrate my recovery? If you don't have to rush off home, that is."

She stopped licking an envelope and looked at him rather oddly. Her large brown eyes sharpened, as though his invitation had frightened her. Then she lowered her gaze, so that he couldn't see her expression any more, and pressed the envelope closed between her fingers.

"I'd like that," she said, giving him her small tuckered smile.

They went to the Compasses, a pub he often used at lunchtime. It pleased him to see the barman give Deirdre a close appraising look, like a Grand Vizier in a slave market, and draw in his lips in a silent wolf whistle.

The pub hardly had any evening trade at all. A smattering of the lunchtime crowd looked in for a pint on their way home but did not stay long. By half past six the private bar was uncomfortably empty, making Huskion regret not having chosen a livelier place.

They took their gin and tonics to a table well away from the bar and talked about themselves, doing their best to ignore the oppressive hush of the empty room.

She told him she shared a flat off Bayswater Road with another girl, which was just what he would have guessed. And inevitably she asked him about Penny.

He talked about the war to see if she would tell him about the concentration camp.

"I hardly remember the war at all. I was only a baby." That was all she said. "You couldn't have been much more, either."

"It ended in my last term at school."

He had to be careful not to give away how much he'd learned about her from Spinwell. So that he wouldn't be caught out, he deliberately slanted questions so that she told him about her school and parents.

"What about going somewhere to eat?" he asked abruptly, as he finished his second gin and tonic. "If you haven't got a date, that is."

He hadn't, until that moment, thought of spending the evening with her, but suddenly it seemed more attractive than eating alone in the Progressive's cavernous dining room.

"Won't your wife be expecting you?"

She said this quite naturally. Whatever it was that had troubled her when he'd asked her out for a drink no longer bothered her.

"I was eating out anyway."

"Then I'd like to."

They walked up to Neville Street, to a Chinese restaurant he'd been meaning to try for some time. She turned out to be knowledgeable about Chinese food and, in consequence, they had a more adventurous meal than the pork pellets in sweet and sour sauce, vegetable chop suey and pancake rolls he usually ordered.

"These are good," he said, gnawing at a spiced spare rib. "Where did you learn about these exotic dishes? Surely not at St. Philippa's?"

"It's a long time since I was at school."

149

It seemed to him that she had a rather shapeless life. Most of her school friends had left the well-to-do homes, where she used to spend lively weekends, to marry and make homes for themselves in the suburbs or provinces and were now absorbed in domestic problems that did not touch her, so she saw them less and less frequently. She seemed to belong to no set, to have no habitual round of activities. She went to dances, theatres, and concerts, but all occasionally and very sporadically. Two or three times a year she would have a weekend in the country with distant relatives or friends of her parents, the invitations usually coinciding with some local festivity such as a cricket week, which bored her, or a Hunt Ball, which she found rather fun.

It all sounded rather cockeyed to him, not quite of this day and age. But then she was past the furious, rootless activity of youth, probably, with her education and upbringing, had never known it. Apparently there had been boy friends, still were, but nothing serious, she said. He wondered if it was because she frightened them. If he'd been younger, he could imagine her collected self-assurance scaring him before he had time to find out it was nothing but protective coloring. Was she already beginning to think of herself as an old maid? There must be times when she was very lonely.

"Why haven't you got yourself transferred to Clerical?" he asked curiously. "You've the qualifications to make the Executive grade."

"I suppose I liked what I was doing."

"Why don't you now?"

"I couldn't, could I? I mean, I'm too old."

"Positively decrepit. But I should think that could be got round."

"Are you trying to get rid of me?" She gave him her odd crinkled smile. "Have you been gorging me on scampi and lichees so that you can get me out of your hair by dazzling me with ambition?"

"We haven't reached the lichees yet."

"I was hinting. Still it's quite a nice way of being given the sack, even if it is underhand."

"Seriously?"

"I just don't want to."

"But why? You're completely wasted as you are, and you'll go on being wasted."

"I like what I'm doing. I prefer being a little minnow, nibbling on the edge of the pond where decisions are made, to being a big fish in an unimportant puddle. I never wanted to be a career woman," she said. "That was why I didn't try for a university place. Of course, I wanted the fun of being a student but I was afraid that by getting a degree I'd be trapped."

He was on the point of asking her if she didn't feel just as trapped now, but bit it back. Though she had spoken lightly, there was a sadness of revelation, as though a tender, rarely seen nerve had been exposed in what she'd said.

The lull that succeeds the exodus of the theatregoers was ebbing and the restaurant was filling up again. A plump Chinese with coarse black hair that looked as though it had been pulled from a sofa, and tangerine quarters under his eyes, wielded long bone chopsticks with graceful delicacy at a table opposite theirs.

"I've always wanted to learn to use chopsticks," Huskion said. "But I expect I'd only make the most dreadful muck because I'm no use with my hands."

It reminded him of His Nibs and his origame and, while they sipped their tea, he told her about it. Together they tried folding paper napkins but achieved nothing more interesting than cocked hats and airplanes.

"Why do you always leave the figures out of reports I

type?" Deirdre asked casually. She had opened up one of the hats and was trying to refold it as a boat.

"I see," she said when he'd explained. She put the paper boat on the tablecloth, smoothing the edges in an effort to stop its falling apart. "Though you may not think it, it's meant to be a boat."

"God bless all who sail in her."

"A blessing is what they'll need. I wondered if it was because you thought I might be a spy."

"There's that, too, of course."

He said it lightly and, in the same tone, told her about the deep positive screening technique. Apparently Security was only a name to her for, though he didn't mention Spinwell's objections to her, she listened with an uncertain concentration, as though she wasn't quite sure he wasn't making it up.

"You mean you're spied on all the time?"

"When they're concentrating on me, yes. Then they'll tap my phone, read my letters, and trail me wherever I go."

"But do they? Have you ever been followed?" she asked suspiciously. "How did you know it?"

"I saw the man because I was watching out to see if I was being dogged. But it may have happened a lot of times when I didn't notice it." He grinned. "Who d'you think is keeping their eye on us tonight."

Her eyes rounded.

"Us? You don't mean that?"

"I do." Leaning toward her he added in a conspiratorial whisper, "Don't look now but under all the padding and yellow grease paint that fat Chinese is really James Bond."

But she didn't laugh. And though he'd joked, he rapidly checked over the people in the restaurant. Of the twenty who were there only the fat Chinese was on his own. What Spinwell would make of his having taken Deirdre out, if he were to learn of it, he had no idea, but he was sure he would not like it.

152

"There's something obscenely frightening about being secretly watched," Deirdre said, wrinkling her nose. "I don't think I could bear it. Being spied on all the time by that two-way television was what I thought was most awful about *1984*. Ugh! I thought this was what we had against the Communists. It seems we're just as bad."

"Slightly better I should say," Huskion said judicially. "After all, it only applies to those of us on secret work. And, though it may look queer to use police state methods to defend individual liberty, it's been forced on us, not chosen."

When they came out of the restaurant it was still early enough for them not to hurry home. After a day that had been dull with the first chill of autumn in it, the evening had turned surprisingly soft and mild. Instead of catching a bus at Piccadilly, they strolled up Regent Street window shopping, intending to take the tube at Oxford Circus. The Central Line would put Deirdre down at Queensway and also give him a connection to Wimbledon.

As they reached the Circus a bus came ambling down Oxford Street.

"That will do me fine, if I can only catch it," Deirdre said, shouting over her shoulder, as she ran off. "Thanks for a lovely evening."

Without thinking he started off after her.

"I'll come with you."

"Whatever for?" she asked in her disconcertingly direct way as he came up with her as she rounded the pedestrian barriers and threw herself across the road without checking her pace.

The bus was held up at the traffic lights. Even so they had to sprint hard to catch it, for its stop was some way beyond Regent Street.

Laughing, they flopped down in a double seat.

"There's nothing wrong with your chest," she said. "I'm much more out of breath than you are."

It was true. But then he never had difficulty in sustaining quite long rallies at tennis. What was inexplicable was the way in which his chest had turned to stone that afternoon.

"We must do this again," he said, after they got off the bus and were walking away from Bayswater Road into the more dimly lit streets and squares toward Paddington.

He meant it, for the few hours away from the tensions tugging at his nerves had raised his spirits. He felt more cheerful than he had for weeks.

"I'd like to. It was fun because it was so unexpected."

"The fun?"

She gave him her little smile.

"I did rather wonder what I was in for. You're rather a scary sort of boss. Haven't any of your other secretaries told you so?"

He found it hard to believe. Still it would explain her look of fright when he'd asked her to go to the Compasses.

"This is where I live."

The house was a towering late Victorian pile of red brick with a steepled portico at the top of a flight of twenty or so chipped flagstone steps. Deirdre's flat was under the roof, in the attic that had once been the servants' bedrooms.

He put his hands on her shoulders and kissed her gently on the lips. She neither pulled away nor hung limply back but matched his pressure with her own. The contact was hardly more intimate or emotional than a handshake, yet as he watched her climb the steps he felt a warm glow of pleasure.

12

Leaves, rust colored and shriveled, lying dankly along the edges of the paths in St. James's Park proclaimed that autumn had arrived. Despite the dampness pervading everything after a continuous drizzle all the morning, there were quite a few people stretching their legs before returning to stuffy offices.

Huskion wondered what would have happened if, instead of drying up, the drizzle had turned to a downpour. Nothing could look more suspicious than two men meeting in the middle of the park in teeming rain. In spy fiction such intractable hazards as the weather never seemed to play a part. Or simple human ailments—such as if he had gone down with flu and not been able to come at all.

But he hadn't gone down with flu and would be there on time, even a few minutes before, for the bridge was nearer to the gate than he had thought. He identified the two trees, for they were immense and an easy mark. On one of the slatted wooden seats beneath them a man was sitting eating

155

his lunch from a paper bag and feeding crumbs to the birds.

Huskion went up to the other seat but not fancying sitting on its damp surface, leaned on his umbrella looking at the birds fluttering about the man. If, as King said, Sherngold's man would be able to recognize him, he could also find a way to attract his attention so they could remove to a more private spot.

The man feeding the birds was fiftyish with a pear-shaped body swelled unnaturally by the assortment of slipovers and cardigans he was wearing under the coarse regulation tunic and dark-blue mackintosh of a government messenger. Thinning rough-textured black hair, parted in the center, clove his brow in a widow's peak. A long acquisitive nose, thin lips and dull brownish eyes behind small steel-rimmed spectacles gave his heavy-jowled face a mean look.

It was the face of a man who was feared by his wife and hated by his children, not at all the type that would be expected to give the better part of his lunch to birds. The birds certainly had no fear of him but flew around him, taking pieces from his hand and even settling on his knees and burrowing in the bags on his lap.

He did not accept this boldness willingly, except from sparrows. Pigeons were allowed to perch and take one peck at a crust and then were roughly brushed off. He was particularly sharp in fending off one pigeon with a game leg who, time after time, flopped onto his upper arm and then slid down to get at the bags.

"Artful, you wouldn't credit," he said, sweeping the maimed bird off his knee. "Presumes, it does, because it's crippled. Presumes on it."

"Oh, surely it's not that intelligent," Huskion said, pretending the antics of the birds was why he had stopped. It was now five past one and, although twenty or thirty men had passed him, none had given him a sign.

"Not intelligent. Artful, artful as a cartload o' monkeys." He held out a crust of bread to Huskion. "Want to have a go?"

"I don't suppose they'll take it," Huskion said, taking the bread. "They don't know me."

But after holding it out for a few moments while the pigeons paraded in front of him, giving him a suspicious eye, one leaped up and gave the crust a cautious peck. Immediately his hand was the center of a flurry of wings as several others decided it was safe to do the same. He was surprised to feel how sharp their claws and beaks were.

"Just guts, pigeons are," the man said disgustedly. "Sit down, Mr. Huskion. Put your paper on the seat if you're worried about getting your arse wet."

Huskion was able to recover from his surprise as he smoothed out the *Times* on the seat. The man went on feeding the birds. When Huskion turned round, he was trying to coax a sparrow to take a bread pellet from between his lips.

"He'd have done it if you hadn't moved and scared him off," the man said reproachfully.

"Not very hygienic games you play. What does the doctor say? I thought he was to be here?"

"He had an urgent call." The man had not stopped shredding bread and scattering it over the path in front of them. He waited for a man and a girl to pass before he added, "He wants the delivery tomorrow."

"He won't have it."

"No?" Pretending to be enticing a sparrow flying low overhead the man swiveled round and peered closely across the sooty grass beyond the trees. "You aren't trying any tricks, Mr. Huskion?"

Huskion had spoken sharply to cover his unease. He wished he knew where King's men were and what they intended to do. The bird fancier's nervousness was catching,

157

too, making him feel guiltier than ever, so that he began to speak in an unnatural whisper.

"Of course not. But there's six loads altogether. I can only deliver one at a time."

The man stared straight in front of him, his muddy brown eyes still and unblinking behind his spectacles. Three pigeons alighted gingerly on his lap and began to tear at his half-eaten sandwich.

"Make the first tomorrow, then. You know the drill, don't you? Here, give over, that's mine," he said, pushing the birds away. "See what I mean about the greedy bastards? I'll tell the doctor about there being more."

Make it natural, King had said, talk about money, it's why you're there, isn't it? But how could he with this oaf, who was only a messenger, a nothing?

"Not tomorrow," he said hesitantly. "It needs some . . . some priming."

"Priming?"

"Three American tons. One and a half before and one and a half after."

The man looked at him, puzzled and suspicious.

"They'll know what you mean?"

"I think so."

It should be clear enough to them as soon as they looked up the table and found there were two thousand pounds in an American ton.

The man whistled through his teeth doubtfully.

"One and a half tons is a hell of a lot."

Huskion thought so, too, but pitch it high, King had told him. They're not buying a twelve-pound-a-week clerk but a three-and-a-half-thousand-a-year Assistant Secretary. Ask for too little and Sherngold'll be suspicious. Six thousand pounds for each file would be about right.

As the trap was about to be closed on the whole charade,

Huskion considered all this pettifogging detail excessive to the point of mania.

"It's what I need. But it'll take a few days to arrange. The delivery will be next Wednesday—if they've fixed the priming by then."

"I don't know if Wednesday'll do."

"Then give me another day."

There was a sudden stir and clatter from the lake. With such beating of wings on the water, two ducks took off, just making enough height to clear the deserted bridge.

The man tensed like an animal. His eyes narrowed and his body hunched ever so slightly beneath its layers of knitwear. Taking a slice of cheese from a sandwich, he crumbled it and flung it as far as he could into the bushes screening the water from the path. Against the blackened shrubs the fragments of cheese flying through the air had the brightness of gems. At once half the birds scratching on the path winged after them. Out of sight, they could be heard squabbling over the titbits.

"They go for cheese," he said, relaxing.

"If I hear nothing from you, it's Wednesday?"

"Yes. Park your car in Fairmile Place."

"Suppose it's full? It usually is."

"That's what I was told to tell you." The man shrugged.

"Suppose something goes wrong at my end and I can't make Wednesday?"

"I'm not here every day but will be next Tuesday."

"Right."

"Here, before you go charging off." The man handed him a chunk of bread. "It's what you sat next to me for, remember? And don't forget your paper. Leaving litter about is uncultured."

Huskion looked at him sharply but he wasn't being ironic. Carefully he coaxed the crippled pigeon onto his finger and, while it pecked away at the bread, discouraged its mates from sharing the feast. He was pleased to see this made the man glower with disapproval.

Tossing the last remnant of the crust onto the ground, he nodded to him and set off toward the Horseguards as though continuing his walk.

He found he was ravenously hungry but had no time for anything more than a couple of sandwiches at the Compasses. With having to meet King that afternoon, this damfool business was eating up his day.

Deirdre looked up from her desk and they exchanged smiles as he loped through the outer office. Neither of them had said anything about the previous night.

Though he had checked his watch with TIM, he was down in the lobby forty seconds early by the electric clock behind the messenger. Giving instructions for a nonexistent parcel from the Board of Trade to be sent up to his room as soon as it arrived filled in the time.

As he went through the glass doors out onto the portico an official Humber was pulling up. Out of it stepped Perkins. He still had his spivy sideburns but his hair was oiled and carefully brushed. In the neat blue serge suit he was wearing he would have been accepted anywhere in Whitehall as a Clerical Officer.

"Hullo," Huskion said. "Are you going straight back to Custom House?"

"I'm not but the car is."

Perkins grinned with just the right blend of cheek and deference. And then, waving a brown paper parcel heavily stamped O.H.M.S. as his excuse for hurrying away, trotted up the steps into Fairmile House.

"Any chance of a lift?" Huskion asked, ducking down and looking across to the driver.

King was sitting behind the steering wheel, an official

driver's cap pulled down to shade his foxy face.

"Certainly, sir," he said. "No, the back," he added quickly as Huskion took hold of the handle to get in beside him.

As soon as Huskion was settled King swung the Humber round, handling it with expert assurance.

"I didn't want to show myself so I couldn't get out to open the door for you."

"It's a bit bloody late to start being courteous," Huskion grunted.

"Sit well back in the corner and try not to show you're talking to me. Don't waggle your head when you speak."

"Are we being followed?"

"Don't look round!" King snapped, sensing Huskion's temptation to take a peek out the back window. "If Semenov isn't slipping, we will be. Well?"

Huskion told him about the St. James's Park bird lover.

"Any idea who he is?" he asked. "I suppose he isn't a government messenger?"

"I could guess but I'll know definitely in an hour from my man who was covering you. What are you going to do about the money?"

"You tell me. It's all in Zurich, intact except for my expenses for the Berlin trip. Do you want me to pass it over to you?"

"Not that. The three thousand you're to get before Wednesday."

"What?" Huskion said in surprise, not having thought about it at all. "If they've been rounded up, we shan't get that." He grinned suddenly. "Unless you're going to wait until they've parted with the cash before knocking them off."

King didn't answer immediately.

"The number of the taxi on our tail is 9840 XCD," he said at length. "You'll go back to Fairmile Place by taxi and you should check whether the same one follows you. Let me know if it does. I don't want to waste time trying to find the driver if it's a phony."

"O.K."

There was another pause.

"You've done pretty well so far, Huskion," King said slowly. "You're right about our not going to pick this bunch up immediately. We're going to play them a bit first. For one thing we want to know exactly how they collect, how they work this garage business. So, on Wednesday you'll put the folder in your briefcase and leave it locked in the boot of your car just as Sherngold told you to."

"No, I'm damned if I do—" Huskion exploded.

"Keep your head still!"

"—I've done as much as I intend to! I want to be shot of the whole bloody nonsense. You've got all the dope you need and now it's up to you. But without me!"

King had dawdled, deliberately allowing himself to be trapped by red lights, but the Strand and Fleet Street were already behind them and they were snarled up in traffic entering Cheapside. There was not much time left for argument.

"You're in this right to the end, Huskion," King said flatly. "You hooked yourself and you'll stay that way until I say you can swim off. That's the only out you have."

Huskion, gripping his soft leather document case, felt it twist in his hands. He was choked with a cold hatred for the man in front and longed to lash out at him with his fists.

"All right," King went on but in a rather more conciliatory tone, "so you'd like to kill me. I've not been straight with you. I haven't. And I don't give a damn. I have to work with anything and anyone I can. I wouldn't have picked you but it was you I got. And with you the chance to do some real damage to the KGB, to clean 'em out, using their own marked cards. For with you they think they've brought off what all of us are always looking for. One that hasn't been tried before. Only we're the ones that have found that, thanks to

162

you. With you we can send them skittering up a blind alley, gain months, maybe even a year or more; maybe they won't even think about Tridon again until the first test firings show they're on the wrong tack. Without you all I've got is a lot of wasted time. Understand?"

"You could have told me—"

"And have you duck out before we'd started!"

Huskion, shrinking down in his seat, didn't argue further. Apparently King wasn't expecting him to say anything.

"So, what about the money?"

"What about it?" Huskion's voice was weary and uninterested.

"You need to play it naturally all the time. But with the money you should be shrewd. As soon as you know it has been paid in, transfer it to your Swiss bank."

"All right."

"Look," King said, sliding his hands forward over the wheel, "we'll be at Custom House two minutes after these lights change. You get out as soon as I pull up. I'll move off at once."

"The farther the better."

King let in the clutch and changed up.

"You've just got to sweat it out, Huskion."

"For how long?"

"I don't know. It depends how hard they chew on the bait. Why don't you try to get some pleasure out of the way you're fooling them?"

Dexterously King slewed the Humber in to the curb.

"At the moment I feel like the one who's being chewed."

He got out and slammed the door behind him. Immediately the car moved off.

He stayed at Custom House twenty minutes, hoping his queries about duty on scientific instruments didn't sound as fatuous as he thought them.

Cab 9840 XCD followed him back to Fairmile Place. And

someone wearing a short raincoat and a narrow-brimmed trilby like the man who had followed him in East Berlin but who had a sharper, keener face and black eyes that swam continually from side to side, dogged him home from the office. Unlike the thickset man who had trailed him on the night Kay Dillon had called him, he didn't come right down Bridle Walk but halted in the shadows halfway between it and the main road. Evidently he knew about the garden exit.

His presence didn't bother Huskion in the least. He was becoming inured to surveillance. The only inconvenience was that he had to ring King from his own phone as it would have looked odd if he'd gone into a public call box at the station when he was nearly home. If the line was tapped, the call would make Spinwell blink but that was King's worry, he no longer cared. He hadn't even felt the smallest zest in singling out his tracker. His ride with King had left him dispirited and resigned.

His mood momentarily turned to something sharper when he arrived back to find Lambert there. He and Penny greeted him briefly and then went on with their conversation as though he weren't there. He shooed them out of the room curtly, so that he could make his call.

"You're right," King said. "There'll probably be someone always on your heels until Wednesday. Don't let it bother you. And don't let them know you know they're there."

"Oh, I was going to ask this chap in. We need a fourth for bridge."

"I thought you preferred three-handed," King said crisply and hung up.

That didn't improve his temper either.

Contrarily, he didn't go to his room after dinner but remained with the others, being calculatingly unpleasant, keeping the atmosphere tense and awkward but careful not to allow it to become so overcharged it would explode in a row. Lambert and Penny pretended they did not notice what he was doing, ducking away to footle with the *Times* crossword whenever his bitching made conversation impossible. None of them enjoyed the evening.

13

The days to Wednesday passed without incident but each one was controlled by King's nonsense. It weighed upon him, separating him from his colleagues, from all the bodies skirling about the grubby stones of Whitehall on government business.

Worst of all was the worry of who had charge of the real Tridon project.

It ate into him. He was suspicious of all the other Assistant Secretaries, wondering which of them it could be and what they had been told. He moved about the department constantly on the alert for questing or appraising glances that would betray who it was.

Before the weekend, Spinwell dropped in on him to inquire about Deirdre. Without superlatives Huskion told him he was entirely satisfied with her, that she was efficient, intelligent and keen.

"But don't take my word. Ask Havelock and Wigstall what they think."

"I have."

"She's too good for the job, really," Huskion added.

"That worries me, too," Spinwell said, his stolid face hard with suspicion. "Why hasn't she ever applied to be upgraded?"

"How the hell should I know? Maybe she doesn't want an E.O.'s responsibility. Or expects to get married."

"Possibly," Spinwell admitted noncommittally. "Or it could be because an E.O. has a lot less chance of getting close to top secrets than an efficient, better-than-her-job secretary who played her cards right."

Ridiculous as he thought Spinwell's suspicions, he said nothing about them to Deirdre nor even dropped a hint to her that the Security man was prying into her life. His training was such that he never even thought of doing so.

One inconvenience of the KGB man who stolidly followed him to work and home again and sat two tables away when he went out to lunch was that he couldn't ask Deirdre to spend another evening with him as a relief from Wimbledon. Though they didn't row, every hour he spent with Penny reeked sickeningly of their rotting relationship.

Though she said nothing, he had the idea that Deirdre rather expected him to speak of their going out together again. At any rate, he hoped she did.

On Monday morning the hall porter at the Progressive phoned to say he had a letter from Germany for him.

"I wouldn't have troubled you, sir, but it's been sent Express and you might not be looking in today."

He had given the Helmstedt the Progressive as his address. Expressing the notification must have been Sherngold's idea.

Deirdre came in as he was hanging up.

"The London Philharmonic are playing Mahler's Fifth at the Albert Hall on Thursday. Like to come if I can get tickets?"

Thursday was safe. By then there would be no need for Sherngold's bloodhounds to be sniffing at his heels.

"I'd love to," she said without hesitation and then, lowering the lids over her large eyes, went on as though she didn't want to talk about it. "Are you going to give me the stuff on the Eindhoven factory this morning? I keep moving it forward in the diary and it'll soon have whiskers."

He collected his letter from the Progressive at midday. Thirty-five thousand marks had been deposited, a generous interpretation of half £6,000. He wrote a check for the whole lot and sent it to the Zurich bank. Sherngold would now know where he was caching the money but King apparently didn't think that important.

The next day he took a walk beside the lake in St. James's Park. It was mild with a brilliant pastel sky overhead and sunlight that was like melted butter on the skin, more like March promising summer than the end of October. The changed weather had brought more people into the park and the man in the messenger's uniform feeding the birds had a ring of interested watchers surrounding him.

The man saw him and they exchanged nods as Huskion stopped near him and leaned on his umbrella. Carefully folding up his packets of sandwiches he flapped the birds away and returned them to his pockets. At once the bystanders began to drift away.

Huskion dropped on to his haunches and tried to coax a pigeon onto his forefinger. The bird, head on one side, its barley-sugar eye full of suspicion, edged away from him.

"Not seen you lately," said the man. "Been missing your constitutional?"

"Work intrudes."

"You picked a good day today."

"Great. And it should be all right tomorrow, too."

"Ah."

Huskion straightened up, saluted with his umbrella and sauntered off.

There had not been the least reason why he should have come to the park today. Except the fine weather and curiosity to know how the bird fancier would communicate with him with more people about. He thought they had managed it very neatly. In a glow of self-satisfaction he looked down the lake to the off-white Whitehall buildings fretting the sky, like an inlay, or an Oriental backdrop, with their towers and onion cupolas, and decided it was one of his favorite views. There was a lot to be said for taking a breather in the middle of the day.

Spinwell was waiting for him when he got back to his office. Huskion had left the agent's slip for two seats for the Albert Hall concert tucked into the ear of his blotter and he had this in his hand.

"Reminded me of something I wanted to ask you," he said, holding up the slip. "You being something of a dab at music."

"You shouldn't believe all you read in my dossier," Huskion told him. "I thought it made it look good to claim an acquaintance with the gentle arts. And if you think I can fiddle you free seats, you're wrong. I had to pay for those. That's a dangerous concert, too, much too dangerous for you. All the music's foreign."

He didn't know why he bothered. Spinwell was armorplated.

"I don't know much about music," Spinwell said. "Thought if I got a hi-fi and started listening seriously that might help. Wanted to ask you about hi-fis."

"Come to the wrong shop." Huskion was put out, disarmed by the unexpectedness of a request so at odds with his image of Spinwell's character. "I know nothing about them."

"But you've got one, haven't you?"

"It's something I've been meaning to treat myself to, for our old radiogram doesn't bear listening to any more. There's a chap called Gellatly in— Here, wait a minute." He leaned down and took his personal folder from the desk drawer. Quickly shuffling through the loose papers he took out the letter Gellatly had sent him doping out the most economical way of buying a reproducer. "It boils down to finding an honest dealer and then telling how much you want to spend, I'm afraid, but Gellatly really knows hi-fis."

Spinwell reached over and took the letter. It ran to two pages and he read it through carefully. He flipped back the first page and glanced at it again before returning it.

"I should have thought with your contacts you could get this stuff at cost or better," he said.

Huskion looked at him curiously.

"Do you want me to see what I can fiddle for you?"

"Could you?"

"I know half a dozen people who, if I were to mention I wanted a hi-fi, would have delivered one as a present before I got back to the office."

"This chap Gellatly doesn't mention anything like that."

"Gellatly doesn't even send me a card at Christmas. That's why it's possible to ask him for advice. It wouldn't occur to him that I was holding my hand out to be oiled."

"Oh, well," Spinwell said, getting up. "I suppose the sets can be got from shops that give civil servants a discount anyway."

"I expect so." Huskion's voice was very quiet. "If you wanted to buy a hi-fi."

Spinwell's marble eyes didn't flicker. He turned toward the door but Huskion stopped him.

"You don't, do you?"

"What makes you think so?"

"The only thing that interested you in that letter was the date. So, what's the game?"

"Where did you talk to Gellatly about hi-fis?" Spinwell asked, coming back to the desk.

170

Huskion stared.

"Here, I suppose."

"You're sure?"

"No, I'm not," Huskion said irritably. "It could have been over a beer at the Compasses. As a matter of fact, I think it was. What does it matter?"

"Someone heard you," Spinwell nodded, "and thought you were looking for baksheesh."

"And you were checking up?"

"Had to."

"Not by trying to trap me by asking a favor!" Huskion was angry. "There's a word for that sort of thing."

Spinwell shrugged his shoulders.

"It put you in the clear. It was just unfortunate your spotting me tabbing the date and being smart enough—"

"—to see you and music don't mix."

Spinwell looked down at his hands, smoothing the palm of one over the large ugly joints of the other.

"I'm not apologizing, Huskion," he said quietly. "There are half a dozen of you here who are too damned important for me to worry about rules, so it's no good your shouting 'foul.' There ain't no such thing. Having me on your neck goes with your job. And putting up with me there whatever dirty trick I play in doing mine. I didn't imagine you were the sort of spiv who would take a bribe however it was dollied up. But I had to know—because if you'd slipped that far you'd be too damned wobbly to have your hands on what's in there." He jerked his thumb toward the safe. "That's all."

"Close the door after you."

Huskion sat drumming on his blotter with a pencil. Beyond his anger, like a small cloud peeking over the horizon, was the unwanted admission that Spinwell's irritation was logically more justifiable than his own.

What bothered him was who had told tales about him.

171

Meeting Wigstall in the corridor as he was leaving that evening he peered into his beaming, unspiteful, malicious face, not listening to what he was saying but trying to remember if he had been in the Compasses the day he had been there with Gellatly. He couldn't remember. He couldn't remember anyone who had been there. Nor could he think of anyone in the department who would have thought it worth reporting what the two of them had talked about. But someone had. And it made him feel dirty. Infinitely worse than being followed about by Sherngold's glum raincoats.

The next day everything went swimmingly according to plan.

In the morning a green Volkswagen was obligingly about to pull out as he drove into Fairmile Place. Part of the Sherngold service, he assumed.

He finished a little earlier than usual, coming out of Fairmile House when there was still a strong trickle of people leaving. Opening the boot of the Morris, he set his document case diagonally across it, using a jack and a spanner to fix it in a position he would remember.

None of his KGB followers seemed to be around. At any rate, he could see none of the four he had identified and who seemed to work such regular shifts that yesterday he had been able to guess which of them would be with him on the tube to Wimbledon.

He put the car in the garage as soon as he reached Wimbledon, locked it and took the key. The garage had a basement where most of the repair work was done and two floors over, all of them with standing room for cars around the walls. As he would be needing it the next day, he chose a space at street level.

No car had trailed him as he had crawled homeward through the rush-hour traffic and he was not shadowed from the garage to Bridle Walk. He had become expert enough at picking out watchers on his heels to be sure of it. The game had entered a new phase. As the significance of the disappearance of his watchers penetrated to him, Huskion's heart tripped. The enemy King was using him against calculated with a computerlike precision that was frightening.

Lambert and Penny had the meal already on the table and they ate at once. He tried to be especially cheerful and relaxed. When Lambert began to fuss because he had overheated the bottle of Saint-Emilion he had brought, he chaffed him derisively, just as he would have done before their friendly relationship had been broken. But, try as he might, his mind kept straying.

Afterwards they all went down to the Odeon, using Lambert's Humber though Huskion would have preferred to walk. But it meant that he was able to buy the tickets while Lambert was parking the car, so avoiding a silly argument over who should pay. Lambert always insisted on picking up the tab if he could when they went out together. Normally, Huskion let him but tonight he wanted the stubs, in case Spinwell should begin asking questions.

On Sunday he'd fixed with Penny and Lambert that they should all go to the cinema Wednesday night. Expecting opposition—why, after weeks of each going their separate ways, should they agree to go out with him—he had prepared the ground by discussing the film, which had had some quite good notices, before suggesting they make a date. To his surprise, after a brief exchange of glances, they had taken up the idea enthusiastically, as though it fitted in with some plan of their own.

In the darkness of the cinema, released from the compulsion to appear sociable, he fidgeted with his thoughts. He resented having to be there, resented having been maneuvered into plotting to block Spinwell's possible suspicions because King refused to warn the Security man off. This not letting the left hand know what the right was doing was being carried to lunatic lengths. In any case, if Spinwell did get wind something was up he'd have to be told before he mucked everything up. It would serve King right if Spinwell boxed his scheme up, Huskion thought viciously, but without much conviction, for any boxing up Spinwell might do was likely to involve him more than King.

He paid so little attention to what was going on on the screen that he was hard put to it to add to Lambert's comments on the film when they came out. Several times he had glanced down the row to see if Lambert was holding Penny's hand as he used to do. Each time she had had her fingers threaded together in her lap, as though pointing that he wasn't. Unreasonably, he took this consideration as an insult, implying they still thought he cared how they behaved.

On the way back to the house he scarcely uttered a word and, as soon as the car stopped, flung open the door and stepped out. With a muttered good night he stalked into the house without waiting for Penny.

When he went for his car in the morning he saw it had been washed during the night. There was nothing significant in this, for it was part of his contract with the garage that they washed it once a fortnight. He was curious to open the boot but restrained himself.

He fumed at the traffic as he drove eastward. At Fairmile Place there was no space, although he was there earlier than yesterday. Apparently the Sherngold service stopped once the goods were delivered. By good luck he was just able to edge into a place in the Mall.

When he opened the boot and saw his document case lying between the jack and spanner apparently exactly as he'd left it, he wondered if something had gone wrong. The thought followed him to the office, where he took out the folder and examined it minutely.

He would have sworn it hadn't been tampered with. Even the little creases he had put on some of the pages were undisturbed.

14

King, when he phoned him at lunchtime, was unimpressed that Huskion's untrained eye had not detected traces of the folder being handled. When it came to making secret searches, Sherngold's men were artists. Unfortunately he still didn't know how it had been done, or what was more important, by whom. According to King, his men had been completely thrown when the car had been taken down to the basement to be washed. It had thus been out of their sight for most of the night. So he still didn't know if the garage was a spy setup or if it was just one of the hands who was a KGB man.

"Forget the softening up," Huskion interrupted harshly. "What you mean is you want me to pass another file in the same way?"

King was lying of course. He was too smart not to have tagged on to the possibility of the car being moved during the night and covered it.

"All right, but next time they get the lot, not just one."

"No," King told him, speaking very quietly. "I don't think that would do at all."

That tied it up. The garage wasn't King's interest. Obviously he'd have been very slow if in the past month he hadn't had it, and everyone in it, checked on, probed and neatly docketed.

"Let me know when the rest of the money is paid in," King said before he hung up.

Huskion pushed through the heavily sprung door of the call box and stood still, breathing in. The air in the kiosk was fetid and its smell of stale cigarette smoke and sodden clothing hung in his nostrils.

He was less depressed about not being finished with the phony folders than he might have been because he had half expected something of the sort, that King would have something up his sleeve for the rest of the files that would include him.

What did surprise him was King's being so sure nothing had gone wrong at Sherngold's end. It all seemed much too simple. One-time pads, messages in hollow trees on Clapham Common, even passing microfilms by switching shopping baskets in Waterloo Road fitted spying, but not just leaving your car in the suburban garage you always used. So long as it remained like that he was willing to pass one more folder to Sherngold.

It wasn't something he had to bother about immediately, anyway. That in itself was enough to give his spirits a lift.

When Deirdre brought him his letters he signed them with a jaunty flourish and then stretched back in his chair, watching her put them in their envelopes.

"You'd do much better to kiss me instead of wasting your lips on that."

She looked at him in surprise, the triangular flap of an en-

176

velope covering her mouth. Then very deliberately she sealed it down, flattening it on the desk.

"I must indent for a pad," she said. "It's a filthy habit."

"And the kiss?"

"An exigency of the service?"

"Certainly."

She pecked him lightly on the lips but, when he tried to take hold of her, swayed neatly out of his reach.

"Do you often take off like this?" she asked, collecting the envelopes.

"Only when the moon is full. Get your bonnet and shawl and we'll be off."

When he came back from the washroom she was not in her office and he went through to his own room. He was humming to himself as he turned over the pages of *Mechanics* when she appeared in the doorway.

"I'm ready."

"Phew!" he whistled, letting the magazine fall on to the desk. "You look as though you've walked off the cover of *Vogue*."

She had, in fact, made only three additions to the clothes she had been wearing all day but the effect was stunning. Her simple skirt in a subtle mixture of dark olive green and black and toning olive sweater were transformed by the completion of the suit with a snug-fitting jacket buttoning to a high vee. She had changed her shoes for black leather knee boots which even without the hat would have justified his whistle. The hat was a cartwheel in stiff black felt turned up at the rim and trimmed with the same dark fur as edged the jacket.

"I pass?"

She was relaxed, smiling, sure of herself and a little excited.

"I doubt if I do, though," he said, nodding. "To walk beside such modish elegance my trousers should be narrower, my jacket shorter, the brim of my bowler much curlier."

After the concert he took her to a Hungarian restaurant in Greek Street which was warm, small and with décor that was friendly, individual and old-fashioned. He ordered Bulgarian salata, paprika chicken and a bottle of Riesling.

Still under the spell of the music, they had spoken little on the way to Soho. There the mood was broken as he tried to park in a barely adequate space, to his chagrin having to have three goes at it, the third time nearly losing it to an M.G. that cut in cheekily. He shouted angrily at the driver and backed sharply into the spot, just clipping the bumper of the car in front. His exasperation made Deirdre laugh.

"You're a real Fascist with a car, aren't you?"

"Hitler, that's me." He grinned. "Show me a carpet and I'll bite it."

They were still laughing when they sat down in the restaurant. But as soon as the waiter had put the menu in her hands, Deirdre went very quiet and looked at him oddly in the same defensively apprehensive way she had on her first day at the office. She made no suggestions, expressed no preferences for what they should eat, but just nodded when he looked toward her as he named a dish.

"Someone stepped on your grave?" he asked.

She was staring down toward the fretted grille at the end of the restaurant behind which the waiters could be heard chattering in a foreign language, presumably Hungarian. She turned her head at his question. Her large eyes were dull and questioning.

"What? Oh, yes, something like that."

"What brought it on?"

She was still looking at him in the same way.

"You can never be sure," she said, "can you?"

"Would you like to go somewhere else?"

"Why should I?" she asked sharply.

"I wondered if it was this place. Not everyone loves fretwork and plush bobbles."

"I'm sure it wasn't the fretwork and the bobbles."

The waiter brought their gin and tonics.

"Here's death to your miseries—from wherever they come," he said raising his glass.

The corners of her lips slid, catlike, toward her cheekbones. But it was only half a smile and it didn't wash the fright from her eyes. That behind her daunting façade of self-possession strange psychic beasts lurked to claw her unexpectedly with intimations of mortality he found appealing and he spread himself to win her from her black mood.

It was not easy, for she seemed to be shriveled within herself. She picked disinterestedly at her salad, only raising her eyes from her plate to shoot querying glances at him, as though she were unsure of the meaning of his efforts to be cheerful.

Slowly she became more relaxed though still subdued, saying little and then only in response to his leads. That was how he came to tell her about Penny and the mess his marriage was in. He had not intended to but when he mentioned Penny casually she had come out of herself to ask him how long they had been married. Her interest had led him on to tell her more. She did not miss the irony in his tone or its meaning.

Through his inadvertently giving himself away, some of their earlier intimacy was recovered. As on the last time they had been out together, he felt an empathy for her that made it easy to talk about himself. He had been carrying so many troubles in silence for so long that to talk of one even in belittling, unserious terms was a relief.

When they went out to the car he stood for a moment leaning on the open door holding her elbow.

"Willies quite gone?"

Her large eyes disappeared behind their scallop-shaped

lids as she ducked down to get into the car, frustrating his intention to kiss her.

"I was an idiot," she said in her exasperated prefect's voice.

Although it was much later than it had been the first time he'd seen her home, she asked him in for a cup of coffee and was out of the car before he had time to reply.

He followed her up the half dozen flights of stairs bounded by dark-chocolate lincrustre. Some of the doors of the flats they passed were painted in pastel yellows and greens with chromium furnishings, the handiwork of the tenants, he judged.

The top flight was narrower than the others and ended in a pale-blue door. Anyone opening it had to step back down two steps to give it room to swing outward.

"Deirdre?" someone called as they went in.

A woman, some years older than Deirdre, appeared at one of the doors that opened off the minute hall into which they were crushed. Deirdre introduced her as Monica Stretley.

"I'd almost given you up."

She had a deep voice, dry and resonant, and a staccato delivery that made everything she said sound snappish. Huskion felt she resented his intrusion, not personally, for she hardly glanced at him, but as a disturber of her habits. In the lines about her eyes and the loosening skin of her throat spinsterish dejection was beginning to set, foreshadowing defeat that would soon have to be accepted.

"We can have coffee right away. I've just put the kettle on for my bottle."

He was left alone while the two of them went into the kitchen. He could hear the rattle of crockery, and their voices, quite plainly for the dividing wall was only a screen of wallboard.

180

The sitting room was still a fair size although part of it had been taken for the kitchen and the side with the window was shortened by the slope of the roof. Some of the furniture, he guessed, must have belonged to Deirdre's parents, a Georgian bureau bookcase, two much worn tub chairs with shell backs, and a heavy Turkey carpet that was too large for the room. The studio couch, nest of coffee tables and the rest were all modern. Lit by silk-shaded standard lamps made from vases, the room, despite the solid reds and blues of the carpet, had a feminine but impermanent look, as though the will had died before it had been completed.

"I told Monica how much you liked her hat," Deirdre said. "She designed it and helped me make it."

Monica, it appeared, worked in a millinery boutique in Beauchamp Place. He could not imagine her in so glossy a job. She told him she liked designing but found dealing with "bloody women" very tiresome.

He and Deirdre sat in the two tub chairs, while Monica remained standing behind the coffee table, gulping her cocoa—"coffee always keeps me awake"—as though she were at a station buffet expecting her train to leave at any moment. It was evident they had planned Deirdre should bring him in that night and she had pressed through with it regardless of the hour. He wished she hadn't.

"Well, I'll leave you," Monica said, plunking her empty cup down on the tray, and adding severely to Deirdre, "You know it's Thursday."

"What's special about Thursday?" he asked when she had gone.

"Nothing," Deirdre said in a whisper to remind him of the thinness of the partition. "She has a beastly journey to her cottage in the wilds of Norfolk every weekend and she says she arrives fagged out if she doesn't get a good night's sleep on Thursday."

181

He stayed for another cup of coffee but Monica had been as effective as Deirdre's willies earlier in blighting the friendly intimacy they had shared when he kissed her at the office.

"I haven't a weekend cottage," she said when he got up to go.

He smiled but did not take his hand from the door.

Downstairs in the car he paused a moment before switching on the engine. Except for the music it had been a mixed-up, unsatisfactory evening. He should have had more sense than to go in when it was so late and the evening already as cracked as a miscast bell.

But if he hadn't it would never have occurred to him to go there on Sunday.

It was on Sunday that Penny told him she was selling the house. The moment she chose was when they were having coffee after lunch, using a flat casual tone as though she were telling him nothing more important than that they had just had the final notice for the gas.

"It's ridiculous to keep this place," she explained reasonably, "when Lambert's is so much more convenient ... and nicer really. What should we do with two houses?"

He said nothing. Afterwards he thought he must have looked idiotic, staring at her over the top of the Business Section of the *Sunday Times*.

"There's some people coming to look over it this afternoon."

So that was why he'd had to be told. With a flash of intuition he knew when she and Lambert had planned it. Last weekend. That was why they had responded so amiably, agreed so readily to go to the pictures on Wednesday. Covering up their guilt. It was as plain as the apprehension that lurked behind her casualness now. Or it might not be apprehension but a flawed purpose, a lurking desire that he would tell her not to be a fool, that he loved her.

Knowing she had rehearsed the scene with Lambert killed any chance of that, whether she wanted it or no.

"Nice of you to tell me," he said, as indifferently as he could.

"I've no intention of moving out until the New Year, so you'll have plenty of time to find somewhere to live."

She moved toward the door as she spoke and slipped out as soon as she had finished and went upstairs to her room.

Not fancying hanging around, functionless and unwanted, like a king termite, while Penny showed a lot of strangers over the house, he collected his car from the garage and drove aimlessly to the West End. He slowly circled Hyde Park, thinking what he should do now that his marriage was finally broken and not just cracked.

By four o'clock, if he hadn't absorbed its meaning fully or made any hard decisions, he had come to accept it. He turned out of the park and stopped the car in front of Deirdre's flat. If she was in she could give him tea.

She was.

15

It was the weekend after he'd left the third of the Tridon files for Sherngold to collect that he and Deirdre became lovers.

Three months earlier the possibility of his risking his prospects by having an affair with his secretary would have been ludicrous. It was a sign of the total derangement of his life. He seemed to be suspended in space. As in a nightmare, the walls of the groove in which he had moved so surely had receded beyond the horizon, leaving him without support.

Yet outwardly his life was unchanged. At night he went home to Wimbledon, in the morning he caught his usual train to Westminster. He walked briskly along the green-painted corridors of Fairmile House, stopped on its elegant staircase to smile and exchange acid banter with the other men. Though he looked harder and harder for any change in their manner toward him, he found none. He sat in on conferences, kept his clerical staff on the go. Conscientiously he batted back and forth to His Nibs the steadily growing phony files on Tridon. When His Nibs brought one of the files back to him he was usually more feyly avuncular than seemed necessary, but what, if anything, that signified he had no idea.

Though everything seemed to be as it always had been, it wasn't. It was not only who was dealing with the real Tridon that bothered him now, though that twisted him cruelly at times. It was all his work. Two more of his Top Secret projects had been dropped and another downgraded without anything of moment being given him in their place. Such projects as remained were going along under their own steam in the control of lower-grade men in his section and required only supervision. He fussed over these and harried his men relentlessly. But it was only shadow boxing. In cold fear, he saw everything seeping away from him, as though his being at the department at all was only a blind. His only real job was working for King. He didn't like admitting it, but it was true. And especially he didn't like the quietly efficient way he'd been freed from his other responsibilities to do it.

He saw little of Penny. She was usually out now in the evenings. When they did meet she would tell him of the people who had been to see the house (three lots were interested but were either dithering about the price or having difficulties over a mortgage) and ask him if he'd found the potatoes Mrs. Tubbs had peeled. If he arrived home after she had gone to bed, there was invariably a note on the hall stand asking if he'd be eating in the following evening. It made him feel like a lodger in a boardinghouse where the landlady had won the pools and lost interest in her boarders. So he stayed out most evenings, going home only to sleep.

Because he had not wholly digested that soon he would not be able to go back to the house in Bridle Walk at all he did not begin to look for somewhere else to live or make any plans for what he would do once the house was sold. His will was paralyzed.

There was nowhere for him to go but to the Progressive. That he found inexpressibly dreary. Like most married men, such friends as he had were not so much his as his and Penny's, and any of those would have thought it strange if he had sought them out without her. Even if there were any he was particularly drawn to, which there weren't. There was nobody, nobody at all.

Except Deirdre.

He was no longer being shadowed. Of this he was certain, for wherever he went he checked that there was no one tagging after him. Curiously, instead of being relieved, he found himself hoping that each time he looked round he would see a Sherngold shortie raincoat or even one of Spinwell's fresh-faced blonds. Being ignored ground at the last shreds of his self-confidence.

Even if King had not said he should, he would have gone to St. James's Park each day to walk past the man who fed the pigeons. Just seeing him made him feel more in touch. On a couple of occasions when he wasn't on his usual seat by the lake, Huskion was quite troubled and walked back the length of Birdcage Walk, in case he was only late.

His name, King told him, was Harry Gamchik. So far as was known, this was the first time he'd been used by the Russians on espionage. For years, the police had known him as a hanger-on of the Eastern embassies and Front organizations, running errands, humping crates of minerals at garden fetes, selling tickets for *Morning Star* bazaars and a regular steward at any protest meeting. Just one of the faithful few so besotted in their allegiance to communism they were incapable of seeing that what was actually done in its name bore small relation to their own vision of it as a synonym for equality and justice. Not at all the kind of character he would have expected in the well-oiled setup the KGB was supposed to be.

"Nothing's ever like we imagine it," King commented dryly.

The Security man was such a cold fish, he was more often dampened than comforted when he contacted him. But there were times when the contact had to be made. As over Spinwell.

The ex-Navy man might be a chump and more than a little stuffy but at least he could learn. This time he hadn't made the mistake of approaching Huskion obliquely, but plunked his screening questionnaire in front of him and sat back.

Huskion glanced at it. It was open at the pages where he had been required to name any of his friends who had or whom he suspected of having Communist or other dangerous associations.

"Well?" he said.

"Not quite complete, is it?" Spinwell said quietly.

Huskion hoped his face wasn't showing what he was feeling. Sherngold! Surely he couldn't have got on to Sherngold?

"Isn't it?" he queried cautiously, making it sound as casual as he could.

"You've left out Dillon."

Huskion was so relieved he could have laughed out loud.

"And there's Phoo Minh, too," he said.

Spinwell's head lifted, not much, just about a centimeter. "Who's Phoo Minh Tu?"

"It's Phoo Minh, not Phoo Minh Tu. A Vietnamese. Though whether one of ours or one of theirs I wouldn't know. There was only one Vietnam in those days; but he might have come from the North."

"But who is he? What does he do?"

"I haven't a clue. He was a boy at my school."

This time Spinwell did not move. Not even a centimeter.

187

"Dillon," he said flatly, in his toneless voice, his eyes holding Huskion's.

"What the hell! It's ten years since I knew him! If I'd put down everyone I'd run across since I'd joined the Service you'd have a list as long as the telephone directory. And about as sensible."

"Dillon's rather a special case, don't you think?"

"No."

"You met him in Berlin?"

"Yes. But I hardly knew him. It just happened that we were once on the same job."

"No social contact?"

"Not to notice."

"But in Cyprus?"

"The odd occasion at the club."

"Give it to me in detail."

Huskion gave it to him, everything he could remember, quite straight. He no longer felt like being funny. Just relieved there was so little to tell.

"And since then you've had no contact with him?"

"How could I? He was always miles away from me."

"How do you know that?" Spinwell put the question in the same flat monotone as the others.

"From the papers. It came out at his trial that he operated from Berlin, Beirut and Istanbul."

"And from Hoverton."

"I don't remember seeing that."

"Oh, well, it's pretty common knowledge where he was during the past two years."

"Not to me."

"So it comes to this," Spinwell said after a longish pause, "since your haphazard meetings in Berlin and Nicosia you have had no contact whatsoever with Dillon?"

"That's right."

As soon as Spinwell had gone, he crushed out his cigarette —the fourth he'd smoked while talking to the Security man— and immediately lit another. From a five-a-day man he was becoming a chain smoker.

He smoked the cigarette right through and then went out to the phone kiosk and fixed to see King.

Finlay Street, in the dark and without the surrounding bustle of the Saturday market, was depressing, almost sinister. Weak reflections of the lamps glistened forlornly from the evening-damp cobbles and cracked paving stones. The ricocheting clatter of footsteps off the yellow brick walls chattered at the nerves like machine-gun fire.

It was coming up to six o'clock and the junk shop was already shuttered and dead. The Bestyet Fish Saloon, in contrast, was ablaze with neon, a plume of steam floating from its fanlight, pungently tainting the moist air. Inside a row of customers, as silently dejected as mourners, stared across the pink marble counter at the white-coated fryers juggling their wire baskets.

At 37c the cadaverous man was sweeping up, watched by Perkins.

Perkins nodded to Huskion and took him through to King in the room at the end of the corridor where the coconut-shy stuff was stored.

The Security man pointed to the same bentwood chair he'd sat in before, made a couple of notes on the file he was working on, read them through, added his initials and locked the file away in the green filing cabinet. When he sat down again he simply waited in silence for Huskion to tell him what was bothering him. It was a mild night but the room seemed very chilly to Huskion.

"I didn't say anything about having seen Kay Dillon," he ended. "I couldn't, you see, because I didn't know how I could skate round it or where it might make him start prob-

189

ing. And after all I'd already reported it to you. And Sir Nigel."

"Not Sir Nigel," King murmured. "When you came to me he was out, remember?"

"What's made Spinwell rake up Dillon?" Huskion plowed on as though he hadn't heard.

"It's his job to rake."

But why now? At the time of Dillon's trial, when it was hot news, it would have made sense.

"Someone's feeding him leads," Huskion said.

He told King about the hi-fi business, how his pub talk with Gellatly had been reported back.

"You may be underestimating Spinwell" was King's comment.

"The point is something's got to be done to hobble the bastard. He's coming in too close. If he prods away at Dillon, he may get on to the Helmstedt Bank. Can't he be choked off now? If he did get on to the Helmstedt he'd have to be told the whole thing anyway."

"It's something we'll have to think about certainly. It shouldn't be impossible. And he's shown us where we've fallen down."

"What?"

"You should be getting jumpy," King said, nodding. "Any day now Semenov will be wondering why you aren't. And we don't want that."

"Why should he? He's getting the Tridon data."

"Too easily for it to be natural. He's not dealing with a trained agent. He's played a long shot and bought a top-grade civil servant who's never dropped a hint before, let alone sold a secret. Such a man would have to screw himself up pretty tight before he could do it. And there'd certainly be a recoil." King looked down at his polished fingernails. "When he hits bottom and realizes exactly what he's done, either he hollers to be let out or gets so jittery he can't see a bed without looking under it for a D.I.5 man. You're altogether too calm."

"You should know," Huskion said.

"You aren't behaving like a man who might meet a thirty-year jail sentence round the next corner. And Semenov won't wonder about it for long. He'll know you're not worrying because it's not something you have to worry about."

"So what do you want me to do?" Huskion asked wearily.

"Let Gamchik know you're jumpy. Ask him for a contact you can reach in an emergency."

"All right. And you'll take care of Spinwell?"

"I'll do my best. But we can't be too blatant at this stage. You transferred the money?"

"Yes. That's another thing I don't like," Huskion told him. "Why does it have to be in my name? Why can't I hand it over to you?"

"I've told you. Those numbered accounts are no longer foolproof. Semenov may not have got on to yours. But he may have. That's why."

"But you're the only one who knows I've got the money. And you're not immortal."

King didn't smile.

"Anyone you find sitting in this chair," he said flatly, "will know all about it."

Huskion grunted disagreeably and got up to go. But King stopped him before he reached the door.

"You read Italian don't you?"

When Huskion nodded, he took a clipping from a drawer in the table and passed it to him.

It had been snipped from the *Corriere di Milano* and the headline was HOMOSEXUAL LINK TO MURDERS? Police, it said, were considering that three murders that had occurred in the past month were directly linked. Though the three dead men

191

were not known to have been acquainted, each lived alone and had no women friends. There were also said to be a number of other similarities that had not been disclosed. Inquiries were still proceeding. It seemed unlikely, however, even if there were a link, that the murders were all committed by the same hand, for Matellotti, the eldest, had been strangled in his flat, Francini found in the gutter of the Via Crosso with five knife wounds, and Gordano bludgeoned to death.

Most of the rest of the column and a half was less concerned with the murders than with the prospect of juicy revelations about the city's homosexual underworld.

"Friends of yours?" he asked.

"Double agents," King said, taking the clipping and returning it to the drawer. "The Russians got on to them."

A wall collapsed in Huskion's stomach.

"They're bound to get on to me, you know, sooner or later."

King nodded.

"They are. But not, I hope, before we've closed the trap on them."

"But what the hell do I do then?"

"Nothing. You'll be in the clear. You're not like those three. You're not a professional agent. You didn't go to them. They came to you. Once the operation's over, they'll forget about you."

It could have been the stench of frying oil pervading the room that was making him so queasy. He had not sat down again after King had called him back, and now he moved uneasily about the room. Without realizing what he was doing he picked up one of the wooden coconut-shy balls from its slatted stand and began to toss it from hand to hand.

"I hope you're right," he mumbled. "Creeping about waiting to be slugged or knifed is not something I relish. I told you I wasn't cut out for your sort of thuggery," he added, tossing the ball back onto the stand.

It sounded a very weak protest. The sordid room, with its small and bizarre fairground paraphernalia, the dust and gray dirt of the floorboards emphasized by the single naked light bulb, made him feel like that anyway, weak, ineffectual and out of place.

"None of us is. Some of us have to learn to live with it, though."

"Not me."

"You'd do as well as most."

King's foxy face was as expressionless as ever.

"I showed you that cutting to stop you getting careless. So watch out and let me know if they seem to be getting the least bit suspicious."

"I'll do that."

"I can't keep you covered all the time," King said, leaning forward in what might have been solicitude, though his expression didn't change, "for they'd be certain to spot a bodyguard."

"They're not following me any more."

King nodded.

"I know. It's not necessary now they know the general pattern of your movements. That doesn't mean they aren't watching you at one or two key points. So see you keep to the pattern. It's impossible to check on a watcher who doesn't show himself. But we can assume they are there."

That was something that hadn't occurred to Huskion and his self-esteem went down another rung. Spotting that he wasn't being dogged had seemed important.

"Don't forget to see Gamchik," King reminded him as he left.

He stood for a moment in the turgid dampness of Finlay Street as, behind him in the now darkened shop, Perkins slammed home the bolts on the door. A paunchy man, whose face under the neon was more putrescently white than his overall, stretched an arm into the window of the Bestyet Fish

193

Saloon and scored "Hake" from the "Frying Today" slate, leaving only "Cod" and "Rock Salmon" on offer for later customers.

Or was that only what it appeared to be and in reality was a message for someone who watched through field glasses from behind a dark, fly-blown window? "Hake" could stand for Huskion and the chalk running through it could tell the watcher Huskion had seen King and had now left.

It was an absurd fancy, which he didn't find funny, though he pretended he did. The ill-lit street was a canyon of black shadows, ideal for an ambush with a knife or a cosh. He moved into the center of the roadway and sped along the length without trying to quiet his footsteps. Coming out into Portobello Road he could not have been more relieved if he had, in fact, been in danger.

Each glimpse he had of King's world had this disorienting effect. King's thought processes were corrupting, insinuating there was nothing so simple or open or ordinary that could not have a sinister interpretation. It didn't only alert to danger but contaminated the familiar and the friendly with suspicion.

And it was hard to tell whether King was on his side or not. At school history had been made repellent by a master who had treated him in the same way as King did, not withholding help but giving it with a frosty, uninvolved indifference that nipped the heart from endeavor.

So he avoided contact with King as far as he could, simply reporting when money was paid into the Helmstedt account. King was always interested in that. Especially when the second installment on the first file had turned out to be only DM.21,000.

Huskion found his own reactions curious. The generous overpayment in the first installment had affronted him, such profligacy with public money offending his Civil Service

194

training in strict accounting. But when the second installment was docked by the DM.14,000 paid in before Sherngold
had come to see him, he was furious. This was tricky and
mean, not at all on a par with King knocking off the price
of the Daks he had bought in Zurich from the chit he had put
in for a new suit. King, on the other hand, was delighted.

"It shows they've taken the bait," he said. "If they suspected they were being given a line they wouldn't have done
anything to upset you. But they're sure of you now, they
think, and they're letting you know who's master. There's
damn little you can do about it, but kick up a row all the
same. And they'll try to cut down the price for the rest of
the files. But don't you stand for it."

King was right. It was with satisfaction that he brusquely
refused to bargain about the "priming" for the next file, telling Gamchik sharply that if there was any shortage, his
bloody pigeons wouldn't be getting any more crusts from
him. After that the payments were regular, DM.33,000 two
days before he left a Tridon folder in the boot of his Morris,
DM.33,000 afterwards.

All this had meant many lunchtimes sitting on the bench
beneath the great elms talking softly to Gamchik out of the
corner of his mouth, while shredding crumbs for the sparrows. The little cockney obviously had no inkling of the
purport of the messages he conveyed. It was enough for him
that he should be helping the "movement" and the furtive
secrecy of their meetings was quite natural since they were
fighting the capitalist class. Naïvely he treated Huskion as a
"comrade." Despite his mean features and grumpy cockiness,
he was infinitely pathetic.

It was a raw day under thick off-white cloud when Huskion
went to see him after his meeting with King, and the walk
beside the lake was wrapped in an early-winter silence more
like death than sleep. Two or three ducks had come up from

the water and joined the sparrows and pigeons swirling about Gamchik.

"Bleak, ain't it," was Gamchik's greeting as he aimed a boot at a mallard duck that had just worked up enough courage to make a waddling dive for a piece of cheese. "Those perishers would eat the bloody lot if you give 'em the chance. Gawd knows where they put it. Like trying to fill a drain."

There was no one about so Huskion dispensed with any pretense of interest in ornithology.

"I want someone I can contact in an emergency."

"Something wrong?"

"Not yet. But if there was I should want someone quickly."

Gamchik tossed several pellets of bread along the path.

"See them gulls?" he asked, nodding toward the bridge where a line of gulls perched disconsolately along the hand-rail. "We're going to cop it this winter. Sure sign it's going to be cold when they crowd up here." Without turning his head or altering his tone, he added, "They'll want to know more than that. What shall I tell 'em?"

"Tell them about the gulls."

"They'd understand that?" Gamchik asked. Behind the steel-rimmed spectacles his eyes were puzzled.

"I should think so. They know my central heating has always been a nuisance. If it became dangerous something would have to be done about it at once. I'd need somewhere to go if it couldn't be put right."

Gamchik nodded. Huskion leaned over him and took a slice of bread from the packet on his lap and began to distribute it among the draggled sparrows lurking in cowardly despair beyond their more aggressive brothers.

"I've got some tickets for the Sharpesville Memorial meeting if you're wanting any."

"No."

"I sold twenty-three. Only got seven left. Going to be packed out, it is."

Huskion dusted off his fingers and picked up his umbrella.

"See you at the meeting, maybe?"

"Maybe."

Huskion had given up trying to make him understand he never took part in politics or protest, just as he had ceased to marvel at the catholicity of the causes Gamchik espoused, for besides tickets for political meetings and socials he had also tried to sell him lucky numbered tickets for a sale of work in aid of thalidomide children, a couple of half-guinea stalls for a recital by a Yugoslav violinist, and a raffle to raise funds for equipping Vietnam snipers, all of which he seemed to find equally deserving. There was something melancholy about his preoccupation with organizations and birds. As though he had to keep the warmth of his emotions at second hand because he mistrusted direct contact with human beings.

Huskion eased his own loneliness by spending more and more evenings at the flat. Which did not at all please Monica Stretley. She disapproved of him, of his impinging on the cozy nest she and Deirdre had made, especially of his being married, and showed it with tight lips and raised nostrils.

A couple of months earlier such hostility would have been effective in keeping him away but his need for a haven, for somewhere where things were still what they seemed, had hardened him. It was only during the week her sulks had to be endured, anyway.

At close quarters, relaxed in her home surroundings, Huskion found Deirdre different both from the personality she wore at the office and the slightly withdrawn girl she had been on the evening of the concert. In the straight blouses left to hang down over the tight trousers that suited her spare long-legged figure, which she changed into as soon as

197

she got back from the office, she had a pliant suppleness that was wholly feminine. At home, without her precise office expression he could call her Calshott, and it was an endearment.

They became lovers on a day when they had been penned in the flat by pouring rain and Huskion had got himself soaked to the skin trying to clear an overflowing gutter that was flooding into Monica's bedroom. So, instead of going out to eat, he had had to sit ridiculously huddled in a blanket waiting for his clothes to dry while Deirdre knocked them up a meal out of tins. As a setting for lovemaking, it was farcically different from the way he'd planned it the week before.

Then it had been fine, a day for tramping in the country in a fitful November sunshine that gave even the barest tree a varnished sheen but had little warmth. They had gone to Burnham Beeches and walked in the woods, surprised to find so few others using the paths where their feet rustled fallen leaves as crisp as new banknotes.

Huskion knew from the looks she shot him, from their silence, from the pressure of her fingers as he helped her over rough patches that Deirdre understood and accepted what this excursion was designed to prelude.

The mood engendered then, gay, slightly self-mocking but also excited, anticipatory, carried over to their return to the flat. Huskion had brought a bottle of Burgundy and they finished it, after steaks and a green salad had sated their hunger, with toasting foolery.

Afterwards, as a tacit sign of their ripening intimacy, he carried the dishes into the kitchen and prepared to wash up, something he hadn't done before.

"Here, wait a mo," he said as he dumped the crockery on the draining board.

Damping the corner of a dishcloth, he took hold of her left arm. Deirdre had rolled back the long sleeves she always wore. Her skin above the wrist was very white but had picked up a sooty smudge which he began to swab with the dishcloth.

As soon as she realized what he was doing, she pulled her arm away from him.

"It won't come off," she said reddening. "It's tattooed on."

"What?"

"My concentration camp number." Being caught off guard had made her stiffen. "I was going to tell you about it later. You would have seen it anyway, wouldn't you?"

He saw it was a number, 680875, in a rough circle, in a matte black pigment. He was completely thrown, unable to speak or move, until Deirdre thrust some cutlery into his hands, telling him to dry it and put it away.

When they were back in the living room she told him how Calshott had found her in the Buchenwald camp and adopted her, nothing Huskion didn't know already.

"You know you could have that tattoo removed?"

They were sitting apart in the two armchairs, the membrane of their contact unphysical and stretched to a brittle tautness. In the kitchen, when the first shock had blurred, he had tried, tentatively, to put his arm round her but she had twitched away, pretending to be engrossed with the sink and not to have noticed.

"I know."

Mrs. Calshott had wanted to have it erased when she was brought to England. Though only a child, acquiescent, even cowed, as a result of her experiences and still a little afraid of her new surroundings, Deirdre had nevertheless flown into a tantrum and kicked and screamed so that Mrs. Calshott and the tattooist were quite unable to hold her when she learned what they were going to do. Because this was so unlike the child, Mrs. Calshott had not tried to subdue her agonized resistance by force, expecting in a few years she would want to be rid of the blemish. But she had remained obstinately against it.

"Because you're proud of it?" he asked.

"I don't know why. But as I always keep it covered up it can't be that. I even have a gold bangle that covers it when I wear evening dress. It's just silliness."

To fight obstinately and so long to retain a stigma any other attractive girl would have regarded with horror argued something deeper, he thought, and Deirdre had been lucky Mrs. Calshott had been sensitive enough to recognize it.

"You remember your mother?" he asked.

"Not very well, nor my father, just sort of impressions, more like pictures or dreams than memories." Her tone was offhand but the words came slowly as though they were being squeezed out. "I was with her after they took my father away. I remember her crying mostly and I know she was crying for my father but I don't know why I do. And that we were with a lot of other people at the time. I think we were traveling but it's horribly confused."

"What happened to her?"

She shrugged but did not answer.

"I mean, after you got to Buchenwald?"

"She was never there. At any rate father—that is, the colonel—said there was nothing in the records that she had come there with me. I remember being in a place with white walls like a cowshed with her and people in white all round us and being frightened and crying because my arm was being pricked and she held me and stroked my hair. But that wasn't Buchenwald. There was no room like that there."

That could have been when their numbers had been tattooed on. It could explain her unreasoning obsession with the brand, clinging to it as a gem of truth, of identity. He did not put this to her, for she was near to tears and he didn't want to upset her further.

200

"It's really the people at Buchenwald I remember, much more clearly than I remember my mother and father. I mean, I can see them clearer."

Now that she had begun to talk about her childhood she went on, answering his questions willingly, gaining release, her stiffness melting as she put into words what she had never freely spoken of before. They became close again as they talked; but not as before, not in a way that made sex possible. The remote strangeness of the horror she had known and his guilt at keeping from her his preknowledge of it constrained them, blighting the urge for communion. When at last they fell silent, both of them had felt physically and spiritually tired. He had gone home to Wimbledon earlier than he usually did when Monica was away.

But the constraint that had plagued them that evening was only on the surface, temporary. Below, their involvement with each other was deepened by it. Deirdre was no longer simply someone he could escape to, someone he could feel was real and safe. He wanted her, needed her, for herself.

With these emotional trip wires behind them, the damp squalidity of the following weekend's debacle became a joke out of which their lovemaking grew naturally.

In the morning he lay for a while looking at the gray light filtering through the curtains, unable to move without disturbing Deirdre, for there was no room for them to lie in the single divan without touching.

Suddenly he was aware she was awake, too, had been for some time, lying with her eyes closed and her head turned away from him. He turned on his elbow and kissed her lightly on the ear.

"I'll have to move now."

"No," he said, "you stay there. I'll make some tea. Want anything to eat with it?"

"I didn't mean that. I'll have to find another job."

Her thoughts had been running on the same lines as his.

"Leave me! Just when you've shown me all your qualifications!" She jabbed him with her elbow. "Ouch!"

"I'm serious."

"And spiteful. What difference does our sleeping together make?"

"A lot, I hope."

"But not to your shorthand."

"You know it's impossible."

"Not if we're careful."

"We can't be all the time. Besides, it's not how I want to be with you."

"I'll make some tea," he said, getting out of bed. "Are you always as serious as this before breakfast?"

They were finishing eating before she spoke of it again.

"There's a possible job in Transport. You wouldn't try to stop me getting it, would you?"

He neither agreed nor disagreed. But he had been thinking. With Deirdre out of the department, there would be one less reason for Spinwell to be on the prowl.

16

As the meaning of his affair with Deirdre deepened, he recovered some of his strength. He still had his moments of panic when he wondered what would happen to him when it was all over and King, having no more use for him as bait, tossed him back into the stream to find his own place in the swim; but now he was able to work, not merely to keep abreast of routine sectional tasks but initiate new ones.

One of these was a theory that policy decisions took too long to hammer out and then, if not entirely wrong, turned out to be slightly off target because they were based on estimates that were sometimes no better than guesses. His idea was for a computer program to predict the statistical effect of all the possible solutions under discussion before a decision was taken. That in itself would eliminate a fair portion of the abortive speculation at policy meetings. But he envisaged that, as the bank of data in the computer grew more sophisticated, the computer would be able to indicate solutions to problems not in themselves statistical.

"It would appeal to our master," His Nibs said when he mentioned it to him. "Pressing a button as a substitute for thinking has a certain fascination even for me. Let me have a piece of paper on it, will you?"

He knew His Nibs was thinking of nothing more than an outline of the idea. But he wanted to back it with detailed analysis. Anything that went to the Minister in a half-baked state which might or might not be thought worth exploring was no use to him. Timed right, something spectacularly proved could be the fulcrum needed to heave his career back onto the rails. That was incentive enough for him to tackle the theory with a will.

"See I was right about it going to be a cruel winter?" Gamchik asked a couple of days after Huskion had demanded to be given a contact.

"What?"

Ignoring the folded newspaper on the seat beside him, Gamchik stretched out and took Huskion's *Times* from him. Turning to an inside page, he folded it and handed it back to him.

"There."

His finger pointed to a story about a collision in the Channel.

What this had to do with the weather baffled Huskion.

"See," Gamchik said, taking the paper from him again and tapping it significantly with his finger, "now them long-range weather forecasters are saying so. But seagulls is better than any ruddy computer."

He folded the paper and put it down next to him, making room for it by pushing his own along the seat toward Huskion. It was done so clumsily and with such babyish furtiveness that Huskion wanted to laugh.

After watching Gamchik crumble fodder for his flock for a few minutes Huskion picked up the paper and walked off toward the Horseguards swinging his umbrella. If anyone had been interested, they could only have missed seeing the switch if they had been blind.

Unfolding the paper when he got back to his office, he found it concealed a plain manila envelope. Inside was a half sheet of copy paper on which was laconically typed:

Kennington 4650
Supply immediately three passport photographs

He was about to destroy the message when it occurred to him King would probably like to see it. Replacing it in its envelope he put it in his wallet.

The newspaper, a *Daily Express*—Gamchik had not even had the good sense to notice that it was a *Times* he always carried—seemed somehow even more incriminating, as he could not remember ever having a copy of it in his office before. As he crammed it into his wastepaper basket he noticed it carried on its front page a headlined warning of a hard winter to come.

"The telephone number is interesting," said King in a voice a degree less freezing than usual. "I hadn't hoped for anything better than DLB's."

"What the hell are they?"

"Dead Letter Boxes, holes in walls, broken drain pipes, refuse bins, anywhere that a message can be left for someone to pick up later. That they're willing to risk the telephone with you shows they are taking you seriously."

"Or know I wouldn't stand for schoolboy larks like leaving messages under loose paving stones. There's such a thing as dignity."

"Agents are usually more concerned about saving their necks than their faces," King commented. "I'll look into that telephone number."

King told him to send the chit for the passport photos to Finlay Street.

There was something snide about King's pettifogging pre-occupation with petty cash vouchers that got under Husk-ion's skin. It seemed intended to imply his thuggish trade was quite normal, even ordinary, really. It sickened him as much as did Gamchik's sloppy conjuring. Meanly filling in swindle sheets for bus fares and playing catch-me-if-you-can round St. James's Park hardly matched with the scientific enormity of microdots and cyanide bullets of modern espio-nage. No wonder Secret Service agents in fiction had nothing to do with such vulgarities but stuck to gambling for high stakes and giving lifts in their Bentleys to fetching young women who, in one way or another, became separated from their clothes four chapters from the end.

Fiction was a definite improvement on reality, Huskion thought as he pushed himself out of the call box. He was be-ginning to associate King with the sweaty, fourth-hand air in the Fairmile Place phone kiosk. That was reality. Still he had Deirdre to separate from her clothes if he wanted to. It seemed a good way to take the taste of King and the call box from his tongue.

Going to the photographers in Trafalgar Square who spe-cialized in passport portraits meant that it was nearly six o'clock when he got back to the office. He had not hurried back from Trafalgar Square because he had to give Deirdre time to get home before he could phone her.

But that turned out to be unnecessary. Entering his room from the door into the corridor, he found her standing behind his desk with one hand resting on the safe.

"Oh!" she said, looking round startled, "I didn't think you'd be back yet."

"That makes two of us. I didn't think you'd be here."

She came round to the front of the desk to make way for him, still a little flustered by his sudden appearance.

"I was just tidying up."

"Well, stop it." He slid his arm round her and kissed her. "I'm taking you out."

"Aren't you working tonight?"

"No. Go on, get ready."

She moved away from him toward the door.

"I'll ring Monica. She'll only fuss if I don't."

"Tell her we'll be back early but won't be using the sitting room."

She looked at him across her shoulder, her head slightly tilted, but said nothing.

By the end of the evening it was plain that brazening it out with Monica had not been such a good idea. Even on their own, in Deirdre's room, her presence in the flat could not be ignored.

"I think she's brooding on what she should do," Deirdre said, putting two cups of coffee on the chest of drawers.

Lying in bed, thinking he ought to get dressed, he had heard them talking together in the kitchen.

"Uh-uh."

Her dressing gown was heavily quilted and so long only her toes showed as she moved. Its cocoonlike bulk and the sheen on her newly brushed hair glinting in the shadow beyond the circle of light thrown by the bedside lamp made her look very young.

"It's all very silly," she said, putting his cup on the bedside table.

It was. But it obviously hurt her. They would not make love in the flat again when Monica was there. Neither of them would want to. Which was even sillier. However many times you jumped through the hoop you could break the paper only once. Monica would make no more hats for Deirdre, whether they did or not.

"Come back to bed," he said, feeling contrite, reaching out for her hand.

"We'll spill the coffee. I don't want a mucky bed to sleep in."

But she bent down and kissed him, rubbing her cheek against his before pulling away.

"Then I'll get up."

"I wish you didn't have to go."

"So do I."

He gulped down his coffee and began to put on his clothes.

"If you had a place of your own you wouldn't have to go."

She leaned back on the bed watching him dress. With his usual precision he had hung his clothes over a chair in the order he would put them on and he slid into them without ever having to look for anything. For so tall a man he was remarkably deft.

"But then it would be me who would be getting dressed to go home."

"I wouldn't like that. Nor would you."

"I'd have to, though. We'd have to be careful until your divorce was through."

He ducked down toward the floor to tie his shoelaces.

She was able to say with casual directness what he shrank from putting into words. He had never mentioned divorce, had only spoken vaguely of their being together in the future.

"Not that I could live with you anyway while I'm working for you," she added. "Your nice boss nose having to be kept clean."

She could say that again!

When he got home he found Penny still up. She said she had only just got back but he guessed she had deliberately waited for him. He wondered if she and Lambert had at last succeeded in becoming lovers and she was going to tell him so. To his surprise, the thought nipped him unpleasantly.

"I was thinking of making myself some coffee. Would you like anything?"

208

Usually, if either of them had a hot drink before going to bed, it was he, as Penny claimed that even tea kept her awake.

"No."

"Perhaps it is rather late."

"Umm."

He was not going to help her. He turned away.

"It's all settled about the house. Completion on January the third."

"So it's worked out as you wanted it."

"They're nice people and very keen to move in but old Dodgett says he can't get it through any quicker."

"Solicitors always hang things out to justify their fees."

Penny, ill at ease, fidgeted with her gloves, picking up one and dropping it on the other lying on her coat.

"I've said they could come in before. They want to re-decorate the hall and your study and rig up the two small spare rooms as day and night nurseries. And they're going to build a laundry out from the kitchen."

"They'll need planning permission for that."

Their usual roles were reversed. He was at the door, half turned toward her, one foot over the threshold, while she was at the settee straining to keep him with her.

"I expect they know that," she said, adding in a rush, "It means we shan't be here for Christmas after all."

It wasn't something he wanted to discuss. If it meant leaving the house just before Christmas, there was still time for him to deliver the last Tridon folders before he had to move. He hadn't given a thought to Christmas. A quiet country pub, not too far away, where he could take Deirdre for the three-day holiday would be good.

"Roy, there are things we must settle."

He was already in the hall. Reluctantly he came back into the room.

"Such as?"

209

"Well, there's the furniture."

"What about it?"

"Is there any you want? We'll have to agree what each of us is to take."

He had thought of this but not seriously, not specifically, because debasing what had been their home to a given number of chairs, tables, beds, carpets and pots and pans had a mortuary taste.

"Now?"

"We haven't much time. Lambert has to make room for anything I take. Not all of it of course. We'll store any we don't want until we can sell it. I want to start moving it right away."

She was still standing, tense and uncomfortable, steeling herself to stay with the kind of emotionally charged situation she hated. Seeing her discomfort and her taut face, he was suddenly sickened.

"Take whatever you want. It's mostly yours, anyway. Take the lot."

Her fingers stopped kneading her gloves and she looked at him apprehensively, obviously fearing the cold way he had thrown the words at her was the prelude to an outburst.

"Do—" she had been going to say "be sensible" but changed it to "—give me an idea what you want. I can't just grab everything. Anyway, there's a lot I shouldn't have any use for."

"Then leave those."

It would be easy to start a row just by being stubborn. Only he could find no zest for it, feeling nothing but a numbness deep inside and a desire to have done with the scene.

"I'll make a list," he said. "And you make one of what you particularly want. If we agree on those, we can go on from there. All right?"

"Oh, yes," she said, relieved, and seemed about to say

something else but the words would not come. "We can be civilized about it, can't we?" He was sure that was not what she had been trying to say.

"Yes, though it'll all have to be fixed up with the lawyers. If you're using Dodgett I'll have to find someone else. For the divorce, anyway."

This hit her. That they were to be divorced, he saw, was as nebulous a notion to her as the practicalities of splitting up their home had been to him.

"Is that what you want? —Right away?"

"It'd be tidier."

When she didn't answer at once, he wondered if she had ever really accepted that they would be divorced, if she had not been looking on this moving in with Lambert as an interlude which could be made permanent or brought to an end as she chose, if she had not expected him to remain as part of her life, in the background but on hand. With Lambert unbreakably fettered to his lunatic wife, she had nothing to gain by divorce.

"Yes, I suppose you're right," she said a little shakily. "You'll sue me, of course, that'll be best."

He was glad she had said it, that she knew without prompting that being the innocent party would look slightly better on his record.

Penny picked up her coat and hung it over her arm.

"It is a mess, isn't it?" Her head was turned away from him, her eyes lowered. "I'm sorry, Roy."

She was nearer to tears than he'd ever known her.

He knew she was reaching out to him, clinging to the familiar and the comfort of habit. He felt the pull, too. It was nothing but a death spasm of the defeated legions in both of them but momentarily powerful for all that.

"So long as we keep our heads, it shouldn't be too bad," he said lightly.

211

For a few moments she kept her face away from him. When she swung round, he saw she was no longer wavering. The fire being put to her boats had caught her unawares, given her a prick of fear, but it had been brief and of no more substance than the flames.

"You've no idea where you're going yet?" she asked.

"None."

"Living here's not going to be comfortable once the furniture starts going. Besides it's a waste keeping this place up just for you to sleep here. I'm not trying to turn you out." She smiled as she crossed the room. He held the door for her. "But it would be sensible if you found somewhere quickly."

Going into his room he found preparations for the move had already begun. Penny had brought two suitcases down from the loft and put them at the foot of his bed. His boats, it seemed, were for burning without a qualm.

17

"Good," King told him when he reported that he had delivered the three passport photographs to Gamchik. He had used the same slapstick sleight of hand with the newspapers but hoped he'd managed it rather better than Gamchik had.

"You did," said King almost affably. "My man says he would have missed it completely if he hadn't been looking for it."

It was news to Huskion that his chats with Gamchik were observed.

"Anything on the phone number?" he asked.

"A little. It is in a furnished flat rented by an embassy attaché called Spolzakov. Connected three months ago and like the other phone in the flat is in the landlord's name. That's to prevent Spolzakov's address and number being listed," King explained. "Spolzakov uses the number twice a day, at a quarter to nine to ask the garage to bring his car round and again at five-thirty to phone his wife to tell her when he'll be home. At all other times he and his friends use the other number. We think the two calls are tests to check if the line is in order."

"I see," Huskion said indifferently. "Have I still got to pass the folders one by one? I'd like to dump the last two together next time."

"That's not on," King told him tersely. "We've had that out already. Stick to procedure."

Huskion slammed down the receiver.

Why did the bloody man insist on keeping him on a string and lying? The trap had to be closed before the last folder was delivered, for that one dealt explicitly with the hardware. It had always seemed this would turn out to be pretty improbable but now the calculations had actually been made it showed up as maniacal. The Russians couldn't be conned into believing all that monstrous junk could be launched into orbit. Not even Intelligence could be crazy enough to think they could. But the little pipsqueak sadistically insisted on keeping him on the rack.

"I've got to find a flat," he told Deirdre as they were clearing up before leaving the office. "Where would you like to live?"

"Are you proposing to me?"

He reached out and took her hand.

"Yes."

At his serious tone she drew away from him, moving round the desk. A moment before she had been playful but now her apprehensive mask had fallen over her features like a shutter.

"Can't we go on as we are?"

"Why the hell should we?"

"Anyway we can't get married."

"When my divorce comes through, we can. Take that prefect look off your face. I've seen you with your pants down, remember? Don't you want to marry me?"

"I don't feel like a prefect. I wish I did."

"Do you want to marry me?"

Quite slowly she moved back round the desk and taking his head in her hands kissed him.

"But it can't be for ages yet, can it?" she said brightly, pressing his face against her sweater.

"Not so bloody long," he told her, his voice muffled in wool. "With luck it mightn't be more than six months."

To celebrate he took her to the Coq d'Or. In a silly mood they competed who could choose the most expensive meal.

"You baffle me, Calshott, at times," Huskion said when they were into the last quarter of their bottle of champagne. "Why did you go all coy about getting married?"

Deirdre's lips set hard and she looked away.

"Coy's nasty."

"It's what you were, darling."

"Please, Roy—" she was looking at him now, pleading but also closed in and determined—"I'm not going to talk about it."

He smiled and pressed her foot under the table, thinking he could allow her her small feminine secrets as she would always be barred from his large male ones.

When the bill came it was large enough for him to hope maliciously Spinwell had chosen that night to put a flatfoot on his tail. He'd have a nasty time getting his expenses passed. Not that any of the diners looked at all likely.

There was much less faking for him to do on the phony Tridon folders now as only the last two were kept up to date. He was kept busy, however, with a number of non-secret chores.

"It's tricky, very tricky," Sir Nigel said of one of these, a highly complex piece of atomic engineering the Authority had asked the department to check for overlaps. "Not to say nasty. Phase Three looks very suspect, very, sails very close to our Plimpton do. So wrap it up tight if you go for it." He

215

handed him the folder. "One of your penances for being our eager bright-eyed boy."

Interdepartmental problems were normally dealt with by Sir Nigel himself. That he was being asked to devil for him meant His Nibs recognized how his ambiguous situation must be troubling him and he felt grateful.

"I mentioned your idea for instant decisions to our master and he was madly keen. How is it coming out?"

Huskion told him how he had been sieving through past department decisions and errors.

"Good, good. Press on, press on, my boy, and let me have something hard on paper as soon as you can."

The following afternoon Huskion was briefing three of his E.O.'s when Spinwell came into the office. Waving him to carry on, the Security man fetched a chair from the outer room and settled himself down under the window.

Huskion immediately broke up the conference.

"You needn't have stopped for me, you know," Spinwell said, "I could have waited."

"I don't like an audience."

"I wouldn't have butted in but the meeting didn't seem very high-powered."

"Just work being done. What can I do for you? Or have you just dropped in for tea?"

Huskion was so furious Spinwell should assume he could sit in on a working meeting of his without a by-your-leave that he forgot that for the past months he hadn't been able to see the Security man at the far end of the corridor without his stomach jerking.

"What's happened between you and the Calshott girl?"

The question might have been a bucket of ice-cold water, it cooled Huskion so suddenly.

"What do you mean?" he asked cautiously.

"She wants to leave you. She's put in for the job in Transport, Agriculture and Education."

"Oh, that!"

"You knew?"

"I encouraged it."

"I thought you said she was good?"

Huskion, his nerves no longer jangling, lounged back in his chair, relieved. "She's better than that," he said with an air of disarming frankness. "After what you told me, though, I gave her a bully-ragging about wasting her talents. And she's decided to have a go at getting upgraded. Takes her exams next June."

Spinwell thought this over impassively, mouth set, as though it were a coin he was testing.

"She doesn't need to transfer to do that," he observed shrewdly.

No, Huskion agreed reluctantly, disconcerted at having what he had thought to be a certain winner returned so smartly. "Unless she's looking for somewhere where the pressure's lower. She's driven pretty hard here, you know."

This seemed to satisfy Spinwell, for he nodded, the merest flick of his long neck.

"I suppose it can't be helped when you've got a full head of steam," he said. "I see you've been staying late, very late, quite often, too."

Huskion told him of the policy analyses he was doing.

"It's not something I can do in the daytime mixed in with all the normal routine," he explained.

"And you take work home other nights?"

"Who doesn't?"

"Any of the Top Secret files?"

Huskion pressed his thumbs together and stared down at the nails without answering.

"Well, do you?"

"I was wondering what answer you wanted, Spinwell. If I say no you'll know I'm lying because we all take home the stuff we're working on without ever thinking of its classification. If we bloody well didn't, the work wouldn't get done. So you'd know I was lying but if one day my briefcase loaded with bumf from there"—he jerked his thumb toward the safe—"is found in the gents at the Corner House you'd be in the clear because you could say I'd told you I never took classified papers out of the office. And if I tell you I do, you point out the regulations and show up snow-white if I come a cropper afterwards. Which do you prefer? You win either way."

"The only sensible thing is to stick to the regulations."

"You don't know how completely I agree with you," Huskion told him grimly.

The Security man stood up and looked out the window.

"You can't be seeing much of your wife," he said unexpectedly, without turning round. "How does she take it?"

"Oh, she's used to it by now," Huskion said with elaborate casualness. "Her father was in the Service—but of course you know that."

Spinwell was facing him directly now.

"Still it can't be much fun for her."

"It's not for any of our wives. I don't suppose yours relishes your being here to all hours sometimes."

"She died six years ago."

"I'm sorry, I didn't know," Huskion mumbled, embarrassed. "An accident?"

"Cancer of the cervix. Stupid because it can be dealt with if taken in time. But she was the shy sort, couldn't bear the thought of being properly examined. So there wasn't a chance."

He hadn't moved away from the window but he was no longer looking at Huskion.

"It must have been hell for you." The silence was so

awkward Huskion felt compelled to break it. "There can't be anything worse than having to stand helplessly by while somebody dies . . . like that."

"I didn't know anything about it . . . not till afterwards." Spinwell's voice was as flat, as uncolored by any feeling or emotion, as always. "She didn't tell me she was ill. I was in Aden and couldn't understand why she kept putting off coming out to join me. I should have guessed something was wrong. But I didn't."

He walked stiffly across the room, passing in front of the desk without turning his eyes to Huskion, and went out by the door into the corridor.

Apart from—or it may have been because of—the embarrassing way the Security man had displayed his wounds, Huskion found the interview disturbing. The questions, quite innocuous in themselves, had been too close to too much he needed to keep hidden. He had thought of Spinwell as a blunt-headed dumbbell whose blundering feet might plunk down where they were not wanted. But the way the Security man's toes kept barking his heels made him wonder if he didn't know exactly where he was treading.

It seemed whenever he was beginning to feel easier something cropped up to drag his nerves as though they were yo-yos that could never be at rest.

And it was beginning to show. Besides chain smoking, he was fuddling himself with four or five stiff whiskeys at the Progressive now when he stayed late.

On Saturday he and Deirdre looked at half a dozen flats she had found on the Bayswater agents' lists. It had seemed an adventure as they set out but as they went from one to another he grew progressively more depressed, they were all so inexpressibly dreary. He marveled how Deirdre could accept their failure as part of the hazards of the chase and not be at all discouraged.

219

"You can't have thought we'd find what we wanted right away, surely," she said.

In the evening the film they went to see seemed to him so piffling that it was purgatory to sit through it. He stayed in his seat because he thought he had been so grumpy and bearish the whole afternoon he ought to stick it out for Deirdre's sake. He had a puritanical dislike for temperaments that showed, even his own.

When they were in bed and had turned out the light he could not sleep but lay on his back smoking, the red tip of his cigarette in the darkness pulsing like the crater of an erupting volcano.

"What's the matter, darling?" Deirdre asked as he lit a third cigarette from the butt of his second.

He'd thought she was asleep. Running his hand down under the covers he found hers.

"Nothing. I'm a bit off color, that's all. Sorry I've been such a drip."

She squeezed his hand.

"You'd tell me if there was anything, wouldn't you?"

"Of course. It's just my liver."

"There's some Alka-Seltzer in the bathroom cabinet."

Because he knew she hadn't believed him, he got up and went to the bathroom and swallowed the draught. When he came back she had turned on her side away from him, pretending to be asleep.

Usually they were late on Sunday mornings, waking slowly in languorous enjoyment of their closeness in the warmth of the bed, hazily relishing their temporary freedom from the harrying hands of the clock. But in the morning he was wide awake at seven. After half an hour trying to doze, he slipped out of bed and went into the kitchen.

"I think I'll go over to Wimbledon and play some tennis," he said when he came back carrying their breakfasts on a tray which he set down on the bed while he cleared the side table. "It looks like being a pretty drear day but at least it isn't raining."

She sat up, pushing her hair back from her forehead and blinking the sleep mist from her eyes. She frowned but said nothing. Leaning over the bed he kissed her, gently stroking her breasts.

"The eggs will get cold."

"You care?"

"I hate them gummy. Give me my dressing gown or I'll freeze."

He threw it to her and she draped it over her shoulders. They ate, saying little, tensions between them.

"What gave you such an urge to get up in the middle of the night to play tennis?"

"Not getting enough exercise. Need to shake my liver up."

He knew she was wondering why he hadn't asked her to play with him instead of going off to Wimbledon on his own. She had told him her game was quite good, although over the past couple of years she hadn't had much practice. That it was not exercise he craved but an escape from the faces that ringed him so closely, even if only to such unexciting ones as his tennis club partners, he could not tell her.

As he dressed he half expected she would offer to give him a game and wondered how he would evade it. When she didn't, he was as much puzzled as relieved. She simply lay back in the bed, not exactly sulking nor even aggrieved but as though bruised and slightly apprehensive.

"Let's mooch around Hampstead and Highgate this afternoon to see if there's anything there we particularly like," he said.

"All right."

"I'll not be long." He kissed her and when he straightened up his hand stayed in her hair, ruffling it affectionately. "With luck I'll come back more cheerful."

"I hope so."

221

Penny had apparently spent the night at Lambert's, for she was not at the house when he arrived to collect his tennis things. She had already started moving the furniture. The missing pieces had a ghostly presence in the lighter patches of wallpaper marking where they had been. He had told her all he would be taking was the stuff in his study and bedroom. There was still an awful lot in the house that neither of them had opted for.

Telling Deirdre that he was off color seemed to have been truer than he had thought. Toweling himself down after two hard sets of doubles, he felt a great deal better, though the problem of the furniture still depressed him. He had a revulsion at the idea of an interminable session where he and Penny took alternative picks at what was left.

"I think we'll furnish with modern stuff," he said to Deirdre. "You know, stainless steel and teak, banquettes and lots of iron-framed shelves."

"You like that kind of thing?"

They had parked just by the Whitestone Pond, the gray, overcast skies, threatening rain, having thinned the usual Sunday afternoon clutter of cars even from Hampstead, and were strolling down one of the streets fanning off from the Heath.

"Not particularly. So long as it's comfortable, I don't care what it is. I'm a philistine, a functional philistine."

"But what about all the furniture you have?"

"I'll sell it. I'd like a change."

"Yes, I suppose so," she said seriously.

He wanted to say it was not like that at all, that he wasn't afraid of old associations and memories but was excited by the thought of buying everything new, of having a home which they had chosen together. But to say it aloud would have sounded as though he were trying to argue away a doubt.

They wandered about until dusk, noting the roads they liked and collecting the names of estate agents to be written to. It was not till they were back in the car and he was feeling for his cigarettes before driving off that he realized he had not smoked the whole afternoon.

Back at the flat they took the stairs in a laughing rush, each of them knowing they would make love as soon as the door closed behind them, the tension of the morning gone as though it had never been.

At lunchtime the next day he picked up the notification of the last payment from the Helmstedt. He had had an unreasoning fear it would not be there and he would be hung up from making the next delivery. But as always it was punctual. He sent off a check transferring it to the Zurich bank and set off to St. James's Park, walking with long swinging impatient strides.

In the park it was raw cold, a stinging wind spinning off the lake, rattling the leafless branches of the trees and nipping his ears. Gamchik, swelled by several extra layers of clothing, a blue bloom on his large-pored, leathery skin, and his flock had the path to themselves. Absorbed in the birds he barely acknowledged Huskion's message that he would be making a delivery on Wednesday.

"Find out who their friends are when the days get a bit of bite in 'em." His fingers tearing at the bread crusts were red and crinkled like half-filled sausages. "New 'uns turn up every day. See that 'un. A thrush. Don't get many of them, not unless the weather's hard. Don't get 'em because they're not partial to bread, see? They like meat, snails and that."

It may have been the cold gnawing at him so viciously he could not stand still without shifting from one foot to the other that made Huskion feel a sudden gush of anger at the man's preoccupation. If it had not been sincere, its incongruity with what brought the two of them to meet would have been bearable. Without another word, he strode on his way, thinking there would be precious few birds where Gamchik was going to be before the week was out.

With the end of the charade in sight, his nervous restlessness increased. To quell it, he suggested to Deirdre they go out somewhere that evening and was considerably put out when she told him she couldn't. As he invariably worked on Monday evenings, she had arranged to go to Petts Wood to see her old nurse and couldn't get out of it. And she flatly refused to let him go with her because she said it would put the old lady in a tizzy if she produced him unexpectedly to her.

"Old nurse!" he grumbled irritably.

"She wasn't exactly that. She was with mother before I was born."

"Just an old retainer. Bloody feudal background you have."

Deirdre didn't fly out at him but plucked nervously at the front of her dress.

"I couldn't know you'd suddenly want to go out—"

"All right, all right, forget it!"

"I'm sorry, Roy, really I am."

And she looked it. When he'd asked her to go out she'd been quite shaken, lost all her color. He knew he was being unreasonable and to prevent his disappointment getting the better of him he stamped back into his own room, hoping his annoyance would make her change her mind.

But it didn't, and as soon as she had left the office he went straight home to Wimbledon, something he hadn't done for weeks, except when he was delivering a folder to Sherngold. Penny wasn't there, and this was another rub. Though he couldn't have said whether he had wanted her there for comfort or to have out with her the row he'd avoided with Deirdre.

In the morning, with one more day behind him, he felt

better and was able to meet Deirdre as cheerfully as usual. She said nothing about her visit, presumably fearing it might stir up his irritation, for she had been apprehensive when he'd gone into her office, only relaxing after he'd given her a kiss that plainly asked for forgiveness.

She said nothing, either, about his tantrum, making it plain without words that, however it had upset her, it was to be forgotten.

But his satisfaction that all was well between them again was short-lived. It happened in the most trivial way. Late in the afternoon his lighter had gone dead and he pressed the key on his intercom to ask her to send one of the messengers to get him some matches. When she didn't answer, he got up from his desk, thinking, as sometimes happened, she was on the phone and had not seen the light flash, and went into her office.

It was empty. Presumably she was with Wigstall or Havelock. For a moment he stood irresolute, the cigarette dangling from his thin lips, debating whether to cadge a light from Wigstall or wait until Deirdre came back.

Not wanting to have to listen to Wigstall's driveling chit-chat, he was turning back into his room when he noticed Deirdre's handbag beside her typewriter. Remembering her magpie habit of always taking the match books left on restaurant tables—"We're always running out of matches at the flat," she had explained—he opened the bag and rummaged through it. There did not seem to be any matches in it but his fingers found an oblong metal object that felt like a lighter.

He took it out. He didn't recognize what it was for a moment. Then his eyes widened in stupefied disbelief.

It was a Minox subminiature camera.

18

"This is unexpected," she said, "but I'm glad you've come. You seemed very morose when I said good night to you."

It was true. He hadn't been able to look at her, let alone speak. He still couldn't say anything but, when she put her hands on his shoulders and lifted her face, he kissed her.

"I've nothing for you to eat. Unless you wouldn't mind an omelet. That's what I'm going to have."

In his office, after seeing the camera, his chest had tightened up and he had to keep emptying his lungs and stretching the muscles behind his shoulder blades before he could breathe again. It had happened again as he climbed the stairs to the flat, making him rest on the second-floor landing until he'd got a rhythm back to his lungs. At any moment they'd go out of gear again.

"Is anything the matter, Roy?"

He had been right. There were just the two studio portraits of her parents and herself in the living room, no other photographs at all. He looked around for her handbag but it wasn't there so, still without speaking, he made for her bedroom.

"Roy, what is it?"

The bag was on the chest of drawers. He brought it back into the living room, flicked back the clasp, and shot the contents onto the coffee table. With his index finger he isolated the Minox from the jumble of cosmetics and odds and ends.

"Oh," Deirdre said quietly, hardly above a whisper, and sat down.

He had wondered what she would do, whether she'd pretend she knew nothing about it or try to brazen it out with some cock-and-bull story or just burst into tears. But she did none of these things.

Like a deathbed watcher at the ending of a vigil that has gone on too long, her blanched, stony face showed relief as much as shock.

"He gave it to me yesterday."

"Who?"

"Medaly."

She said it as though surprised that he, that anyone, should have to ask. It took some time before he understood how she came to have a Minox camera and who Medaly was. But at last he got the pieces together.

When the Hungarian Revolution had broken out, Deirdre, then a sixth former at St. Philippa's, had thrown herself into the work of caring for and resettling the fugitives from the Russian tanks in the streets of Budapest. Beyond the humanitarian reasons, she had a personal interest in the work. Though Jews and people from every part of Middle Europe had been housed in Buchenwald, by far the largest group had been Hungarian. With no real evidence to go on, she believed she, too, had been Hungarian before the Calshotts adopted her. So, as she saw it, she was helping her own people.

Later, when the first flush of enthusiasm was over, most of the helpers drifted away, leaving the bewildered Hungarians to find their feet as best they could among the frustrating disappointments of a strange foreign land. But not Deirdre. She was not put off by the seeming ingratitude and continual grumbling of the refugees. Having taken sides, she refused to hedge her loyalty. During school holidays and after she started work at the Board of Trade, she went to a club center off the Fulham Road where she took a class in English, helped them with their letters and served cups of tea and cakes at socials.

She also began to pick up a smattering of Hungarian. Her teacher was a quiet, sad-eyed, middle-aged man called Stepan Kovacs. They became friendly enough to visit each other at weekends when, after her lesson, Kovacs would talk nostalgically of his youth in Budapest and holidays on Lake Balaton. It was at one of these sessions that Deirdre told him about the Buchenwald camp and that she believed she might be Hungarian.

Kovacs was intrigued. He said he was sure she was Hungarian, for he had felt the affinity between them. He would call her his little sister. It was all very lighthearted, a joke between them.

But some time later, very seriously, he had asked her if she had attempted to trace her parents. She told him she had no starting point, not even a name to go on. Kovacs then told her that many Hungarians who had been in Buchenwald were still alive and maybe one of them might remember something of her and her parents. He would see what he could find out.

The next Sunday he brought Medaly to see her, saying if anyone could help her Medaly was the man, for he had worked in the department for the Rehabilitation of Concentration Camp prisoners. Medaly was a very different type from Kovacs, fifteen years younger, better dressed than any of the refugees at the club could afford to be, with a white, thin-lipped, unsmiling face and hard, almost black, eyes. Even at that first meeting he had made her uncomfortable.

Very deliberately Medaly drew from her all she could tell him—which, as he pointed out, was little enough. He could promise nothing. It would not be easy and the investigation would take time, quite a lot of time.

It was almost a year before she saw him again and by then had given up expecting to. He didn't come to her— by that time she had moved into the flat in Bayswater with Monica—but asked her through Kovacs to meet him in a small café at Hammersmith Broadway. She had found him there alone—she had expected to see Kovacs too—with an empty cup in front of him. Instead of offering her a seat, he shepherded her along the road to a coffee bar, where a jukebox going full blast ensured no conversation could be overheard. (She was to become familiar with this pattern, for, wherever she arranged to meet Tibor Medaly, they always moved somewhere else to talk.)

He had news, he told her, some good, some bad. He had found twenty Buchenwald survivors who remembered her at the camp, three of whom were able to contribute rather more than a memory of an orphan child. These three had been in the same party as Deirdre and her mother when they came to the camp. Almost as soon as they arrived, her mother had known she was to be removed and, fearing the worst, persuaded the other women to hide her daughter so that she would not share her fate. One of the three even remembered the woman's name was Serly. Her mother had been mistaken, however. Instead of going to the gas chambers, she was sent as a slave laborer to a leather factory near

Linz, where the director's wife had chosen her as a maid. As such, though she escaped neither cruelty nor hardship, she was better off than those who went to the works.

Her father had had a much more adventurous time. Sent to a labor camp at Regensburg, he had escaped during an air raid, crossed the Alps into Yugoslavia and joined the partisans, was twice wounded fighting the Germans and decorated by Tito. As a war hero and a party member he was given a government job when he returned home after the war.

Unfortunately, Medaly told her with thin-lipped disapproval, it seemed that he had received more than medals from Tito, for Feodor Serly had been killed by a Russian bullet in the student revolt, not a stray one either, for he had fallen with a rifle in his hands.

Though ailing, her mother was still alive. As a traitor's widow, Medaly explained, Marthe Serly could not expect to have an easy life, but she had a job as school cleaner in a village on the outskirts of the capital which enabled her to exist. He had brought photographs of her, taken only a fortnight before.

One of these showed a woman in a shapeless print dress and peasant head scarf, with felt slippers or broken-down bootees on her stockingless feet, standing listless in front of a wilting paling fence edging a dirt road. The other photograph, taken at the same time, was a close-up of the woman's head, very sharply focused to bring out all the details of her features. In it it was possible to see the lined and roughened skin, the cheeks sagging over almost toothless gums. The expression in her dull lackluster eyes held nothing but defeat. It could have been the face of a well-preserved woman of eighty or the ruin of a fifty-year-old's.

"Is it your mother?" Huskion queried, looking at the photographs.

"Yes," she said. "I wasn't sure at first but I am now."

For the first time her eyes filled with tears.

She asked Medaly whether she could do anything to help her. He was doubtful about being able to send her money —receiving presents from someone in the West could be embarrassing to her—but said he would try. Helped by Medaly, she wrote a letter to her which he said he would see was delivered. She also gave him twenty pounds.

About six weeks later he brought a reply. And after that she had more letters every week or two, not through Medaly but sent to her direct.

The letters were full of reminiscences of her childhood, few of which meant anything to Deirdre, though one, which must have happened on their journey to Buchenwald, when her mother had put her to sleep in a hammock made from her coat slung across the corner of the truck in which they were traveling, came back to her vividly. These were mixed up with expressions of Marthe Serly's delight that her daughter should not only be alive but thriving and touching gratitude for the help she was receiving.

Though she was now in direct contact with her mother she was still seeing Medaly, for he was the channel through which she could send money to her. He continued doing this for about a year.

Then came the day on which he told her the government would no longer tolerate the widow of a traitor being made more than comfortable with foreign money. That would have to stop. But—

If Deirdre was prepared to make amends for her father's treachery and work for Hungary by passing information they needed, then the government itself would take over looking after her mother. And, as though he knew the first thought that jumped into Deirdre's mind, he added, she must know that his government could not only help her mother, it could harm her as well. The choice was up to her.

She had not given in at once. But the more she thought

about it, about her mother's plight, about the unlikelihood of her ever being able to pass any information that would be in the least valuable, let alone vital, from her work with BoT's Film Division, to play along—or, at least, pretend to —seemed the most sensible thing to do.

Wryly Huskion recognized the reasoning.

For quite a while Deirdre was able to string Medaly along. Every six to eight weeks or so he contacted her and seemed satisfied with the snippets she passed to him, all of which either were in BoT publications or soon would be. She dug out for him the policy of the Board over the Czech Film Festival because he said the Hungarians were considering mounting one, too.

He was especially interested in any details she could tell him about the organization of the Civil Service and the union activities of the Civil Service Clerical Association, but, as she was almost totally ignorant of both, she was able to tell him less than he could have learned from annual reports.

Her mother continued to write regularly. By now conditions in Hungary had begun to ease and several of the refugees she knew went home. All of them Deirdre asked to look up her mother and let her know how she was. Two of them, Kovacs and another man, confirmed that, though frail and in poor health, she was being well looked after.

"Kovacs!" Huskion said contemptuously. "How could you trust him?"

"He'd tried to help me. He didn't know what Medaly wanted me—"

"Didn't he? Be your age!"

"You don't understand." She was almost angry, defensive. "The poor man was dying to go home. To clear the way he'd made contact with Medaly and wanted to help me by sharing his contact. He meant no harm. You didn't know him or how he felt."

It was no use arguing. After all, the woman might be her mother. If she had survived, it would be easier to use her than to invent a substitute.

"Go on."

Medaly's attitude had suddenly, and without warning, changed. He said she was not giving value for money. If she couldn't get hold of secret information where she was, she must get herself transferred somewhere where she could. She explained to him, as she was not British born, she would never be allowed near classified material; but he insisted she try.

So, to pacify him, she began to apply for any job at the Foreign Office or atomic establishments that was advertised. And, as she expected, landed none of them.

"What made you put in for Gilly's job?" he asked, curious because the department's Top Secret work was not generally known.

"I didn't. I'd applied for one that was going in the Harwell Registry but, when I went for the interview, they offered me Gilly's which they said had just come up."

He could have laughed. The haphazard British method of selection by grades, irrespective of the character of the job, had decided. The applicant of the right rank who happened to walk through the door got the job that happened to be on the top of the pile. Later, generally not much later, Security caught up with the bad risks.

A lot of things were becoming clearer to him. For instance, the panic fear that had seized her when she heard the waiters talking in the Hungarian restaurant he had taken her to the first night they went out together. She must have thought he was warning her cruelly that he knew all about her!

"I suppose it was Medaly's idea that you should seduce me?"

She nodded. "He was always suggesting I could find out

233

more than I did with sex but I kept telling him it was something I just couldn't do. It . . . it wasn't like that, Roy. That was why I was so awkward when you asked me to go out with you. I was terrified that without meaning to I was doing what Medaly wanted. It was even worse when you asked me to marry you," she added quietly.

He said nothing.

Medaly had been extremely pleased that Huskion was taking her out but not at all that she was able to give only the sketchiest idea of the work they did. Now that she was handling official secrets she had great difficulty in stalling him. She held him off by pretending she saw only bits of the projects they were handling and didn't know whether these were important or not.

That was the reason for the Minox camera. She had been with Medaly the previous evening, while he taught her how to use it. She was to photograph as many papers as she could so that he could evaluate them and instruct her on which she should concentrate.

"They wouldn't be much use without the formulae. How were you going to get those?"

"I wasn't. I told Medaly it was impossible as you had only one of the two keys needed to open the safe."

But the safe needed only one key, the one he had. There had been more than a dozen occasions when she could have got it from his pocket and made a wax impression of it when he was out of the bedroom. He also remembered how flustered she'd been that night when he'd surprised her near the safe.

He upended her bag again and shook it. A bobby pin dropped on the table but nothing else. With a set face he examined everything he had tipped out of the bag, even throwing the powder from her compact into an ashtray and taking her lipstick out of its case to make sure nothing was

234

concealed in them. Picking up the bag, he ran his fingers slowly over every inch of the lining. There were only two keys, on a ring in a purse, one for the flat, the other for the outer door.

He looked up. She was watching him, sitting slightly hunched in her chair, totally dejected.

"Take your clothes off."

For a moment she looked puzzled, not understanding. Then the penny dropped.

"But Roy, I haven't got—"

"Shut up!"

She dragged herself up and started for the door but he stopped her.

"Not in the bedroom. Here."

"But Monica—"

"To hell with Monica! There's more light here."

For several seconds she didn't move, standing irresolute like someone trying to get her bearings. Then she drew her dress over her head and handed it to him, staring straight in front of her while he went over it hem by hem.

With the same deliberation he examined each garment as she passed it to him, taking particular care with her bra, girdle and shoes. As he finished with each one, he didn't hand it back to her, but threw it onto a chair.

The shoes were the last to go on the pile.

"Open your thighs."

"Roy, you're hurting!"

But he hadn't finished with her even then.

"That was vile of you," she murmured, as he stood back and she was able to straighten up.

He couldn't tell her that he'd had to be rough or he couldn't have done it. Her body always excited him. Even now.

"Can I put something on?"

He went with her to the bedroom to get her dressing gown.

She kept her eyes away from him as she slipped it on, cowed and desolate, not from what had been done to her but because it was he who had done it.

He was not up to this sort of thing, either. The sight of her belongings so roughly strewn about the living room sickened him.

"Sorry about that," he could not prevent himself from mumbling.

He felt deflated, embarrassed, his dynamic and anger all gone.

"Have you told Spinwell?" she asked at last when their silence had stretched into minutes.

He shook his head.

Her story could be true. Which meant she had been caught, just as he had been.

"Have you used this?" he asked, picking up the Minox.

"No. I told you I only got it yesterday."

"But you were going to?"

"I hoped I would get my transfer before I had to. If I didn't I was going to mess up the exposure or the focusing so the films wouldn't be any good."

"What does your friend Medaly think about your asking for a transfer?"

"He doesn't know. I was going to tell him Security had vetoed my appointment and insisted on my being put on nonsecret work."

That clinched it. Her having tried to get away from the department's secrets was a hard fact that couldn't be read two ways. It lit up everything else she had told him, making it all true.

The atmosphere between them slowly changed. He still had questions which he put desultorily, unaccusingly, just filling in the gaps. They had reached this point when they heard Monica come into the flat. A moment later she was standing in the doorway, frostily eying the litter.

"Well!"

"Just catching up on my sewing," Deirdre said, and started to collect her clothes. "I must put them away."

"Don't bother for me. I simply must eat. I'm starving. And after that I'm going to bed."

She went out and immediately they heard her clattering saucepans in the kitchen.

"You'll have to resign," he said.

"I can't do that. There's mother."

He wanted to say that, even if she existed, her mother could hardly mean anything to her as she hadn't known her in any real sense. But she looked at him so piteously, pleading for understanding, that he said nothing. Her feelings, born out of the strange circumstances of her life, were her own.

"But damn it all you can't just go on as you have been."

"If I get the job in the Ministry of Education—"

"That could take months. Besides, it's still spying—you don't seem to understand what that means!"

Or how to go about it, he thought. Nothing could be more backhanded than Medaly's mania for hopping from one café to another. That was the kind of thing calculated to raise suspicions, not avoid them. Not to mention giving the girl a subminiature camera to carry in and out of the department in her handbag.

Somehow she had to be put in the clear. And she certainly couldn't be left loose in the Service. But how could it be explained she wasn't a spy when it was patent that was exactly what she was? And who to explain it to? Certainly not Spinwell. There was King, of course . . .

"Would you be willing to help the Secret Service?"

"Of course."

"If they gave you some fake secrets, would you pass them to your Medaly?"

237

"I don't know," she said, frowning. "Suppose they found out they were fake?"

"Medaly might wring your pretty neck."

She shook her head.

"It's what they would do to my mother."

They talked for another hour without getting any further.

"You're not to come in tomorrow," he said when he got up to go. "Go sick." The important thing was to keep her away from the office. It couldn't be a permanent solution but it gave him time to think of one. He could give his whole mind to it after he had delivered the folder tomorrow.

He put his hands on her shoulders and kissed her. She clung to him.

"I'm glad you know," she said, her cheek against his lapel. "It's always been there, spoiling everything. Now it isn't any more."

"It's bad enough," he answered ungraciously, still bruised from the shocks he'd taken.

19

"Take it."

"Oh, thanks. You know what I am about fridges and Lambert's is such a tichy one and as we had the van here—"

"I told you to take whatever you wanted."

"I know but I had said I wouldn't need anything from the kitchen and—"

"Forget it. I'm glad you called, though. I was just going to ring you."

"Oh, yes."

Huskion smiled at the note of caution that had come into Penny's voice. The divorce was making it impossible for them to behave naturally to each other.

"Only to say I'd be back early tonight and how would you feel about picking up the Peter Sellers film?"

"Oh, dear, I'd forgotten it was Wednesday."

Huskion frowned. He hadn't thought she would have noticed that it was invariably Wednesday that he picked for going to the pictures.

"I'm terribly sorry, Roy, but we're going down to Bath."

"Oh, well, it doesn't matter," he said shortly.

"I'll leave something for you—oh, but the fridge will have gone—"

"Don't bother, I'll eat out."

Huskion sat back in his chair feeling put out, disgruntled. As she had always been ready to go to the cinema with him before, he had depended on it and felt let down. His earlier tolerance toward her picking whatever she liked from the home evaporated, and he thought blackly she was taking altogether too much, rooking him without compunction.

On impulse, he wrote her a sharp little note saying that, as she was taking far more of the home than she had originally indicated, it would be fairer if all of it were to be valued professionally and they then divided it according to its money value. To show that he meant not only what was left in the house but also what she had already taken, he underlined "all."

Before leaving the office he rang Deirdre. She said she was feeling much the same as she had yesterday. She had been to see her doctor who had put her on a light diet and told her to keep warm. There were a lot of unpleasant bugs going around and she seemed to have picked one up.

Leaving his car at the garage with the Tridon folder locked in the boot had become routine, causing him none of the furtive flutter he had once felt.

Before going to sleep he decided to put Deirdre into King's hands. King had got him off the hook and could do the same for her. Besides, to keep quiet, hoping to find some other way out, was too dangerous—to him as well as Deirdre.

Halfway through the morning Spinwell dropped in on him, coming in through the outer office.

"Hullo, where's your Miss Calshott?"

"Sick. She was very dicky on Tuesday so I sent her home and she didn't come in yesterday."

Spinwell nodded and sat down.

"Did you take a Tridon file out of the office last night?"

Huskion froze.

"Yes."

"Ever taken one before?"

"You know damn well I have. It's what I'm working on."

Spinwell nodded.

"How often?"

"God knows."

"Remember any of the times you did?"

"The dates, you mean? I've no record. What I take home is decided by my in-tray."

"And on Wednesdays it's Tridon?"

All Huskion's muscles snapped tight.

"What?"

"It's always Wednesdays when you take home the Tridon files, isn't it?"

Huskion's mind was racing trying to guess what Spinwell knew. Had he spotted that he always came to the office by car on the day he took a Tridon folder home? He cursed Sherngold's efficiency in ensuring he would always be able to park in Fairmile Place.

"I wouldn't know the days. I told you I don't keep a record."

"Did you work on the file last night?"

A rivulet of sweat broke from his armpit and ran down his flank.

"As a matter of fact I didn't," he said as coolly as he could manage. "By the time I got back to Wimbledon I was feeling thoroughly shagged and went to the pictures instead."

"Have you somewhere at home, then, where you can leave papers of Tridon's priority safely?"

"I left them in the boot of my car. In the garage."

"You're not serious."

Spinwell said this in his usual flat, uncolored tone but

241

there was incredulity in his sharply leveled gaze. Huskion had a momentary impulse to tell the fool to stop meddling in things he didn't understand and get the hell out of it. But that would have been mad, now he was almost out of the woods.

"The boot was locked."

"Any sneak thief has a key for a Morris boot."

"In an open garage? With people about all the time?"

This was too weak for Spinwell to bother to knock over. He just stared rather more woodenly at him.

"It comes to this," he said. "You establish a pattern of taking home papers on the department's most secret project every Wednesday and have so little care for them you leave them in the boot of your car in a public garage. Can you think of anything more dangerous?"

That was the point, of course. That he could have done anything so maniacal was totally unbelievable if Spinwell could only see it. Or did he? That was an even more chilling thought.

"It won't happen again."

"We'll have to make sure of that," Spinwell said, getting up from his chair. "But you can't expect what's happened to be shrugged off, you know. You chaps make things very difficult for us. And for yourselves."

After he'd gone Huskion was able to think more clearly. King had got to see Spinwell off. And quickly. It was ridiculous that he should be so scared. But he was. He couldn't have been more frightened if he really were a bloody traitor.

But there was worse to come. Just as he was going out for lunch Spinwell looked in again. He no longer seemed a comic idiot to Huskion. The mere sight of the man made him start.

He was holding Huskion's questionnaire in his hand.

"I forgot to ask you something when I was up here before. Your list of banking accounts has got us a bit foxed because you didn't put them down in date order."

The bastard had got onto that, too!

"Now, let's see. Oh, yes, you went from Berlin to Cyprus and there you used the Nicosia, is that right?"

"Yes."

"And you went on using it when you went to Alexandria?"

"Yes—no, I don't think so. Wasn't it a branch of Barclay's in Alexandria? I was there only a couple of months and I'm a bit hazy about it."

"Ah, that's what was throwing us. Yes, Barclay's. We hadn't thought of an English bank as you usually used a local one when abroad. So you closed your Nicosia account when you left Cyprus?"

"Yes."

"And you didn't go back to Germany again, did you? Presumably, then, you would have closed your account with the Helmstedt Bank before going to Cyprus?"

He was momentarily saved from replying by the telephone. With Deirdre away it was switched through to his desk. He was so fuddled he let it ring three or four times before clutching up the receiver.

It was Penny, all apprehensive over his letter.

"I'm rather tied up just now."

"I only wanted to say of course we agree. We didn't know you were getting all prickly and—"

"Yes, of course, my dear—" that was for Spinwell, who was impassively turning over the pages of Huskion's questionnaire and apparently not listening—"but I can't talk about it now, Penny, I've someone with me."

But Penny, having screwed herself up to call him, expecting unpleasantness, wasn't being put off.

"I'll only be a second. Lambert and I think—"

"Good. 'By for now."

He hung up.

243

"Sorry about that," he said but couldn't manage a smile to go with it.

"I'm through anyway," Spinwell said, looking up from the papers he was holding. "Just to recap. You said you closed the Nicosia and Barclay's, Alexandria. And the Helmstedt when you left Berlin?"

Huskion swallowed, trying to get some saliva into his parched mouth.

"There was hardly ever anything in it after about the third of the month. You know what my pay was then."

Even if he'd thought it would have been any use, his tongue just could not have formed the direct lie. If Spinwell was checking those accounts—

"Well, that's it," Spinwell said, making a note in the margin of the questionnaire. "Going away for Christmas?"

"I thought of trying a country pub. If I can find one that looks possible."

"If you do, don't forget to leave your address. In case we want to contact you."

He went out.

If Huskion had been frightened before, he was now terrified. This was no blundering oaf officiously throwing his weight about. Spinwell was acting like someone who knew, knew it all, and was just needing to tie up the ends.

Grabbing his hat and coat he shot out of the office, only by an extreme effort preventing himself from running down the long Fairmile House staircase.

"Now?" King queried. "Can't be done, I'm afraid. I've a lunch date."

"To hell with that. This is urgent."

The sour stench of the kiosk penetrated his consciousness even through his agitation.

"Everything all right last night?"

"No, it wasn't."

King took his time before speaking.

"All right," he said at last with evident reluctance. "Get here as soon as you can."

Huskion found Finlay Street busy. The Bestyet Fish Saloon was frying and a queue of customers ribboned out through the door to the pavement. There were even signs of life in the mole-like interior of the junk shop next door. Amusements Unlimited's windows positively blazed with Christmas novelties, rather astonished-looking fairies, tinsel chains and winking colored lights predominating. Inside there was a gaggle of buyers, Notting Hillians, not fairground types, picking over the toys and Christmas tree decorations.

Perkins excused himself from the woman he was serving and without a word took Huskion through to the back room.

"Not bad," King said after listening in silence to what Huskion had to say. The comment was not exactly approving but as near as he ever came to it.

"Glad you think so!"

"Spinwell's not such a fool. And for a plodder he's got onto the ball very smartly."

"He's got to be got off it even more smartly."

King looked down at his hands.

"I don't think that would be a good idea," he said quietly.

"But he's going to have the Special Branch on my neck any minute now!"

King nodded.

"I should think he'd have got round to that by the weekend."

"Well, then?"

Leaning forward on the table, his foxy head cocked over his right shoulder, King looked at him very straight.

"You're not going to pass over the last Tridon folder, you know. Because it would bust the whole operation open. And we wouldn't like that."

245

"I was coming to that. I'm glad you've grasped it, too."

"Nor would you like it."

"What do you mean?"

"You'd probably be fished out of the Thames with a broken neck."

Huskion felt a great wave of relief.

"You're going to grab the lot now?"

"There really isn't anything to grab," King replied, pursing his thin lips. "Semenov—Sherngold, that is—is back in Moscow and all the rest are operating with diplomatic cover. We could have them declared *persona non grata*, which would simply mean they'd be recalled and replaced by a new lot in the same line of business. That would leave us with Gamchik. And, as a spy, Harry Gamchik scarcely rates the cost of keeping him in prison for five years or so. Besides . . ."

He stopped and his eyes drooped toward the table.

"Besides what?"

"It's just possible," King again looked straight at Huskion, "that if we scooped up their men, Moscow would know we'd been fooling them all along over Tridon—particularly if one or two of them had begun to wonder about that already. But whether they did or not, it wouldn't get you out of trouble."

"Why not?"

Huskion did not like the way King kept harping on him.

"If we knocked them all off but not you they'd know it was you who had blown them. That wouldn't please them—not after having paid you rather more than twenty-five thousand pounds."

"Oh, no!" Huskion growled angrily in something near to panic. "I'm through. I don't care what you're cooking, I'm not letting Spinwell arrest me."

King nodded slowly. Unbelievably, as far as it was ever possible to read what was in his mind from his foxy poker face, he seemed to be giving judicious consideration to the suggestion.

"No," he said, "I wouldn't choose that either if I were you. I think, though, if you're to avoid it, this is the time for you to go."

"Go?"

"Defect. Ring Spolzakov and tell him you want a ticket to Moscow fast."

Totally stunned, Huskion could only gawp at him.

Once—and not so long ago—he would have kicked the table over. Or, more likely, burst out laughing. But the long defeat he had endured since meeting Sherngold had cowed him, robbed his spirit.

"You're not serious?" was all he was able to get out.

King was silent for a moment while he looked at Huskion sitting bunched up, as though his body had fallen in on itself, eyes rounded, the cigarette between his fingers unheeded.

"I'm quite serious," he said coolly.

"Then you're mad," Huskion told him through his teeth. "Why the hell should I run? I've only done what you told me to. I'm not a spy."

"Spinwell doesn't know that."

"Then you can damn well tell him."

King shifted his shoulders slightly.

"I can't do that—for lots of reasons. One is that, so far as Spinwell is concerned, I don't exist. And he's done a pretty good job. It would be bad for the morale of his department if they were to learn there had been another branch of Security on their ground unbeknown to them."

"To hell with that! What about me?"

"That's what we're talking about, isn't it?"

Huskion stood up. He'd got back his self. Some part of it anyway.

"You're crazy," he said quietly. "I don't pretend to understand this lunatic idea you've cooked up. I don't care what it is, it's not for me. I've finished with you, as of now. If you won't tell Spinwell, I shall—as I should have done right from the beginning. I'm going to tell everyone who will listen just what's been going on, the way I've been used."

He hadn't realized how much he craved to do just that until he said it.

"The stink of fear, which is all the air your kind breathe, corrupts every decency," he added. "I can't tell you how glad I'll be to be free of it."

He swung on his heel and strode out.

But immediately he was on the other side of the door he stopped short.

Perkins and another man he'd not seen before, a thickset, sandy man, with a scraped, round face and pale, unintelligent, blue eyes, blocked the corridor. Despite their barrow-boy rigs, they didn't look like yobs. They were not exactly standing to attention but, for all that, were so militarily starched they might have just left a guardroom inspection, with webbing ambitiously blancoed and side arms polished.

"The colonel hadn't finished what he had to say to you . . . sir," Perkins said politely.

They were not going to let him pass. They were like automata, mindlessly obeying an order. If the order had been to break his neck, their attitude seemed to say, they would have done it with the same disciplined indifference.

Huskion fumed for a moment and then, to save himself being manhandled, went back into the room. One of the thugs closed the door behind him.

King was still sitting in his chair behind the table. He looked very spare, even frail, with Huskion looming over him.

"You'll be more comfortable sitting down," he said.

Huskion, deciding being awkward would only delay his release, sat down.

King turned on the sympathy. He understood how Huskion must feel. It was rough to be forced into a dirty and dangerous game for which he had no training. But it was a rugged world. Countries struggling to keep their independence had to accept the rules of the game or go under, rules that gave the individual no rights that could be counted against the national need. He added a lot of embroidery about the meaningfulness of a life dedicated to the protection of one's country. If the role was being foisted on Huskion, it didn't alter its reward or significance. He was sorry it was against his will but Intelligence wanted a good man in Moscow and he was the one that had come to hand.

"If there's one thing that proves you're round the bend," Huskion broke in contemptuously, though he had resolved to keep his mouth shut, "it's imagining the Russians would want me. I'm not a scientist like Fuchs or Pontecorvo. I'm a civil servant."

"So were Burgess and Maclean. And with Burgess dead and Maclean quite out of touch after all this time, a replacement is just what they need. And, in modern terms, you're more valuable being a technological administrator while they were diplomats. You're just what they need to evaluate the Western secrets and processes they get hold of."

"And I'm supposed to fool 'em into thinking they're no good?"

King's eyebrows shot up.

"Of course not. Try that and you'd be in the Lubianka before you could brush your hair. You'll do what they ask you efficiently and to the best of your ability. You're too much of a civil servant, anyway, to do anything else. Just as knowing the files were faked made no difference to the quality of your work on Tridon. You did a damn good job there, by the way."

Huskion didn't rise to this.

"All you'll have to do is to let us know every month or so what you've been working on. Next in importance to collaring the other fellow's secrets is knowing which of yours he has penetrated. That's what you'll be able to tell us."

King went on to explain how, once he had settled down in Moscow or wherever he was based, means would be found to contact him. He would be given "dead letter boxes" where he could leave his report. He would be in touch with no one directly. That would be too dangerous.

"Fine," Huskion said. "Except I'm not playing. I'm not giving up my career, my life, to do your dirty work. I'll spill the whole thing to the Russians first."

King shook his head.

"That would be suicide. And what I'm offering you is all the career you'll have after Spinwell is through with you. You'll not be giving up as much as most either. No wife problem anyway."

So he knew his marriage had cracked up.

"And you needn't go alone," the Security man added softly.

And about Deirdre, too! Had King planted her on him—? Was Deirdre working for King too, as a double agent? It didn't seem possible that she wouldn't have told him. Except that where King was, lies and deceit were the only constants.

As though the whole thing was now settled, King again went over all he had said, adding only very precise instructions as to how he would be able to identify the contact who would give him his orders in Moscow. Huskion hardly listened. He was damned if he was going to be blackmailed in this way. There had to be a way out.

How the hell had he been such a fool as to get himself in so ghastly a mess? Damn it all, he'd done nothing.

"What made you pick me?" he asked when King seemed to have finished what he had to say.

"I didn't. Semenov—your friend Sherngold—picked you."

"Why?"

King shrugged.

"I can only guess. And you're probably as good a guesser as I am."

Huskion stood up.

"Can I go now?"

"Yes. I shan't be seeing you again. I'm sorry that it's been so rough. If I'd had a choice, I wouldn't have picked you. But you'll do. Good luck."

He held out his hand. Huskion ignored it.

There was no one in the corridor. His shoes rattling on the bare boards set up a forlorn, deserted echo.

20

"I'm afraid he's out, Mr. Huskion."

"Out?"

Huskion blinked unbelievingly down at Miss Hartopp.
Away from the bizarre atmosphere of Finlay Street, it had all
suddenly seemed so easy. All he had to do was to see His Nibs,
let him know what King was trying to do to him, and that
would be that. It hadn't occurred to him that His Nibs would
be out.

"Is it anything urgent?"

"It is rather."

"And nothing I can do?"

"Afraid not."

Miss Hartopp looked at him keenly. She enjoyed maneuver-
ing Sir Nigel for the benefit of the young men of the department she liked. Huskion was one of them.

"He was seeing the Minister at the House immediately
after lunch and then going to a meeting with the Permanent
Secretary. Some sort of bother with the Ministry of Works,

he said. I hope they're not trying to push us out of Fairmile House again. But he's sure to look in before going home."

"Thanks, I'll catch him then."

On his way back to his room he passed Spinwell in the corridor and they nodded to each other. Because of the man's normally blank face, he could not be sure if his greeting had been even more aloof than usual. But it worried him. He would have preferred it if he had spoken—even if it had been to say he knew all about the money going through the Helmstedt Bank.

During the afternoon he buzzed Miss Hartopp three times but Sir Nigel had not come back.

He also had to endure Wigstall hilariously brimming over with a typically Civil Service scandal that had almost submerged their Bristol office in carbon paper.

"The salesman chappie convinced this clot, who thought he was ordering a two-year supply, it would be fresher if deliveries were made each week, instead of in bulk. But when he signed the order he didn't notice it was for the whole lot to be delivered every week. Two years' supply every week! And ever since it's been coming in. And nobody noticed, not till it had spewed out of the stockroom and half filled the general office! Over five thousand quids' worth! Would you think the whole department uses more than a quarter of that in a year? If some M.P. picks it up, won't there be the juiciest row!"

Huskion had to pretend to be amused. But he showed his irritation when Wigstall went on repeating the story to ring every ounce of ridicule from it.

Not that it was any better when he was left alone again. Even pretending to work was impossible. He could only wait through the dragging minutes until enough of them had passed for him to buzz Miss Hartopp again.

At a quarter past five, instead of calling her again, he went along to her office. It was empty but through the open communicating door he heard His Nibs talking to her.

"Oh, Mr. Huskion, I was just going to ring you," she said when she came back into her office.

She looked guilty, seemed to be avoiding his eye as she fussed with the correspondence folder she put down on the desk, so that he wondered if His Nibs hadn't been in his office most of the afternoon.

"He's just going, so you mustn't keep him long," she told him.

His Nibs looked up as he entered.

"Ah, glad you dropped in." He took up a piece of paper and began to fold it. "This will interest you."

"I need help."

"Devised by a chap in Lima—that's in Peru, you know—I didn't until the invaluable Hartopp told me—I thought it was in Chile. Peasant with sledge. It's extremely elegant."

"I know it sounds mad, but that man King is trying to blackmail me into defecting to the Russians. To spy for him."

"No, I've gone wrong." Sir Nigel crumpled the paper into a ball, tossed it into the wastepaper basket, and took up another sheet. Instead of beginning to fold it he held it stretched between his hands, looking over it directly at Huskion. There was nothing babyish in the blue of his eyes, nothing fey, only the cold sheen of polished steel. "In origame there's no going back. Each fold is forever. Nothing can ever make the paper smooth again. Each fold is a choice which dies when we make it, leaving us with a new shape and a new choice. Just like life there, isn't it?—Something we all have to learn."

Very deliberately he began folding the paper between his wax-white fingers.

Huskion knew it was no use. King had reached Sir Nigel before him. But he had to try.

"Spinwell knows I've been taking out the Tridon folders," he said despairingly. "And about the money being paid into my Berlin bank. Or if he doesn't he soon will. If he's not stopped, I'm done for. And King won't stop him."

With a wringing motion, His Nibs twisted a corner of the paper into the bullet head of the peasant, and set the figure down on the desk.

"There. Just eleven folds. Intricate but extraordinarily elegant, don't you think?"

Huskion didn't know how to grovel. With their job security, it wasn't something civil servants were required to learn. But he did his best.

"Please help me. You're the only one who can. You're the only one who knows the folders are faked. And about King."

His voice faltered away to nothing, taking with it the last pale candle of hope. If His Nibs had been enjoying his role, or supported its purpose, an appeal might have had a chance. But beneath his suave exterior was only a gritty anger against Huskion for trying to thrust on him a responsibility that not only was not his but which he repudiated as intolerable. To be moved by, even to hear, an appeal would mean involvement in the foulness.

"You're looking very peaky, my boy," he said. "Spinwell tells me you've been staying very late most nights. Doesn't do to overdo it, you know. Why don't you take a few days off? Best thing for you, I'd say. Don't want you cracking up. How's your paper on—what was it we called it?—I remember, instant decisions? As soon as you let me have it, I'll put it up to the Minister. I told you that, didn't I? Always do what I say. I think we all should."

Miss Hartopp had come quietly into the room and was waiting to show him out.

Back in his office he sat down in a daze. He had expected His Nibs might be difficult, give him a slamming. What he had not imagined was that Sir Nigel wouldn't be revolted by what King was trying to do to him, would not take his side.

How long it was before he left the office and started walking he didn't know. He was in Oxford Street when he came to his senses, through a series of collisions with the Christmas crowd thronging the pavement for the Thursday late-night shopping hours. His car, he remembered, was parked in Fairmile Place.

He called a cab. For the same reason that he felt it necessary to collect his car—that Spinwell should not have anything to see that he might think unusual—he stopped the cab in Whitehall and walked the last block.

If someone had been tailing him he'd got lost in the thick West End traffic. Nor was he followed when he drove to Bayswater.

Monica opened the door to him. Deirdre was in her room. The doctor, having diagnosed a chill on her stomach, had advised rest and keeping warm.

"He wasn't all that wrong," she said. "Whenever I have an upset it always goes to my tummy."

She was lying on the bed, wrapped in her quilted dressing gown. Her makeup did not quite hide her pallor or the lines of strain round her eyes.

She got up and went into the kitchen to cook him a chop and some instant mashed potatoes. After he'd eaten, they went back into her room. Normally, they would have gone into the living room but neither thought of doing so, as though feeling subconsciously what was between them could only be supported in the closest privacy.

Deirdre sat on the bed and Huskion hunched himself up on the one small chair. In the dim light from the bedside lamp he thought the tiny, overfilled room had the crushing spacelessness of a cell. The way they were sitting, like prisoner and visitor, added to the impression.

Deirdre sat with her hands loosely clasped between her knees, looking straight in front of her. Since the quick perfunctory kiss he'd given her when he arrived, they'd had no physical contact, and it was clear she had interpreted his somber withdrawal as rejection.

"Well, what have you decided?" she asked in a dry whisper. "About me."

The little alarm clock he always dumped on the mat outside the door whenever he slept there because of its furious tick, jangled the silence with its aggressive beat, seeming to go faster and faster, like a heart run wild.

He couldn't tell her he'd almost forgotten her troubles, that if he'd remembered he probably wouldn't have come tonight. He had come to Bayswater blindly, because, for so many weeks, it had been a sanctuary. But she was no longer someone separate from his tribulation, with whom he could find comfort. She had become another piece of flotsam in the slipstream of the juggernaut he was trying to ride, another burden.

"Do you know a man called King?"

"No, I don't think so. What department is he in?"

"A small, foxy-faced tyke, with a yellowish skin and a clipped way of speaking?"

She shook her head.

"No. There was a King at the Board but he was very tall with a mustache, with one of the import divisions. And H.E.O., I think."

"And there was never any sign that Security knew what you were doing. They never approached you—in any way at all?"

"I've told you, no."

But she had been spotted. Given the fatheaded way Medaly performed, it was almost inevitable. Why had they left her alone? Because they hoped through her to pick up some

257

larger fry than Medaly? Because the damage she could do from the Films Division of the Board of Trade was too marginal to bother about? You needn't go alone, King had said. There was no getting away from it, she'd been planted on him. Which could only mean that King had planned to turn him into a defector right from the beginning.

That it had been done so coldbloodedly had not occurred to him for, like himself, King had seemed to move from one expedient to another. It was illogical to feel it was so much worse to have been planned.

"What were you going to do if you were found out?"

"What could I do?"

"Wouldn't your Hungarian friends have helped you?"

"How could they? Medaly said something about getting me away to Hungary, where I could be with my mother, if I found myself in danger."

That was how it could be done if they were to go to Russia, for he certainly wouldn't be able to take her with him. There'd be no time to arrange it.

It was the first time he had even thought of going to Russia as a possibility. Not that he intended to; it was just a thought.

"That could be a way out."

She looked up at him, thoroughly startled.

"You want me to . . . run away?"

"It hasn't come to that yet."

If he called the bluff, dug his heels in, and refused to be panicked, they'd have to pull Spinwell off his back. And it was a bluff. When it came to the crunch, whatever King might be capable of, it wasn't credible His Nibs could stand aside and let him go down.

"You're not going to tell Spinwell, then?"

For answer he reached over and took her hand. She rubbed her cheek against his finger.

If he spat in King's eye and beat him, King would still have

Deirdre. Though he might be badly mauled if he hit back, he could do it because he was in the clear, being framed for patriotically accepting a dirty Intelligence job. But Deirdre was genuinely guilty.

"You shouldn't have come tonight, Roy. It's too dangerous for you. Even after I get my transfer, Medaly will make me pass stuff to him. And if we married it'd be worse because he'd badger me to get things out of you." In the two days she'd been at home alone in the flat, thinking had ground away false hope. "We can't go on. I was a fool to let it start," she added miserably, "but I never thought—being found out was something too nightmarish to happen."

Like death or winning the pools.

For King, though, spying wasn't a fantasy but a business. If he, Huskion, didn't go through the hoop now the whip had cracked, King would drop on Deirdre. The terms of the trade demanded it; bad payers had to be crossed off. Like the three corpses the Italian police were "investigating." King had said nothing of this to him, hadn't needed to, because it was certain he'd get around to understanding it without it being spelled out. A good craftsman didn't go on bashing at a nail after it was home.

"Keeping away from each other would be pointless," he said. "I think Security was on to you a long time ago."

"How could they be?"

Angry as he was with King, training and habit inhibited him from telling her of the trap that had been laid for him. Even if this built-in loyalty hadn't restrained him, caution would have kept his mouth shut. How much he would ever be able to tell her depended on whether they escaped the trap—and how.

"Why do you think you got Gilly's job? You'd been turned down for every Top Security job you'd ever applied for—and you knew why—and then you were pushed into one you

259

didn't know was going. You were deliberately planted there."

He told her how Spinwell had attempted to veto her. How flummoxed he'd been when he was overruled, only able to assume that she had some high-powered protection.

"But why?" she asked, puzzled.

He shrugged.

"Who the hell can understand what Security is up to? As bait, probably. By putting you in touch with some genuine secrets, maybe they thought they would catch someone a bit larger than the idiotic Medaly."

"Oh, no!"

She began to shiver. Though she tried to hold on to herself by pressing her arms together between her thighs, the tremors ran right down through her body. He slid off his chair onto the bed beside her and put his arms round her shoulders, holding her tightly against him. But it was some time before she was still.

"I'm sorry, Roy." She was pressing herself against him now, seeking comfort. "To be used like that is so . . . so filthy, disgusting. Worse than being put in prison."

It was on his tongue to say that spying was filthy and twenty years in jail no prettier.

"Bear up," he said instead. "Everyone is used in one way or another."

"But what am I to do?"

"You could tell Medaly to go to hell."

"There's my mother."

There was more than that but he didn't tell her. If she tried to duck out, the Hungarians might leak what she'd been up to to Security—just in case they didn't know.

"Won't you stay?" she asked when he got up to go.

He shook his head.

She didn't want him to stay any more than he did. They didn't know each other well enough to sleep together without making love. Neither of them wanted the guilt of pretending an unfelt desire.

Monica had shut herself in her room and the flat had an eerie, deserted feeling as he let himself out, the only light in the little hall coming through the glass transom from the staircase. In the unnatural hush he walked on tiptoe, closing the door behind him with furtive care, as though he were making an escape.

21

He slept well, so deeply that in the morning the sheets were completely unruffled, holding only the contour of his body. It was as though his mind, like an overbeaten mule, had suddenly struck. As he'd climbed into bed, the sap had seemed to run out of his veins and he was out as soon as his head was on the pillow.

As he came awake he knew exactly what he would do, knew without thinking.

Yesterday he'd behaved like a dumb cluck because he'd been caught unprepared. Instead of losing his temper, he ought to have laughed in King's foxy face. Told him that if he let Spinwell carry on with his investigation, he'd blow the lot, make a real stink. If there was one thing the British public got steamed up about, it was bureaucrats monkeying with the liberty of the individual. Nobody had been very happy at the way Wynne had had his arm twisted in the Penkovski affair. What King was trying to do to him was a hundred times worse.

Finlay Street, under a bright December sky of the palest washed-out blue, had a frowsty, sickly appearance, as though just awakened after too little rest. What movement there was was slow and cautious, respectful of raw nerves.

An elderly man in a musty, long-dead suit and cap was setting up a trough of tattered paperbacks on the pavement outside the junk shop.

The fairy lights blinking in the window of Amusements Unlimited were reflected on the flank of a small van standing outside the door. As Huskion approached a man came out, calling over his shoulder.

"At half a bar you can't go wrong. I'll drop you in a couple of gross."

He got into the van and the self-starter began to whine, grating as painfully as a dentist's drill in a hollow tooth.

Neither Perkins nor the blue-eyed thug was in the shop. The cadaverous man was there, though, and he came forward to meet him.

"I'd like to see Mr. King."

"Who?"

"Mr. King . . . the boss."

The cadaver looked at him mournfully. As usual, he was coatless and his waistcoat unbuttoned.

"There's no Mr. King here."

"The boss," Huskion said quietly, adding, "the colonel."

The man put his thumb and forefinger in his waistcoat pockets and jingled the medallions on the heavy silver watchchain stretching across his wasted middle. His heavily hooded eyes gleamed with amusement.

"The boss is Mr. Fink—short for Finkelstein. And he's no colonel, just a lance corporal, he was. Like me."

"I want to see him."

"What about?"

"The same business as yesterday."

263

"You were here yesterday?"

"You know I was. You saw me. You've seen me here several times."

The man looked bland.

"Can't remember it, can't remember ever seeing you before."

"Look, each time I've seen your boss I've gone through that door down a passage to the room at the end. There's a coconut shy stored in his office."

The man seemed impressed.

"You'd better come through then," he said, but at the door he stopped. "You ain't selling anything, are you?" he asked suspiciously.

"No."

"That's all right then. He ain't partial to seeing salesmen first thing."

He led the way down the passage and pushed open the door at the end.

"Some cove come to see you, Sammy," he announced.

The M.O.W. filing cabinet had gone and the table had been moved in front of the window. But the coconut shy, the encrusted dirt, and the stale taint of the Bestyet's frying was still there.

Mr. Fink was sitting at the table with his back to the window.

"Herbie Condon's been in with a line of cowboy outfits," said the cadaver. "I told him we'd take a few. Sale or return."

"Cowboy-schmowboy," Mr. Fink scoffed. "It's nothing but space suits now."

The cadaver went out.

"Now what can I do for you, Mr. . . . ."

"Huskion."

Mr. Fink was a cherubic little man with pale, kindly gray eyes which held a sadness even when he smiled, which he did almost all the time.

"Well, Mr. Huskion—" The telephone on the table shrilled. "All the time it goes! A fire station you'd think we had! Sam Fink," he said into the receiver. A voice scratched at the earpiece without Huskion being able to distinguish any of the words. "Are you mad, 'Orrie? Not since I didn't know from nothing have I touched pier kiosks." The voice scratched again. "I know it's a nice place, got a bit of class—Maurice and Mamie was there a couple of years ago. But it's on the east coast, 'Orrie, the weather! And the wind! On my life you wouldn't believe the wind!" More scratching. "Oh, if it's not on the pier . . . You'll be at Sadie's tomorrow? We'll talk about it then."

He hung up.

"Today they're being born two a minute. Now, Mr. Huskion."

"I want to see Mr. King. Or perhaps you know him as Colonel King."

Again the telephone rang.

"Sam Fink . . . Oh, Jake, I heard you got a new line in bingo gear . . . Very nice . . . Lovely . . . Do me a favor, of course I'm interested, if the price is right . . . I'll be over Monday for a butchers. If it's what you say, there's a nice order for you, Jake." He dropped the receiver back on its cradle. "The only King I know has a fun arcade up by Clapham Junction. Is that who you want?"

"I want the one I spoke to in this room yesterday."

"Here? In this room? Yesterday?"

Mr. Fink's normal voice which he used to Huskion was much more refined and gentle than the one he used for business.

"Yes."

"But you've not been here before."

"Yes, I have, several times. To see Mr. King."

"Yesterday I was here all day myself. Got here at eight-thirty and didn't leave till after six. In this room. Didn't

265

even go out for lunch. The Bestyet did me a nice bit of steak and a few chips. It's not kosher, but what the hell. At home we're strictly orthodox, for the sake of the children, you understand."

Again the phone rang.

"Mr. Huskion," Mr. Fink said after he'd dealt with the call, "what is it you want with me? This is a legitimate business I have here. Started by my grandfather over fifty years ago in Middlesex Street. My brother, Morrie, still trades from the same shop. So . . . what do you want?"

"Stop playing the fool," Huskion said harshly. "I've been seeing King in this room for two months. I know what's in the coconut shy."

"In the coconut shy?"

Huskion got up and went over to the crate that held the shies. Before his hands had grasped the wooden slats, he suddenly knew what was going to happen. The crate rocked a little on its legs but no tray came off the top. He reached inside it, scrabbling the wooden balls aside. There was no false bottom. And no tape recorder.

"There was a tape recorder in it," he mumbled, lamely.

"A tape recorder?" Mr. Fink said blandly. "What was this business you had with this Mr. King?"

He couldn't say it. He knew the little bastard was lying, was part of the plot, but he couldn't say Secret Service. Not in the face of that polite, cherubic, innocent interest. It was too damn silly.

"You know damn well what it was."

Mr. Fink leaned forward excitedly.

"You know something," he said eagerly, "you could have been here. Not yesterday, not during the day like you said. But here you could have been. Dematerialized. Such things happen, you'd not credit. I know, I was a member of the Psychical Research Society. Before I was married, of course

266

—my Bessie, coming from the family she does, wouldn't have so much as a ouija board in the house. Harry Price it was then—but he's dead now. That's what you should do, go to the Psychical Society."

If he could have believed he could beat anything out of him he would have slugged him. But he was sure it would be useless. The little sod would just be sadly helpless and take all he could give. His act was too good to be cracked by a sock on the jaw. Besides, King had almost certainly thought of such a possibility and placed a pride of his thugs in earshot.

He leaned over the table and hoisted Mr. Fink out of his chair by his lapels.

"Tell King it's no go. Just tell him that."

He pitched the little Jew back into his chair and stormed out.

For him, it was quite a display of violence and he didn't like it. As he made his way to Notting Hill, all his muscles were trembling. Touching this kind of pitch left its mark, dragged you down, took away all dignity.

Somehow he had to reach King. Leaving messages was not enough.

At the tube station he found a phone booth and checked whether Amusements Unlimited was listed as a subscriber. It was—but the number was not King's. He dialed and immediately it was answered, "Sam Fink." The little man could have been sitting there waiting for him to call. King thought of everything.

King's number produced the high-pitched whine of the "number unobtainable" signal. After calling the operator and having her confirm that the line was out of service, he asked for the supervisor and demanded to know what was the matter with the line.

"There is no subscriber connected to that number," she told him after keeping him waiting several minutes.

"But that's ridiculous. I got through to it yesterday."

"I don't think you could have done, sir," she said politely. "You must have made a mistake."

"Look, I tell you— Am I likely to make a mistake about a number I've been ringing for months?"

"It couldn't have been that one, sir."

"What makes you so sure?"

"The number you are calling belongs to our reserve block. No subscriber has been connected to it for several years."

She didn't sound as though she was lying. More probably she didn't know that Security used those "reserve" numbers.

That number was the only link he had with King. And now, like his office in Finlay Street, it not only had gone but had never existed.

His Nibs must know that King at least existed somewhere apart from that telephone number and Amusements Unlimited. Somehow he had to persuade Sir Nigel that it was imperative for him to contact the Security man.

He took a taxi to Fairmile House and without waiting for the lift took the stairs to his floor two at a time.

"Oh, Huskion," Wigstall called to him as he reached the landing, "I've been looking for you. About Fellingham's. There's been—"

"Not one of my flock, laddie."

"I know. But as His Nibs isn't available—"

"Isn't he here?"

"Not till Tuesday. Having a checkup—in the London Clinic no less. Rich and colorful lives our Undersecretaries lead. Now Fellingham. You were in on it at the beginning, weren't you? So you'll remember the ding-dong over the alterations Braithwaite insisted—"

"Not now, Wigstall. Later."

Wigstall pouted huffily.

"Very well," he snapped. "I'll be in my office when you feel you can spare a minute of your extremely valuable time."

Huskion didn't even notice his annoyance.

So His Nibs had gone to ground, had he? Like King. It would, of course, be King's idea to get him out of the way in case he cracked. And Sir Nigel wouldn't have needed much persuading now that the crunch had come.

They were forcing his hand, crowding him, certain that, even if he thought of putting up a fight, knowing he would be the first casualty would stop him.

They couldn't be more wrong. If he was going down he would take King and His Nibs with him.

There was still the Minister. Though the department had a small opinion of him as a brain, he was a great one for individual liberty. In his backbench days, he'd been a persistent questioner on behalf of the National Council for Civil Liberties. Telephone tapping and similar clandestine practices of the Security forces had been his specialty. He'd love an opportunity to stamp on some cloak-and-dagger fingers.

What was more, he could show him the fake Tridon files without breaking security. More important still, he knew enough to see they were fake, proof of his story—which Spinwell couldn't do.

Without waiting to take off his coat, he walked across his office and opened the safe. He wouldn't bother about getting an appointment with the Minister, he'd go to him straight-away, camp in his office until he saw him. And if he was away somewhere, he'd go after him wherever he was.

But as he pulled open the drawer he had the same premonition he'd had as he took hold of the crate of coconut shies, and his heart missed a beat.

But they were there.

In a surge of triumph and relief, he whipped them out and dropped them on his desk. For once King had missed a trick.

He would take them all with him, of course, but it was important to show the Minister the most obvious phony first so that his interest would be caught at once. The third would probably be best, the one that dealt with the triggering mechanism.

He shuffled the folders across the desk and found it, flipping it open.

For a moment he froze. Then, thoroughly flustered, he began to scrabble among the other folders. He looked into all of them but he knew it was useless.

The genuine Tridon files had been substituted for the fakes!

Like King and his Finlay Street office, the phony files had evaporated and he had absolutely nothing to prove they had ever existed.

Game, set and match!

The door was pushed open and Spinwell came into the office.

"I thought we'd lost you."

Startled, because Spinwell had used the door from the corridor, Huskion, still in his overcoat and with the Tridon folders spilled across the desk, thought he must look as ridiculously guilty as a child caught at the jam cupboard. He could think of nothing to say.

"Either it's flu or Christmas shopping, for half the department is missing this morning," Spinwell painstakingly explained. "I thought you were another."

"You can't win all the time," Huskion said as lightly as he could. It wasn't very bright but the best he could manage.

"Wigstall was looking for you."

"I know."

"You're looking a bit off color, you know. Is everything all right?"

"With Calshott away, His Nibs in the London Clinic, and Wigstall maundering about the Fellingham cockup, I'd say they were just about perfect."

Spinwell nodded, thoughtfully rather than in sympathy.

"Mustn't let it get you down. Sir Nigel was saying he

thought you ought to rest up for a few days."

When could he have said that? Huskion wondered. His Nibs had been on the point of leaving when he'd seen him last night. And Spinwell hadn't been looking at him when he spoke but at the folders with their large TOP SECRET stamps. Did he know about the phony ones? Was he another of King's men?

"I've the weekend to dose myself—if I need to."

"Oh, well, if you think that'll be enough . . ."

"I do."

After the Security man had gone, Huskion stuffed the Tridon folders back in the safe and hung up his overcoat. Before he got back to his desk the phone was ringing.

It was Penny.

"Lambert's arranged for a man from Pilchard and Evans to do the valuing," she said a little breathlessly. "He says they're as good as anybody in the district. Is that all right?"

"Of course."

"If we met at the house on Sunday morning, we could do a final sort-out."

God, why couldn't she get into her head that he didn't care a damn about the blasted furniture? He never had and certainly didn't now.

"I don't think I can make Sunday."

"Oh." In the pause that followed he could see the martyred expression she always wore when she was thwarted as clearly as though she were sitting opposite him. "I rather wanted to finish moving the rest of the things I'm taking on Tuesday."

"You do that."

"Oh, thanks. I suppose I'll be getting the writ soon?"

"The what?" he asked, unable to follow her.

"For the divorce."

"Lawyers always take their time."

"I suppose so. I'll be at the house anyway on Sunday morning. So if you can come . . ."

He was quite calm now. His mind was so concentrated that almost before he had put down the phone he had forgotten Penny. Even while he had been speaking to her not more than a quarter of his mind had been engaged.

All that there was left for him to do was to make a decision.

He doodled a tunnel on his scratch pad, a long tunnel with a small circle of light at the far end, a gaping maw of an entrance in the foreground. There was no longer any hope of finding a side alley or an escape hatch. It didn't have any. He could go forward or back. At the far end he wrote "Shern-gold" and across the entrance he put "Spinwell."

If he chose Spinwell, he must see him now, before he learned about the money being paid into the Helmstedt Bank, and tell him the whole story. He wouldn't believe him. Nobody would. It was altogether too bizarre. There certainly was no hope of King or His Nibs coming forward to save him. That would only have been possible while the secret still held. Once it was out in the open, admitting concocting and taking part in such a scheme would be damaging to them. He wouldn't even have the satisfaction of blowing his story at his trial—whether anyone believed it or not—for Security would insist the court went *in camera* while he told it. The only question was whether he would get more or less than twenty years.

The alternative was to do what King wanted. That would mean being condemned to a lonely life in a country he didn't know, cut off from his own people, surrounded by suspicion, his value as a defector depreciating year by year as isolation blunted his usefulness. Not a future to choose if there was a choice, but better than prison. He had made himself at home in foreign cities before and could do so again. There were worse places than Moscow. And Deirdre would be there, too.

So that was it.

With just one proviso. Once in Moscow, King could go whistle. He had done with spying. He was, and always would be, a civil servant, a professional. If the British didn't want him, he'd be as loyal to the Russians as he'd tried to be to his own people.

He tore the sheet off the scratch pad, crumpled it into a ball, and was about to toss it into the wastepaper basket when he changed his mind. Smoothing it out again, he burned it in his ashtray, carefully crumbling its ashes.

With his course resolved, he began to feel a certain excitement. It was a relief to know what he was going to do, to be making decisions again. He tried to imagine what it would be like, his mind running on such trivia as what he'd be able to take with him. Just a traveling case probably. It would pay King out if he took the genuine Tridon folders! It was a nice thought but he couldn't do it. As, of course, King knew.

For Spinwell's benefit he had to act more normally than normal. So he went along to Wigstall's office. He even managed a brutal imitation of Braithwaite being officiously obstructive that made Wigstall forget his affront and laugh. And he dawdled away ten minutes beyond the hour he usually broke for lunch before going out to phone Spolzakov.

As he put his hand on the receiver it crossed his mind that he wouldn't be smelling the sour stench of the Fairmile Place phone booth again. And just for a moment it made him pause; for there were other, sweeter things he'd be missing, too. The Samarkandlike view from the bridge in St. James's Park, walking on the North Downs, the special earnest bustle of Whitehall, having a career, a future. Moscow was a long way from all that. But so was prison.

He dialed carefully.

"Kensington 4650. Yes?"

It was a woman's voice, foreign and cautious.

273

"It's about the central heating. I'm afraid it's developed a fault, a serious one."

"Thank you."

And then there was only emptiness on the line. She had hung up.

He didn't know exactly what he'd expected but certainly not to be left in the air. He dialed the number again.

This time, although he let it ring for a full two minutes, nobody answered.

22

Huskion left Fairmile House at five-thirty and turned up Whitehall among the swirling race of homeward-bound clerks and typists.

All the afternoon he had been in a lather of uncertainty. If, as it seemed, King had miscalculated and the Russians had no use for him, what then? With Spolzakov's phone being monitored, King would know all about his brush-off. He must now let him off the hook. He had carried out his instructions and could not be blamed for the Russians' refusing the bait. The cloak-and-dagger ethic that demanded a nasty death for double agents must surely, as a *quid pro quo*, insist that loyal ones be protected, even rewarded?

He hoped.

Each time his phone rang, he leaped on it expecting it to be King. As the afternoon wore away and he heard nothing from him, doubt began to nag. But not enough to destroy the euphoria his rejection by the Russians had induced.

Was this how it was going to be? he wondered as he walked

along. Was he to be left alone now, without a word, expected to go in on Monday morning and take up his work on the genuine Tridon project as though the past weeks had never happened? Surely he couldn't be shrugged off as indifferently as that? After all he'd been through, he rated a benediction, some tacit recognition if an open salute was impossible. Like an OBE in the Birthday Honors. This odd thought made him smile cynically. That would cause a stir in the department, for he was nowhere near due for the award yet!

At Trafalgar Square, just as he joined a clot of people waiting for the traffic to be stopped, he felt a hand being pushed into his pocket. He was about to yell and lash out but, swinging round, he saw Gamchik worming his way past his elbow.

The backhanded idiot with his stupid clumsiness! Feeling in his pocket, his fingers made out an envelope.

Gamchik had edged his way forward to the curb and was gazing fixedly in front of him. In his messenger's uniform, a cardboard attaché case clutched in his hand, he had the ideal protective coloring for the neighborhood. He probably thought he was being very clever in ignoring him. But, as they were old park acquaintances, it would have been natural, and much less significant to anyone watching, if he'd spoken to him. Gamchik would never get anything right.

The traffic came to a reluctant halt and Gamchik shot across the road like a sprinter out of his starting blocks. On the corner of Cockspur Street he dived down the subway, another stupidity, for if he'd wanted to take the tube he hadn't needed to cross two roads.

At the Progressive Huskion locked himself in a lavatory and took out the envelope. It was quite plain and bore no address. Inside was a single sheet of very thin paper on which was typed in capitals:

BE AT THE THIRD LAMPPOST FROM THE BUCKINGHAM PALACE

END OF THE MALL ON THE LEFT-HAND SIDE FACING ADMIRALTY
ARCH AT 7:08 P.M. TONIGHT.

There was no signature.

Presumably, 7:08 had been chosen instead of 7:05 or 7:10 to impress on him the importance of precise timing. Anything so plain and natural as seven o'clock for a rendezvous hour would, of course, be abhorrent to the devious mind of a spy.

He tore the paper into small strips and flushed them down the pan. The envelope he crumpled up and threw in the waste bin.

In the bar he ordered a pint of bitters and some sandwiches. His euphoria had died when he had seen Gamchik at his elbow. Now he felt neither fear nor excitement, only dead, empty of purpose. Like a canoeist who, having steered his craft into the channel for shooting the rapids, knows there is nothing more he can do but hope the flood won't overwhelm him, he waited, numbly watching the hands crawl round his watch.

He was alongside Queen Victoria's statue in front of Buckingham Palace as Big Ben struck seven. He had marked the third lamppost and measured the time it would take him to reach it. It was safe for him to linger by the statue, for he would be unnoticed among the loiterers hopefully waiting for their spirits to be enlivened by a sight of passing royalty.

The rendezvous had been well chosen. The wide well-lit unfrequented sidewalks gave little cover. He had no difficulty in identifying his shadower, a biggish man in a dark overcoat with a trilby hat pulled down over his eyes, whom he hadn't seen before. King's man? Or Spinwell's? Or Sherngold's?

Not Sherngold's, for his interest would be in any shadower, not in him. Spinwell would have checked that the Tridon folders were all in the safe immediately he had left and, finding them intact, would have had no interest in having him followed.

At five past seven he began to saunter up the Mall, making it as difficult as he could for his tracker by varying his pace, stopping to kick pebbles, and staring aimlessly around with the air of someone ambling away time.

But as he passed the second lamppost he began to feel nervous and his heart started to pound. He misjudged his pace and went too quickly so that he had to stop and very deliberately kick another pebble into the road. Even so, he was a good twenty seconds early when he pulled up beneath the lamppost. He covered up by scuffing his shoes and examining them carefully as though he had trodden in some dog's dirt.

The car came round the bend in front of the Palace high up on the macadam, traveling quite slowly, a Hillman family sedan, indistinguishable from a dozen others that had rolled past while he had been waiting. Huskion, expecting something more impressive with CD plates, paid no attention to it, until it suddenly darted into the side and pulled up at the curb in front of him. It had barely stopped before the door was slipped open.

He got in. Out of the corner of his eye he saw the man in the dark overcoat running frantically, trying to get close enough to read the number. He wished him luck but doubted if he made it, for the car was moving again before he had the door shut.

There was nobody else in the car but the driver, a man in his mid-thirties with flat, deeply concentrated features who gripped the wheel hard with large efficient hands.

"Who are you? Spolzakov?"

"Don't talk now."

Huskion saw why he didn't want to be disturbed. His mind was as much on what he could see behind them in his mirror as where they were going.

They didn't go up into Trafalgar Square but turned off into St. James's and then down Piccadilly.

A plate screwed to the dashboard read "Godfrey Davis Self-Drive Car Service." That wasn't really clever. Unless the number plates were changed, a hired self-drive car could be easily identified from its number and King could be there waiting when it was returned to the garage. Not that he would be, of course, even if his minion had managed to get the number. King would consider Big Hands was doing very nicely on his behalf as it was.

At Hyde Park Corner they went round the island twice before turning up into the park. They headed north but were no longer hurrying.

The driver took out a packet of Senior Service, flicked it open dexterously with his strong, competent fingers, and offered it to Huskion. Huskion took one and supplied the light for both of them.

"This emergency, what is it?"

Huskion had not been expecting the question, for he had assumed they were on their way to a meeting place. Apparently the preoccupation with whether they were being trailed had simply been force of habit since, if the interview was to be in the car, whether they were being followed or not was purely academic.

Huskion told him how Spinwell had closed in on him. They were on their second circling of the park before he finished because Big Hands, mistrusting his command of English, asked for much of it to be repeated, and wanted the whole system of Security precautions at the department explained in detail.

"So," Big Hands said at last, drawing on his cigarette— he had been chain smoking ever since they entered the park —after a long silence. "Your Spinwell knows you took home files on Wednesdays. Nothing more."

His accent had the thickness of those who have learned a

279

language when well past their childhood but the deliberateness with which he spoke was temperamental, not because of lack of fluency.

"It would be enough for your people."

"But not for yours," he said shrewdly. "It is a pattern. That is a bad thing. But it is not proof."

"But when he finds out about the Friday payments into the Helmstedt Bank it will be."

"Will he be able to find out that?"

"You know he will," Huskion said impatiently. "If your people could forge my account there—" he was about to say "our" but trapped the slip just in time—"the British Secret Service should be able to get a copy or at any rate a sight of it."

It had started to rain. Big Hands pressed a switch and the windshield wipers began to thump. In the darkness his cigarette pulsed evenly from red to white. The thick fug in the car was making Huskion's eyes sting.

"When will he hear from Berlin?"

"I don't know. Some time next week, I should think. It depends when he asked for the information. I don't think he could have done it before Wednesday and maybe not until today. You'd know more about how long it would take to get it for him than I do."

"It is not necessary for you to hide tonight, then?"

"No. I think I'm safe until Monday at least."

Big Hands nodded and went on nodding for quite a while. Then he took out a large manila envelope from inside his raincoat and tossed it into Huskion's lap.

"There is your passport. You must fill in your description and sign it. You are Hermann Fierstengl—write it down—F-I-E-R-S-T-E-N-G-L—Fierstengl. Born in Dortmund, now living at Ringstrasse 12, Düsseldorf. An electrical engineer. Yes? Very well, repeat it."

280

Huskion did so.

"When you have filled the data in your passport, tear that leaf out of your diary and destroy it. It is bad to write things down but there's no time for you to remember accurately."

"I can get rid of this altogether," Huskion said, holding up his diary. "I shan't need it any more."

Big Hands acknowledged this with a flick of his eyes.

"In the envelope there are also two hundred French francs. And a ticket for the noon flight to Paris tomorrow."

"Tomorrow!"

The other man ignored his surprise.

"You know Paris?"

"Very little."

"This?"

He handed him a business card.

> Hotel Guillemin
> Place Guillemin
> Paris 6.
> 42 chambres (6 avec bains). Restaurant. Ascenseur.

He shook his head.

"The Place Guillemin is off the Boulevard Raspail"—Big Hands pronounced the French names in the English way, "min" to rhyme with "pin" and "Raspail" with "mail"— "through a small gap between a tobacconist and a per-perrukier." He had difficulty getting his tongue round the unfamiliar word. "It is beyond where the boulevard crosses the Rue de Vaugirard."

"On the St. Placide side?"

The other man frowned sourly. Huskion guessed he knew nothing of Paris and resented it. He was just repeating instructions that had been given him.

"I don't know St. Placide," he said shortly. "It is in the

281

direction of the Boulevard du Montparnasse. You understand?"

"Yes."

"For the flight you use your own passport. At the hotel a room has been booked for Hermann Fierstengl. This is the name you will use there. Stay there until you are contacted."

"When will that be?"

The answer was a shrug.

"Escape routes have to be arranged. I have only to get you to Paris."

"I see."

"Repeat the instructions."

Huskion did so.

"Again."

He went over them five times before Big Hands was satisfied.

"You can drop me here," he said as they came up to Lancaster Gate on their next circuit, "unless you have any other idea."

The KGB man braked and pulled in to the curb.

"You are under discipline now," he said stiffly, "keep to your instructions."

Huskion pushed open the door.

"See you in Moscow."

But as he looked at the disappearing tail light of the car, Huskion rather hoped he wouldn't. If Big Hands' bleak and unimaginative temperament was a sample of those with whom he would be working in future, life in Russia was going to be anything but gay.

He strode along quickly, not feeling exactly excited but wound up and pressured, his mind racing. Stray thoughts, like what clothes he should take with him, how many shirts and pairs of socks, where he could get hold of a Russian grammar and dictionary, kept popping up to wreck the coherence of his thinking.

He was troubled about Deirdre, about how she would react when she learned he was defecting. In many ways she was still very much the St. Philippa's prefect. All that side of her would be horribly jolted. He didn't doubt she loved him but there were influences welded into the soul that could override love. As he couldn't tell her about King, he had no compelling, personal reason, like her mother's plight, to explain what he had done. Inventing an explanation for his flight that was not despicable was not easy.

Before going into the house he walked past it and came back on the other side of the road, to make sure no one was watching it. No one was.

In front of the flat door he hesitated a moment. Without an iota of evidence he had taken it for granted she would come with him and now, in something like panic, it hit him how important it was that she should. He had to make her.

He pressed the bell and heard her feet come scampering across the hall. The next second he was almost knocked down the stairs. Deirdre, blazing with excitement, flung herself on him, kissed him furiously and dragged him inside.

"Darling, I thought you were never coming! And it's all right, darling. It's all right! Mother's dead."

"What?"

"Mother died. Last Saturday."

"Oh."

He slid down onto a chair, feeling very limp. She knelt beside him, putting both arms round his shoulders.

"Darling, don't look like that. I had a cry when I heard. But she wasn't young any more and had been ill for a long time, poor dear. And . . . and . . . don't you see, I'm not responsible for her any more. I'm free."

He saw it only too well.

283

"Poor darling, you're all flaked out. Has it been a beastly day? Have you eaten? I'll make some coffee, then. You flop down, put your feet up. I'll only be a second."

She flittered out, as gay and frothy as a deb at her coming-out party.

Huskion went to the sideboard and took a bottle of whiskey from the cupboard. He gulped down a stiff tot and moved back to his chair.

The problem raised by Deirdre's news, he decided, he'd have to play by ear, though God knew how. Putting it out of his mind, he took out the passport Spolzakov, or whatever his name was, had given him.

It was a long time since he'd seen a West German passport but it looked all right. It was three years old and over that time it showed its owner had visited Spain, Argentina, Egypt, Norway and Turkey. There was no entry or exit stamp for France. That showed imagination, for more often than not French immigration officers didn't bother to stamp the passports of people on short visits. The places chosen, too, were all likely ones for an electrical equipment salesman to go. A very neat job.

His curiosity satisfied, he slid it back in its envelope and put it away in his breast pocket.

How the hell was he going to persuade her to come with him now? He was not, repeat *not,* damn well going without her. That was for certain.

But he knew that was just bravado talking. He'd go, with her or without her. Because the price of staying was too high. And didn't include Deirdre either.

"How did you hear?" he asked when she came back with the coffee tray.

"Mother had arranged for a neighbor to let me know if anything happened to her, given her an addressed envelope. So I naturally thought it was a letter from mother. You can imagine what a shock I had when I found this other one inside." She handed him his cup. "I've been wondering . . . Do you think she could have guessed?"

"What?"

"That they were using her as a hold over me and wanted to be sure I knew it was no longer there."

It was clearly what she wanted to believe. It seemed to him, though, it would be normal for any mother to arrange for her daughter to be informed of her death.

He found her excited, almost hysterical gaiety at her release hard to support. She clung to him, rattling away breathlessly about how she'd resign from the Service, give Medaly back his camera, and try to get a personal assistant's job, doing temporary work until one came up, and couldn't they go somewhere marvelous for Christmas to celebrate?

"Like where?"

"Oh, anywhere. So long as it's quiet . . . and luxurious . . . somewhere very special that we'd never think of going to normally."

He said he'd try to think of somewhere like that and she kissed him, telling him it didn't really matter as she didn't care where she was going so long as she was with him.

It was very daunting.

"Would you mind living abroad—if we had to?" he asked.

"Darling, is that what's making you so glum? Are you being posted overseas?"

"It could be."

"If it's your job, of course I won't mind. I've told you, so long as I'm with you I don't care." She pulled away from him and sat up, her young girl's eyes rounded and alight. "Roy, is it South America? That would make the day just too wonderful!"

"Why South America, for God's sake? Have you ever been there?"

"No. But it's the place I've wanted to go more than any other."

"Why?"

"I've always had a thing about it since I was at school. It was the only geography I could ever learn. There are such fascinating places like Brasília and Lima and Caracas and Mexico and Rio. Rio's so marvelously beautiful—darling, that's what we'll do for Christmas! We'll go to Rio! I can sell my Premium Bonds—the beastly things never come up anyway. Four hundred pounds would be enough, wouldn't it? It's just the kind of mad wonderful celebration—"

He wasn't listening. When she'd started cataloguing those South American cities, the "Ezeiza, Buenos Aires" stamp in Hermann Fierstengl's passport had swum into his mind. And then it had hit him.

King had made it impossible for him to stay in England but *that did not mean he had to defect to Russia.*

Treason was not an extraditable offense. Especially in South America. That was why the Israelis had to kidnap Eichmann.

In Argentina he would not only be safe from Spinwell but free of King and the whole nauseating spying mallarkey.

Dierdre was punching him in the ribs.

"Roy, why're you looking like that? What's the matter?"

He pushed her away from him.

"Shut up!"

"But—"

"Just keep quiet! I've got to think."

He got up and went over to the sideboard, where he stood with his back to her, leaning forward, letting his weight rest on his outstretched hands. Dierdre looked at his taut back with amused tolerance, puzzled by his sudden change of mood.

She refilled their coffee cups and when he turned round handed him his without a word.

"I'm leaving England tomorrow . . . forever," he said quietly.

He told her everything. Even about King and the phony Tridon files, of his plan to turn him into a double agent, for now they weren't going to Russia, there was no danger in her knowing.

Her reactions mirrored his own. Interest, even amusement at Sherngold's blunt approach, sympathy for his predicament, rebellious anger at the ruthless way King had used him and, finally, incredulity, at once furious and fearful, that what she could neither have imagined nor believed could be true.

One thing he didn't tell her was why she'd been planted in the department as his secretary. That King had been his pimp was altogether too raw. That they were lovers as part of King's plan was something he didn't want to believe himself.

"I want you to come with me," he ended. "Will you?"

She didn't answer but came across the room to where he was standing and kissed him on the lips. He clung to her.

Suddenly it was all quite different. In place of the sullen resolve to gyp King of his press gang victory, there was excitement at the prospect of starting a new life.

With feverish elation they began to plan.

"There's not much time if I'm to be ready by tomorrow," Deirdre said.

But as soon as she said it, he saw she couldn't come with him to Paris in the morning. He had to elude both King and the KGB and that would be doubly difficult if she were with him. Besides, he hadn't even worked out how he was going to get to South America. And at that hour of the night.

He began to scrabble through the S-Z telephone directory.

287

Finding the *Daily Telegraph* number, he dialed it.

"Ask for information," he said, handing the receiver to Deirdre. "I don't suppose there's anyone there but I can't think of anything else to try."

But for once his luck held.

"They're putting me through," she said. "What do you want to know?"

"When Charlemagne lived. Ssh!" he added, when she looked at him as if he'd gone mad and opened her mouth to speak. "I'll be in the telephone booth at the corner. Come down when they've answered."

He shot out and went leaping down the stairs. It was just possible King had the phone in the flat tapped. He was probably being overcautious but it would be damn silly to be caught through being too lazy to avoid risks.

He was holding on, waiting for the cheerful young man who had answered him from the *Daily Telegraph*'s Information Room to find out if there was a plane out of Paris for anywhere in South America the following evening, when Deirdre joined him. She squeezed into the kiosk beside him as it had begun to rain again. She didn't ask any questions, so he guessed she had worked out for herself why he hadn't used the phone in the flat.

He didn't say anything but pecked the tip of her nose with his lips. Behind her head, the sodium vapor street lamps made the raindrops on the square panes of the booth as iridescent as pearls.

"There's a plane that leaves Orly at 20:35 on Saturdays," said the young man. "That any good to you?"

"Just about perfect. Where's it go?"

It arrived at Rio de Janeiro at 10:20 the following morning. Yes, it was possible to book a seat even at this time of night. The airlines maintained a twenty-four-hour booking service. And there was a flight out of Gatwick for Buenos Aires on Thursdays that seemed tailor-made for Deirdre.

He dropped the receiver onto its cradle and hugged her tightly as he told her. With so much coming good the world lost some of its menace.

For once Heathrow's telephone exchange worked efficiently and put him through to the right department first time.

Whether there was a reservation available on the Rio plane had to be checked with Paris. If the tourist seats were full, would he accept a first-class booking? He said he would and was told to ring back at midnight when they should have the answer on the Telex.

They went back to the flat and their planning but in less of a euphoric mood than before.

First, they had to settle what it would be best for Deirdre to do until she caught the plane on Thursday. The more they thought about it the clearer it became she couldn't stay on at the flat. If there should be a hue and cry after him, she would certainly be roped in by Spinwell for questioning. He couldn't make up his mind whether Spinwell was working hand in hand with King or whether King was using him like a clever dog to harry the game.

Finally, they decided she would disappear on Monday. She could cook up some story for Monica about going into the country for a few days to convalesce and then find somewhere within easy reach of Gatwick to stay.

There were other niggling details that had to be worked out. She would have to clear her banking account and cash her Premium Bonds and buy her plane ticket before she left. And post her letter of resignation to the office. Though she thought the money she had would be sufficient he gave her a blank check in case it wasn't. It was necessary for them to take with them all the currency they were allowed and he didn't want her to have to cut into her allowance of traveler's checks to pay for her ticket. Once in Argentina, money would be no problem. He saw now why King had insisted on his keeping the numbered Zurich account in his name. It was compensation for his wrecked career. And that was exactly how he was going to treat it.

Then they had to decide where they were to meet in a strange town neither of them knew. That necessitated another trek to the phone booth to get a list of hotels from the A.A.

"I'd never have believed it possible to lay so much on at this hour on a Friday night," he said. "What do you say to the Crillon?"

"It sounds horridly expensive."

"They'll all be, I only asked for first-class ones. And what the hell, a little luxury on the Avenida Santa Fe will be just what we'll be wanting by next Friday."

"Is the Avenida Santa Fe very posh?"

"You're the South American expert. I haven't a clue."

"It's got a nice exciting sound anyway."

"That's why I picked the Crillon."

While they waited for midnight he made her repeat over and over again exactly what she had to do and in what order. He thought he sounded like Spolzakov but it didn't bother him. He hadn't had King on his neck these last months for nothing.

There was only first-class accommodation on the Rio plane. The fare, two hundred and sixty pounds-odd, rocked him a little. It looked as though Deirdre would need his check if she had to go first class, too. He could pick up the ticket at either London Airport or Orly. He didn't like that at all. If there were KGB men around keeping an eye on him, collecting plane tickets would strike them as decidedly odd. And Orly was out, anyway, as he wouldn't have enough francs for it. Wasn't there anywhere else where he could pay for the ticket? With some reluctance, it was admitted he could collect it from any accredited travel agent. He wrote down

the details of the flight number and the seat they were holding for him and then rang off.

Deirde had come down to the kiosk with him and he walked
her back to the flat with his arm round her waist. He didn't
go in but said good-by at the foot of the steps that led up
to the front door of the house. Their leavetaking was brief.

"See you Friday, Calshott."

"Be careful, won't you?" she whispered as his lips closed
on hers.

He held her until he felt her tremble slightly and then
separated himself from her.

"Look after yourself."

She nodded and ran up the steps. At the door she turned
and made a small gesture. He answered with a brave and
confident sweep of his hand. And then she was inside with
the door closed behind her.

In Bayswater Road he picked up a cab, telling the driver
to set him down at Wimbledon Station. From there he went
to his garage. As he drove the Morris out he wondered if
the Russian's contact in the garage would report his having
collected his car and if he did what Spolzakov would think
of it.

In Bridle Walk he parked the car and went into the
house without bothering to look about for King's man. He
would be there all right, he had to be. And he ought to be
pretty uncomfortable by now for the rain, a deep, penetrat-
ing rain, had settled in in earnest. He hoped Perkins had
drawn the job. That would be a nice bonus to the night.

He was tired but he still had a lot to do. In his room he
sat at his desk and set down exactly what he was planning
to do next day, numbering each in order like King. Then
he made a list of what he intended to take with him, ruthlessly
jettisoning everything that was not of essential and immedi-
ate practical value. In his small suitcase he would put a

291

summer suit and as many shirts, socks, underclothes and handkerchiefs as he could stuff into it. His briefcase would take his night things.

He wrote a note to His Nibs saying he'd decided to take his advice and go off for a few days' walking in the West Country. That, he decided, would keep Spinwell quiet—at least until his inquiry about the Helmstedt account was answered. He also wrote to Zurich telling them they would be receiving instructions to transfer funds to Buenos Aires and enclosing a check to clear his Helmstedt account of the payment that would have been made for the folder he had delivered on Wednesday.

He checked his bank account. Although his current account had the best part of his month's salary in it, it would not be enough for his needs. But he'd have no difficulty in getting an overdraft against the £500 he always kept on deposit. It was a nuisance that he'd not be able to take it all with him but it couldn't be helped.

And then he nearly made a dreadful bloomer.

With his own passport in front of him, he opened up the Fierstengl one. After practicing a dozen signatures for his new name, he was about to copy in his identifying particulars when, with his pen almost touching the paper, he stopped. Of course, they had to be in German and his height in centimeters! That was something that meticulous fool Spolzakov hadn't mentioned, the key detail that could have wrecked everything! He sweated with the thought of how near he'd been to making a complete box-up.

Nor was it the only slip he uncovered. He suddenly realized that, though they'd arranged to meet at the Crillon, they hadn't agreed which of them should make the reservation there and in what name. He drafted a cable booking a double room with bath in the name of Fierstengl. That meant he had to write to Deirdre telling her what he'd done.

He didn't like doing that but it was safer than phoning her.

When he had finished he burned all the papers he'd used and carried the ashes through the dark house to the kitchen where he flushed them down the waste disposal unit.

Then he went upstairs and packed. By the time it was all done it was about four o'clock.

He decided to shave and bathe then as, after a little more than a couple of hours' sleep, it would be a tiresome chore when the alarm woke him with an inevitable thick head.

The bathroom was in the front of the house and even with the curtains drawn he was not sure a light in it could not be seen from outside. So, as he didn't want any watcher to know he was still about and busy, he had to make do with such light as was reflected through the bathroom door from the landing.

God, he thought as he stretched out his tired limbs in the warm water, how glad I'll be to be rid of all this bloody foolery.

Staring up at the murkily lit ceiling, he felt so weak, so worn out, he could have wept.

23

King had laid on a car, a black Wolsely. It was too dark for him to see the man in it but he was sure he was there. Parked thirty yards down on the other side of the road, it was waiting for him to leave.

He came from the window, and went into his bedroom to collect his bags, looking carefully round for anything he had forgotten. He retrieved his brush and comb and stuffed them into his briefcase. There were bound to be things he'd only remember when he needed them.

Penny would be puzzled by the Morris standing outside when she came on Sunday, but he could think of no note of explanation he could leave her that would make sense.

As he came downstairs the *Times* came through the letter box and thumped onto the mat. He picked it up and took it into the kitchen.

He could have allowed himself another half hour's sleep. In his anxiety not to miss the dark, he had imagined that it began to get light around seven o'clock. Today, with the sky curdled with thick clouds, the night would still be lingering at eight, possibly even later.

He sat down to wait. The longer he could delay starting the less time he would have to fill until the shops opened.

When he saw the clouds through the window beginning to turn an oily gray he picked up his bags and went out through the back door.

Not being able to lock it behind him was awkward because finding it open would be another thing Penny would think strange. He hoped she wouldn't start making a fuss at the office or going to the police.

He went across the garden to the service alley. The one weak point in his plan was that King knew he could leave the house this way. Everything depended on the watch being concentrated on his car.

There was no one in the passage and, when he came to the exit in Bridle Walk, he saw the car was too far away for anyone in it to recognize him or even to be certain he had not come out of one of the adjoining houses. But they probably weren't even looking.

All the same, as soon as he was round the corner, he waited, hunched up in the first shop doorway, as on the night he met Kay Dillon, to see if the car would appear. It didn't. Nobody did, except a man, whom he knew by sight as living somewhere on the other side of Bridle Walk, hurrying toward the station.

He found a workman's café that was just opening and had a plate of greasy bacon and eggs. When he asked for some marmalade for his toast and the sullen woman behind the tea urn told him surlily she had only jam, this breaching of his normal habits fretted him disproportionately. He supposed it would be little things like this that would make exile hardest to bear. But, presumably, there would be marmalade in the Argentine. If there weren't, there was always Harrods and the Army and Navy Stores.

He was waiting in the doorway of the Equator Travel Agency when a slip of a wench, with three-quarters of her

295

mind still on her pillow, opened up the Agency. But he had to wait another ten minutes for a youth, older than the wench in experience though apparently not in years, who could attend to him. Even so, there was an interminable amount of phoning and hanging on before his booking was confirmed and taken up.

By then the bank was open and, leaving his bags in the agency, he went along to draw out his money while the youth filled in the tickets. That took time, too, for the overdraft required that he see the manager. While he was waiting he made the sudden decision to draw out all the money he could and spend what he couldn't take out of the country on realizable valuables at London Airport.

Even then there were his traveler's checks to prepare. He left them to get on with that while he went back to the Equator to collect his ticket. Back again at the bank, there were still the traveler's checks to be completed and he fumed with impatience as he scrawled his name on them.

Even after discarding all the unnecessary folders and bits of paper he had been provided with, his breast pocket was uncomfortably loaded. James Bond, he thought with inward amusement, would certainly have taken him for a left-handed gunman using a shoulder holster.

He sent off the cablegram to the Crillon and then, on impulse, seeing one of the phone boxes momentarily unoccupied, dialed Lambert's number. He was still faintly worried about Penny. He would feel much safer if she believed he was going on a walking tour and had been warned about the car and the back door. But apparently she was already out, for there was no reply.

He was on his way to the station when he remembered he hadn't posted the letters he had written. That meant he had to go back to the post office again to join a queue for stamps.

By the time he finally got to the station it was after half

past ten. Too late to make the Cromwell Road Air Terminal and the airport bus.

"How much to London Airport?"

The taxi man looked at him squarely before replying.

"Three pounds ten."

"That be damned. Three pounds?"

"All right," the taxi man said mildly. "Get in."

Knocking the man down gave Huskion a kick and he leaned back in the cab smiling to himself. He had been too sleepy while in the café having his breakfast to feel any excitement at having eluded King but now he gloated. For the first time he'd managed to beat the devious bastard and he couldn't have put a price on how good it felt.

At the airport, after handing over his suitcase, he made a round of the shops, buying himself an Omega watch, a lighter and a gold Parker pen set and, for Deirdre, an enamel and gold compact. And, because he found the extravagance exhilarating, added some Pinaud after-shave lotion though he never used any kind of cosmetics normally.

He only just had time to complete his purchases before his flight was called. He had made no attempt to conceal himself. If there was anyone keeping tabs on him, it couldn't be one of King's men. And if it were the KGB, they knew what his flight was and had only to note when he joined it. But as far as he could see there was no one.

What was of no importance at Heathrow would matter at Orly, though. He had a half-formed plan of not going to Paris, but to somewhere nearer, like Sèvres, and waiting there, returning to Orly just in time for his flight to Rio. But that depended on there not being anyone on the lookout for him when he landed.

There was.

He was standing behind, and seemingly aloof from, the knot of people waiting beyond Customs. Unlike the others, who were pressing forward, craning their necks, straining to catch a glimpse of friends or relatives before they reached the barrier, he was standing quite still, intently watching each passenger coming into the lobby, a slight man, with narrow features and thin lips in a bloodless face, wearing a raincoat and a low-crowned felt hat with the brim turned down.

Huskion wasn't sure why he should be so certain of him. It could have been the way he stood with his hands thrust into his pockets or the immobile carriage of his head while his eyes constantly moved. Or his hat. He rather thought it was the hat. Whatever it was, he would have picked him out of a lineup of all the men in the concourse.

Still, he had to check.

He went down to the washroom. When he came out Felt Hat was there fiddling with a weighing machine. Instead of collecting his suitcase from the luggage bay, he went back to the lobby and began to leaf through magazines on the newsstand. Felt Hat followed, seeming to have found an urgent interest in the Arrivals and Departures board.

Huskion was puzzled. The KGB man was not being clumsy but was obviously indifferent whether he spotted him or not. Half-expecting him to come up and speak to him, Huskion lingered by the newsstand. But the man ignored him.

He fetched his suitcase and found a taxi. As he was tipping his porter, Felt Hat came through the beam-operated glass swing doors and got into a black, shark-nosed Citroën that was waiting for him. When the taxi turned onto N.7, the Citroën was behind, with two cars between them. And though dozens of other cars passed them, there it remained.

They were halfway to Paris before he realized why Felt Hat hadn't cared whether he saw him or not. He wasn't there to watch him but to protect him, a bodyguard to take care of any trailing British agents. He was the KGB's property now and they were taking care of their investment.

For the first time since escaping from Bridle Walk he felt thoroughly frightened.

He had relied on Spolzakov's shrugging "Sunday or Monday perhaps" in reply to his question about when he was likely to be contacted. If the KGB's car was too close, his problems were not doubled but multiplied a hundred times.

But to his relief at Porte d'Italie, where his cab swung across Boulevard Kellermann, the Citroën drove straight up on the Avenue d'Italie. Apparently Felt Hat and his mates had decided, with no one on his tail, he had no need of their assistance.

Entering Boulevard Raspail from the Boulevard Saint-Jacques, the cab slowed and, after crossing Boulevard du Montparnasse, they were going at no more than a crawl, while the driver peered uncertainly about him. Presently he pulled up in front of a shabby café-tabac. The driver turned to Huskion and let out a torrent of explanation, emphasized with much ill-tempered gesturing, which he eventually understood to mean there was no room to take the cab into the Place Guillemin and this was as far as he was going.

Huskion paid him and carried his suitcase through the archway beside the café, which was wide enough for a ten-ton lorry, let alone a cab. But once inside he saw what the cabby meant.

Place Guillemin belonged to the days before Baron Haussmann laced the city with straight boulevards designed to give artillery a clear line of fire at any barricades the rebellious citizenry might throw up. Wedge-shaped, like a chunk of cheese, the place was entirely enclosed by buildings. Behind iron railings, which somehow had eluded the scrap-metal collections of two wars, a litter-strewn patch of mud supported a gaunt, leafless tree and a rotting wooden seat. There was just enough room outside the railings for a cobbled way, the width of a car. It ended abruptly at the apex of the place in front of the hotel entrance, a surprisingly modern entrance, with a revolving door beneath a circular canopy.

He pushed his way through it into quite a sizable lobby with a reception desk and, beyond it, a lift. In the far wall there was another revolving door that apparently led out into another street and was rather more impressive than the one to the Place Guillemin.

"You have a room for me, Hermann Fierstengl?"

The young man at the reception desk nodded and made a tick in the ledger in front of him.

"You can let me have this later," he said, handing him the regulation police registration form.

An elderly man in a green baize apron with a pronounced stoop and a highly polished pate came out of the lift and picked up his suitcase.

"One-o-three," the clerk told him.

The old man lurched to the lift and waited for Huskion to enter it.

The lift climbed wheezily to the first floor. From the landing, corridors ran off in the shape of a Y, two long arms that he guessed ran along each side of the place and a short shaft pointing toward the front of the hotel.

It was along this last section that the porter led him. He opened a door on the right-hand side without using a key and stood back for Huskion to pass him.

A man was sitting on the bed, lolling back with a glass in his hand, a man in an expensive Italian-cut suit with a silk handkerchief spewing out of the breast pocket in a way that was no longer fashionable.

"Hi!" said Spiller Martin. "Nice to have you with us."

He dug a handful of loose change out of his pocket and flipped a franc to the porter, who stowed it away and then left.

"Surprised, eh?"

Huskion walked across the room and put his briefcase down on the dressing table.

"Our friends asked me to come along, thought you would like to have an old buddy to welcome you aboard."

With his back to Martin he slowly took his overcoat off and hung it in the wardrobe.

He was shocked and scared but that wasn't what was making the muscle below his jaw tighten and pulse. That was blind fury. He knew now, as King had known all along, why Sherngold had come to him, who had pointed him out as a likely victim.

Spiller Martin.

"I'm to hold your hand as far as Prague."

"When do we leave?"

"Tonight, on the quarter to nine plane for Zurich."

Only by a quarter to nine tonight he ought to have been in the air ten minutes already, flying west instead of east.

"So you've bags of time to freshen up and relax before we leave."

If they were to be cooped up in the room together until they left, that put the kibosh on his being able to make a move until they reached the airport. Playing hide-and-seek around the "Gents" at Orly, in the hope of being able to sneak onto his Rio plane unseen, was not exactly a bright prospect. Spiller had to be shaken off before it came to that.

"Semenov is waiting for you in Prague. He'll take you on to Moscow. He told me to say that he's looking forward to meeting you again."

Huskion nodded, and then remembered he ought not to know who Semenov was.

"Semenov?"

Martin grinned.

"You knew him as Sherngold."

301

Martin knew it all. Maybe he hadn't just pointed a finger at him but dreamed up the whole plan when the Russians became interested in Tridon. The muscle in his throat began to throb again.

"He's a colonel in the KGB. And that's a lot better than it sounds, for Intelligence doesn't go in for high ranks. In fact, he's a genuine big shot, one of the biggest. And a hell of a good chap."

Huskion thought he sounded exactly like King talking.

Martin shifted himself into a more comfortable position on the bed. He was carelessly relaxed, a successful professional, pleasantly savoring a job well done. Huskion noted that his once-sharp features had coarsened and he was thicker round the middle. But his birdlike eyes hadn't changed. They were as alert and as shrewd as ever. If it were to come to a sprint or a roughhouse, Huskion would not have backed himself to come out best.

"You're looking a bit slugged. How are you feeling?"

"Tired."

Martin nodded sympathetically.

"It's a hell of a shock, having to uproot yourself suddenly. But you'll find it'll work out all right. The Russkies are a great crowd to work for. They're bloody generous, too. So long as you deliver the goods, you won't find them fussing over your expenses the way the old Treasury does. Remember the rows I used to have with them?"

He grinned reminiscently, and then went on:

"Mind you, I don't say you won't find it a bit lonely and strange at first, not being able to speak the language. But Moscow's a marvelous city. You'll love it. And you'll be privileged, able to get tickets for the Ballet and the theatre whenever you want to, the best theatre in the world. And the opera! Until you've seen *Boris Godunov* at the Bolshoi you've seen nothing. *Aïda* at La Scala is a shambles com-

302

pared to it. Having to learn Russian may be a help, too, give you something to do while you're settling in."

"That reminds me, I ought to get myself an English-Russian dictionary and a grammar. Where'd be the best place for me to pick them up here? Hachette's?" Huskion asked, without much hope that it was a good enough excuse to get them out of the hotel.

"Don't bother, everything's being fixed for you. You've the key of the castle and anything you like to ask for whether it's a dictionary or—" Martin's grin didn't quite mask the appraisal in his eyes—"your wife. Just supposing you might want her, that is."

"She knows nothing about this."

"Nothing at all?"

Huskion shook his head. Walking over to the bedside table, he lifted the glass from the throat of the water carafe. Head turned across his shoulder, Martin watched him with amused contempt.

"That stuff will give your guts damp rot. Shove the bell and get something that'll put some life into you."

Huskion smiled weakly but took no notice. He had half filled the glass when he suddenly stiffened.

"What the hell's that?" he said sharply, looking at the floor just in front of Spiller's feet.

The oldest gag in the world, Cain probably used it on Abel. But it worked. Martin jerked forward.

"What—?"

Huskion swung the carafe in a wide arc. It wasn't very well aimed and would have caught Spiller a glancing blow on the side of the head if he hadn't suddenly sensed his danger and ducked away. That made it just about perfect. The sharp edge of the heavy base of the carafe bit deep into his neck just where it met his collar.

A water carafe is a clumsy weapon but, given the right

angle, is more lethal than a cosh or the butt of a gun. Spiller Martin pitched forward on his face without uttering a sound.

Huskion, heedless of the water slopping from his glass onto the carpet, watched as he twitched with weird involuntary movements. When the twitching ceased he moved cautiously forward to see how badly the man was hurt. As he bent down, there was a sound from where Spiller's face was pressed against the carpet that made him start backwards, a sound like the draining away of the last inch of bath water.

But Spiller didn't move. It was his lungs emptying themselves of air. Without having to touch the body, Huskion knew he was dead. He set the carafe and the glass back on the bedside table and sank onto the bed. He was trembling a little and his legs felt weak. But his brain was clear.

After a couple of minutes he got up and turned Spiller over. His head rolled free like a marionette's that had lost its strings.

He began to search the body, looking for a gun. His accidental straying into violence had left him feeling naked, unprotected and craving a weapon.

Spiller hadn't carried one. But in his fob he found a folded wad of hundred-dollar bills. His wallet was fat with 'French, Swiss and both German currencies. He guessed the dollars were Spiller's reserve for emergencies and the other money trip expenses.

He left the East German marks in the wallet and pocketed the rest.

Beside the wardrobe there was a second door. Opening it he discovered it led to a private bathroom.

He dragged the body into it. Getting the corpse into the bath was difficult, for though Spiller was smaller than he, he was heavier. In the end he managed it but not without a certain amount of noise as his shoes scraped the sides of the bath. He maneuvered the body into a sitting position, with the head between the taps, then drew the shower curtain so that it was out of sight from the door. With any luck, Spiller would lie there undiscovered until the morning.

He went back into the bedroom. Looking at his watch he was surprised to see it was twenty to five. He had forgotten the hour he had put it forward at Orly and was still thinking of London time. His bag would have to stay on the slatted trunk stand where the porter had left it. He couldn't walk out of the hotel carrying it. The risk of the reception clerk seeing him and becoming suspicious was too great.

The suitcase, a light inexpensive one he had bought for business trips, had no identifying marks except the maker's name. As they were always washed at home, his shirts and underclothes were free of laundry tags. But the jacket of his suit had his name and address on the tailor's label. After attempting unsuccessfully to squash it into his briefcase, he cut the label out and put it in his pocket, then refolded the jacket and returned it to the suitcase.

He picked up Spiller's overcoat from the bed. His passport was in the inside pocket. After a moment's hesitation, he decided to leave it there. To take it would be pointless as Spiller probably had a dozen things on him proclaiming his identity. He simply hadn't the stomach to go back into the bathroom and paw the body over looking for them.

With his briefcase under his arm, he checked the room from the door. He went back and opened the suitcase, so that its lid lay against the foot of the bed. That made it look as though the occupant of the room expected to be returning soon.

He went out into the corridor, locked the door behind him and slipped the key in his pocket. There was no one about.

Just inside the door of the hotel, he had seen a staircase. But that came out into the lobby beside the reception desk.

305

He hoped there was another on the other side of the lift.

There was. He guessed that at one time the hotel's only entrance had been from the Place Guillemin, and what was now its front had been a separate house added to it later.

He went down the stairs. When he reached the foot he heard someone at the reception desk talking on the telephone, but the lift shaft shielded him from sight. In the lobby a man reading a paper and two women looking idly about them sat at a table, evidently waiting for someone to arrive and complete their party. No hotel servants were hanging around to see him pass through the revolving door.

It was a narrow cul-de-sac he found himself in, blocked off to his left by what looked like the back of a warehouse. It led into another equally narrow street along which he turned left and then right at the first intersection. He tried to keep track of his direction by relating it to the only point he knew, the Boulevard Raspail, which was somewhere behind him.

Presently another turn brought him out into a larger street with the iron railings of a public park running down one side of it. Peering through the bars at the graveled waste disappearing in the dusk beyond a fringe of trees, he guessed it was the Luxembourg Garden. He skirted the railings until he came to the Rue de Vaugirard. There he found a taxi, telling the driver to take him to the Champs-Elysées.

As they wormed their way through the first hesitant wave of rush-hour traffic on the quais, he looked out onto the stone parapet of the Seine sliding by, not thinking of what had happened. From the moment he had seen Spiller sitting on the bed his actions had not been planned, thought out, but reflex. The spring that had been released then had not yet fully unwound and he leaned forward in his seat tensely, urgent to be moving again.

They crossed the river between the arrogantly flaunting

eagles of the Pont des Invalides. Huskion waited until they were a little beyond the Rond Pont and then stopped the cab and got out. The Champs-Elysées was thick with people. The first person he saw was a little old woman dressed entirely in black, the skin over the spiky bones of her face webbed with fine lines like cracked enamel, feeding pigeons from a paper bag. Paris, too, had its Gamchiks.

He walked up the slope toward the Etoile until he came to a men's shop. He had to replace the things he had left at the hotel. People didn't fly across half the world with nothing but a briefcase.

Inside, the shop was bright with neon and quiet, a separate world from the anonymous noise of the street. A group of Americans, three youths and a girl, were choosing Christmas presents with much self-conscious guffawing.

". . . You don't think it's awful pansy?" the girl was saying.

"That's my old man, baby, hip, hep and hop!"

"Pop!" yelled one of the other youths throwing his arms in the air. They all laughed.

Their voices jarred on Huskion. Though there was nothing sinister about them, he felt himself begin to tremble. Unfamiliar surroundings and a foreign tongue in his ears had made it easy to imagine he was acting naturally in a dimension divorced from his own. Hearing English spoken made him feel exposed, naked, as though he had waked from a nightmare to find it was reality.

"But it's silk, Ginnie. He'll sure go for that. Genuine silk from old Europe."

"For Chrissake, El, pick something and let us get out of here."

"M'sieur?"

It was the assistant. Huskion realized he had been standing on the other side of the counter for some time waiting for him to speak.

307

It was quite an effort to think of his neck size and translate it into centimeters.

Not till the Americans finally made up their minds and left the shop was he able to focus his mind. He bought half a dozen nylon shirts, socks, underwear and a dressing gown.

The sallow-faced assistant, oddly formal in his black single-breasted suit with all the buttons done up, without becoming exactly eager, lost some of his indifference as the purchases mounted.

His long legs were an insurmountable obstacle to finding a suit that would fit him. But the assistant produced a pair of slacks that would do, though rather baggy in the seat, and a striped sports jacket, in two shades of green, to go with them, that he would never have dreamed of buying in England.

He used his traveler's checks to pay for them. His purchases made up into a formidable parcel. From another shop he bought a fiber glass suitcase into which he stuffed the parcel without undoing it. Shoes and slippers, he decided, could be left until he got to Rio.

At a travel agency that had a *bureau de change*, he cashed what remained of his traveler's checks into francs. It had occurred to him quite suddenly that, if he didn't get rid of them, they would be useless, as to cash them in Rio would give away his being in South America.

It was now getting on for seven, still too early for him to go to Orly, for the airport was, of all Paris, the place where he was likeliest to run into someone who knew him.

A bitter, knifing wind blowing from the Tuileries Gardens up the rise to the Arc de Triomphe made him shiver. He had not realized Paris could be so cold in early winter. And he was hungry.

He found a café and drank a cognac. It was unpleasantly sweet and sticky but took the chill out of his belly while he waited for the omelet, which was all there was available at this between-meal hour.

Suddenly he felt all in, exhausted. That he had killed Spiller Martin did not disturb him. With his first meeting with King in Notting Hill Gate he had stepped into a world where to kill was natural. That, given time, the moment would come when he would have to had been as inevitable and inescapable as that water would rise in the bath when the taps were turned on. That it should have been Spiller he'd killed was neither here nor there. The momentary satisfaction he'd felt as he'd swung the carafe at his head was all gone. Beyond a craving to put his head down and sleep he felt nothing, nothing at all.

Two cups of black coffee before he left the café sharpened him enough to be sure there was no one on the lookout for him at Orly. When his flight was called he was the first one through the door to Customs. And he was first up the steps into the plane.

There were only five passengers in the first-class compartment. Three were obviously a family party, mother, father and a teen-age daughter, who had a certain sultry attractiveness and might have been the younger sister of the heavy-featured stewardess who had shown him to his seat.

Across the aisle from him was a plump, nattily dressed Latin type, heavily pomaded and overwhelmingly scented. He fussed about the disposal of his hand luggage, and, as soon as he was in his seat, took out folders of papers from his briefcase. Before they had begun to taxi down the runway, he'd called a steward and ordered a large brandy and asked the stewardess to find some ink for his fountain pen.

He had shaken off the dogs—all of them.

After the Comet had leveled out from its steep climb, he unfastened his safety belt and told the stewardess he didn't want to be disturbed. Ten minutes after tipping his seat back, he was in a deep sleep.

When he woke it was to a heavy hush broken by a rhythmic snoring. The plane had touched down. He had a feeling it had done so once or twice before during the night. The snoring came from the girl. Of the others only the father was awake, staring dull-eyed at nothing, resigned to sleeplessness.

His watch said it was just after nine and for a moment he thought they must have arrived at Rio ahead of schedule and was puzzled by the dark outside. And then he realized they had been speeding ahead of the sun all night.

He stood up. The night had staled the scent on the man across the aisle and the brandy fumes coming from his open mouth did not sweeten it. The tourist compartment was half empty.

A stewardess told him the missing passengers were over in the airport buildings, freshening up, and there was time for him to do the same if he was quick. Yes, she would find him something to eat when they were airborne again. It would be nearly three and a half hours before they reached Rio. This was Recife. They had gained three hours since taking off.

Whatever the local time said, he had slept for more than eleven hours. Shaved and fed, he looked down, trying to catch glimpses of the lush Brazilian seaboard. It was the first time he had been in America and though he had known it was vast, it was impossible not to be impressed when it was actually seen. Twelve hundred miles from Recife to Rio and they would still be in Brazil. And beyond Rio there was yet another thousand miles of coastline.

From the air as they planed down to land at Galeao airport, the great cup of Rio's harbor, glinting gemlike in the morning sun, looked as beautiful and inviting as Deirdre had said it was.

24

Huskion put his watch back half an hour. Argentina was thirty minutes behind Uruguay. In five days constant time adjustment had become a fact of his life.

Flight RG 834 from Montevideo was due in Buenos Aires at twenty to five. It was the first time he'd been on a Boeing 707 but it gave him no satisfaction. That he was on it at all was the final frustration of a frustrating week.

He had flown down from Asunción the previous evening intending to surprise Deirdre by joining her plane when it touched down at Montevideo, only to discover there were no seats to be had on it. The Boeing had been the earliest flight he could get. Deirdre would feel let down when he wasn't at Ezeiza to meet her. The cable and flowers she'd find awaiting her at the hotel wouldn't make up for it.

It couldn't be helped; just one more thing that hadn't gone quite right.

In five days he'd been in as many countries, plane hopping in and out of Brazil, Paraguay, Bolivia and Uruguay, crossing into Argentina from Asunción by car, without ever find-ing an immigration officer who did not carefully stamp his passport. He had wanted just one country that wasn't fussy about such things so he could switch to his Fierstengl pass-port.

Not that it was a disaster, only a minor irritation. He had no intention of becoming Fierstengl permanently, only as a first stop to assuming a completely new identity.

How he would be able to do this he still hadn't a clue. But in a country where a phony passport was as unremark-able as a hammer toe, buying false papers ought not to be too difficult.

The police wouldn't be fooled, of course, but that didn't matter. He doubted if there were many aliases they didn't know, probably fewer than were missed by the police in England. The difference was that, in South America, know-ing was enough, no one felt any compulsion to do anything about it.

From Montevideo down the estuary of the River Plata was scarcely more than a flip but he chafed with impatience to have it over. He longed to be with Deirdre again.

The great plane was full of Argentinians going home for the holidays. Nearly all were men and they kept the steward-esses scurrying with their drink orders. Huskion, his thoughts hurrying ahead, hardly noticed them. He'd given up check-ing for possible followers.

If Buenos Aires was as attractive from the air as Rio he was not to know, for after crossing the river they suddenly planed down before the city came in sight. Ezeiza airport, he learned, was thirty-odd miles south of Buenos Aires, farther away than Gatwick from London. Which meant at least another hour before he would be with Deirdre. For the twentieth time he cursed himself for a fool for not flying direct from Asunción.

He was first off the plane, having let go some of his ill temper by barging his way to the head of the queue. As he went down the gangway he thought he could do without airplanes and airports for a very long time.

His thrusting hurry did him no good. The plump Customs officer ignored him in favor of regular commuters, casually pawing through their belongings as an excuse for a gossip. Or so it seemed to Huskion. When at last he turned to him, he accepted his assurance that he had nothing to declare with a nod, chalked his two cases without opening them.

Stepping out into the concourse he looked round eagerly, half hoping to see Deirdre waiting for him. She wasn't there. It wasn't really to be expected. After twenty hours in the plane she would not have felt like making the long trek back to the airport to meet him.

He didn't hear the announcement the first time, when it was made in Spanish, for he was not listening to the loud-speakers. But he got the repetition in English clear enough.

"Will Señor Fierstengl go to the Information Desk where there is a message for him. A message for Señor Fierstengl, Señor Hermann Fierstengl, at the Information Desk."

What the hell was wrong now? It could only be from Deirdre. No one else knew he meant to be Fierstengl in Buenos Aires.

"Señor?"

The porter carrying his bags had gone on ahead of him when the loudspeaker had pulled him up short. Now he had come back and was gazing at him with melancholy curiosity. Huskion gave him fifty pesos and told him to put the cases down.

When the man had gone off, touching his cap and smiling in a way that made him think he'd overtipped, Huskion picked up his bags and circled the concourse until he came to the Information Desk.

313

Taking out his Fierstengl passport, he held it open to the clerk.

"Usted tiene un mensaje para me?" he said hoping his rudimentary Spanish would be intelligible. It hadn't always been during the past week.

The clerk glanced at his passport.

"Sí, sí, Señor Fierstengl."

He handed over an envelope. It was from Deirdre all right. His name on it was in her writing.

Huskion didn't open the envelope at once but wove his way through the crush in the concourse to a bench where he squeezed himself onto the space at the end next to an elderly mink-coated woman wearing a capriciously inappropriate hat covered in summer flowers and fruit.

In the envelope was a single sheet of paper, undated and without an address.

Darling,

Don't go to the hotel. It's too dangerous. Spinwell knows what happened in Paris.

I will find somewhere else for us to stay and meet you tonight at the Corucca. It's a café-restaurant down by the docks the man I sat next to on the plane told me of—right off the tourist track, he said it was, and great fun. Nobody would think of looking for us in a place like that.

It's not easy to get to because it's on the waterfront. You take a taxi to the corner of Guidacha and Anduloba streets, they're somewhere beyond the Hippodrome tell the driver. Walk along Anduloba until you come to the Paseo de Rochas. This will lead you down to the river. Turn left along the quay and it's only a little way to the Corucca.

Be there at 9 o'clock—it can't be any earlier as the café doesn't open until then.

Longing to see you—and so much to tell you.

All my love
Deirdre

He didn't read it all at once. The first time he didn't get beyond the opening paragraph.

"Spinwell knows what happened in Paris."

Since he landed in South America he'd hardly thought of what had happened there. It had belonged to that other world he had temporarily and so reluctantly inhabited but which was not, and never could be, a part of him.

He had known, of course, that when Martin's body was found it wouldn't just be ignored. But he hadn't doubted that the police would at once understand. The Deuxième Bureau was certain to have a file on Spiller Martin as, with hindsight, he was now sure King had. In Paris, of all places, action over the violent death of a spy could be expected to be no more than token.

But that Spinwell should know about it changed everything. Spinwell was a part of his world, the real world. Killing Spiller had been logical, unexceptionable, within the terms of war by which King and Sherngold lived. But in the real world, the world where truth had meaning, killing was murder, inexcusable, foul, like everything about King and Sherngold.

For the first time he felt he'd broken the law, was a criminal.

He went over to the bar and ordered a large brandy, putting half of it away in a single gulp. Propping his elbow on the bar, he looked around carefully. There seemed to be no one watching him, no one in the concourse he'd noticed near him at any time since he'd come through Customs. But then there wouldn't be. If Spinwell had been there, he'd have been arrested the moment he landed.

He drank the remainder of the brandy more slowly. Instead of calming him, the spirit brought back the queasiness that always affected him in the last few minutes before landing as the air pressure in the plane was adjusted.

315

Rereading Deirdre's letter, he wished, instead of writing, she had waited at the airport for him. She was only trying to be helpful but it was damn silly for her to dash off on her own. They could very well have looked for somewhere to stay together. And then he wouldn't have been left for hours on his own, worrying about what she was going to tell him.

At the newsstand he bought a Thursday's *Daily Telegraph*. There was plenty about France in it. About the decline in the number of tourists, the fierce competition being offered by the Italian and German car industries to Renault and Citroën, the importance of Saharan oil to the Common Market countries. Nothing about a murder at the Hotel Guillemin.

If Martin's body had been discovered on Sunday, it would have been very old news by Thursday, unless something new and sensational had been unearthed since. Whatever had been reported about it would have appeared on Monday.

The only Monday English paper the newsstand had left was a *Financial Times*. Spiller would have had to be the French Finance Minister at least to have ranked as much as a paragraph in that. A Tuesday's *Daily Mirror* had nothing about it either. The current French papers had not arrived yet, and the newsstand was out of back numbers.

Not till he was on the bus scudding toward the city did it come to him that the German papers would have been the best bet. Spiller Martin was well enough known in Berlin for his killing to have made real news for them. But by then it seemed hardly to matter for in an hour he would be with Deirdre and know it all.

Because it seemed to offer safety, he had hung about the airport until it was time for him to go to the Corucca. With Spinwell in Buenos Aires, looking for a place to loiter away the hours there would have chewed what was left of his nerves to rags.

That the Security men should be so close behind him no

longer seemed unbelievable. With a dreadful clarity he now saw that all his efforts to cover his tracks lost their value once his Fierstengl alias was broken. Knowing his connection with Spiller Martin would have put up King's foxy snout the moment he learned of the body being found. He would have had no doubt who was the Hermann Fierstengl the Sûreté were anxious to "interview." Routine digging would fill in the gaps. His bank, the travel agency, his cable to the Crillon . . . bingo! Put like that, it was childishly simple. It was still staggering, though, that it had been unraveled so quickly. But then he'd always underestimated Spinwell.

There was nothing to be seen from the bus, one main road being indistinguishable from another in the dark. The outskirts of the city, too, were as featureless as those of any other.

Unreasonably this sameness depressed Huskion. Bricks and concrete remained bricks and concrete wherever they were. Foolishly he had imagined it would be different in South America.

Nearer to the city's center the scene became less drab. There were taller buildings and lighted shop windows, many with special displays for "Navidad," mostly crude tableaux of the Crib in the Manger.

His nerves tautened as the streets broadened. He sat hunched forward in his seat, his eyes on the people on the sidewalk, as though expecting at any moment to see Spinwell among them, looking for him.

The danger point was the terminus in the Avenida Cordoba. He was the last to leave the bus, hanging back to study the faces of the loiterers before getting up from his seat. There was no one who looked even remotely English.

He hadn't taken a taxi from the airport in case the cabby should remember picking him up. For the same reason he didn't look for one now but picked up his bags and should-

317

ered his way through the cloud of touts.

One little man in a shabby, shapeless coat that almost dragged the ground, the sleeves so long they hung down over his fingers, clung to him tenaciously. No doubt the services he had to offer were so crummy they could only appeal to a foreigner so eccentrically mean as to hump his own baggage. In imminent danger of tripping over his dragging coattails at every step, he trotted along beside Huskion, like a worried terrier. He tried to seize his bags, to take him to a hotel—"Ver' cheap, muy bueno"—a brothel, a night-club—"mucho espectaculo"—to be his guide. At each suggestion he raised his hand to the once-shiny, much-cracked peak of his chauffeur's cap, causing his monstrous sleeve to concertina back to his elbow, exposing a naked fleshless forearm. For half a block he shambled wheezily beside Huskion, who pressed on as though he were not there, and then suddenly stopped, stamped his foot and used what was left of his breath to gasp abuse in an affronted wail, like a child who had just seen the luscious crown of his ice-cream cone fall into the gutter.

Relieved of this importunity—really relieved, for though Huskion had learned in Alexandria that giving them money was the last way to get rid of beggars, their wretchedness always embarrassed him—he went on rapidly down the Avenida Cordoba, crossing the first intersection and turning right at the next.

He had no idea where he was or whether he was going toward or away from his rendezvous. The intersection brought him into another broad avenue parallel with the one he had just left.

Again turning right, he waited, leaning against the wall, just round the corner. He'd been too preoccupied with shaking off the touting scarecrow to check whether he was being tailed.

318

There weren't many people about so near the dinner hour. In as many minutes only three men came after him, two going straight on and the other walking rapidly away from him on the other side of the avenue.

Teetering on the curb, Huskion wondered which way was most likely to bring him to a taxi rank. The mountain came to Mahomet. Like a spider darting on a fly, a cruising cabby spotted him and skidded to a halt. He directed the man according to Deirdre's instructions.

Once the cab began to move he felt more secure. Anticipation that he would soon be with Deirdre, his loneliness at an end, smothered his dread.

His excitement gave him new eyes, so that he no longer saw himself surrounded by nondescript piles of cement and glass. He was struck by the great breadth and straightness of the boulevards and the opulence of the buildings. Buenos Aires was quite a place.

He looked out for the Hippodrome Deirdre had mentioned and thought he recognized it, but it turned out to be a polo ground. The Hippodrome was beyond, a giant oval of towering terraces. He wondered what it was used for. Bullfighting? Football? It looked huge enough to house both at the same time.

They left it behind and also the wide avenues and came to a tangle of dark little streets through which the driver wove uncertainly. Once he missed his way completely and had to back out of a cul-de-sac, cursing sibilantly. Finally, after much peering about at intersections, he pulled up beside a great black hulk of a building with a grunt of satisfaction.

"Est' aquí?" the driver queried. "This you want, eh?"

Clearly he didn't believe it.

"Esta Calle Guidacha?"

"Sí, esta Guidacha. Aquella esta Calle Anduloba."

319

He paid the man and got out.

Deirdre was certainly right. No one would think of looking for them in this district. Except for a scrawny dog scavenging among the refuse littering the cobbles, there was nothing living to be seen in either of the ill-lit streets.

The driver hadn't moved but was watching him, head cocked, evidently expecting him to get back into the cab. When Huskion waved him away, he shrugged and let in the gear. Swinging the taxi round in a wide arc, he made off back the way they had come. The surge of the engine as he changed to top gear echoed eerily in the empty silence.

Calle Anduloba consisted of nothing but warehouses, all dark and shuttered, with hoists jutting from their upper stories like gallows. Guidacha was a cutting between the windowless walls of two of them.

The quiet was oppressive, thick and menacing, though the air was full of sounds. Distantly the city hummed; from somewhere close, beyond the lowering walls, a shunting engine coughed and snuffled and trucks banged their buffers against each other ill-temperedly, while in the warehouses ropes and baskets whispered as they eased. Only the deserted street was silent. Silent in a peculiar way, as though it had passed out of time or was holding its breath.

Carrying his bags he picked his way through the litter. Each warehouse had its own smell. Headily pungent spices, fruit scents and revolting stenches he was unable to identify, breathed out on him as he passed, momentarily quenching the general reek of decaying garbage. Though he trod lightly, the walls were like sounding boards magnifying the soft pad of his shoes on the cobblestones.

He nearly missed the Paseo de Rochas for it was no more than a yard-wide slit in the wall. There was a lamp on a bracket over its entrance and another at what he took to be its end. Between there was a Stygian blackness. The fetid air in Calle Anduloba was quite still but a breeze blew down the Paseo into his face, a damp breeze from the water he presumed lay beyond the farther lamp.

It was a forbidding place. Deirdre's plane friend must have been drunk or one of a party when he came here to have suggested it to her. If she was not already at the Corucca, he would come back to meet her, borrowing a flashlight if he could. It was no place for a woman to walk down on her own.

He stepped out rapidly, anxious to reach the other end of the alley as quickly as he could. Despite the breeze the air between the walls was dark and smelt of urine.

He had gone no more than twenty yards before he looked back over his shoulder nervously. Whether it was a sound, or the habit of months of looking out for followers, or the creepy darkness of the alley that caused him to, he didn't know. But whatever it was the instinct was right. He saw a man quite clearly outlined against the light of the lamp. Just momentarily. A split second later he had disappeared, flattened into the shadow of the wall.

Huskion didn't stop to question whether his presence in the Paseo de Rochas might not be as innocent as his own but began to run. But after half a dozen strides he stopped dead.

Two men had stepped out into the lamplight at the quay-side end of the alley ahead of him. Their low-crowned soft hats and belted raincoats told him what they were. And that the man behind him would be another.

He was completely trapped.

Without a weapon he couldn't even make a fight of it. Forward or back, they had him.

Desperately he looked up at the alley's prisoning walls. One was sheer, the blank side of a building. The other didn't reach up indefinitely into the sky, as he'd thought, but ended abruptly ten feet or so above the ground. If he could find a foothold he might, just might, be able to get over it. If the top wasn't glassed.

Six paces on he found what he was looking for, a buttress.

Jamming his suitcase into its angle, he stood on it and reached up. The top was smooth, unprotected. But he could not stretch far enough for his fingers to find a purchase on the farther side of the brickwork.

He filled his lungs with air and bunched himself for the leap.

He had to make it in one. If he missed, they would know what he was trying to do, and the man behind him would be on him before he could try again.

Getting as firm a handhold as he could, he flung his briefcase over the wall and, almost in the same movement, heaved himself upward. For a moment he hung in mid-air, his feet scrabbling madly in the cleft by the buttress. One toe held and he pushed first his hand, then his elbow, over the top of the wall and swung himself up.

In case they had guns, he kept himself flat, rolling over the wall like a polevaulter straddling the bar. As he went over he braced himself for the drop on the other side.

Only there was no drop.

With a shuddering crash, his feet and knees fetched up in a gutter less than a foot below the top layer of brickwork. He was in a trough between the wall and a steep roof attached to it.

He lay there panting, winded as much by the shock of not finding the free space he'd expected as the sudden check to his fall. Hardly aware of the pain in his jarred joints, he tried to collect his wits.

There had been no shots as he went over the wall. But they must know where he was. If they hadn't seen him, they'd certainly heard him.

He was damned sure they couldn't see him now. The alley was too narrow to see anything beyond the front rim of the wall. That was why he hadn't seen the roof, despite its sharply angled pitch.

322

Not a sound came from the alley.

Moving silently and keeping flat, he pushed himself up the roof until he was upright with his feet in the gutter. But he got no farther. The tiles were covered with a damp film of fungus on which his shoes could find no bite. Each time he edged a few inches up the steep roof his feet skidded back into the gutter as soon as he put his weight on it. After the third attempt he gave it up.

He turned over onto his back. Face down he couldn't see what the bastards were doing.

Only they weren't doing anything. He'd made himself as helpless as a treed cat. And they knew it.

He reached out and picked up his briefcase. It was something he could throw, though it wasn't much of a weapon.

How the hell had the KGB found him? Had the whole menagerie moved in to Buenos Aires? King as well as Spinwell?

And what had happened to Deirdre?

Had she deliberately trapped him?

The thought ran through him like a powerful electric current, turning his muscles to water. It was impossible, he told himself frantically. He didn't believe it, mustn't even think of it as a possibility, or he'd lose all will to resist. But if it wasn't true—God, what had they done to her?

He almost moaned out loud.

The next second all his sinews whipped taut.

Someone in the alley was whispering, whispering so quietly it seemed like a susurration in the bricks immediately below his feet. From somewhere in the direction of the quay there came a brisk command in reply. He couldn't catch the words or even identify the language, but it sounded like a query answered in the negative.

And after that nothing. No more whispering, no shoe-scraping betraying movement, no head cautiously raised above the top of the wall. Nothing. Only the silence settling ponderously, like explosion debris in a slow-motion movie without a soundtrack.

He couldn't just sit there. He had to move, to do something. But what?

From away behind him, beyond the roof and toward the quay, came the metallic rattle of a winch running free over its ratchet. He'd heard it before without realizing its significance. Down on the quay a boat was being unloaded.

That meant people.

People were his only chance. There would be none coming down the Paseo de Rochas, that was for sure. But on the quay . . .

Cautiously he slid himself sideways two or three paces. Though he chewed his lip in concentration as he tried to move noiselessly, he couldn't prevent his shoes scuffling the grit in the gutter. If they were able to hear what he was doing, he might as well stay where he was.

His breathing had changed. His chest was seizing up, turning into a solid lump. Lying back on the tiles he emptied his lungs and relaxed his shoulder muscles.

Deirdre, Deirdre— He mustn't think of her, of what they might have done to her.

When his lungs had recovered their rhythm, he sat up and took off his shoes. Knotting the laces together, he slung them round his neck so that they hung down his back. The laces cut into his throat uncomfortably but that couldn't be helped.

The alley was as hushed as a cemetery. He could have been utterly alone in the silent night.

Were there more than the three he had seen? Not that it mattered. Three were three too many.

Bending his knees and balancing his briefcase on his belly, he put his hands behind him, bracing himself against the roof, and waited for the winch to run free again. When it

324

did, its noise, because he was listening for it, sounded comfortingly loud. Before it died he had moved four of five yards like a crab. And without making a sound.

But moving like that was a hell of a strain and he was glad to flap down on his back and get the weight of the briefcase off his stomach.

Who the hell had tipped off Sherngold? The KGB couldn't have tracked him to Buenos Aires unless someone had. Not so soon.

Confident he could move noiselessly now he was shoeless, he started off again without waiting for the cover of the winch. But after a couple of shuffling steps his stockinged foot came up against something sharp and hard. It was a tile that had come loose and slid down into the gutter. Dumping his briefcase, he picked it up and stuffed it in the top of his trousers. It would make a better weapon than the case. And he had the whole roof to draw on for more.

Small though this gain was, it bolstered his resolution. Purposefully he shed his overcoat. Not only was he freer without it but would no longer have to worry about the dragging tails catching on the edge of a tile and giving him away.

He couldn't be sure but he didn't think they knew he had moved. That also increased his confidence.

He cast about for some means of putting them off still further, to make them imagine he was making for the Anduloba end of the alley. But he could think of nothing. Chucking the tile along the roof would be plain silly. They'd never fall for that. His best bet was to keep absolutely silent.

Why didn't one of them come over the wall after him? Were they afraid he had a gun? It wasn't likely. They must be damn sure his nerve would crack if they left him alone, that he wouldn't be able to stick it out up there indefinitely.

He began to move again. Very slowly. Though he was less encumbered now, the strain of holding himself inverted like a crab was still enough to force him to rest every few yards before his pumping breathing became loud enough to be heard in the alley.

Suddenly, as he was taking his third rest, the silence was split by the blast of a ship's siren that seemed to come from right beside his ear. A liner, with its upper decks sparkling with lights, slid past the end of the roof, so close it seemed to be in touching distance. Though he knew its seeming nearness was an optical illusion, the sight encouraged him. It confirmed that along the quay there was plenty of wakeful life.

Once more he started to move.

King! Bloody King! King could have tipped off the Russians!

He'd been a blind fool to think Martin's killing would be shrugged off. By the Russians, anyway. And King, though he'd be happy enough to have Spiller out of the way, would be coldly vindictive because he'd gypped him. No one could be allowed to get away with that. He hadn't been kidding when he showed him that Italian newspaper clipping. That was the system. Using the KGB as executioners would be a neat stroke according to his hideously twisted ethic. Cheap, effective and leaving no awkward questions to be answered.

The anger surging through his veins made him travel farther this time. When he eventually lowered his aching arms, he had to bite his lip to prevent himself from gulping for air.

He didn't shrink from the idea of King's betrayal as he had from the possibility of Deirdre's. Fevered by his peril, it seemed to him not only conceivable but eminently believable. It was the last piece of the jigsaw, completing the pattern. Right from the start it hadn't only been Sherngold, but Sherngold and King in cahoots, trying to destroy him.

326

He was so burned up he could hardly contain himself until he'd recovered his breath.

Where were the bastards?

He wanted to see one of them come over the wall, come near enough for him to hit out. His whole body raged with desire to get at them.

Looking toward the end of the wall, he reckoned the way he was going it would be all of half an hour before he reached it. And by then he'd be so whacked he'd be fit for nothing, let alone a fight.

Rolling over on his belly, he raised himself on his hands and feet. Face downward he could move about four times as fast with a tenth of the effort. True, that way he couldn't keep his eye on the top of the wall. But there wasn't anything to see.

Now he could really move, making about thirty yards before he had to rest. One more dash like that would get him to the end of the roof.

There was still no sound from the KGB men. Not a sign they knew he was moving.

Regular as a heartbeat the winch ran back over its ratchet. It had grown louder as he neared the quayside.

Overhead the sky had taken on an opalescence as though somewhere out of his sight a moon was coming up. He didn't know whether more light was something he wanted. His eyes had become accustomed to the dark. On the quay, with the open estuary beside him, there'd be light enough for him to make a run for it. If he had the chance.

As he approached the end of the wall he went more slowly, stopping altogether ten feet short of it. The lamp at the mouth of the alley spread an uncomfortable radiance over the far corner of the roof.

Lying flat along the gutter, he cautiously raised his head until he had an eye above the wall. At first, he thought the

327

third man must have pinned himself against the wall immediately below him, where his head would be nicely teed up for him to swipe at it with the tile. But no such luck. Snaking his way forward to recce the waterfront, he suddenly saw him.

He was standing out on the quay smoking a cigarette, relaxed yet alert, head pointed toward the alley, like a dog waiting for a rabbit to be flushed from its burrow. A tough, thick-shouldered man with square jowls.

Huskion wormed his way backwards out of the man's line of vision. He had not been able to move close enough to the edge of the roof to see down the wharf to where the ship was unloading. But he guessed it was farther off than he'd hoped, maybe a couple of hundred yards or even more. Now he could hear the steely ripple of the winch directly, instead of its echo bouncing off the warehouse walls, its edge had gone soft, as though melted by distance.

He put on his shoes. He chewed his tongue in agonized concentration as he drew them on and knotted the laces, for the slightest sound would ruin his plan. It seemed to take him an eternity.

After wiping the sweat from his palms, he weighed the tile in his hand. Thrown edge first like an ax, it was heavy enough to stun. On even to kill. If the aim was good.

With his shoes on, crawling back along the gutter was torture. One clumsy movement, a scrape of his toe, and whatever chance he had would be gone.

He made it and rested his face on his hands, lying prone and filling his lungs with air. Slowly he lifted his head above the wall.

The man had not moved. As Huskion looked at him he flicked the butt of his cigarette over his shoulder. It sent up a spray of golden sparks as it went wheeling across the quay.

Worming himself round until his back was against the

roof, he settled his feet firmly in the gutter. Then he poised himself, hunching forward and swinging the tile backwards and forwards to gain momentum.

He screwed up his muscles until they hurt. Then he let them go and shot upwards. From his full height he whanged the tile at the center of the man's forehead.

As Huskion appeared over the parapet, the man's head jerked up in surprise. It was complete enough to freeze his reflexes momentarily. He was still gaping wide-eyed when the tile landed. But its direction wasn't quite good enough, off to the right and too low. It caught him a thumping blow just under the left shoulder blade.

He gave a yelp of pain and nipped out of sight behind the wall. Footsteps pounded down the alley but stopped abruptly when the man on the quay shouted a warning. There was a brisk exchange between him and the others. Then one of them trotted back toward Calle Anduloba. This time Huskion recognized the language as Russian.

Cowering back against the roof, he waited for the attack, swiveling his head from side to side. Frantically he began to tear at the roof tiles. But they were set tight and would not give at his tugging. In desperation he stamped on one until it broke. Now they came loose, unraveling like a laddered stocking from the hole he'd made.

He ripped away at the roof, building a little coign of tiles on either side of him. But as the piles grew bigger and there was no attack his hands lost their urgency.

He sat down on the roof and listened. All was as still and serene as it had been before he'd sprung his surprise. Their indifference to what he'd done and—even more depressing—what he might do was frightening.

He seemed to have been on the roof for hours but he saw from his watch it was not yet ten o'clock. He had no idea how long it was to dawn but it could hardly be less than eight hours.

329

A tug, its navigation lights seeming to float in space, swam across the end of the alley, well out of hailing distance. Its siren chirruped twice, and then it was gone. He strained his ears to catch the plash of oars or a voice from some small craft feeling its way along inshore. But, except for the occasional slap of water against the timbers of the wharf, the silence was complete.

The rills of sweat on his flanks had grown cold and he began to shiver. He couldn't sit there interminably, a tile clutched in either hand, eyes darting nervously up and down the parapet.

Tearing out the tiles had made a long gash in the roof. He enlarged and widened it hopefully. But the rafters were too close together to allow him to drop through the hole. All the same he tried, getting his buttocks stuck and hauling himself out in a panic in case they caught him trapped like that.

Through the hole he saw he'd been right in guessing the roof belonged to an open shed of some kind, for the quay was plainly visible beyond its far side. The ship that was being unloaded was berthed at a pier running out into the estuary at right angles to the wharf. Floodlights were on its decks and the dockside. They were so bright that anyone working in their radiance would be blind to anything beyond it.

The quiet in the Paseo de Rochas weighed on him like lead.

It wasn't feasible that this brick jungle beside the waterfront could be utterly deserted. It must be full of hidey-holes. The sort of places sailors crawled into when they were broke and had missed their ships, homes for tramps and other riffraff.

He sent a tile winging over the roof ridge and heard it splinter forlornly as it hit the ground.

330

"Help! Murder!" he shouted, flinging tiles with each word.

It sounded foolish. Debased by a thousand childish games, not even the strained anguish of his voice could make the words ring true. But they killed the choking silence.

He had thrown more tiles and yelled again before he realized he was shouting in English.

"Asesinos! Socorro!"

It sounded better in Spanish.

"Aquí! Aquí!"

If there were people lurking near, none answered.

"Asesinos!"

In desperation he flung tiles higher and higher, putting all his strength behind them, while his shouts rose in a crescendo.

"Socorro! Socorro! *Socorro!*"

He stamped his feet on the roof and screamed.

"Hi! Hi! Hi-i-i!"

Nothing.

He slumped down on the roof. It was useless. He was just wearing himself out bellowing at the empty air.

Insensibly, like a pond recovering its smoothness after its surface has been ruffled by a stone, the quiet of the night locked over him. The KGB men stayed where they were. They waited, their presence thickening the silence. It was as though they'd expected him to break out like that and, like doctors at a sickbed, left the fever to exhaust itself. Their discipline had a shriveling, professional certainty. As though all the decisions had been made, the outcome concluded, and he was already nothing.

"Come on, you bastards!" he yelled in impotent fury. "Come on, damn you!"

The Paseo de Rochas stayed as quiet as a vacuum. No hand appeared over the wall. He could have been alone with the night.

Since they apparently didn't want to tackle him on the roof, that's where he ought to stay until the hours ran away and they could hold back no longer. That way he could keep whatever advantage they imagined the roof gave him.

But he couldn't do it. To wait like that he would have had to have their cold skill and professional training in murder. He wasn't even an amateur at the trade. Each dragging, silent minute wrung him cruelly, so that he gulped convulsively, near to tears. Like a child menaced by bullies who cannot stop himself swinging ineffectually at the grinning faces of his tormentors, he couldn't contain himself. He had to find some way of forcing their hand. However desperate the throw, he had to see how the dice would run.

To jump down onto the quay wasn't impossible. When he'd done his parachute course, he'd jumped from higher than the wall many times. Though that had been a long time ago and he'd had grass to land on, not cobbles. The snag was, he'd almost certainly end up on all fours. Even if he didn't do himself an injury, the thug he'd hit with the tile would have him before he could get to his feet.

But if he could be got out of the way or put out of action . . .

As quietly as he could, he inched himself along the gutter, stopping just short of the man on the quay's line of vision.

He measured the distance to the mouth of the alley as well as he could, picking the spot from which to jump. If luck turned his way. If it didn't, he'd have to stay where he was until he could dream up something else. He wasn't looking for suicide.

Holding two tiles in his left hand, he crept toward the end of the wall. When he was inside the radiance of the lamp and could see the deserted quay beyond, he stood up.

As though skimming pebbles across a pond he sent the tiles spinning as hard as he could along the length of the alley. They clipped the far wall and ricocheted backwards and forwards over its narrow width, making a great clatter.

There was a sharp grunt of pain as the second one collided with something that wasn't brick.

The man on the quay broke cover. Crouched like a Rugby fullback he moved out to block the alley's exit.

Seeing him, Huskion felt a great surge of joy.

Then he was in the air, going for the man's chest with his knees.

The man saw him but had no time to dodge. He was off balance, looking up, when Huskion crashed into him.

They went down together in a confused ball. He heard the KGB man's head hit the stones. And at the same moment an excruciating agony blazed in his knee.

But he didn't let go the hold he'd taken as their bodies met. His fingers were tight on the man's collar. Hauling upwards, he crashed his head down onto a jutting paving edge. Blood spurted and the man's mouth fell open stupidly.

He began to scramble up at once. But he couldn't free his leg. Something was holding it, making it hurt like hell when he tried to move it.

Struggling wildly, he got his right leg in position and pressed himself up on his hands. But still his left leg wouldn't follow. It seemed stuck in a deep hole. It—

He didn't see the man in the raincoat come out of the Paseo de Rochas. But he felt the knife. It began as a burning low down in his back and traveled up in a raging fire as though he were being consumed by lightning.

The man in the raincoat eased the knife out of the body. At the Fifth Directorate's School for Special Operators he had been taught that a knife driven upwards from just below the rib cage could always be withdrawn easily. A bonus on a stroke guaranteed to kill efficiently and suddenly.

He snapped the blade back and dropped the knife into

his pocket. Kneeling down beside the body, he began to empty Huskion's pockets systematically.

The third thug came out onto the quay. At a nod from the kneeling man he bent over their colleague sprawled on the stones. Raising his head, he examined the mash of tangled hair, blood and splintered bone, muttered "Ppht!" and gently set it down.

Satisfied there was nothing more to be retrieved from Huskion's clothing, the man in the raincoat got to his feet. Again he nodded. Together they dragged the body across the wharf and let it slide over the edge into the water.

After checking the pulse, the man in the raincoat unstrapped the shoulder holster from the body of the man Huskion had jumped on and handed it to his companion. He didn't search the pockets for papers for he knew there wouldn't be any.

When they had put the second body in the water, they stood side by side for a few seconds, watching it bob and settle in the swell.

Then they turned back into the Paseo de Rochas, moving like shadows, and as silently, on their rubber soles.

The room, with only an M.O.W. filing cabinet, a table and two chairs for furniture, had a bleak monastic austerity. Except that the window looked down on the Horseguards and the dirt and coconut shy were missing, it might have been the one behind Amusements Unlimited in Finlay Street.

"I'd never have agreed to it if I'd known what you were planning."

His Nibs, looking out the window, did not turn around as he spoke.

The man sitting at the table, who was sometimes known as King, didn't answer, thinking Sir Nigel ought to know that was precisely why he hadn't been told. The Undersecretary had to be allowed his beef but he would have to get it over quickly as he, King, was due at a GDS meeting. For it he'd had to put on the red-tabbed uniform he wore so rarely it still looked as though it had come from the tailor's that morning.

"He was too good a man to lose."

"You'd lost him already," King said frigidly. "He was finished the moment Semenov approached him. You couldn't have used him on classified stuff after that."

"A ghastly shambles."

That depended how you looked at it, King thought. The neighbors would have to find a new leader for their Berlin circuit and a replacement for their strong-arm squad. All pure gain even if the main plan had misfired. And at no cost at all—not to his department, anyway.

"With something that hasn't been tried there's always a risk. This one would have worked if your man had gone along with us."

His Nibs turned away from the window. There was no trace of feyness in the grim, drawn lines of his face.

"I suppose it was the girl?"

King nodded.

"I didn't think they'd know about her. Usually the satellites are pretty cagey about their agents—there's no love lost between their secret services and Moscow, you know—but once in a way they work together. Like us and the French."

"What's happened to her?"

"We've nothing definite. Probably she's been smuggled out of the country by now. Though whether dead or alive—"

"God!"

King straightened his gloves and stick across the cap lying on the table beside his elbow.

"Has it occurred to you she may have been acting for them all the time?"

The Undersecretary looked at him sideways.

"No," he said very quietly, "I'm glad to say it hasn't."

King stood up and began to draw on his gloves.

"My masters wait."

His Nibs shuffled indecisively.

"Look, Jimmy," he said placatingly, "isn't there something we can do to soften it? A pension for his wife?"

"Out of the question," the Security man snapped curtly. "There's Spinwell to consider. If he were to suspect Huskion had been acting under my orders, it'd throw him completely, wreck his morale."

"There's the Zurich money."

King balanced his cane on the table and rested his gloved hands on it.

"Yes," he said thoughtfully, "I don't see why Mrs. Huskion shouldn't have that. Spinwell will be on to that account any day now—he's still digging, you know—but we can let him believe we can't prevent her having the cash."

He straightened up.

"Best that can be done, I'm afraid, Nigel. I know what you must be thinking—"

"I'm sure you don't!"

Sir Nigel's voice was full of bitterness.

"I'm thinking the service to which I've given my life is now so cankered by what is laughingly called Security, I can only thank God I'll be rid of it in a couple of months."

He went out.

King settled his cap on his head. Authority was very wise, he thought, to insist senior civil servants retire at sixty. By then their cozy blinkered lives had made them all like Nigel, completely out of touch with the real world.

About the Author

R. Vernon Beste was born in London in 1908 and attended St. John's College in Britain. As there was little for the "unskilled and partially educated" in the Britain of the late 1920's, he took up writing.

Besides writing, which he finds agonizing, Mr. Beste has held various positions in publishing and the theatre. From 1939 to 1942 he was general secretary of the Unity Theatre Society, then became managing editor of Fore Publications, Ltd., and editor of *Our Time.* He took the same post of managing editor in Burke Publication, Ltd., and Shaw Publishing Co., Ltd., in 1945.

Four years later Mr. Beste entered film journalism as associate editor of *The Daily Cinema.* He held this position until 1958, when he began to give most of his time to writing—theatre, television and radio plays as well as novels.

During World War II Mr. Beste was one of those responsible for forming the first groups for putting on entertainment in air-raid shelters and factories in England. In conjunction with the British Drama League, he formed the Play Encouragement Committee, whose members included Sir Julian Huxley, Sir Michael Redgrave and Stephen Spender.

Mr. Beste is also a founding member, and until 1958 chairman, of the Soho Association, which presents the Soho Fair.

Repeat the Instructions is the second book Mr. Beste has had published in the United States; the first (his first novel) was *The Moonbeams,* published by Harper & Brothers in 1961.

Format by Sidney Feinberg
Set in Linotype Caledonia
Composed, printed and bound by The Haddon Craftsmen, Inc.
HARPER & ROW, PUBLISHERS, INCORPORATED